Desire

for

TRUTH

BY

DIANA DIRIENZO

A Tale of Romance, Comedy, Mayhem, Mystery, & Travel

Novels
By
DIANA DIRIENZO

Escape

Desire for Truth

Shake the Glitter

Disclaimer:
This story is a work of fiction and any similarities to persons living or dead are purely fictional. I have utilized a period in real history with famous persons' names, music, movies, and celebrities only to honor them and create a setting that brings the reader back in time with my fictional characters. The situations created are based in my imagination; yet give realism to my settings, plots and subplots. Attention readers this story is a love story and does contain sexual encounters and some profanity.

Dedication
To Kevin,
My Super-hero

Thanks to the history makers in 1984 i.e. NYC personalities, celebrities, playwrights, musical artist, NYC businessman, Donald Trump, Fashion designers, and the Super-hero Police Officers and Undercover Detectives that put their lives on the line to defend our laws to uphold justice.

Special thanks:
To my friends and family in Wisconsin
You inspire me.

Honorable mention:
Geraldine Ferraro
August 26, 1935 - March 26, 2011
An inspiration to women everywhere.
America is still the land where dreams come true.
A great example and inspiration:
NYPD's first African American Police Commissioner.
Retired Commissioner
Benjamin Ward
Aug 10, 1926–June 10, 2002

A personal thank you to:
Former New York Mayor and NY Attorney:
Rudolph Giuliani
For his diligent work on the
Mafia Commission Trials and 9-11 Terrorist Attacks

You are all American Heroes

QUOTES

In many works of fiction some truths are evident. Here are some quotes that have inspired me to write–
"Desire for Truth"

"There is no God–higher than TRUTH"
Mahatma Gandhi

"In the chamber of death, I prayed in very early years,
'Give me truth; cheat me by no illusion.'
O, the granting of this prayer is sometimes terrible to
me!
I walk over the burning plough shares, and they sear
my feet,
But nothing but the truth will do."

Sarah Margaret Fuller
May 23, 1810 - July 19, 1850
Journalist, writer, critic, women's rights advocate,
and Poet who lived at 116 Waverly Place NY, NY

"When we choose to live in denial with false illusions and lies, we live in fear of truth. Truth can become an uncontrollable monster that cripples us. We cannot move forward unless we face the truth. No matter how mobile truth may seem or how damaging it appears–lies do more damage and ultimately the Truth will set the innocent free. Truth can free one and imprison another."
-Diana Dirienzo–writer 2012

Chapter 1

The truth was that every step clicking the sidewalk, every honk, and blaring siren paced Amanda Lindas closer to her ultimate dream job. Just minutes after leaving her apartment on West 35th and 8th Avenue, she strutted down 34th Street en route to the Empire State Building. She paused only to watch Macy's Memorial Day displays being dismantled in the early morning hours. The temptation to scrutinize her distorted reflection in Macy's windows overpowered her urge to return to pounding the pavement.

Subtle she shifted front to side admiring her decision to wear her well-tailored black pencil skirt with a padded shoulder peplum blazer. And although it wasn't a Donna Karan or Coco Chanel original, she assured herself that someday it would be. Her trendy business ensemble was complete with her no-nonsense two-inch black pumps, black sensible purse, and briefcase. The serious down-to-business look won her debate against a red skirt suit or her light-weight white blazer and slacks combo. Each reflected her new and improved 80's look keeping up with business fashion trends.

The unmanageable issue was her hair. After wrestling with it for thirty minutes that morning, she twisted it into a shapely tight bun. Too bad her chestnut brown mane had treacherous ideas to unravel and dance wild and kinky in the humidity. *Thank God,* she brought extra hairpins to keep it under wraps. It frizzed unruly naturally and today was no exception, yet she desperately needed today to be the exception. Today ended her first rainy thunderstorm filled weekend in New York City.

Today, Monday, June 4th1984, was the day after she attended the Broadway Tony Awards held at the Gershwin Theatre. She was thrilled to accept the nosebleed seats that her new boss was able to obtain at short notice. Nothing but today could top seeing Julie Andrews, Robert Preston, Liza Minnelli, Dustin Hoffman and a whole slew of Broadways' best. She was especially enthralled by the productions and songs by phenomenon playwrights, and composers: Harvey Fierstein, Jerry Herman, Stephen Sondheim, Tom Stoppard, and James Lapine. And so many more that she took notes on in hopes of getting to interview them. Mr. Underwood promised she would after she attended their epic Broadway shows.

1

Today began her new life and career in New York City. She was convinced beyond realistic measure that today was going to be spectacular and perfect rain or shine.

Energized by self-empowerment, Amanda careened in and out of a moderate crowd of New Yorkers presumably headed to their work destinations. Signature yellow taxis and black town cars maneuvered around orange construction barriers and multicolored pedestrians; while she remained happily undistracted on her mission.

Purposely she had left an hour earlier; to avoid being the least bit late. She prided herself on promptness.

Perspiration settled at her nape, she blamed the mugginess that hung in the air and not the new job jitters.

It was a risk taking an entry level journalist position to boost her career. The first day of her TV journalism career would begin at NYCB– *New York Communication Broadcasters* an edgy up and coming TV network news venue, backed by prime wealthy investors. Her mind was made up; she left Chicago for a fresh start in New York. Mr. Rich Underwood pitched the idea to her at a charity function in Chicago. A function in which her gregarious mother, Florence Lindas, forced her to attend. When Chicago's top social/gossip columnist insists on your attendance, you go and be happy.

"Work the crowd, you never know who will change your life forever," that was her mother's way of prompting her to mingle.

Fortunately for Amanda, Frank Houston was also in attendance, her favorite journalism professor. He taught her everything she needed to know about digging deeper, by going beyond trusting her instincts to search for and oust the absolute truth.

Professor Houston formally introduced them, "Amanda meet my good friend, Mr. Rich Underwood, the owner/producer of NYCB. Rich this is Ms. Amanda Lindas, my star student."

For once her mother was right, well maybe.

"My pleasure, Miss Lindas at NYCB we have the perspicacity to hone in on the top stories. We're small enough to set up and be on the air before the big conglomerates. NYCB will sway the viewing public to edgy timely truthful news; we have to in order to compete with ABC, NBC, and CBS. Of course, we'll need the right reporters and investigative journalists in place. Are you tough enough to handle the cutting edge on truth? Are you willing to take risks?"

"Rich, her desire for truth is stronger than any natural desire, it outranks relationships, eating, and even shopping. She has tenacity, drive, and a killer instinct better than most men." Professor Houston said jovially implanting an elbow jab into Mr. Underwood's side.

They all laughed. But sadly pitiful–that was the truth.

So now, here she was in New York City living her dream standing at the base of the Empire State Building. The massive concrete building engulfed her with its looming shadow. In awe, Amanda craned her neck as far back as she could to catch a glimpse of the radio mast top. Too close to see it, she shuffled across Fifth Ave. to encompass its enormity. Her free hand cupped above her eyes as she gazed upward squinting at the reflected morning sunbeams gleaming on the glass and silver lined masterpiece. Its brilliant splendor jolted her childhood memories.

At age ten she had gazed up at the impressive skyscrapers in Chicago– a tender morose time when her mother divorced her father. Tears welled in her eyes; Amanda was as frightened and excited now, as she was then. Unfortunately her father had a chronic habit of twisting the truth and chasing women on more occasions than she cared to evoke. Her love-hate relationship with him prompted her to steer herself into her career. She despised liars and arrogant womanizing men. And what woman didn't? That was all behind her now.

Hugging her briefcase, she inhaled deep to embrace New York City's energy. The city captured her spirit and vehemence pushing her towards success and her desire for the untainted unabridged truth.

At the Empire's glass doors entrance a vacuum force sucked her inside the prestigious building that epitomized the top real estate in the Big Apple. Dizzy with excitement, blood rushed to her head, her breath escaped as people squeezed past her. Straight ahead inlaid in the gray and burgundy swirled marble slab walls was an astonishing shimmering replica of the building, it stopped her. But, to the right, office attired groupies crowded into the elevators resembling packed sardines, less the smelly fish oil.

Yet plenty of floral perfumes and spicy colognes wafted through her nasal passages causing her dizziness to return when she merged to become one with them.

To the 30th floor she rode with the strangers she believed could become friends or at least daily acquaintances. The elevator stopped at each floor like an endless slow motion ride, her heartbeat skipped at each level. The humming of the lights and the mechanical clatter of the doors kept her mind entertained with white noise. She was grateful NYCB offices weren't on the 102nd floor, although she entertained the thought of spending some lunch hours on the observation deck. Amanda was enthralled with New York City and its endless possibilities.

Finally at the 30th floor, she glanced at her watch. Forty-five minutes early, she stepped out feeling the freedom of becoming one again with herself. Nervous she tucked a few loose strands of hair back into the tight bun desperate to keep it under control. She possessed the type of hair with a dreaded natural spiral curl. Or did it possess her? She wasn't quite sure.

The first day as an official investigative TV journalist/reporter she desired to look confident and poised. Of course, she realized this was strictly an entry level position as Mr. Underwood had made it perfectly clear at several interviews. Her ultimate success depended upon her ability to obtain leads on edgy newsworthy stories, special first interviews, and exclusive celebrity leaks before the other hungry news mogul sharks could sink their piquant teeth into them.

Journalism was a vicious cannibalistic career. It was easy to get eaten alive, but she was up for the fight.

Containing her fears she walked up to the familiar double glass doors labeled with the NYCB tastefully designed blue and white logo. In early May, she had interviewed in the office afterhours with Mr. Underwood, so she was familiar with the layout.

Apprehensively she peered in, clutching her purse and briefcase to her chest, she entered. The semicircle teak receptionist desk topped with glistening blue-pearl granite sat empty. The design was an appropriate choice that reflected an inviting professional image. The journalism office was on the left flanked on the right by a glass enclosed conference room. It contained an elongated oval teak conference table corralled by not less than twelve oversized black leather chairs.

Amanda walked left and entered the bay of gray metal desks with smaller black leather mobile chairs on a not-so-chic gray-tweed commercial carpet. The desks were lined up like a schoolroom labeled with the various positions and name plates. Everyone had a place and every place had space just for that certain someone. She glanced at each, spotting hers in the back closest to a huge glass office enclosed like a fish aquarium labeled: Chief Editor and Producer–Richard Underwood.

No one was around just yet, so she made her way to her desk. Content she sat at her designated desk with her very own official name plaque that rested on the front edge. She stowed her briefcase and purse in the side desk drawer.

Across the room to her left, a small white cabinet with a gray Formica countertop was covered with coffee condiments and an oversized smudged chrome coffee urn. A momentary urge to polish it flickered in her, but she restrained her inner Martha Stewart from taking action. Attached to a coffee splattered wall was a shallow metal box layered with cream colored slot cards. Time punch cards, she mused, what an outdated method being that IBM computers had replaced electric typewriters on each desk. Certainly an up and coming tech-savvy corporation would log into the computer to start the day instead of punching an antiquated time clock. And instead of printed paper memos they should receive interoffice memos via the computer.

Typical of Amanda, her natural inclination was to over analyze; perhaps she over thought and assumed too much in all situations.

To pass the time and to be abreast on office protocol, Amanda sorted through the myriad of office memos stacked on her desk. After reading a memo stating that it was acceptable to have personal items on ones desk she bent over to pull her briefcase from the side drawer. While gathering a few small inspirational wood plaques, she heard the rustle and murmurs of others arriving as the wall clock ticked closer to eight.

What she had not anticipated was the firm behind of a male co-worker perched on the side edge of her desk toying with her prized name plaque. Who was this guy?

On alert, she cautiously gazed up at the clock while evaluating him with her peripheral vision. His lean physique fit well in his guise of designer black slacks, she guessed Armani. A suitable choice complemented by his perfectly pressed white dress shirt, probably Ralph Lauren. The sleeves were rolled precisely a couple of turns to his elbows as if he was determined to delve into his work. So why was he sitting on her desk chatting amicably with others?

With vested interest, she took notice of his slightly longer than collar-length feathered sandy-brown hair. Styled in the top fashion for men, but covered with a strange, not in a bad way, black fedora. He reminded her of a sophisticated 1930's press agent, with exceptional taste in clothes. His fashion forward look fit his male-model figure, and was praiseworthy if she had the desire to mention it. *Which she did not.*

Who was he? Why was he sitting on her desk? Was he her equal? Or an office manager she was not made aware of? And if he was, why was he tossing her name plate up in the air?

A bit taken aback by his intimidating stature planted on her desk. Amanda cleared her throat mustering courage to speak her mind.

"Umm... Umm...Do you mind?" In a split moment he glanced at her with his effulgent emerald green eyes putting an immediate halt to her revolt. Her mouth gaped, but nothing came out. Not a peep or even a squeak, she felt mousey in his presence.

And yet, his towering presence didn't shrink her journalistic mind. She studied him; summarizing he was about six-two, maybe taller and around one hundred eighty pounds, maybe thirty give or take a few years. No wedding ring, clean shaven, and smelled of musk cologne, possibly

Polo by Ralph Lauren. Manly and fresh, not that it mattered in the least bit to her. He was definitely not her type. *Not at all*, she curtly reminded herself patting her brow and smoothing her hairline. *Not nervous, just a case of first day jitters*, she told herself. Waiting for his latent response, her attention waned momentarily to her other office comrades flowing into the office bay like an organized school of fish. Everyone went about their business obtaining morning coffee and checking the mail cubbies. They chattered and gazed lazily at the industrial clock for the precise time to punch-in to begin another exciting day of their journalism careers. But not him, he stayed with his long legs comfortably extended into the aisle still juggling her name plate.

She asked again, "Do you mind?"

With a cocky boyish grin he said, "Yes, I do mind...sometimes. So, you're Amanda Lindas. Hmm... a 1982 graduate of Marquette University in Milwaukee, Wisconsin. You obtained high honors in journalism and communications. You made the National Dean's list not once, but twice for straight A's during your four year stint. 'A promising up and coming news star,' reported in the Chicago Tribune. Your parents are divorced. Your mother, Florence resides in Chicago and your father, Archibald resides in Miami. You'd be an only child except you have an older sister, Dory who... let me think, is not married and lives in Pennsylvania. Have I left anything out?" His suave voice hinged on another quirky smile.

Smugness looked good on him. It oozed from him as he tossed her name plate again in midair just high enough for her to seize the opportunity to snatch it. She bolted up from her chair, reeling it backwards against the metal rail just below the large glass windows attached to Mr. Underwood's office.

The chair crashed discharging a huge BANG! Loud enough to traumatize their officemates, they hunkered down as if waiting for the A-bomb to explode. Amanda missed the plaque.

The anonymous squatter paid no mind, not missing a beat, he smirked and asked. "Oh, may I call you Mandy?"

Snatching her newly acquired name plate from his grip she quipped, "No, only my *friends* call me Mandy. It is Ms. Lindas to you." Her icy-blue eyes glared. "I see you've done your homework. What were you in college–the class clown?"

He flinched, as if her words wounded him or he believed she would strike him with the name plate hovering by her head clenched in her slender fingers.

"Well if you insist... my name is..."

"No, I did not insist. Get your facts straight." She interjected sarcastically shifting her position from victim to foe.

"I am here to work. And furthermore, if I want to be entertained by a clown, I will go to the circus." Her icy words and eyes nearly frostbit him.

From behind her, Mr. Underwood's firm baritone voice rattled through the office, "Mandy, please come to my office? Mr. Kilawee remove your backside from her desk and get some work done today."

Mr. Kilawee didn't move.

Amanda's face pinked. Sure enough, Mr. Underwood felt the glass shake in his office when her chair slammed into the metal rail. And sure enough, it was her first day and already she was being reprimanded. In less than an hour, she had caused a huge splash in the peaceful fishbowl skirmishing with an oversized piranha.

The bay of business attired fish-faced workers swirled into tapping on keyboards while sending swells of murmurings through the press office.

Amanda fidgeted with her name plaque and placed it *exactly* where it was, before she was so rudely accosted by–*Mr. Kilawee. What sort of name is that?* She wondered.

Absentminded, she turned into her opened desk drawer. Surely it left a bruise on her knee. "Damn it!" she hissed, slamming the drawer. She walked towards Mr. Underwood who waited patiently. His brow furrowed. She wasn't sure if it was because of her or Mr. Kilawee. She surmised she was about to find out.

Closing the door to the press tank, Rich Underwood pointed to one of the black leather bucket chairs sitting opposite of his oppressive teakwood desk. Amanda sat like a well trained show dog.

Silent, he poured a fresh cup of coffee at the credenza on the backside of his desk, "So, I see you've had the pleasure of meeting Kurt Kilawee?" Nonchalantly he plopped two sugar cubes into the steaming white mug that donned the blue NYCB logo. "Care for a cup of coffee?" His eyes never sought hers, until he lifted the freshly brewed coffee to his sandy-blond mustached covered lip. He eyed her over the cup rim.

She'd love a fresh cup of coffee; the aroma made her nostrils tingle and teased her into believing it was superior to the mud brewed in the pressroom coffee urn.

Her hands twisted in her lap, she wet her parched lips, and stared respectfully into his tired blue eyes. She managed a slight nod.

"So does your nod mean yes on both accounts?" He inquired as he set his mug down and cordially poured another cup. "Cream or sugar?"

"Ah, both," Amanda managed to find her voice under a layer of fear.

"Okay, let's get something clear. Were you answering my first questions or my second?" His eyebrows rose almost eliminating his frown.

7

Amanda allowed a small smile to creep across her warm blushing face. "Yes, to the coffee, cream, and sugar. And – a definite, no – to the *pleasure* of meeting Mr. Kurt Kilawee." His name rolled comfortably off her tongue.

Rich handed her the fresh coffee, she accepted. He casually sat at the edge of his splendid desk with one leg extended and his other knee bent close enough for her to touch. She automatically retreated into the comfortable chair with her coffee clutched in both hands. The mug was hot, nearly as hot as her cheeks. It was highly irregular for her to be reprimanded. Studiously she waited for his reproof.

He stared at the ceiling, his left forearm rested on his thigh with his coffee mug gripped in his hand. He scanned the office as if taking inventory. His bent leg kicked slightly possibly assisting in his contemplations.

Finally he quelled the thick silence. "Hmm... how can I put this to you?" he looked squarely into her eyes. "We need to be on the same page. Open honest communication is of the utmost priority. My personal and professional advice to you is to avoid too much interaction with Mr. Kilawee. He has the reputation of being a womanizer. And he will, if given the opportunity steal any leads you may have on all big stories. He's the hungry wolf in sheep's clothing. A cutthroat– he takes no prisoners. But don't misunderstand me, he's a topnotch reporter. Quick. And so far the best journalist/anchor we have. Kurt will be your biggest pain and downfall if you let him rattle you." He leaned over and stared into her eyes. "Mandy can you keep it professional?" He stood and walked to her side.

"I think so. When you say he's a womanizer, do you mean at work or outside of work?" Amanda bet he saw fear rising up from her inner most sanctuary. After all, she was new on the job, she didn't want to rock the boat, cause a ruckus, and sink it.

"Both. Kurt Kilawee has the propensity for being a fast-paced playboy. But don't worry sexual harassment at NYCB it is never permitted. It's a new era and by law we are required to protect everyone from injustice. Just remain professional with him and let me know if any problems arise. I am here to help launch your career. You can be the next star reporter at NYCB." Wearing a pleasant smile, he placed a comforting hand on her padded shoulder giving it a reassuring squeeze.

Then without premise he clicked his coffee mug to hers and flashed a toothy white grin covered slightly by his bushy mustache. For an older man of forty-something, she guessed, he wasn't half bad, even sort of attractive. Although today he looked ragged around the edges, unshaven with bloodshot eyes as if he hadn't slept. Maybe he was just having a bad day, she could relate to that.

Amanda suspected that her day was going to get better when he refilled her coffee cup and let her take it to her desk. The best part was when he released her into the sea of desks; he hollered. "Kilawee get your ass in here now!"

Mr. Underwood's expression was not nearly as welcoming to Kurt as it was to her. She made her exit expressing an enigmatic smirk at Kurt. He yielded, held the door wide allowing her to pass. His face reflected grimness, not panic. Signs of wild mischief sparked in his eyes.

His eyebrow quirk charmed her as he tipped his fedora inducing an unbiased flutter from her lashes. She felt his intense gawking before he entered Mr. Underwood's open forum. He was much too tall, she confirmed. *Not her type at all.*

Inside the bullpen, Kurt sat on the edge of the leather chair back; his arms crossed his chest, unwilling to surrender to Rich's boorish dominant nature. He waited. He knew what was coming and he suspected the underlying reasons why.

Rich's eyes met his darting and furious, his hands clutched his hips. "What the hell are you doing terrorizing the new help?"

Kurt stood straight overshadowing Rich by a few inches, placing his hands on his hips in retribution, "Oh, come off it. I was just having a little fun; just *feeling* out the pretty new acquisition. What is she, your new office toy? Getting a little younger these days huh?" He knew Rich knew where he was going with his innuendos.

"Knock it off, Kurt! What the hell do you know about where this company is going? We need new blood to get better stories and more coverage. Just so you know she's not only pretty, she's bright. And I don't need you interfering with her career." He pointed at Kurt's chest, his face pumped deep red, wicked intent accompanied his words. "FYI... she's up for your job as top investigative journalist, so watch yourself Anchorman. Now get out of my office and stay out of my sight."

Kurt grimaced, feeling the sting of bile rise up his throat. His face flashed with indignation. He had no response that wouldn't have gotten him thrown out into the street. He needed this job, so keeping his cool was essential. Besides, he and Rich went way back a few more years than he cared to remember. Rich was his mentor and gave him his first real break as an anchorman. Rich was the big brother type you loved to hate.

Kurt shrugged off Rich's threats and strutted out the glass door slamming it so hard he nearly broke it off its hinges. A cacophonous rapture spread through the office. He suspected the other NYCB personnel cherished when Rich and he were at odds; it kept Rich off their backs if only for an ephemeral period. With a dour glare he scoured the room daring anyone to speak. His lovely competitor kept her eyes attached to her computer screen.

He'd address her again, later. Glancing at the clock it was a quarter of nine; time to leave. Maybe a short city walk could dissipate his aggravation. Too bad it was too early for a drink; he could use one to celebrate his new competitor, as if he didn't have enough competition in New York City.

Besides that he had an appointment with Sarah Underwood, Rich's wealthy oversexed wife, the main investor in NYCB.

Earlier she called Kurt about a special assignment asking him to keep it under wraps away from Rich. She promised to pay well. And money was all Kurt needed right now for motivation. The disagreement with Rich made it easier for him to escape quickly and make the appointment without anyone prying.

Outside, Kurt flagged a taxi and instructed the driver to take him to *The Tavern on the Green* on Central Park West. He was pissed at himself for leaving his Armani suit jacket back at the office. It would force him to return to the office later, preferably after Rich left for his late liquid lunch by three with Daffy, the receptionist.

During the cab ride across Midtown, Kurt unrolled his shirtsleeves and adjusted his black tie. Leaning in close to the rearview mirror checking his hair and hat, he thought about why Sarah petitioned him.

She had mentioned it wasn't a news lead. So it meant one thing. Well, possibly two, but he hoped it was his first instinct and not his second. The first inclination was she wanted him to use his private detective skills to flush out some unworthy associate in her social circle. Dig up some dirt, or drag some unethical skeletons out of someone's closet. The unanswered questions were–who? And why him? Then that triggered his second option which she had approached him before on addressing her sexual urges.

He was in no mood to suppress or conquer her urges then or now, so he hoped to God it was the former and not the latter.

Chapter 2

Frustration was rapidly becoming a chronic disease for Kurt Kilawee. After his morning meeting with Sarah Underwood had stretched into afternoon, he escorted her to a waiting town car. She awarded him with a somewhat freakish gesture, a warm peck on each cheek for his compliance to her wishes.

Weary he returned to *The Tavern on the Green* bar hoping to find resolve in a couple more highballs of Irish whiskey. Although he was wise enough to realize that alcohol was just a temporary solution to the greater turmoil he just agreed to; his wisdom did not curb him from drinking more.

Not that he had a choice–*not* to accept Sarah's timely monetary bonus for his services. At times he wished he would have stayed in Chicago coddled by his mother's sweet but overbearing indulgence. His ultimate desire was to be free from money worries and the women who came with them. *God, the things a man does for money and sex makes him the most pathetic of the two sexes, possibly of all creatures.*

The minutes and hours passed as he contemplated his life and unstable career. It was evident that his talents were squandered at NYCB, yet the *avant-garde* news venue opened doors to obtaining lucrative opportunities with affluent clients and permitted him freedom to moonlight as a private detective. His passions amply supplied not only adrenalin-junky adventures, but lined his pockets and bank accounts. The day would eventually come when his mother would stop dumping money into his account. She insisted on generously supporting him as he pursued his tremendous dreams of obtaining a high profile anchor job or opening a prestigious detective agency.

He surmised her motivation was her aversion to having 'her baby' serve on the Chicago police department with his older brothers and his father.

Kurt was torn between his passions. Every business adventure takes capital and his required an expensive wardrobe to properly convey competence and perceived success. Ill-at-ease with his surreptitious agreement to Sarah, he felt confident he'd have an ulcer by the end of the summer.

Sarah was cunning and convincing, fully admirable by letting him keep his top position at NYCB regardless of what Rich's new protégé could accomplish. The underlying truth was if he did as Sarah requested then he could *keep* his job–period.

With that premise, Sarah had slipped a fat envelop under the table. A considerable advance towards his future work for which she assumed with his astuteness he would deliver. What else could he say, but yes. It wasn't as if she gave him any other options, like what's behind door #2?

Trapped like a starving mouse on a glue board or mousetrap greedily nibbling on cheese; he was destine to suffer predation or suffocation. Unethical entrapment was a traditional trap in the rat race called life.

Perhaps he misjudged Sarah, either way he had no choice.

Go ahead enjoy the bait until the trap–snaps! He automatically coached himself. *After all wasn't it Emerson that said, "Build a better mousetrap, and the world will beat a path to your door–"*

Problem was Sarah was playing and paying him well–to set a bigger trap for a large rat–perhaps too well.

Her puzzling words spooked him. Spoken in her best dramatic Marlene Dietrich alto voice, "Darling, you can do this; all you need is a little thread of information. This could get twisted. But you have the ability to turn it into a huge ball of truth. Spin it and weave it into a story we will both be proud of. Wrap it up as a befitting gift for my return from Europe. I promise there will be more." Her sultry sophisticated looks and words mesmerized men and women alike. Kurt decided if she was going for the Joan Collin's lookalike contest. She nailed it. She was a dead ringer.

Frankly, it wasn't that he was absolutely appalled by her or his new assignment, but it was going to be as difficult as performing surgery with a butter-knife. The goals were obtain the evidence and avoid getting caught spying while following up on his regular work leads.

Glancing at his watch, already quarter to four, he drank the highball libations. Time to return to the office to collect his weekly lead folder and his jacket, he tarried awhile longer hoping Rich had plenty of time to leave for his sex filled liquid lunch. To deal with Rich in his alcohol infused state would be like stepping into the ring with Mohammed Ali without sparring gear. Self-induced manslaughter–.

Kurt rubbed the rough stubble on his chin and called out in his best English-Italian accent. "Hey, Tony, Antonio, or whatever you call yourself, pour me another." Primarily he wasn't a big drinker, but lately he had gotten tied up with leads that took him on New York's tour of the finest bars and exclusive clubs. Sometimes to get the best stories you had to "sleep with the enemy".

Kurt evil eyed the Italian swing shift bartender busying himself cleaning the glassware maintaining the elite reputation of *The Tavern on the Green*. "Hey, you speaka da English?" he tapped his empty glass on the bar.

Antonio Casali extended his buff arms to the bar ledge, leaning in he studied Kurt's bloodshot eyes, "You sure you need another? Or should we just close your tab and pour you into a cab? Or is there a car service at your beckon call?" Subtle contempt augmented his voice.

Kurt looked up with a wry half-smile, "Hey, I will let you know when I'm finished. And if I wanted a limo service at my beckon call I'd have one, so you just do your job and pour. And I'll do my job and drink. I do appreciate your attention to detail. The lady is just a business associate not my keeper."

"Hey man, no offense, but you're pretty tanked and the evening has just begun." Antonio smiled warmly and poured.

"No offense taken, thanks for your concern. I need fuel–I have to go... *to face the Ice-maiden*." He murmured the latter, shot down the whiskey, and followed with a sharp wince. "Now, you may pour me into a taxi." Kurt staggered reaching into his front pocket for cash. The fat envelop noticeably bulged his opposite pocket, reminding him he was still pissed at himself for leaving his expensive jacket at the office. He needed to get back. It was not every day that he wore or could afford custom Armani suits. Just recently, he purchased two suits and a tuxedo attempting to impress his high-class clients. To fit in, he dressed and acted as any affluent anchorman would; playing celebrity was a key part of the job.

Kurt slammed a fifty on the bar, "Keep the change." He backed up, almost tipping over the heavy wood barstool into a couple of early diners strolling pass.

Antonio came around the bar catching the chair sparing the elderly couple from injury. He directed Kurt towards the exit.

"Hey, can I get a cup of Joe to go?" Kurt said with a slur. "You know, *a cup of Joe,* is Joseph Daniels fault. He was Woodrow Wilson's Secretary of the Navy. He reformed drunken sailors by making coffee the strongest beverage on the Navy ships. I'll bet you didn't know that?"

"Sure man, whatever you say." Antonio motioned a waitress to get the coffee. "Where are you headed sir?" He asked as he poured Kurt in the taxi.

"I told you, I am going to see the Ice-maiden of Hell. Hell will freeze over before she gets my job. To the Empire State Building–." he glanced over at the driver's name plate, leaving Antonio confused about the Ice-maiden. "Okay Bob. B-o-b that's a nice name... Bob is a palindrome. Simple forward or backward... Bob's the man."

Mild mannered Antonio pushed Kurt back into the seat and handed him his hot coffee. "You heard him Bob, to the Empire State Building."

"Cheers!" Kurt toasted his host, as the waitress brought his fedora to the taxi. Antonio placed it on Kurt's head. "Thank you, thank you very much." His Elvis impersonation was garbled.

Bob took the scenic route winding through Central Park from West 67th to the eastside southbound on 5th Ave. to 34th. The thick afternoon traffic gave Kurt the advantage to gather his sober bearings. A few deep breaths and sips of hot black coffee, he'd be back on his game.

At the office, Amanda studied her lead list from her blue folder. There were several lead folders: orange, yellow, green, pretty much the whole gambit of the rainbow. She contemplated the hierarchy of which color folder was coveted and which lead would catapult her into the "Star Anchor" journalist position.

Curious she investigated the cubbies earlier finding that Kurt Kilawee and Jeremy Meyer, the lead cameraman, both contained blue folders. She had the delight of meeting Jeremy that morning. A pleasant effeminate black male, if she were to guess, mid-twenties around her age. He was very informative about office protocol as they rode the elevator to the top of the Empire State Building. A virgin to seeing the city from the sky, Amanda was totally enthralled with its majesty. Jeremy patiently pointed out landmark buildings she hoped to see up close.

During their lunch tour, he explained on how, when, and where she was to page him for emergency reports. But for scheduling offsite interviews she was to go through dispatch. Jeremy reminded her of a younger Lionel Richie which to her surprise, several of his co-workers referred to him as Lionel. She politely inquired as to which name he desired.

He looked at her with a genteel sparkle in his brown doe-like eyes, "Listen, just be sure to call me before Kilawee does, and I won't care what you call me." He smiled and winked, as if forewarning her of her co-worker's habits.

"Is he mean?" she had to ask.

"No sugar, he's just hungry for the truth and wild for women. It's his nature to be an arrogant jerk sometimes. Most times he's harmless. Just be careful and call me, I'll take care of you like a mother hen with a baby chick." A bright white grin flashed across his face. "Remember we are all wearing the same jerseys. Teamwork will win in the end. I noticed Rich put you on the best team." He fanned his blue folder. They strolled around another lap on the windy deck, the view put spectacular back into her day.

The best team. Teamwork will win. Amanda repeated in her head. She wanted to be a part of a winning something–anything. It would be a welcomed change in her life. Just as she researched her list of leads, she heard someone at the front entrance. The blonde-bombshell receptionist, Delphina had left shortly after Mr. Underwood, around three. The others left soon after they received their assignment folders.

The intruder had a key, so it eased her initial fear. That was until she saw him, Mr. Kilawee. He appeared disheveled and devilish.

By his aroma he must have had an interview with a brewery. She glanced up at the clock, it was not quite quitting time, a quarter to five. She feigned reading. From the corner of her eye she noticed he wasn't swaggering with his earlier overconfidence and he had a strange bulge on the right side of his tastefully fitted dress-slacks. She couldn't help but notice; it seemed to throw his lanky physique off balance.

He went to his cubby silently, well as silent as a drunk trying to be sober could.

More curiosity peaked; she continued to spy to see his reaction to his blue folder contents. He browsed through it and threw it. "Damn it Rich!"

Amanda continued to study him. He caught her.

"What are you looking at?" He inquired with a hostile noticeable slur.

A small smile cracked her face, her eyes cut to her computer. "Oh nothing. Did you have a good interview with a bottle of scotch?"

Awkward and slow he gathered his folder from the office floor, keeping his emerald eyes glued on her. "It was a great interview with a fine bottle of Irish Whiskey, if you must know."

"Well, I hope you accomplished what you wanted. Looks like we are going to have a busy schedule tomorrow," she raised her blue folder like a prized award.

"Yeah, looks that way. Guess we will have to become fast friends, Mandy," he cocked his hat in an alluring fashion, "since we will be working hand in hand, and side by side." A natural sexual charm radiated from him as he approached her.

"Well, I wouldn't presuppose that we will be the hand in hand type of work associates. I am professional. And I assure you that I will not be sucked into clownish sophomoric antics." She stated the facts as she saw them.

Ambivalent, offended and challenged, he ambled close to her desk. Should he buy into her hectoring sarcasm or set her straight with his credulous intelligence that she simply pretended to ignore?

"Ms. Lindas, I assure you that I was not the class clown of my graduating class. I happen to have a degree in criminology and journalism with top honors from the University of Chicago. I was on the National Dean's List before you entered college. And I worked as a private investigator in Chicago until about three years ago when I decided New York was the place for me and my hat." He tipped his hat forward shadowing his brilliant laughing eyes.

Her icy eyes darted into his soul, "Hmm, I don't recall inquiring about your background Mr. Kilawee or your hat. I simply stated that your future would not involve doing anything hand in hand with me." She shuffled and straightened the papers on her desk several times before standing them on edge and tapping them on her desktop.

He was so close she could practically get drunk just off the fumes that emanated from him. Not to be towered by his stature, she rose to meet his glare. There was an awkward standoffish silence between them.

As if he didn't know any better; she thought he was going to lean in and kiss her. She flinched, turned her face to the clock. Thereby escaping his flirty green eyes; the clock hands slipped past five. She shifted right to avoid his advancement. But he quickly shifted in front of her.

"Now wait, Ms. Lindas, I think we've started off on the wrong foot. Maybe we should go somewhere to discuss our differences of opinion. Particularly the one you have of me. I am not the enemy. I am the lead reporter, and I believe you are my understudy."

She shifted left, he followed. "Mr. Kilawee, I am not anyone's understudy. I was hired to do special interest stories that you obviously are not qualified to do. Otherwise, Mr. Underwood would not have selected me for the job."

"You can drop the formalities, by all means, call me Kurt. What do you mean that I am not qualified? I assure you Sweetheart that I am totally qualified to handle any special interest stories that you can handle with just as much or more finesse."

"Really, you have quite the remarkable opinion of yourself? Maybe you should look over our leads with more scrutiny Mr. Kilawee. Mine pertain to women's special interests from a woman's point of view. Funny, but you don't look like a woman to me," she scanned him. "Now, refrain from calling me Sweetheart and following my footsteps, I would like to leave."

Kurt's demeanor softened, "Well, at least you recognized that I am a man." He smiled.

"You appear to be of the male species. Whether that makes or breaks your qualifications to cover stories for women, I wouldn't know nor do I care to speculate. I believe in a strict professional working atmosphere. I am here to launch my career as NYCB's top news anchor." Her cold blue eyes were unwavering pools of darkness.

"Ah yes, you are qualified to be a woman. And Rich likes 'pretty' qualified women. Pretty goes a long ways around here."

"Thank you, I am almost flattered that you think I'm pretty. You're correct about one thing; I am going a long ways–preferably away from you." Her face pinked. The uncontrollable urge to be sarcastic wasn't professional. She didn't want to become prey to his banter. "Now please, excuse me."

Kurt stepped aside allowing her to pass. She turned to collect her briefcase and purse. Cordially he stretched for them. "Here, allow me." He slipped her purse strap on the firm shoulder pad of her power-suit.

Admittedly he thought she pulled off the fashionable feminist power guise well. From her neatly pulled back hair to her perfectly rendered makeup to the fitted pencil skirt that ended discreetly at her attractive knees above her well formed calves, maybe it won't be so terrible to work with her. Mandy-Candy was a delight for his acute eyes.

"Thank you, but I don't need or want your self-aggrandizing help." Amanda clutched her briefcase under her arm and strutted towards the exit.

"See you tomorrow, Mandy." He said flipping his fedora airborne and landing it on his head.

After Amanda's exit, Kurt staggered to his small office passing the restrooms, the supply room, and the janitor's closet to collect his Armani suit-jacket. Collecting it and his blue folder, he shuffled out of the office door locking it behind him.

By the time he arrived to the lobby, Amanda was walking out the large revolving door. Definitely a nice curvy piece, not bad on the eyes, at least that was one benefit. If he was forced to work with a woman; she might as well be attractive. Problem was–she smelled nice too. Another hindrance, just looking wasn't his forte, he liked touching. And Amanda Lindas was definitely the untouchable kind.

He followed to watch her hips sway confidently in her appropriate power-suit and black sensible heels down 34th Street. He kept vigil until she was just another speck in the maddening crowds of New York. Too bad, he thought, she wasn't going to disappear as the proverbial thorn in his side anytime soon. *Word of advice Kilawee– she's strictly business– deal with it.*

He slung his Armani jacket over his shoulder, lowered his mirrored aviator sunglasses shading his tired bloodshot eyes. He headed east to his

Kips Bay area apartment on East 33rd and Lexington. It wasn't the Waldorf Astoria, but it was clean and almost completely renovated.

Time to sleep off his drunk and maybe later he'd workout in his newly renovated basement gym near his lower apartment. His place was the opposite direction from Amanda Lindas' apartment. He knew her building well, just off West 35th. He found it for Rich and Sarah, not realizing that it was for his competition.

Now, that mystery was solved. But Amanda Lindas didn't know, and what she didn't know was to his advantage.

Amanda huffed to her apartment. Overheated by the June heat and the fact she was seriously miffed at her new co-worker and his obvious arrogance. His roving eyes practically undressed her, how was she going to deal with him every day?

Entering the redbrick building she slipped her key into her brass mailbox. Sure enough, her luck, she received a credit card bill and junk mail. At least she had an official place to call home in New York City.

She was so excited when Rich phoned to say *he* had found her the perfect two-bedroom corner flat on the eleventh floor, stating she would have a slight view of 34th Street. It was her favorite street ever since she was a little girl watching Macy's Thanksgiving Day Parade. And even better her apartment was the eleventh apartment on the eleventh floor which was her and her best friend Shelly's favorite lucky number.

Rich paid attention to details. The building was also one of those real historical gems kept in pristine condition. The massive wood doors matched the dark wood wainscot that lined the dimly lit parchment colored halls. She was grateful for the working elevator.

When Amanda unlocked her apartment, the eerie feeling of being watched sent slithering chills through her. The click and slide of metal against metal caused her head to jerk and peer over her shoulder. Across the hall, a large violet-blue eye laden with fake eyelashes, thick black eyeliner, and dark blue eye shadow spied at her from a chained door held slightly ajar.

With sly and slow inspection she gathered the eye was connected to a petite dark-haired woman; her bare feet were exposed at the bottom of the door crack. With her door unlocked; Amanda looked back at the decorated eye and said, "Hello, I'm Amanda Lindas. Who are you?"

The door slammed shut.

Amanda shrugged. *I guess the spooky-eye owner is not ready to meet me, yet.* The agenda for that week included meeting new friends in her neighborhood and at work. Just one long weekend in New York and she already missed Shelly and home.

In her living-dining area she dropped her purse and briefcase on a wicker side chair. The apartment appeared more spacious than most New York flats simply because she didn't have many furnishings. To cover purchasing furniture, she was waiting for a belated birthday slash Christmas slash College graduation check promised from her unreliable unpredictable father. Maybe she could buy a real bedroom ensemble instead of using her red sofa with a beat up coffee table that doubled as desk slash bed stand. She flicked the wall switch to illuminate the sparse room with her alien like chrome and white orb floor lamp, a reject from the 70's. However, she did have her prized possession; her tall bookshelf filled with a plethora of books and news magazines. To complete the homey look was her boom box with her collection of cassettes organized in alphabetical order. Her music and her books sufficed as perfect company until she was able to purchase a television. Rich promised once her stories sold to special interest groups or became syndicated she would receive royalties in sizable bonus checks.

Her hottest lead focused on the election with Geraldine Ferraro selected as the first woman on the Democratic primary ticket. Still another fascinating lead was on feminist groups protesting unfairness to lesbians and gays in the work place. Amanda snickered. *Love to give that one to Kurt, just to watch him squirm while the ladies detested him and the men goggle-eyed him.* Kurt was the type women and men liked to watch and touch. And the arrogant bastard knew it.

Before she finished her thoughts someone rapped on her door. She flipped her sensible black work shoes off and proceeded with caution to the peephole. Through the fishbowl lens she spied the impish raccoon eyed spy from across the hall, within her grasp was a white ceramic coffee mug. No guns or knives visible, so it must be okay to open the door. The girl like woman was tiny. Amanda believed if she had to, she could take her in a fair fight. But just in case, she hinged the chain lock before she unlatched the large deadbolt.

She opened the door the length of the short chain, she stared at the girl and the girl stared back. They sized each other up as everyone does when they first meet.

The pixie-sized Joan Jett look-alike lifted her mug. "Can I borrow a cup of sugar?" her voice raspy, but soft.

Amanda shut the door. Quickly she unlatched the chain and reopened the door. "Hey, sorry about the chain, but you never know?"

"Yeah like, I hear ya." The neighbor said and stepped in. "Wow, this place is real *bad*, like real clean, like I can see the floor. You're not Euro-trash or a JAP, are you?"

Amanda's face was covered with confusion. "What? JAP? Euro-trash? Ah no, I'm from Wisconsin originally then transplanted to Chicago. Do I look Japanese?"

"No, not at all. You know JAP–like Jewish American Princess or Euro-trash–like a Richie from Europe? The place is crawling with them." The strange girl whispered as if the room was bugged.

Amanda chuckled inside. Her strange neighbor wore black other than her rainbow striped legwarmers. She was some sort of punk-rocker who rambled on about invaders while Amanda went to the cupboard to find sugar. To her amazement she discovered her shelves loaded with food. Mr. Underwood must have filled them. He kept a spare key and said he would help out, and it appeared he did. Nice to know some people follow through on their promises unlike her father. No check in the mail, again.

Grabbing the sugar, she thought, *a cup of sugar such a nineteen fifties Midwestern neighborly thing to do, for a woman who barely looked out of her teens.* "What do you need the sugar for? Do you bake?"

"Bake? Me? Oh shit no." The mysterious girl blurted then clamped her hand over her small bow mouth. "Oh sorry, for my wicked mouth," she sank onto the red sofa tucking her bare feet hiding the rainbow striped legwarmers. Her short blackish-blue hair was ratted up and pulled to one side with a black banana clip.

"No problem, I've heard worse wicked words, believe me. My parents fought most of my life and they used all the choice words. If you know what I mean?" Amanda took the cup from her neighbor's hand. "Say what do you call yourself? Got a name or nickname? You look like Joan Jett–the rocker girl."

"Wow, thanks. At the clubs they call me *The Wanna-be Joanie*, but my real name is Belinda Blaskowski. Kind of Polish, but really I'm part Russian, Hungarian, or something. Not a Commie."

Amanda handed Belinda the sugar. "Hey, I'm no judge of people's names or backgrounds. What's the sugar for if you don't mind me asking?"

Belinda lowered her eyes and clutched the mug close, "Well, honestly I am learning to like coffee, I really need a pick-me-up because I'm dead at work sometimes. But I found out I only like coffee with lots of sugar in it. Kind of lame huh?"

"No, I wouldn't say that. I take sugar and cream in my coffee. As a matter of fact I like my coffee like I like my men– sweet, tan, and hot."

Belinda chuckled. "I guess that means I like mine extra sweet, strong, and hot. Oh, I suppose I should go. I'm probably cutting into your chill time."

"My chill time? Ah no, not really. I was just getting home from the office still hot after a confrontation with a co-worker. He's a guy." She frowned and plopped down on the opposite side of the sofa.

"Oh, I see. What is he a dickhead, dweeb, or just a barf-bag?"

Amanda shifted up straight, a bit shocked at Belinda's assumption that Kurt was an undesirable hick. "Oh no, he's quite the opposite, damn smart and damn good looking. A sharp dressed man with amazing green eyes–" She stared into the distance evoking his flirtatious gaze.

"Hey Earth to Amanda–wake-up. He must be someone's boy toy if he's that bodacious unforgettable. So what's the absolute problem? Find out who's got him on a leash and set him free. You're a real looker. I can help if you want."

"No. He's not my type. He's too tall and lanky. And did I mention horribly arrogant."

Belinda's wide eyes widened. "Say, I've seen a guy like that around here. And I think I've seen him out at the hot clubs too. The kind of model like guy, like jock type, the kind Calvin Klein puts on billboards in tight jeans and no shirt for the world to gawk at–one choice hot-blooded guy. Not my type either. A little too good looking, the kind you can't trust."

Amanda bit her lower lip, "Yeah, you're right that kind. But you have seen him around here?" This alerted Amanda in a queasy weird way.

Belinda stood shaking her feet awake, "Sure, he wears fantabulous duds and a cool hat like detectives wear on TV. I nicknamed him Hot-n-Yummy Vice. He has a cute tight ass, nice front package view too."

Amanda raised her eyebrows, "I wouldn't know that, but the hat is definitely his signature. Wonder why he was here? When did you see him last?"

Belinda opened the door, "Oh, maybe a couple of weeks ago. He hasn't been around since you moved in. But some older blond guy with a mustache and sideburns was here, he brought groceries. Does that help?"

Amanda went to the door as Belinda made her exit, "Yeah, sure does. Let me know if you see either of them around." Belinda walked across the hall. Amanda had a whoosh of inspiration, "Hey, maybe we could hang out sometime or do lunch on the weekend? Not like a girl date, but like friends–you know?"

Belinda smiled, "Like yeah, just friends, 'cause I'm into dudes."

"Yeah me too–totally into dudes," Amanda said doing a lame midair fist pump.

.

Chapter 3

The New York summer heat struck seasonably early with high humidity leaving Amanda perspiring in her power-suits, but her vain ego refused the compromise of dressing down.

Kurt, on the other hand, was Mr. Cool. Perfect hair, perfect attire for whatever occasions they encountered. She hated his timely appropriate appearance and quick witted responses. It was like he couldn't fail. Maybe hate wasn't the right word–maybe envy was more correct, but she kept herself in denial.

Anchorman Kurt Kilawee attended every parade, festival, grand opening, and society party that was listed on their lead sheets. When Amanda failed to get her foot in the front door, Kurt finagled his way in the back and met her with Jeremy in tow. A man of several disguises, waiter, doorman, and even a dog walker in the gay and lesbian parade, he excelled beyond compare. The parade was her story, but he landed the interview. He even protected her from a gregarious woman who pursued her, by introducing Amanda as his girlfriend. It burned her, but it worked.

Kurt Kilawee worked the system and he was damn good at it. She reluctantly admitted he was cleverly entertaining and enlightening.

They fought like two King cobras giving Jeremy migraines and fits, each time they rode in his camera van. He threatened them with bodily harm and worst of all with divulging their unprofessionalism to Rich.

It was the end of June when the transit and sanitation unions threatened city wide strikes if demands were not met. By, Monday, July 2nd, the heat of the strikes and violence had Kurt anxious to tackle his leads. Amanda had her own agenda. Simultaneously, they reached for the front passenger door of Jeremy's camera van.

"Shotgun!" Kurt called.

"Oh hell no, I need the air-conditioner. I have an interview with the sanitation union leader." Amanda snapped. "The humidity is torture to my hair."

Kurt inadvertently touched her hair, "I like your wild side."

She slapped his hand away.

Jeremy reached and locked the door. Like he channeled an old southern woman, he shouted, "Y'all get in the back seat! I ain't havin' none of your shit today. It's hotter than Haiti and the air-conditioner is broken, so shut the hell up, get buckled in, and don't give me any lip." He often slipped into his country roots when his frustration level skyrocketed.

"Well, Jeremy don't you think ladies should go first?" Amanda demanded.

Kurt yanked the backside door handle, "Lady my ass, when did you get the premonition that you personify a lady? Seniority should have precedence Lionel." It was essential for Kurt to get to the transit garage off 116th before his snitch ditched him. He squeezed into the back with a money roll lodged in his pocket.

Earlier Amanda had cunningly addressed the wad with a snide comment. "Hey Kurt, are you happy to see me? Or are you trying to impress everyone?" He wondered where she was getting her overtly cocky attitude and script.

When she started at NYCB she was demure and accepted a few pointers from him. The longer she worked the more perverse and strikingly witty her comments evolved. It seemed someone trashy was feeding her lines. And Amanda was quite the pro delivering them at just the right time in front of their close knit co-workers. Because of her blatant observation that morning, he was forced to put on his linen suit-jacket to divert attention from his bulging pocket. *Happy to see her–my ass. Damn her.*

He promised himself when the chance presented itself he would insist Rich switch her off the Blue team. He had worked too many nights on Sarah Underwood's project spying on Rich and his own underground union leaks to lose anymore sleep competing with Amanda.

Squished together on the bench seat with the camera equipment, they managed to keep a few inches between them. Kurt scrunched his cream blazer sleeves up trying to get reprieve from the heat.

Next to him she looked as cool as ice in her fitted short-sleeved navy shirt dress with a red patent leather belt. Her fresh showered scent perked his manly senses into overdrive. Lately she'd been having that affect on him.

Problem was he was so busy watching Rich skirt chasing he had no time to chase skirts for himself. Another problem–Amanda was the innocent kind a man could really care about, not that he was to that point. But spending eight to ten hour days with her and several nights when they had to tag team at social functions was wearing down his resistance to her. Christ, he was only human, and she flaunted her wholesome purity act everywhere.

At least from what he gathered, she wasn't seeing anyone in particular. When he saw other guys making moves on her, she pretended not to notice, or she was just naïve to her natural charms. His thoughts of her made him swelter as they pulled out of the parking garage off 33rd Street.

"Lionel, you sure the air isn't working? God it's hot, roll the window down more. Mandy must you sit on top of me?" Kurt complained and shoved her,–just a little.

"Oh, you wish. Keep your paws to yourself. And don't call me Mandy." She adjusted the lower half of her tight dress. "Jeremy tell animal man to leave me alone."

"Whoa showing a little leg this morning huh?" Kurt commented after his eyes roved her. "Hey Lionel, the professional career girl isn't wearing nylons. Must have a hot date today or she's already starting the Fourth of July long weekend early," he reverted back to Amanda, "or are you trying to tease me?" It was working.

Just the thought of coming close to touching her long slender legs sent his carnal mind and senses to a roguish mood. Undoing his shirt another button and fanning for air, didn't help one bit. His eyes drifted up and down her smooth tan legs. And when she caught him looking longer than usual, she swatted his shoulder, crossed her legs, and turned away from him. That didn't help divert his attentions, he just lingered a little longer taking in her three inch red heels.

"Do you mind?" she shoved him. "Try keeping your eyes in your head. Jeremy tell him to stop staring at me."

Jeremy slammed on the brakes and glared over his shoulder, "If you two don't stop that bickering, I will beat some sense into you. Now knock it off! I'm done. The last three weeks have been hell. You're acting like an ornery old married couple, you both need counseling. Now shut up and don't touch each other, don't look at each other, and don't even breathe the same air– you hear me?"

"Woo Lionel, don't hold back." Kurt retorted. "Just let me out at the next subway, it's probably cooler underground and hassle free compared to you and Miss Hottie."

"Don't start with me Kurt." Jeremy warned. "You know how I get. You two give me migraines. It takes days to get rid of them. And I have plans to go out to *The Garage* on the Fourth. I don't *need* any of your sass."

"Well, excuse me for breathing." Kurt turned his eyes and thoughts back on Amanda, "So, hot date tonight? Where are we going for the long holiday weekend *Lime Light*, *Roxy's* or *Ritz*?" He quirked an eyebrow towards her and extended his arm comfortably on the seatback just shy of her shoulders.

"What? Are you writing a book?" she quipped.

"Well what if I am?"

25

"You'd better leave my chapter out." Amanda barked and scooted forward, "Jeremy, please tell Mr. Kilawee – WE are not going anywhere with him. Not tonight or any other night he might have in mind."

Jeremy jerked the van to a stop. "Well, I can see we are going nowhere with this idea of you two either hooking up or separating for good, so Kurt remove your skinny tight ass out of my van. Here's where you get off."

"What? Picking sides again, come on cut me some slack, man." Kurt pulled out a small black book double checking some numbers. "Well, you two ladies have fun then." He crossed over Amanda to pry the sliding door open, almost toppling onto her.

Jeremy steamed, "Get out Kurt before you embarrass yourself even more." His eyes widen like he was putting a voodoo hex on Kurt.

"Okay, okay, I get your drift, I'll call you later."

"Fine, you do that. Now close the door, Mandy and I have work to do."

Kurt slammed the door so hard it bounced back open giving him one last shot at Amanda's striking bare legs. "Damn you have sexy legs." he heard himself say aloud.

"See, what did I tell you? You just can't keep your mouth shut." Jeremy scolded. "Now shut the door, Fool."

Amanda sat shocked and silent.

Taxi drivers and New York drivers blasted their horns causing the scene to erupt into a worse debacle. Kurt leapt to the curb, flipped his mirrored sunglasses down, and flashed his middle finger to his irritated audience. Jeremy was right; he did open his mouth too many times and inserted both feet.

He ducked into the subway welcoming the clattering of the trains and the cool breeze that accompanied them as they rushed by. To contact his informant he had to get to 116th Street before ten a.m. His big story was just about to break, and then he'd show Amanda and Rich he was the bomb reporter.

Amanda was glad to be free of Kurt and his lewd staring. What was his problem? *He acted deprived like he hadn't seen a woman's bare legs in years.* She knew that wasn't one of his problems, more like a fault, but not a problem.

Jeremy invited her into the front seat after Kurt left.

"Wow Kurt is right. You do look exceptionally hot today." Jeremy said innocently. Jeremy was a great friend and co-worker; he was openly gay and always told her how well she did with her news spots and how tastefully she dressed.

Amanda laughed, "Thanks, coming from you it sounds like a compliment. I'm just trying to keep cool. What are you doing looking at me that way?"

"Hey just because I like guys, doesn't mean I can't appreciate beauty in a woman. Besides Kurt is right–you are one fine looking smart lady."

"He really said that about me?"

"Damn girl, you better pull your head out. That guy has got the 'hots' for you something awful. He doesn't know how to handle feelings. Hell, he confessed he hasn't been... you know–horizontal in a long time."

"Jeremy, please," Amanda blushed. "I don't need to know details on Kurt's sex life. Remember strictly business. Kurt has plenty of women at his beckon call. He always has arm-candy at the society parties." She was escorted by Rich for most of the parties while Rich's wife was supposedly out of town, getting some European body lift. At least that was the gossip in the fish tank.

"You're killing me with your love-hate relationship. I can't keep playing umpire. We are supposed to be a team girlfriend."

"Well, I will try harder not to push his buttons for your sake."

"Maybe you should push his buttons, go out with him. Might relieve all the stress he's been under."

"Oh no Jeremy, did he put you up to this? Did Kurt ask you to ask me out? That is so lame." She rolled her eyes tipping her head back.

Jeremy's mouth opened and closed several times in denial, "Well, sort of, he asked me to tell you where we are going on the Fourth."

"You and Kurt going out? Well, I never saw that one coming." She said astonished.

"No you got it wrong. Kurt is cool about me. He knows *The Garage* is my place where my type brothers hang, but it's a mixed crowd too. We go there, *The Lime Light*, and *Roxy's* or sometimes to old *Studio 54*. You should go. Kurt gets us into the VIP lines. I can pick you up."

"No thanks, although I would love to hang with you, I don't think I am ready to deal with Mr. VIP Kilawee. Belinda and I have plans. But maybe we will accidentally run into you at one of the clubs."

Amanda fanned herself trying to move the thick air while taking in Jeremy's revelation. *Well, well, Mr. Hotshot Kilawee has the "hots" for me. How nice.*

Well, whatever turned him on; as long as he kept his distance everything would be just fine.

Amanda was enjoying her career at NYCB and loving New York. Belinda was a great friend to hang with. They attended award winning

Broadway shows: *La Cage aux Folles*, – *The Tap Dance Kid*, Off-Broadway plays, and underground new wave punk concerts. They fulfilled their quest to try food at each of the street venders. And they became connoisseurs of the pizza joints from the Bronx to Midtown.

This Fourth of July weekend was going to be a blast! Belinda planned to help her dress as a Madonna-wanna-be and they were going to hit the clubs. No way was she letting Kurt know their plans. His smug two-cents on her new attitude weren't needed. She loved to dance and she finally had the cash to afford a couple of nights out.

Just that morning, she dropped a thank you note in the mail to her millionaire father thanking him for paying her rent for the year. Rich had advanced her salary paying for the first and last month's rent, she was set financially. Belinda had helped her find good used furniture, so she finally had an awesomely comfortable bed and a TV. Life was good. And it could only get better.

After the Fourth of July long weekend, she had a private lunch meeting scheduled with Rich at the famed *Tavern on the Green*. She had never been and she was stoked to go.

He said his private town car would pick her up at the office Monday. Maybe he planned to offer her the traveling anchor job. Kurt was the face of NYCB, but maybe, just maybe they needed a woman's touch on the edge of truth digging.

Rich praised her documentary on "The Controversial Life and Loves of Lillian Hellman." Always intrigued by playwrights and political farce, Amanda had interviewed Lillian earlier in the month at her Martha's Vineyard home. NYCB aired it shortly after Lillian's unexpected death on June 30th. The well received documentary interview became Amanda's first jaunt into semi-stardom.

Even Kurt complimented, "Hey Amanda nice job on the quality and quantity of truth, everyone in New York knows Lillian Hellman as a great truth enhancer, and she's a damn good dramatist giving excellent journalism a witty stirring."

"Well, it just proves there's hope for your enhanced pretentious journalism style." Amanda quipped.

"Yeah, so I hear. Any chance Hellman mistook you for Mary McCarthy? It seems your agendas for the absolute truth match."

"Thank you, you're so keen. It wouldn't hurt you to put some truth in your stories.'

"Ouch, hey I was giving you a serious compliment, a simple thank you was enough."

"Newsflash, save it for someone who cares for your opinion."

Lately he'd been suspiciously complimentary and always around, like a nascent stalker.

Later that night, Belinda transformed Amanda from Miss Preppy into a knockout Madonna-wanna-be. After they searched several thrift shops they decked themselves out in tight leather minis, lace leggings with matching lace gloves, and off-the-shoulder swanky torn T-shirts. Huge hooped earrings and tarted red lips completed her totally awesome rocker look. Of course, her untamable hair sprayed up wildly big.

Ready to party, Belinda encouraged her to take a few swigs from a fresh bottle of Jack.

Not Amanda's style, but hey this was her first Fourth of July holiday in New York City. It was time to P-A-R-T-Y the next few nights!

Over the course of the weekend they went to small clubs starting out around ten. New York clubbing didn't get tempestuously wicked until midnight. They checked out the scene at the old *Studio 54*, it was nothing like its heyday in the late 70's, but it had a decent flow of celebrities slinking through the VIP lines. Belinda wanted Mandy to see it just for the pop culture history. And it was easier to get into than the other hot spots.

As they stood in the not-so-celebrity line, Amanda spotted Kurt in the "celebrity" VIP lane with not one, but two sizzling beauties. They looked like they had just jumped off the fashion runway, as tall as him with their stilettos. She tugged on Belinda's sleeveless jean jacket, "Hey, look who's in the VIP line."

Belinda squinted hard. She really needed her glasses, but refused to wear them because they made her look too smart, so she claimed.

Amanda had had the foresight to bring them in her handbag. "Here put your glasses on."

"Alright, hold your panties," Belinda put on the bug-eyed glasses, her mouth dropped. "Oh my Gawd–Tom Cruise and Kevin Bacon?"

Amanda pushed her out of the way and used the glasses herself, "No not them, the guy behind them with the two super-models!" She shoved the glasses back at Belinda. The line moved forward, probably as close as they were going to get, now that _real_ celebrities were showing up.

It was at that exact moment Jeremy hollered, "Hey, is that you Amanda Lindas?" He shouted loud enough that everyone within 8th Ave. and Broadway heard him. Everyone stopped talking and looked. Amanda stepped out from the crowd and did a short wave, her bangles rattled to her elbows.

Kurt lifted his head over the few celebrities standing in front of him. His eyes met hers. He raised his eyebrows and mouthed, "Wow".

She merged back into the line tugging on her miniskirt trying to make it grow. She was embarrassed having Kurt see her out of her professional attire, damn that Jeremy for spotting her.

Belinda stood on her tip-toes and read the weather report, "His eyes haven't moved, he's still staring, I think he's coming over." Amanda shrank behind her petite friend. "Nope, he's moving forward. Oh, he is saying something to the muscle at the door, yep he's pointing over here. Now he's in. Damn girl, you need to be nice to him, so we don't waste party hours in long lines."

Defeated by her arch enemy, Amanda slipped into a grumpy mood. Kurt proved he had "celebrity" status and she did not.

About an hour later, they were just about to give up when the muscle doorman came up to her, "Hey are you Amanda Lindas?"

She gulped, "Yes. Is there a problem?"

"No, just need to see your ID. Is this little pip with you? Need her ID too." He scrutinized them and their IDs like he worked for the FBI. Finally he said, "Follow me ladies, it is your time to shine." He smiled a gold filled toothy smile.

"Must have been in a few bar fights in his time, bet he won." Belinda whispered as they followed him into the loud flashy nightclub.

The club was a far cry from the dive bars that Amanda had enjoyed dancing in Wisconsin. Filled with half-dressed gyrating men and women on several lighted bars and pedestals, this club was way-out of Wisconsin's bar top dancing league. The deafening bass boomed through her body. The club muscle escorted them to a small roped off area encompassing two red leather sofas with bottles of booze lined up in the middle of a low rectangular table.

The lights flickered and flashed to the beat of the DJ's mix. Belinda took one of the bottles and poured them both a drink. She handed the clear liquid tumbler to Amanda, "Drink up and let's set that dance floor on fire. Time to party!"

Amanda looked around as she sipped the not-so-familiar alcoholic beverage nervously. She knew Kurt was in the wild crowd. But she'd bet she could find a *needle in a haystack* before she'd be able to locate him and Jeremy. Maybe he had a private booth to entertain his lady friends who were probably doing him unmentionable favors.

Belinda pulled her from her thoughts and onto the dance floor. They danced to the Police, Culture Club, Hall & Oats, and Bon Jovi tunes. Stopping only for shots and highball drinks on ice to quench their thirst; they were having the time of their lives.

Amanda slowed her pace and started drinking water; she could not afford to die of a hangover before her big break on Monday.

Someday soon, she would be recognized as a celebrity. Still half wasted she went in search of Kurt and Jeremy just to show her appreciation.

Each time Belinda or she tried to pay for drinks the scantily clad waitress just shook her head and pointed up to the second or third level. She said a smart dressed man was paying their tab. That had to be Kurt. He wore his new dark platinum Hugo Boss custom suit; it was dropped off at work by his tailor. *God, Kurt did look sharp.*

Suits do make men look smarter. Maybe she should do a piece about– "Sharp Dressed Men and Their Power over Women". Not that she was interested in Kurt, but she did owe him a thank you. Of course, she could wait until Monday when she saw him at work. But it would be easier to face him in the dark while intoxicated, to avoid seeing him gloat.

She excused herself to the little girl's room, and then squeezed through the groping crowd to a spiral staircase attached to the second floor.

A bouncer guarded the base; with a bulldog look, he eyed her. "Name Miss?" he asked gruffly. He leaned, making it possible for her to scream her name in his ear. He nodded and flashed a green cone flashlight. They waited for a waitress to descend the spiral stairs to escort her.

Amanda heard him say, "Kilawee's booth."

The arrogant son-of-a-bitch was expecting her to search for him like little Red-Riding Hood tracking the Big Bad Wolf.

Tempted to turn around, but she was already halfway. She would just say thanks and leave. That was it– short, sweet, and to the point.

When she arrived on the scene, he was busy sucking face with a starving model.

"Oh, excuse me, Mr. Kilawee," she cleared her throat, "sorry to interrupt your mouth to mouth resuscitation." Sarcasm was a gift she acquired from her mother.

Kurt looked up shocked, dismayed, or ashamed, she couldn't tell which. He adjusted his shirt which was unbuttoned past his sternum, exposing sparse chest hair, she hadn't noticed before. She watched his Adam's apple struggle as he swallowed. Looking guilty like a husband caught cheating; he grasped a whiskey tumbler from the table and ingested its contents within seconds.

"Hey, hey Amanda," he scooted out of the cushioned booth to stand next to her. She didn't match his height in her three-inch spiked heels, but she managed to lock coolly onto his eyes.

"Hey Amanda," he said again wearing a sly smile that matched the wicked glint in his eyes.

"Ah, hey Kurt you're reiterating. Now that I know you recognize me, I just wanted to thank you for your hospitality. So thanks, now you can go back to saving your girlfriend." She turned abruptly dismissing him.

What was that strange twinge in the pit of her stomach? She wrapped her arms around her exposed midriff. Belinda had gotten a little carried away with the scissors earlier.

With his hands on her bare arms, he turned her to face him. His cool composure was back. "Hey you, join me for a drink."

Still clutching her waistline, she shook her head. "No, I wouldn't want Belinda to think I deserted her. I should go. You go back to doing what you do best." She sensed the starving model wasn't leaving voluntarily.

He turned her and pointed at the dance floor, "See you can watch Belinda from here. Looks like she's having a good time, she's a club savvy girl, she can handle this crowd."

He was right; she hated it when he was right. In direct view was their designated table. Belinda was having a blast with newly acquired dance partners.

"Satisfied? Come on, stay with me, have a drink, relax." He said pulling her into his booth. He scooted in giving her the outside seat. At least she possessed the advantage to escape.

The starving girl sulked, shifted over perturbed, and retouched her red oversized lips. *A skeleton with lips and ghoulish eyes, what was the attraction?*

Kurt poured three drinks. Amanda surmised it was the same expensive whiskey she encountered on his breath her first day.

"Mandy, here's to friction and friendship," he elevated his glass.

Her eyes flashed cold at the nickname. She took the glass reluctantly and reached for ice from the sweating silver ice bucket.

Kurt grimaced with an apology in his eyes, "I'm sorry. I know you prefer Amanda, but..."

"But nothing Kurt, you don't respect me or any other females." She plopped two large cubes into her glass splashing the expensive liquor onto the table.

"Sure I do. I respect my mother."

"You're required to do that. Let's just keep this on a professional level." She toasted him and took an obligatory sip.

"You look great," he said glowing with romantic charm. "I love watching you dance. If it weren't for Lionel, I wouldn't have recognized you in line. You should wear leather miniskirts and let your hair loose more often." His voice was smooth as velvet. He sat so close the warmth of his breath tickled her neck, sending shivers to her core. His strong hand covered her glass holding hand just long enough to piss-off the skinny bitch.

The six-foot girl stood, tossed her drink at him, and screeched, "Here Jackass, I have better things to do than watch you play up to a twit."

Kurt jumped up, brushing the spattered liquid from his expensive suit; he nearly hurled Amanda to the floor. Aghast he shouted at the model, "Oh go on, go eat something before you pass out!"

Amanda grabbed a cloth napkin. Habitually she took charge and patted the drink off his jacket and shirt. Without forethought she reached inside his shirt to wipe his bare chest. When her hand touched his skin, evident unsettling electricity shot between them. She immediately stopped at the edge of his slacks, "Ah, I think you should handle the rest." She said awkwardly shy and handed him the napkin.

"Yeah, sure thanks," he said staring deep into her eyes. Mechanically he dabbed the liquid, not taking his eyes off hers.

It felt as if he could read her mind. She turned and pulled away from his toxic hypnotic look thinking life would be easier if she could fly down to Belinda.

Up from behind her, his arms circled her waist, he placed himself strategically at her backside gently letting her know just how hard and interested he was. "Amanda, let's not fight our energy," he whispered. "Let's get out of here."

Her head shook as she twisted to lock eyes with him again. "No, no, no, we can't," she pushed him back. "I can't. You don't understand. We can't mix business with–pleasure. No Kurt!" She ran before he revealed more pressing ideas about them connecting.

"Amanda stop, wait–damn it!" He slammed the table, raked his hair, temporarily limited by his obvious physical condition to pursue her. He sat disgusted. He had to cool his jets

Jeremy rushed across the crowded dim room.

"What the hell did you do man? You had her in your hands. What happen? Did you do what I think you did?" Jeremy's eyes bulged. Kurt's head slumped, he glanced up dourly.

"You did! I knew it! I knew it! You scared her away with that tool. I told you, she isn't that type. If you want to land a chick like her, you're going to have to use different bait. Damn you! Now I'll have to tolerate your high strung sexual tension again. You're gonna give me a migraine and a heart attack. I hope you're satisfied, man." He cuffed Kurt alongside the head and stormed away in a huff like a mother disgusted with her child.

Well, the Fourth of July is supposed to be filled with explosives. Kurt agreed he got his fill of explosives that night. He definitely got more bang for his bucks.

Chapter 4

Within minutes, Amanda hustled Belinda out of the club.

"What's the hurry?" Belinda shuffled three steps to Amanda's one.

Out of breath, Amanda worked to get as much distance as physically possible between her and Kurt. How could he just assume she'd leave with him? What did he think she was a promiscuous whore out for a one night stand? Well, she wasn't. And he'd better keep his distance from her. She gritted her teeth as she bolted down 54th Street to Broadway in high heels.

Belinda caught up clutching Amanda's arm almost pulling it out of socket. "Hey, slowdown chick! What is the absolute problem here? Spill it!" Belinda gulped for air.

Amanda faced Belinda, huffing. "Let's get a taxi."

"Yeah well, that would have been easier by the club. What the hell is your big hurry anyway?"

"That lascivious jerk pressed up against me and asked me to leave with him! He has the audacity to think that I am like his cheap trick dates! I am not. I am his co-worker. I am a professional. And he should treat me with a lot more respect!"

Baffled, Belinda reached to calm her, "Well girlfriend, you look like an escaped lunatic from a mental hospital, a tragic hot mess. Your face is beet-red, your mascara is smudged like raccoon eyes, and one side of your hair is flat and the other is like Einstein's. Let's grab a taxi, a Ray's pizza on 57th, and go home." She yanked Amanda to the curb and waved a taxi. "Umm–so, what does lascivious mean to me?"

Amanda smiled halfhearted, "It means, Horny Bastard."

"Really? What a frickin' jerk." Belinda voiced her alliance.

Back at Amanda's apartment, Belinda prodded for straight answers about Kurt's alleged lewd actions; it wasn't easy. "Mandy, it can't be all that bad. Go clean up." She said wiping Amanda's tears with a dish towel.

They changed out of their hip dancing garb and settled into comfortable Badger and Packer jerseys. Facing each other on the red sofa, they popped open chilled Diet-Cokes and chowed down on their favorite Ray's bacon cheeseburger pizza.

"So, let me get the story straight," Belinda began *her* commentary. "So the rat bastard already expected you. Right? And then he's like sucking serious mouth with the no-tits skinny bitch, and like he has you drink with them. Wow some balls, like he was thinking *Ménage-a-trios*, what a sick-o. How could he think that you're into that?" After a huge gulp of soda she belched, "Ex-cu-se me! Wow where'd that come from? So like then you threw a drink on him?"

Amanda devoured a cheesy bite of pizza, shaking her head. "No, no, that's wrong. Remember a good reporter gets her facts straight; the twig threw her drink on his Hugo Boss suit. His *new fancy* Hugo Boss suit. Oh my Gawd, like you should have seen his face–totally un-cool distorted like pissed, but totally trying to keep his composure."

Still feeling the buzz from the free drinks, they laughed to hysterics. Soda spurted out of Belinda's nose. She grabbed pizza napkins to wipe the mess.

Still laughing Amanda continued, "So then Kurt jumps up and tells skeleton she should go eat something. A skeleton with lips–no boobs, I wonder if that's his type."

"Ah, no I don't think so. If she was he would have pressed his boner on her ass not yours. Mandy you just don't give yourself credit. You are one hot chick and you need to dress-up your positives and stop being such a downer. Ok–so, he tells her to go eat and then you rubbed a napkin all over him?"

"No, I only dabbed it. You never rub a spill into a fine fabric. You pat to absorb the liquid. He was doing it too."

"Okay, thank you Martha Stewart for the dab lesson, so like then how did dabbing evolve to him gyrating on your ass?"

"He wasn't gyrating. It happened so suddenly. I was patting his shirt and I just slipped my hand inside to his chest to prevent the liquor from drizzling downward. It was all perfectly innocent–I swear. But oh my Gawd, his chest is rock solid like hard ripped muscles. I didn't think he was the exercise kind of guy. I wished I would have torn his shirt off just to see his chest in all its glory. I could use a little fantasy material. Oh you know what? I should have licked the whiskey off him." She stuck her tongue out doing a licking motion; taking another gooey slice of pizza she gnawed the tip. The cheese stretched off in a long string.

"Okay, that's the booze talking. So, the electrifying connection was you touched his chest, but no licking right? Hell, that poor dweeb had the hots for you from the beginning. His rise is evidence; he's had nasty thoughts before. How's that for reporting?" Belinda sat cross-legged and smug.

"Well maybe, but this is all circumstantial evidence. He's a guy. And most guys can watch girls dancing and get lustfully hard, so it doesn't mean he's had prior feelings towards me personally. Plus he was sucking face with the bean pole too. I speculate that he assumes he can get any woman he wants just by charming them. I'm not that kind of girl."

"Well, I am," Belinda laughed. "I like a good lay now and again. Keeps the stress away. More people die from stress than anything else. And no sex equals lots of tension. And sexual tension is the type that explodes!" she popped up off the sofa doing a jumping-jack.

"You could be right," Amanda agreed. "Crap I haven't had sex since college, that's almost two years. I just don't care for one night stands. I like having a friendship first and then a physical relationship."

"Oh you're the prude preppy type, the worst kind of teasers." Belinda accused.

"No, I just like to have someone to do things with–like dating not bedding. Some women think that a guy pinching them or rubbing himself on them is a compliment. But I think if you're not seriously dating or already intimate then the guy has no business touching you especially with his private business. It is so disrespectful and violates your private space."

"So you're a new wave feminist. You want the power to pick when some guy rubs up against your booty. Control issues?"

"Yeah, I guess so." Amanda sheepishly agreed.

"So Kurt letting you know he's physically attracted to you turned you off instead of on?"

"No," Amanda stopped to think, "No his actions intrigued my physical senses and stroked my ego, especially since he chose me over the model. But we are co-workers and work in the public spectrum. He could ruin my professional image. And he assumed I'm a one night stand." She hoped that she wasn't sending that message to him. Guilt washed over her. "Honestly, I like that he is attracted to me, but I wish he was man enough to ask me out. You know, like why didn't he ask us to be his arm-candy tonight instead of those two sticks with lips?"

A quizzical look crossed Belinda's face. She walked across the floor like a trial lawyer doing closing arguments. "Hmm... maybe he's afraid you'd say no. And rejection from his arch enemy slash hot chick at the office would be too embarrassing and torch his ego. You did say Jeremy wanted us to hang at certain clubs. But we avoided them on purpose. Why... because you didn't want to face-off with Kurt outside of work. I got it! I nailed it! You both fear rejection. It's like a human tug of war. Neither wants to admit you dig the other, you are both scared shitless." Belinda did a double-fisted victory air pump.

Amanda cleaned the pizza mess, making several trips to the galley kitchen. "Well, that sounds like an iron clad theory, but it doesn't solve anything. I can't work with him, I can't quit my job, and I can't shoot him, so what do I do come Monday?"

"What do you mean Monday? Today is only Thursday. You won't see him tomorrow?"

"No he's going to Wimbledon to report on the McEnroe–Conner tennis tournament. Lucky bastard," Amanda slammed the pizza box on the counter.

"Whoa is that a chunk of jealousy girlfriend?"

"Yeah, you're right again. I am jealous he gets to travel, do the top stories, and gets paid the big bucks. I want that guy's job. And that's the blatant truth."

"Then go after it! Don't let him keep you down. Show him who the best man is! Or best woman!"

"Yeah, that's what I will do. I refuse to let this escapade control my career. I did not come to New York to have some good looking smart-ass stud steal my joy. You're right Belinda this is war! I refuse to lie down and let him get on top. I will show him, I am more woman than he can handle. He will learn to respect me. I will be on top!" She went over to the boom-box and popped in her Helen Reddy cassette, "I Am Woman" lyrics filled the room. Amanda felt invincible.

They danced around the small apartment until they dropped from exhaustion. Amanda adopted a whole new perspective and attitude. She would use her physical and mental talents to her advantage.

To get where you want to go, you have to conquer the source of fear first. She wanted to be on top. And Kurt Kilawee was not going to stop her. Relieved he wouldn't be back until after the long weekend, she had time to plan. Besides Monday was her luncheon meeting with Rich, she'd do just about anything to get the local or travel interviewing spot. Well, just about anything.

Monday finally arrived. Amanda dressed in her Donna Karan crimson red power-suit accented with black lapels and cuffs. This wasn't her typical knee-length skirt. This skirt exposed more leg about three inches above her knees. Her black patent leather three-inch pumps completed her provocative ensemble. She clipped her shoulder length chestnut spirals into a black beaded bun holder and shoved the black lacquer stick through to hold it in place. She mused she'd use it as weapon like a ninja, if needed.

She arrived at work gun-shy not knowing when Kurt or Rich would appear. A small neatly wrapped gold-foil package was placed squarely in the center of her desk. Surprised by it, she picked it up. It felt weighted, possibly contained glass with liquid. Beneath it was an envelope, simply scripted with an all too familiar handwriting, written in red ink was *Mandy, I am sorry.*

Appalled not flattered, she mumbled, "You're not sorry, not yet." Immediately she placed both unopened in Kurt's office cubby. As she did, she noticed a yellow lead folder.

The dreaded yellow folder; the one Kurt derogatorily referred to as the "pee-on team". The Yellow team was assigned the crappy un-newsworthy stories no one wanted. So, Kurt must have brought the gift in earlier because World War III hadn't been broadcast that morning, nor was the Empire State Building wrapped in yellow crime scene tape.

Kurt would hit the ceiling or wipe up the floor with Rich, once he realized he was switched to the bottom of the barrel.

Amanda shuddered.

Well, serves him right. He'll get a double whammy once he sees the yellow folder weighted down with his unopened returned gift. Hell, he could re-gift it to one of his twiggy models.

When Kurt arrived he was casually dressed in tight creased Tommy Hilfiger stonewashed jeans with a crisp white dress shirt. He had no tie–no Hugo Boss suit–he was just scrumptious eye-candy.

What was he up to? Did he know about the yellow "pee-on" folder? Did Jeremy warn him ahead of time, yeah that was plausible? Jeremy must have placed the gift on her desk too. Kurt probably paid him to buy the gift and the card! She made herself sick thinking about it.

Here she was dressed for the kill, up for a fight, and Kurt was laying down his weapons.

Very calm with begging-dog sincerity in his tired eyes, Kurt approached. He leisurely planted his firm butt on her desk, extending his long legs; he crossed them at his ankles.

Amanda sighed heavily.

"Hi," he said looking at her over his left shoulder, his voice whisper soft. His eyes searched her face for acceptance.

"Hi," she muffled low, shifting her eyes back and forth befuddled at where to place her gaze.

"Did you get my apology?" his self-restrained large hands rested on his tight jean covered thighs.

Swiftly her eyes switched from his thighs to his quiet emerald eyes. No sparkle–no comic relief–just calm. It was unfortunate that her mind flashed back to their exploding July fourth encounter…his arms were wrapped around her while his privates pressed her backside, the vision hinged her breath.

Her wide crystal blue eyes locked on his calm green pools, "No, I did not. Are you apologizing for your rude, lewd, obnoxious, forward presumptuous behavior?" her lips pressed together, stopping her from raising her voice as the other sharks swarmed the fish tank.

Everyone was now considered her direct competitor. To seize every opportunity in the cutthroat society of celebrity journalism, she had to prevent making an unprofessional scene. That was not her style. Although his agenda seemed quite personal and not professional, she did not trust him one iota.

Dismayed, his eyebrows raised, "Well, if that is what you made of my actions, then yes, but Mandy..."

She stopped him. "My name is Ms. Lindas to you! Got it?" She stood exposing her balled fists tight to her sides. Her red power-suit befitted her mood. "I don't know what your deal is, but you can save the acting for your academy award." She kept her voice low and steady not to rouse an audience. "What do you want from me a brownie? Will that pacify your damaged ego Mr. Kilawee?"

Kurt twisted his upper body to face her. A glint of humor bubbled in his chest, "Well, if it would make you feel better. Yes Ms. Lindas, throw me a brownie–or better yet..." he said crossing his arms over his chest keeping his demeanor in check, "why don't you throw me a bone?" He gritted his teeth showing a false pretentious smile. "Why don't we settle our differences over lunch and not air our grievances at work?"

With her arms crossed over her chest, she leaned towards him as if to grant him a reprieve, "My dear Mr. Kilawee, I have no intentions of tossing you a bone, or accepting your invitation to lunch. I have a lunch date. Now would you please remove your Gluteus maximus off my desk? I have professional work to do." She picked up her blue lead folder and fanned it, "Don't you?"

"Sure, I'm available for an anatomy lesson–you available?"

"Oh kiss my ass Kurt." She rasped.

"Honey, I'm not ready to go there, but thanks for the invite."

She rolled her eyes, he had rendered her speechless.

Thank God Jeremy walked in with his blue file in hand; he strutted straight towards her. With bugged out eyes, his head jerked signaling her to remove Kurt before he made his final approach. Kurt remained on her desk wielding a subtle arrogant smirk.

Jeremy slowed keeping his distance. Amanda glared at Kurt.

With one more last ditch effort; Kurt stood and adjusted his crisp collar with both hands. He got into her personal space-bubble popping it intentionally, putting her on the defense. "Come on, Mandy..."

Not about to cave, her expression flared with deep-rooted derisive aggravation.

Oblivious to heeding her warning signals, Kurt stepped closer, "Come on… I am only human."

She stepped back a half step putting a few inches between them, ready to claw his eyes out. "Oh, really, you are *only* human?" Her voice raised an octave, her hands went airborne. "Wow! Newsflash! Kurt Kilawee is only human and not the immortal Demi-God we thought he was. Damn now I have to change my religion and rewrite the Bible."

As if bewitched, she strutted to the center of the office so everyone could hear. Then she turned to him. His face red with embarrassment or anger, she couldn't tell which and she didn't care.

"So you're only human! Well great, what the hell does that make the rest of us? Aliens, Martians, or just little peons? Why is it that some men think that they have inalienable rights to make sexual advances and suggestive innuendos? It is as if you think your need, or desire for sex supersedes everyone else's. We are all humans here– some choose to use self-control while arrogant losers make lame excuses for their poor choices forgoing the common decency to respect others!" Her rant caught everyone off guard including herself. So much for keeping up her professional charade, she was a train wreck that stopped in front of an explosive geyser.

Like Old Faithful, Kurt unleashed, "Well, don't hold back; please tell us how you really feel." He followed her path through the office. "Are you through? May I take the floor Ms. Lindas? Are you ready to climb off your soapbox? Your manipulative, controlling, self-righteous pedestal– Jesus Christ, Amanda I said I was sorry! What the hell–why don't you just crucify me and get it over with?" hands on his hips, he was in her face breathing heavy and perspiring.

Their intense glares heightened the estrogenic emotional tension and spurned the testosterone dominance throughout the office. This was a no win situation and they all knew it, every last one of them. They all knew that the battle between the sexes began way before their time and would continue long after they were dead and gone. An explosive-relief, an oxymoron, the unspoken truth finally exploded in the office.

Kurt and Amanda had it bad– passion for success, desire for exposing the truth, and the tenacity to be the victor. Was there room at the top for both?

As the tidal wave of tension tumbled around her, Amanda gave Kurt another dose of reality. "Well, there you go thinking you're God wanting to be crucified for all you've sacrificed–your manly ego. Bring out the cross let this Saint be hung. You're a pathetic egomaniac–so delusional you think every woman wants you."

With arms extended he posed as a cross, he relinquished his apology. "Well, at least I'm not a teasing, incorrigible uptight Bitch!" The disgusted shock on her face indicated he had step on an emotional landmine.

"Thanks for the insight; I'll add that to my resume. Can I use you as a reference?"

"Sure use me; add-on qualified for defamation of character, just finish me off. Put a spear in my side."

Amanda crossed her arms refusing to banter further, she let the fallout settle.

After a long pause, Kurt looked at the floor, scratched his head, and coolly said, "We're done here, huh?" he turned towards Jeremy, "Lionel we have work to do."

"No Kurt," Jeremy said interlocking one arm through Mandy's. In solidarity he wagged his index finger, "*We*–do not work with you. You are off the Blue team!"

Kurt looked astonished. "What? What the hell are you talking about? Jeremy–you and I are the Blue team. We have always been the Blue team. Jeremy?" his tone went stern.

Jeremy continued to finger wag, "Oh no you don't! You can call me Lionel, only my friends call me Jeremy. Come on Mandy we have work to do." They strutted out of the office.

Kurt examined his cubby. A bright yellow folder mocked him along with his sincere apology package and card. He was sorry, he was clueless on how to make amends, but obviously now was not the time or place.

Rich did not go to NYCB directly, he had his town car pick Amanda up promptly at noon, just after she and Jeremy finished filming her interview with Geraldine Ferraro. The interview with the prospective first woman vice-president was exhilaratingly inspirational and televised perfection.

After the fallout, Amanda was a ball of energy, released from the tension of Kurt's approval. No more fighting or bickering or jumping through hoops for him. Jeremy was happy too, no more migraines, everything was perfect. She kept Kurt out of her head.

When she arrived at *The Tavern on the Green*, Rich opened the passenger door and escorted her into the restaurant. Such a gentleman, he had a private table reserved in the garden room. The subtle white twinkle lights added ambiance to the intimate lunch. The floras and trees in full bloom emitted a fantastic fragrance emanating elegance and romance. Rich ordered two Lobster bisques and Caesar salads, with a table-side chilled bottle of Chardonnay.

They laughed about Amanda's contrived truth of the office disparity. Conveniently, she left out the details about sex and men; concluding it was not table conversation. Kurt's antics couldn't ruin this perfect moment. Life is good.

Life wasn't good for Kurt, and far from perfect. He had to obliged Sarah; she wanted proof of Rich cheating. The manager Gus, at *The Tavern*, let Kurt slip in through the kitchen to obtain photos of Rich's secret rendezvous. Daffy had tipped him off; he had plenty of leisure time, since he was degraded to "pee-on" patrol.

Using his zoom lens he zeroed in on Rich's hot new little number. The lighting was perfect for taking compromising photos. Her warm smile enchanted the patio even more than the white sparkling lights. Her blue eyes flickered with flashes of luminous glitter. This beauty looked like she was dancing on air, but what the hell was she doing with Rich? Kurt refocused; it was her– Amanda Lindas! So this is how the self-righteous bitch got him kicked off the Blue team? *Just do your job, Kurt. He instructed himself.*

He snapped Rich caressing her smooth hand on the table. Another click of the shutter; Rich extended his knee contacting her shapely tan legs under the table, no nylons again. Kurt's camera and eyes adored her. Her red power-suit exuded professionalism and sexuality simultaneously. She was a classic beauty.

What was she doing dating Rich? The sincerity in Rich's eyes embodied that he was promising her the world; a master engineer, probably promising her Kurt's job as he placed his slimy married hand on her knee. Snap. Snap. Snap.

Kurt couldn't keep spying, he felt conflicted and guilty especially after her sermon that morning. It sickened him to watch them chatting and laughing over lobster bisque. *Christ,* the guy wasn't even funny.

What were they laughing about? Curiosity sparked the urge to get closer to read her lips. During years of detective surveillance, he had developed the deft skill of lip reading. In a quandary over whether to cure his cotton-mouth with a liquid quencher or continue, he continued.

Technically he was done for the day, and after all, he was doing a good deed, saving a worthless marriage. Wouldn't Mandy be proud of his moral standing on helping marriage partners be faithful? Even God would approve, so why did he feel like shit spying?

He set the camera down. "Hey Antonio, can I get an Irish whiskey on the rocks, make it a double?"

"Yes Sir Boss." Antonio eyed the expensive camera and poured. "What's with the camera?" He handed Kurt a tumbler of iced whiskey.

"Well, it's a deal-maker and a ball buster." Kurt smiled and sipped his drink. "Just a little assignment."

"Yeah, now I recognize you. You're that news anchor guy. That was a great interview with McEnroe you did over the weekend. Must be nice to travel and meet athletes. I loved McEnroe's line about the moron. Good funny lines."

"Thanks. Yeah, it is nice to travel. I get tickets to the World Series and Super Bowl." At least he still hoped he did.

Kurt swallowed his drink and turned to scrutinize the lunch meeting. They appeared a trifle cozier, alerted he decided to move closer. Maybe increasing his odds at getting a kiss shot that would add a big bonus to his deal with Sarah. Marginally torn, he analyzed the area seeking the best location. He needed camouflage. A waiter about his size walked by with a tray of food hiked on his shoulder, Kurt moved deftly alongside to get at a table near a large potted plant. There he could spy on his victims.

Just as he focused in, Amanda pulled Rich's thick greedy hand off her knee and placed it on the table. Her gritting smile said all too clear—do it again and you'll feel my hand across your face. Kurt knew. She had given him that feisty look more than once.

"*Good girl, Mandy.*" Kurt whispered under his breath. Satisfied she removed it, yet disgruntled that she never let *him* get that close to those beautiful sexy legs. Given that he was already focused on her legs he took a snapshot for himself. *I'm only human, Baby.*

At least from his new position he could gather a little one-sided conversation. Rich's broad back faced him. Amanda's delicious red lips were a joy to watch. They matched her red suit exactly. She was talking about her college swim team practices and touched her shoulders indicating how she thought they were too wide. Kurt disagreed. He saw her shoulders and they were perfectly balanced like the rest of her.

What was the deal with shoulder pads? Why did women want to dress like Joan Collins on Dynasty or Linda Evans on Knot's Landing? Ok that's enough of night soaps for you.

Amanda stood up and b-lined straight towards him. Had she seen him? He hid his camera. Lucky for him a cute blonde was sitting alone at a table adjacent to his. Nonchalantly without introducing himself; he kissed the blonde's cheek, sat down, picked up a menu and proceeded to have an amiable conversation with the receptive yet astounded woman. Amanda spotted them his eyes gaped at hers. Then he smiled.

Amanda did not.

When she passed, Kurt dropped a twenty on the table, "Thanks have a drink on me." He snatched his camera and exited before Amanda returned. He escaped into the sublime peace of Central Park.

Chapter 5

Amanda reluctantly returned from her restroom reprieve, still disconcerted by Rich's implied advances. Thankfully, he broached the subject of the top anchor position and he offered it to her. Which was a relief, yet she felt degraded by his presumptuous propositions. She certainly was not interested in advancing her position by joining him in compromising positions. What was she going to do?

Dejected and pallid she approached the intimate table rubbing her temples warding off a migraine. A few career damaging choice words rattled relentless in her mind, but she suppressed them preventing a whirlwind exodus of her senses.

And of course seeing Kurt on a lunch date didn't help her uneasy disposition. How long had he been there? Just how much did he see, if anything? Flustered she had to escape, "Rich can we discuss this matter at a later time?" Her voice quivered.

His clever blue eyes sparkled bewitching her. He was a conniving handsome man, and married, and her boss. Three strikes against him. Her future was in the grip of his licentious hands.

Taking her hand he squeezed it gently as he circumvented her rejection, "Hey, no pressure. You have already earned the position. And beginning next week it's yours. No strings attached. You are our star news anchor of NYCB– *The New Edge on Truth*. Your new contract includes a substantial raise, a private town car, and sizable bonuses for exclusive reports. I've created the deal with our sponsors and board members. They are impressed with your tenacity and astute style."

"What about Kurt?" She inquired for her peace of mind, not wanting to be teamed up with him or deal with his prattle.

Rich patted her hand, "Don't worry, I will take care of him. You will only have to do a few duo anchor spots. I'll be your mentor." His smile overstated enthusiasm. "Now, here..." he slipped a company credit card into her hand, "this is for you. Take the rest of the week off– go shopping, buy an expensive professional wardrobe, go to the spa, and get ready for your launch into illustrious stardom. I have great faith in your innate abilities." He glanced at his Rolex, "Say, I have to leave. Thank you for a captivating lunch." He paid the waiter.

Amanda stood frozen and speechless.

Rich had the audacity to give her a peck on the cheek, "Oh by the way, there's no limit on that card. I will deliver your shooting schedule, before next week." He strutted out with a royal good-bye wave. Mission accomplished.

Still in shock, Amanda ran her fingers slowly across the credit card as if she could read Braille. Several patrons were being seated as she lingered statuesque.

The Italian bartender approached her from behind speaking softly, "Hey if you're trying to spruce up the décor you certainly are pulling it off well. But is it okay if I move you to a better spot–like maybe by the bar, so our other customers can be seated?" He tugged her elbow cautiously. She relented to a seat at the bar.

Cordially he poured her a white wine, "So, what's on your mind beautiful? You can tell me? I'm a psychologist studying to be a bartender." His infectious smile caught her attention snapping her from her stupor.

Exasperated by what just transpired she leaned forward pointing to her forehead and asked, "Excuse me, but is there anything written on my forehead?"

Taken aback, his big brown eyes squinted suspiciously. Then he played into her ploy. "Well, let me see. Can you lean over into the light a little more? What should I be looking for?"

"Does it have anything like 'stupid, naive or dumb bitch' on it?"

"No, no let me see..." his fingertips smoothed her creamy skin. He said seriously, "I do see intelligent, beautiful, and a remarkable good sport."

Satisfied with his answers she sat back. "Thanks for that reading. Sure you're not a psychic instead of a psychologist?"

"No, I'm not sure of anything. Just your friendly neighborhood bartender at your service." A glint of humor and humility wavered in his eyes.

Not presumptuous, non-assuming, not arrogant, just friendly. Amanda needed an outsider male friend. Besides he was an adorable nicely wrapped package with his wavy dark hair, warm dark brown eyes, bright smile, medium muscular build and neatly trimmed mustache–a real catch by any woman's standards.

They chatted in between his tending to his other customers. Amanda was attracted to his droll sense of humor and his outlook on the world was refreshing and bright. He alleviated her worried disposition, as he energetically spoke about his love for New York and all its cultural pleasures. After two hours of unexpected intriguing conversation; Antonio's shift ended.

It was obvious neither of them wanted the stimulating conversation to end. They took an innocent stroll in Central Park, slightly east to the small pond where they sat and chatted more. Antonio made her feel morally right about her choice to keep the credit card and convinced her to put it to good use. She need not feel guilty for doing her job professionally. And since she had the whole week off to shop he offered to meet her back at the same park bench around three the next day. They both agreed he should take her on a private tour of his hometown–New York City. Then go on a shopping spree fit for a queen on Fifth Avenue. *"The new NYCB Queen."*

He hailed a taxi, assisted her in, bowed like a pauper while kissing her hand, he said in a playful Shakespearean tone, "My Lady, I must bid you adieu until we meet on the morrow."

"Thank you, my Lord Antonio, for a splendid end to an almost disastrous day."

"You're welcome and my friends call me Lord Tony, Queen Amanda." His brilliant smile genuinely made her heart skip a beat.

"My friends call me Mandy." She blushed.

"Hey you twos wanna get a room?" grunted the impatient cabbie.

Reluctant to release her hand, Tony said, "See you tomorrow. No high heels, we'll be doing a lot of walking."

"K, see you." She smiled as he closed the door. Tomorrow– shopping and exploring New York City with Tony. Her joy was out of control.

When Amanda arrived home, Belinda met her at her apartment with a huge bouquet of red roses. Handing them over, she turned away, "Just wait there's more." She slid across the hall as Amanda unlocked the door. Belinda returned with an even larger bouquet of beautiful wild assorted flowers, she set them on the small counter where they barely fit side by side.

"Hey Belinda, you will never guess! I got the job! You are looking at the new NYCB Queen of primetime. *'The New Edge on Truth'* reporting by Amanda Lindas."

They did a happy dance.

"Oh my Gawd! You're the luckiest girl I know."

Amanda flashed the credit card, "Correction Belinda, *we* are the luckiest girls in New York."

"What? What is the credit card for? Who did you have to sleep with to get that?" Belinda let out a squeal of excitement.

"Not funny, Belinda, I earned this. I put up with Kurt's shit for a whole month and I tolerated, my boss, Rich assuming he was getting sexual favors from me. Which he will not. I am sick of men trying to coerce me into having sex with them to advance my career. This card is buying you and me a whole new wardrobe–no limits Cinderella. We just have to use it before Rich changes his mind. He even gave me the whole week off. Oh, I almost forgot–I also met this awesome guy at *The Tavern on the Green*."

"Woo when you hit the jackpot girl–you get cha-ching! Do you want to know who the flowers are from?"

"Sure, what's in the notes?" Amanda smiled; she knew Belinda's patience was weak. No way could she wait for Amanda to get home before she peeked.

"Well the huge wild one was delivered personally by Kurt. Damn girl what did you do to him? He was fidgety as a dork. His card was a sincere apology. He really wants to make it up to you. He gave me his card, told me to have you call him."

"Right, like he's really sorry. I saw him out on a lunch date with a blonde. Me call him, yeah like that's ever going to happen." Amanda pulled the card from the roses. "Oh from Rich, thanking me for a lovely time. How nice?" she tossed his card into the trash with Kurt's.

Belinda popped the cork of a fresh bottle of white wine, "Well let's celebrate! And tell me about the other stud in your life. Hey do you think Kurt would go for me?" she poured two glasses and toasted her friend's success. They celebrated their new plastic treasure.

The next few days Amanda was in shopping Heaven. Credit card in tow and her arm interlocked with Tony's they strutted on Fifth Avenue. She got a complete makeover from MAX, suits from Ann Taylor, Donna Karan, and Coco Chanel along with sensible shoes for every outfit. She felt like a princess modeling extravagant gowns for Tony and Belinda's approval. The gowns were selected for the charity balls and black-tie affairs. They had a spectacular week together.

As time progressed Amanda did concede to extravagant dinners at The Plaza, the Waldorf-Astoria, and Café de Artistes on Central Park West not far from *The Tavern on the Green* with Rich. Just to keep up appearances and her charade, but no huggy-touchy feely crap was going on between them.

Kurt made his presence known on several occasions, but she avoided him. Antonio Casali became her confidant. She wasn't sure if it was her hatred for Kurt or her loathing of Rich that pushed her into a closer relationship with Antonio. It wasn't easy. He worked most nights, and attended Columbia University. And with her grueling glamorous star schedule she saw even less of him. But they managed a dating schedule all through July. Life couldn't be better.

As for Kurt he was miserable inside watching Amanda blossom into the anchor star he conceded she always was. But outside, he was exceptionally successful on his monetary gains. He landed several moonlighting jobs and extra journalism assignments. He also received lofty bonuses for sending Sarah exclusive photos of Rich and his new squeeze– *The new Queen-B of NYCB.*

Kurt had to admit Amanda was strikingly vibrant. She was the complete package. And becoming one of the top sought after woman interviewers. Other news media and cable shows televised clips of her first interviews. Showcasing the U.S. Representative of New York, Geraldine Ferraro, the first woman Vice-Presidential candidate, it was a masterpiece in journalism. Amanda invoked a super laugh when she mentioned Walter Mondale's comment ridiculing Gary Hart's polices lacking depth by asking, "Where's the Beef?" back in March. Who knew a single comment could stir action in the political arena? Amanda had cleverly interjected that having a woman in the race would corral the 'beef' into addressing the in-depth serious issues. She reiterated that Geraldine was proof that the USA is the place for women to embrace their dreams.

Her next gripping interview was with Lynn Ripplemeyer, the first woman to Captain a 747 across the Atlantic Ocean. She caught the viewers' attentions on what women could conquer and accomplish in the 1980's.

She accomplished a tastefully brilliant interview with Vanessa Williams, the first Miss America to resign after posing nude. In closing Amanda posed the questions, "Can a woman's body be considered art? Can she use her freedom of expression to choose its exposure no matter what position she holds in society?"

Kurt was secretly proud of her objective perspective on her high-profile interviews. Amanda reflected the natural beauty of rural Middle-America meeting and bridging the gap to the glamour of High Society.

She hit the new nerve of Celebrities being *real* down to Earth people. The girl next door introduces popular interests, new designers, playwrights, and tackles serious issues like AIDS, drugs, and world hunger into New Yorkers' living rooms.

Kurt was one of her biggest fans, but she remained his biggest hindrance. He channeled his aggravation into his commissioned articles for *Pleasures, Players International,* and *Hustler.* Somehow her success was fueling his pent-up energy and creating a force of magnitude success. It was cannibalistic how they fed off one another's success.

A couple of weeks into August, Kurt and Rich had a confrontation that spread like a dry brush fire through the office. Kurt regarded that the first sparks ignited when Rich had his intimate lunch with Amanda.

The Yellow "pee-on" folder was just the fire-starter. Amanda's continued rejection of his apology was the burning torch that fed the inferno.

Rich arrived early; the sheer look of aggravation covered his face. Someone was going to get the brunt end of his revulsion. He stormed to Kurt's office before Kurt headed to make up for his interview with Eddie Murphy on his new movie *Beverly Hills Cop*.

"Kurt, I need you in my office immediately." Rich barked and returned with a stomping gait. Kurt followed with concern written on his face and his yellow lead folder clutched in his hand.

Once inside the soundproof fishbowl, suppressed sparks flew like the Fourth of July all over again.

"Kurt, I have an outside job for you and it takes precedence over anything else. You will be compensated well." Rich pressed his fisted knuckles on his desk and stared unflinchingly. He resembled a linebacker at the line of scrimmage.

Kurt maintained his own game face and playbook agenda. He'd be damned to get another offhanded shitty assignment when he already had a fistful. He threw the yellow folder on Rich's desk, "Not until we discuss this crap that you've been feeding me! Why the hell am I chasing around town covering Dog Shows and Fashion Shows for anorexic women? Huh? Answer me that!"

Rich threw the file just missing Kurt's face. "Dammit Kurt, you did that to yourself! You pissed Jeremy and Mandy off every day for a month. I had to switch you out before they both quit or committed murder. We are running a news station here not some fucking petty playschool! I need you to do a job as an investigator outside of work." He walked around his desk his hands on his hips.

Kurt didn't back down, he had the advantage of stature by a few inches, "Oh sure, I'm your Anchorman and top reporter on shit detail and now you want my personal time too." He didn't dare confess that he was already being stretched thin by Sarah's demands. "I don't have a life outside of this job. I would love a few hours of sleep at night. But you have me running my ass off chasing shit stories, so I have to moonlight to pay my fucking bills. You knew damn well Mandy and I wouldn't get along. Hell she's got more balls than you when it comes to getting at the truth. You set me up!" He forcefully pointed his finger in Rich's chest.

A Pit-bull ready to pounce, Rich growled, "I warned you when I hired Mandy that the competition was going to get tough. Toughen up. Don't be such a pussy. When I was your age I raked this town for hot news stories and had plenty of time for hot babes too. You don't need sleep, news reporters live on caffeine and adrenaline. Do you want the job or not?"

Kurt's chest heaved with atomic reserves, "You Son-of-a-bitch, we both know why you hired Amanda. She's a bit young for your taste in women–don't you think? What about Daffy your receptionist, she can't even make a pot of coffee much less copy a report, what about her? Are you tired of her?" Kurt worked to keep his temper in check; his hands firmly clamped his hips. He didn't look, but he felt the hungry onlookers swarming close to the glass like greedy blood-suckers just waiting to latch on to the winning shark.

"Her name is Delphina, not Daffy. Maybe you should start dating her; she could ease your cockiness or that sexual repressed energy you tote around. When's the last time you got laid?" Rich whittled him down ruefully guessing the reason he was sleepless.

Livid at Rich's veracity about his sex life Kurt rescinded with strident hostility, "I am guessing that you did not drag me here to discuss my sex life." He raked his feathered hair, "What the hell do you want?" His surveillance on Rich, had forced him to witness some x-rated scenes, something he could have lived a long happy life without.

"Well now, that's more like it," Rich smiled valiantly. "I want you to follow Amanda."

A quizzical looked contorted on Kurt's face, "Why? What do you want with her? You already take her to the society parties and charity functions. Why don't you just leave her alone? What is she to you?"

Rich smiled sheepishly, "I like her. I like my women feisty and smart and shapely. And she's the total package."

Although Kurt agreed about the "total package" he was totally disgusted. "What? Why don't you do it? Is she even interested in you? You make me sick–can't keep your dick in your pants while your wife is out of town?" Kurt was mortified. Besides technically, he was already being paid to follow her. She attended several functions with Rich. It worked out well for him because he was required to attend the same parties. "No Rich, I won't do it! I can't do it!" He felt like a rat on a sinking ship chomping on leftovers getting his fill knowing he was about to drown.

An indignant frown covered Rich's face, "What do you mean you can't? You will... if you want to keep your anchor position and get off the "pee-on" team. I'm concerned Mandy is seeing some lowlife bartender." He stroked his mustache with his forefinger and thumb.

"What? She's seeing someone?" Kurt was shocked, a hint of jealousy triggered deep in his gut. "Who is he? When and where did she meet him?" He thought out loud.

Dumbfounded Rich replied, "Well how the hell should I know? That's why I'm hiring your ass." He reached into his top desk drawer, pulled out an envelope, and slipped it into a blue folder. He handed it to Kurt. "I hope a bonus of five grand will suffice. And welcome back to the Blue team."

Kurt shoved it back at him, "I said–No! Under no circumstances am I trailing her for you." He thought, *maybe for myself, but not for you scumbag.* "Take your Blue team and money and shove it. Get a life–you're pathetic!" Kurt gallantly turned away, but not before Rich cold-cocked him with a right hook. The blow sent Kurt to the floor. Blood splattered from his split lip onto his silk shirt.

The hungry gawkers lined the windows. If Kurt needed witnesses on who threw the first punch he had plenty. But then he realized he was fighting a losing battle. He tasted the blood from his lip and rubbed his bruised chin. Annoyed with Rich, the dire situation, and himself for what he was about to do. He crumbled. He caved like a sinkhole.

"Okay fine, what the hell is your deal?" He grumbled with less than honorable intentions he stood, brushed himself off, and gathered the blue file and its contents.

Rich backed up, his fists raised for boxing.

Instead of blasting back with his fists, Kurt surprisingly blasted out requests, "Five grand? You'd better double it. Amanda gets less alone airtime. And I am her escort to the major functions–all expenses paid, while I verify her every move."

Kurt thought, *this is my turn to get something out of this mess. At least she will be my charming co-star and date for several days and nights. Something was awry and he'd play along until he found out what.*

Rich lowered his fists and nodded to Kurt's stringent weird requests. He extended his right hand to confirm their deal. Kurt obliged with a grimace and sneer. Somehow he couldn't help but think that he just stole the poison bait from the most devious rat he knew. Rich's adamant request of Kurt's personal time detonated an explosive conquest.

Before Kurt left the office he turned, "You better call your Star–girlfriend to cover the Eddie Murphy interview. I am not going on camera with a cut fat lip. Oh, another thing, I wear fitted large shirts, a seventeen and a quarter neck, with a thirty-six sleeve. Deliver a few Armani shirts to my place and transfer the other money to my direct account. Thanks Boss." His words brittle and sarcastic, "You do want the laundry job? If you don't, I will chat with Amanda about our deal." He patted his blue folder and the right front pocket of his slacks, "Or maybe Sarah will be entertained by our conversation. I'm sure my mini tape recorder picked up just exactly how you like your women." He flicked his hair back, strutted out slamming the door, scattering the busybodies back to their desks.

Chapter 6

Amanda woke that same day with a vestigial hangover. Nothing pressing at work, she had stayed out late celebrating her July interviews' bonus with Tony. So subsequently she was caught off guard when Rich called her to cover the Eddie Murphy interview. Originally she coveted it, but of course the *favorite* anchor got it.

Forcing herself out of bed she asked Rich to send a car. She needed an energizer shower desperately.

Promptly after Rich's call, donning her new black Coco Channel suit with matching heels; Amanda stepped out of her apartment into another sweltering New York mid-August day. Good thing she didn't bother with makeup it would have melted off anyway. Work was minutes away she barely had time to enjoy the air-conditioning before getting out of the gleaming black town car. Exiting, she encountered her nemesis.

Kurt opened her car door, his quirky smirk partially covered by an icepack, "Well, welcome to NYCB Ms. Lindas, so glad you could cover for me at such short notice. What no makeup today? Did you have a late night?" He grinned. Not that she needed makeup on her smooth tanned skin, but he usually saw her in full camera makeup, he had almost forgotten how beautiful she was *au natural*.

She leered; "Hello Kurt." The sight of his swollen jaw and lip momentarily stopped her. She collected her Louis Vuitton handbag and briefcase from the town car as he exposed the deep cut in his lip, "What truck hit you?"

He leered back, placing the icepack back on his swollen lip. "Like you care, but if you must know I got into a fight over a woman."

"Well, it looks the other guy won."

"Well, who said it was a guy?" he smirked lowering his icepack. "The fight isn't over, in fact–the war has just begun."

She scrunched her face at him.

He couldn't tell if she was repulsed by his bruised bloody lip, or his smart-ass attitude, but during war sometimes you have to lose a battle to gain some ground.

"Well soldier, you'd better retreat," she patted his smooth cheek. "You may need stitches, and I'd hate to take all your Hottie Honeys

55

interviews for the next two weeks until your pretty-boy face heals." She pouted her lips vexing him.

He slipped into the waiting town car, "Oh don't worry Ms. Lindas I have already called and rescheduled my Hotties..." Closing the door she heard him exclaim, "Home James and through the park, please."

"Arrogant bastard, he knows the driver's name is Leroy." she said huffing into the building. Inside she went straight to makeup next to studio B where the interviewee was already cutting jokes with the staff. This was going to be a treat. She was a great fan of Eddie Murphy.

The interview went off without a hitch. It was plastered all over the up-and-coming comedy cable channels. Even MTV did a spot later that night. Amanda was so thrilled she telephoned her mother, so she could watch her youngest daughter on national TV. Amanda was in her glory, she even called Shelly back home. And she surmised Kurt was stewing over her success.

Kurt barely spoke to her at work after all the hoopla.

Over the next couple of weeks, he seemed preoccupied with some secret project. During that same period they were forced to be a couple to attend dinners, movie premieres, and two top Broadway shows– *Sunday in the Park with George* and *The Real Thing*.

Amanda was pleasantly surprised he enjoyed Broadway shows, and that he was a very attentive cordial date. He brought her drinks, opened her car doors, and escorted her genteelly on the red carpets. Was he working on a call-back for the overly attentive boyfriend lead? Or worse yet, was he patronizing her by acting like a hired professional escort? *He was acting, wasn't he?*

Ushering her with his natural swagger, Kurt edged through a crowded charity function using his broad shoulders. His guiding hand on her exposed lower back caused an electric current to race from his skin to hers giving her heart a jolt.

They were photographed together at every function. They posed like a typical real couple their arms wrapped each others' waist. The paparazzi dubbed them, "New York's Golden Anchor Couple".

She noticed he was losing weight. And that he was drinking more than usual, and then he started smoking cigars and cigarettes. He appeared anorexic and exhausted.

But in his defense, she felt tired most of the time herself. She and Tony were seeing each other twice a week. Not intimate yet, but she felt her resistance waning. She hated to break her "two month dating rule" before getting horizontal.

The rule of thought was men could only act for two months then they became their *true* selves. If after two months, she liked the *real* man then she would consider intimacy. Antonio was attentive, smart, funny, an excellent kisser and dancer. But time wasn't on their side, their schedules were so opposite.

The real shocker came when Antonio mentioned he wanted her to meet his mother. What man would want a woman to meet his family before they were on an intimate level? If she didn't have to straddle her time between Kurt and Rich as a trophy date, she could have met his mother. Antonio never mentioned any other family, so she knew meeting his mom was a monumental relationship step.

The problem was Amanda felt like she was triple dating. For whatever reason Kurt's propinquity every night had Antonio perturbed, almost jealous.

Prior to Antonio's arrival to the clubs, Kurt bought drinks for her and Belinda. She just thought Kurt was trying to fit in; he didn't seem to have any close friends. Of course, he had the knack to attract glam-girls hanging on him, his every word, and kissing his handsome face promoting a public spectacle. More like a public nuisance.

He and Jeremy were still at odds. Kurt did something major to lose Jeremy's respect and jilted their friendship; she couldn't extort a confession from either. Jeremy was tight-lipped especially when Kurt was around, which lately was all the time. If she didn't know better, she'd swear Kurt was stalking her. He kept a safe distance most of the time, at least, no more privates on her behind.

He acted like a big brother, not the type of big brother like– I am here to protect you, but more like the creepy *Big Brother,* from George Orwell's 1984 novel. The scary type like– I'm watching your every move, like the popular Police song. He seemed fascinated by the lyrics.

She also heard him singing another under his breath at the studio. Something about magic and how the little things the woman does turns him on, and the guy has feelings for her, but he loses his nerve to tell her, definitely a strange song for Kurt to repeat over and over.

In fact, he was doing it again, as they sat in the makeup room getting painted for–*The New Edge on Truth* telecast. His hands drummed the beat. She couldn't stop herself, she interrupted his chanting, "Who are you going to call to marry you in an old fashion way?"

"What?" he asked returning from La-La Land. His emerald green eyes wide with wonder.

"Who are you going to ask to marry you?"

With eyebrows raised, he pointed to himself, "Me?"

"Yes you. You keep singing that song, so I thought it was something heavy on your mind."

The makeup artists finished painting their lips, his soft masculine pink and hers bright seductive red, they were left alone to dry before camera time. Usually in separate rooms, but today all the actors from the hit movie *Footloose*, were on, so they were forced to share.

Kurt shifted uncomfortable in his chair, he sat straight up and pointed at his chest again, "Me, ask someone to m-marry me? Oh no, I am not the Mmm type." He stuttered, way out of his persona.

Amanda didn't believe his act for one second. She felt his jitters all the way over to her chair. "You can tell me. Who's the unlucky girl?"

He laughed at her subtle jab, "Wouldn't you like to know?"

"No, not really," she lied flat-out. Honestly, she was curious as to what type of woman he would choose. Hell, half of New York was probably interested in who NYCB's Anchorman was interested in marrying. Just from rumors she heard he had dated and bedded plenty runway models and Broadway starlets. And he left them brokenhearted.

"If you're not interested then why did you ask?" His Irish eyes twinkled with amusement.

"Oh just curious as to why you constantly sing that song like a broken record."

"What you don't like my voice?" He seemed genuinely concerned.

"*Au contraire*, I like your voice very much. In fact you have a sexy smooth voice like the lead singer of The Police."

"Really?" he blushed even through his makeup.

She couldn't believe it. "Kurt Kilawee blushing? You're cute when you blush." She said as her face pinked, sharing a flirtatious smile.

Kurt stood, removed the makeup tissues and the white drape protecting his new Armani pink shirt, a tribute from the boss. Pink never bothered Kurt; he was secure in his manhood. He buttoned the top button and slipped a burgundy silk tie around his neck. "Well, as much as I'd love to sit around discussing how cute we look when we blush. We've got a show to do."

She peered down at her new Gucci watch; he was right, she stripped her tissues and cape off exposing her royal blue Anne Taylor suit.

It made her gray-blue eyes pop, causing him to struggle with his tie. She squared his shoulders towards her, "Here let me help. We wouldn't want you to smudge your new pink shirt."

As Mandy adjusted his tie, he became uncontrollably mesmerized by her beauty. *Damn*, he thought, she'd better get her hands and eyes away from me before something of an embarrassing nature rises.

58

He swallowed hard, "Hey, I'm good now. You can stop mothering me." The word mother should have suppressed his urge to seduce Mandy right there in the makeup room. *Well, that vision was no help.* Quickly he turned her so she wouldn't see the effect she was having on him. "You go; I'll be right behind you…" *Now, that would be great.*

Rich's baritone voice vibrated, "Ready on the set!"

Yeah, I'm ready… for hot sex or a cold shower. Kurt had promised himself to stay away from her. But she touched him; he didn't touch her other than turning her away from his inherent arousal. He did take liberty and eyed her ass, but that was natural for him.

Now he had to stop thinking about her to regain his composure–easier said than done.

"Ready on the set!" Rich started the countdown.

Kurt walked out with his suit-coat on; he slipped into his anchor seat satisfied that his jacket covered the other part of him that was ready for something other than show business.

At Rich's pointing cue, Kurt flew into action, "Kurt Kilawee and Amanda Lindas reporting live– *The New Edge on Truth.*"

After their successful group interview, Kurt exchanged numbers with some of the actors. He could convince anyone that he was their best buddy. Even Kevin Bacon was joking like they were college frat buddies.

Amanda excused herself and went to the office to the same little desk she started with. On the desk was black and white striped Spotlight Shoes designer shopping bag. A note attached, *To Mandy – Dance the night away.*

She didn't recognize the handwriting, but she delved in. Just as she pulled out a glittery black five-inch platform stiletto, who but Kurt would make his presence known?

Within seconds, his long gait launched him to her side. After whistling a wolf-call, he tsked, "Whoa sexy shoes, a new office dress code?" He scrupulously eyed the other shoe handling it like a fine artifact. "Well, everyone is gone–you could model them for me? I've covered plenty of fashion models." A single eyebrow arched, matching his facetious smile.

"I'll bet you did," she said. His bragging about his sexual prowess on bedding models wasn't her idea of entertainment; she wanted to smack the smile off his face. But she refrained.

Instead she shot him a glare and snatched her new possession from his loose grip. "I'm not your type of model, so wipe that smirk off your face!"

Kurt picked up the shoe she had discarded. Now he scrutinized it like evidence in a courtroom. Noting it was size seven, so whoever purchased them knew her size. Vexed his eyes roved to the package, up and down her person, and then back to the sexy shoe, "Where do you suppose a lady would wear these shoes, Amanda? Oh wait the note says Mandy, must be an intimate friend to buy you expensive '*fuck-me*' shoes."

"I don't owe you an explanation. They are a gift! Furthermore, why don't you go mind your own business?" She held the shoe like a weapon with the heel extended.

Kurt snickered at the irony. "*Au contraire*, but I am minding my own business–you are my business." He spoke in an obnoxious TV Game show host voice. "Ladies and Gentlemen, Amanda Lindas is Kurt Kilawee's business." The more he thought of them as "*fuck-me*" shoes he emitted a tense rush of jealousy. "What kind of woman are you becoming Mandy?"

"Oh my God, you're jealous." It finally dawned on her, perfectly clear. "What do you care who buys me '*fuck-me*' shoes as you so endearingly call them? It is none of your business what I wear or where I go to wear it! Who do you think you are? You despicable–deplorable Jack-ass!" She nailed the five-inch heel into his meaty shoulder, "That's for your raunchy thoughts and accusations!" She left a dent in his neatly pressed shirt and seized the other shoe from his grasp.

"Whoa, I like it when you talk dirty," he winced and ducked as if she would hit him again. His hands raised in surrender, "Hey, no need to get violent over an assumption. I thought you were better at obtaining the facts, without attacking your audience." He massaged his sore shoulder. "And don't assume that I'm jealous." He ascertained that he was going to have a serious bruise on his shoulder along with his ego.

Shoving the designer shoes into the black and white striped Spotlight Shoes bag, Amanda crunched it under one arm and clutched her purse under the other. She was late for a dinner date with Tony before his shift. "May I leave now? Or will there be more insinuations and interrogations? Or would you just prefer to stalk me on my date?"

Still rubbing his smart wound with a trace of embarrassment on his face, he replied. "Well, I suppose with those weapons you won't need an escort to *The Tavern on the Green*. I'm just a little envious and put-off that you'd hit me with them, yet refuse to model them for me. I was thinking they'd look good resting on my shoulders." His sheepish crooked grin did not help.

"That will be a cold day in Hell. Now, allow me to pass, I have a date with a *real* man."

"Ouch," he scowled. "The Ice-Maiden strikes again. I get frostbite just from her words." He narrated like a movie trailer commentator.

His hands rose, surrendering again; he shifted over allowing just enough space for her to squeeze between him and her desk. Her sterile cold glare bewitched him. Just as she passed; his hand closest to her dropped and slapped her firm rump hard. "That's payback for the dent you left in my shoulder."

Flustered by his forwardness, she jumped nearly dropping her package, "Oh, cry me a river. And don't you dare ever touch me again!" Her behind throbbed from his masculine swat.

"Oh don't dare me–that would only lead to another swat, and I could enjoy that one too." He pushed his face close to hers. Close enough to feel her soft breath and smell her subtle fresh scent. She was one hell of a hot tease. Her spark ignited his inner flame like no woman ever did. "So, call me when Hell freezes over Ice-Maiden?" He rasped.

Heat rose to her cheeks, forcefully she bit back more harsh words; she didn't want to entice him into a huge blowout. The inclination occurred to her that he was purposely trying to make her late.

Her pulse raced and her heart pounded offbeat, she felt faint. In a hurry to leave, keeping her cool was imperative, "This conversation is over. I wouldn't call you if you were the last man on Earth, in Heaven, or Hell." She spun on her heels, strutted to the exit, and smacked into the locked glass doors.

The glass rumbled. *The cunning bastard had locked the doors. Damn, he was so self-assured.* She turned the hand bolt releasing her from his brazen presence.

Not to be out done, Kurt shouted after her, "Well, you don't impress me! You're no frickin' picnic Amanda Lindas. And you're no Barbara Walters or Connie Chung either!" He rubbed his sore shoulder consoling himself.

####

Later that same night Kurt and Jeremy went clubbing only after Kurt begged and pleaded like a little sister. It was Labor Day weekend and anyone who was somebody would be out clubbing.

"Man, you need to chill, stop acting like you have ants in your pants." Jeremy slugged Kurt as they stood in the VIP line at Roxy's on 10th Ave and 18th Street.

"Ouch! Damn it Jeremy, that's my sore arm." Kurt flinched.

"Geez, you're such a baby. I don't know why I let you talk me into this shit. I'm tired of being your babysitter. You owe me big time."

As they fought like kids, Kurt noticed Amanda and Belinda a few sets of people behind them in the VIP line. He smiled. His little protégé had made it. She was tarted up with wild hair and spandex leggings, a *Flash Dance* girl-wonder. Mandy was now a New York City local celebrity; she earned the VIP status, thanks to him.

He approached the bouncer, slipped him a Ben Franklin, whispered and indiscreetly pointed to Amanda and Belinda. The bouncer chuckled with him.

Kurt and Jeremy entered into the inner sanctum of Roxy's flashy strobe-light, black-light, disco-rock jungle. The air reeked of cigarettes and pot. The vibrant scattered rainbow lights made the smoky billows into colorful poisonous clouds.

Outside, just moments later, the bronzed bouncer weaved through about a dozen people to reach Amanda, "Hey you're Amanda Lindas that new hot Anchorwoman. You're looking mighty fine, I have instructions, from the boss, to escort you and your friend to your private table."

Belinda and Amanda were escorted past a plethora of ogling guys and girls. Amanda thought she saw envy in their eyes. They made it! Finally thin enough–pretty enough–rich enough and maybe even tabloid material. The paparazzi lurked about like cockroaches just waiting for photo ops.

Inside, she scoped the club scattered with black lights looking for Jeremy's bright eyes and smile. The club's trippy cosmic atmosphere with blaring music added to the edgy mystery that hung in the background of Amanda's mind. She was interested to know how Jeremy and Kurt "kissed and made up". They were a strange breed, a hilarious couple.

The black lights made most of the clubbers looked like they had Florida orange Q-T tans.

Her eyes immediately gravitate to Kurt with his white jacket sleeves crunched to his elbows covering a bright aqua T-shirt. His hands rested on his hips covered in tight white jeans. Captivated by him, she could hardly breathe. He resembled the character detective from *Miami Vice*, just taller. He was so hot he made her blood boil in a manner she'd never discuss with anyone. His presence demanded her attention.

Too bad, he was a Jekyll and Hyde. She couldn't believe the jealous guy at work was the same attentive date she enjoyed as her private escort to the surplus of summer events–he even paid attention to Shakespeare's *Henry V* at the Delacorte Theater.

What was his deal? A mystery her mind wanted to solve, but her heart didn't dare contemplate him further. He had too many red-flag warnings all over him.

Another bouncer accompanied her and Belinda to a private roped off area with white modern lounge chairs and a low black granite oval table topped with two cosmopolitan martinis and a note.

The note stated: *You look awesome, please save a few dances for me– don't look for me–I will be watching you.*

No sooner did she finish reading it; she glanced up. Kurt was talking with the DJ, he lowered his aviator mirrored sunglasses and trigger pointed his hands in her direction. *What a dweeb*, she thought. So, *not cool*. She turned her back to him and laughed at his dorky quirkiness. The DJ switched the song to The Police–"Every Breath You Take".

Belinda pulled her onto the dance floor, "Not to freak you out, but he's standing at the balcony above the dance floor watching."

Tentatively she looked over her shoulder finding Kurt with his arms crossed and his long legs straddled shoulder width apart still wearing the mirrored sunglasses. He was singing the words.

Amanda officially had the creeps. She made the executive decision to ignore him. Tony was meeting her later and last thing she needed was Kurt messing with her relationship.

Drinking the cosmos' like Kool-aid, she was amazed at how quickly they lit her. The endless martinis kept coming. She lost count of her mandatory three drink limit. The club was so dark she couldn't tell the real celebrities from the "wanna Bs". Maybe they were all "wanna-Bs".

At eleven Kurt made his move through the cigarette smoke and generated fog. On the dance floor, Amanda was spellbound by the glow in his hypnotizing gorgeous eyes. His warm strong hands touched her bare midriff, gently pulling her close swaying to the music. She accepted his friendly gesture; he leaned and asked, "Having a good time Mandy?"

She shot him her, *you-know-my-name* look.

"I know I know..." He rolled his eyes, "I want us to be friends. I'll bet Antonio Casali calls you Mandy."

She twirled with his assistance; facing him she shouted over the music, "Listen, Tony calls me Mandy because he is my boyfriend. Got it?" She stepped in closer sprawling her hands on his chest. "By the way," her thick lashes fluttered exposing telltale bedroom eyes, "thank you for buying our drinks again, you really shouldn't." Ambivalent she stopped herself from telling the truth. Tony was coming to the club and he didn't appreciate Kurt's generosity.

"My apology for what happened today. I don't know what came over me. What can I do to be your friend? Why shouldn't I buy you drinks?"

"Because I am capable of purchasing my own drinks," she smiled pretentiously. *Well, it was a version of truth, just like reporting the news.*

The song "Beat It" pulsated through the club. Kurt spun her away and started dancing like he was born a Jackson. She reeled back to him tango style and ran her fingers through his wonderfully soft hair something she had wanted to do since day one. The alcohol loosened her inhibitions; she took advantage of their close connection. Out of control, her hands trailed down his body to his muscular thighs and across his tight butt. He was quite the mover and shaker–gyrating to the beat.

They were magnetic. The crowd circled them pushing them to the center of the dance floor. They swayed into each other, bodies not touching but close enough to generate an electric spark. If anyone could make love on the dance floor this was as close as they could get.

Self-conscious Amanda made the mistake of glancing at her watch.

Unwilling to let the moment end, Kurt noticed, took hold of her wrist, and skillfully removed the watch placing it in his pocket. The timing was right for his ulterior plan to kick into action. Any moment Tony would walk into the club and see them together. If Kurt couldn't get Mandy to break it off with Tony– then Tony would have to do it.

Dirty dancing with her required assiduousness; she was very responsive. She wasn't quitting. If anything she up the ante with deeper dips and gyrations. Mandy could dance; but he already knew that. She danced in his dreams keeping him awake and needy.

No more sleepless nights–he was going to collect what he wanted–hopefully tonight. If she'd agreed to be his girlfriend, he could put an end to his reports to Rich and Sarah. Just that action would lift his burdened conscience to focus on the other shady deals he feared included Rich.

The bewitching hour approached; Jeremy reticent stood sentry watching the door for Antonio's arrival. In plain sight he waved his arms like a fool flagging an airplane on a runway. Kurt finally noticed and twirled Mandy into his chest where she belonged–according to him.

Their hips swayed completely synchronized, no rubbing, he knew better now. Their explosive chemistry stunned the crowd. Ready to burst with emotion, he said, "You feel so right to me." His evident passion raged, he went to kiss her perspiring neck, but then the music changed to "Thriller".

The crowd interrupted and congratulated them on their dance moves. Midway into the song Amanda stopped and pushed him away. The magic dissipated.

DESIRE FOR TRUTH

Darkness seals your doom... she thought making her way to the flashing dance floor edge. Her eyes met Tony; dressed in all black, his hands shoved into his front pockets. She reached him; he crossed his corded arms over his twitching chest beneath his polo shirt, obviously holding back anger.

Kurt followed her off the floor. Awkwardly he reverted into 'best buddy' mode. "Hey big guy, thanks for letting me borrow her. Can I buy you two a drink?" He flagged a waitress, ordered their libations of choice, knowing from his surveillance time, the longest fucking three weeks of his life. His investigation wasn't superficial like Rich had requested. *Yeah, he was better than that.* He did an extensive background check on Antonio Casali. He traced him to his roots. There was plenty background bullshit that Amanda didn't need to know. Kurt couldn't tell her the truth or that he was spying on her. *And by the way, getting paid a bundle.*

Somehow he had to earn her trust and woo her away before he could thrust the cold hard truth in her face. He was working on the biggest feature article of the decade and couldn't risk jeopardizing or leaking it because of her "boyfriend", the bartender.

God, he hated that she had confirmed the boyfriend-girlfriend status–a certified couple. He wanted to scream and vomit. Just watching her soothe Antonio's ruffled feathers increased the slow burn in his throat.

Turning away would have been merciful. But he chose longsuffering by not shifting his gaze from her silky hands. As she caressed Antonio; her tart-red lips nibbled his neck until a wave of forgiveness flooded the boyfriend's tense face and body. Hell, Antonio was like putty in her hands. And the only thing that pissed Kurt off more was for the first time in his life he wanted to be someone else. The honest truth was he wanted to be– Antonio.

He should have left, but instead he chose more torture by watching them slow dance to Foreigners "Waiting for a Girl Like You".

Away from her eyes and the dance floor, Kurt plowed his fist into his palm repeatedly, with grievance.

Jeremy tried calming him. "Dude don't make a scene. Go outside get your cool back on. If she sees you flip-out you're a goner."

Taking Jeremy's advice, Kurt paced outside stroking her Gucci watch. He bummed three cigarettes; chain smoked them, and then decided he was *well enough* to go back into the club. Like an insane patient writing his own prescription.

The first hot chick he encountered, he lured to the dance floor. They danced every song that Tony and Mandy danced. Move for move it soon became an unofficial dance competition. Although he was on fire with the new girl, the chemistry wasn't the same.

Off the dance floor, Kurt was getting loaded. In the chaos of the club, Jeremy lost track of him, he headed outdoors on a search-and-rescue mission. And there he was sucking face with a hottie propped up against his waiting town car. Jeremy tapped his foot and cleared his throat like a cat hacking up a hairball.

Kurt stopped necking long enough to catch Jeremy's disgusted motherly glare. He peered through his slits for eyes from too much alcohol. "What Lionel? What? Can't you see I'm busy?"

"Don't go there Kurt, you come here when I'm talking to you." Jeremy waved his index finger. "This is not the plan. You let that girl go. Let's leave before Mandy sees you in all your horny glory. And don't call me Lionel we've talked about that. Now let the lady go. I don't want any more lip from you, Fool."

Kurt excused himself from his more than voluptuous and willing newest fan club member. With gritted teeth he asked, "What the hell are you doing man? You're cramping my style. Dude you're killing me."

Jeremy's eyes widen and then squinted. "You don't want to do this Kurt. You've been drinking and you know how you get when you drink."

Kurt leaned in and whispered, "Yeah, I know... I get horny. I am a man that hasn't been laid in almost three months, and I can't wait anymore. Amanda's not into me man." The truth gripped and twisted him to his core, having to admit he had fallen for a woman who didn't want him. It ripped his heart out and crushed his ego. She was driving him completely insane. "Mandy is into Antonio–her boyfriend. We lost. I lost, and I'm not waiting in line for my turn."

"So that's it?" Disappointment washed Jeremy's face his voice rose to the occasion. "So you just give up! What's so manly about that? I told you love takes time, but no-o-o, you can't wait for the real deal. Well, Mandy is the real deal. Can't you see that? You try too hard. Just stop and be yourself–stop the competition shit. You're too smart to be this damn stupid."

It was close to four in the morning, they stood shouting at each other on the sidewalk as the club started to empty.

Amanda and Belinda spotted them arguing while the bimbo waited next to the town car. It appeared they were close to blows. Amanda pushed Tony over to separate them. Kurt would end up killing Jeremy if it came to blows.

Kurt swayed as he stated his hopeless case to Jeremy. "You don't understand, man, I can't... I am done... I'm leaving with Rachelle or Raquel here." He whispered his last intent. "I want to get laid."

With his chest puffed, hands on his hips, Jeremy portrayed his best motherly stance, "So, how does it feel to want? How does it feel to *not* get your way? Don't you dis me; I know how it feels to want. If you do this we are through!"

Just then the paparazzi and the crowd gathered to view the confrontation. Camera bulbs flashed.

Tony approached laughing; he became vindictive, trying to affront Kurt. "Hey are you having a lover's quarrel here?" He pointed to Kurt and then to Jeremy. "You two need to cool off. Take your lover's quarrel home. You don't want to air your dirty laundry out here."

The paparazzi cameras started flashing again. Amanda and Belinda could not control their laughter. Kurt was going to end up in some smutty tabloid.

Kurt stood speechless. He rubbed his hands through his hair, befuddled as the crowd swarmed viewing him and Jeremy as a couple. Covering his face first, he then raised his arms in protest. "NO! NO! Oh hell no! We are not a couple! We are not having a lover's quarrel." Frantic he pointed, "Tell them Jeremy" his face distorted and stern, "Tell them the truth, I'm warning you."

Jeremy stood defiant with his arms crossed and shaking his head. "You're pathetic man."

Raquel moved away from the town car. Jeremy yanked Kurt's arm. "Get in Dear," he said and turned to smile at Mandy. He tucked Kurt's head down pushing him into the back seat, and jumped in shutting the door to the din of the laughing crowd.

Inside the town car, Kurt and Jeremy looked at each other and in unison screamed, "Don't you ever do that to me again!"

Kurt slouched as Jeremy crossed his arms and sulked.

"I cannot believe you did that to me." Jeremy whined.

"Me? You? I'm the one that's ruined. I wish I had a gun."

"You do have a gun, but shooting yourself isn't going to straighten this mess out." Jeremy scolded.

Kurt glared at Jeremy, "I wasn't going to shoot myself."

"Then what do you need a gun for?"

"To shoot you with, Lionel."

"What are you jive talkin' 'bout Fool?"

The chauffer opened the glass panel between the seats, "Where to Mr. Kilawee?"

"Home James, but drop Lionel off on the way.

"Oh no, you don't. You made me promise to help you get Mandy. I'm going home with you, so you don't pick up some street sweet-tart and get a disease. The driver's name is Leroy not James. Leroy you take us to Mr. Kilawee's apartment." Jeremy slid the glass panel shut.

Kurt passed out.

Jeremy patted him on his tousled hair, "That's a good boy. Take a nap you will pay for this in the morning, fool."

Chapter 7

The next morning, Jeremy catapulted Kurt off his platform waterbed. The free flowing water mattress allowed enough movement to project Kurt up and out. Not a conventional technique, but it worked.

"Come on man, we have to get to work." Jeremy coaxed Kurt up off the floor and scuttled him across the antique hardwood floors to his newly renovated, *you-could-have-a-party-in-it* shower.

"Dude what's with this bathroom? All mirrors, Hollywood lights, and this big ass shower with sprayers everywhere. What do you do in your spare time that you can afford this?" Jeremy seriously questioned and sat Kurt in the shower on a *Cesca* chair he had confiscated from the dining room. Without warning Jeremy turned on the jetted spouts and drenched Kurt–clothes and all.

Kurt jumped, "I'm awake–I'm awake." He plopped down cradling his head in his hands, "Damn man, what the fuck? What did I drink last night?"

"The question is–what didn't you drink? You scarfed down a bottle of expensive Irish whiskey after I hauled your ass into the house."

Kurt peeked through his fingers the water-jets pulsated his face, "Really? Damn, I hate myself when I drink my good stuff after bar time. What a fucking waste. God, Jeremy what time is it?"

"It's time for you to pull yourself together. You have that controversial AIDS documentary with you know who today."

"Man, I can't face her after last night." Shock spread across Kurt's face as he suffered a flashback of the end of the night. Stumbling around the bathroom he stripped to his underwear. He looked in the mirror, on automatic pilot he washed his face with cold water and smoothed his long wet layers of hair back. "Find out what smut tabloid took those photos last night. That bastard Tony saying we were a couple didn't help!" He squeezed toothpaste on his toothbrush, fiercely brushing he muffled, "Go–go find out."

"I already did. You're too late."

Kurt stopped. Toothpaste drooled around his open mouth. He slammed his hand on his forehead. "Shit! When Rich sees them I'm screwed!"

Jeremy stood stoic, arms crossed wearing one of Kurt's too large dress shirts. "He already did. He's called three times this morning."

Hurrying Kurt splashed his face again washing off the toothpaste residue; he lathered the lower half of his face with shaving cream.

"Slowdown or you'll cut yourself?"

"What are you my mother?" Kurt shaved fast.

"Yes, unfortunately I am the closest thing you have to a mother or friends for that matter. You sure know how to piss-off people lately. What the hell has gotten into you?"

"It's her, ouch damn it!" Kurt nicked his chin. "See just mentioning her gets me all messed up."

"I told you to slowdown. You have some time. Rich wants to see your ugly mug in an hour."

Kurt patched his cut with a dab of tissue. A splash of aftershave and cologne stung his face knocking him back to life.

"Rich won't fire me. He can't–can he? Nope, not possible he doesn't have the balls to do it. Besides Sarah is my ace in the hole. She'll protect me – I'm her love child." He combed his feathered hair almost satisfied that he no longer looked like a zombie. But a shade of death warmed over wasn't all that appealing. *Thank God for makeup*–did he really just think that?

"Yeah that's another call I took. Your 'Mommy' or should I say 'Sugar Mamma' called this morning while you were dead. She's not sending flowers she's flying out today either to save your ass or kick it."

Kurt stood with his hands on his hips, breathing so hard that his abdominal muscles contracted. "Really? You might want to leave now. I'm totally going to be sick." Jeremy ducked out quickly, just as Kurt spun around to vomit into the sink.

Jeremy gave Kurt some alone time. In the interim, he answered several phone calls. Annoyed he answered offhandedly, "Kurt's cookie house which crumb do you want? Kilawee's Mortuary you stab 'em we slab 'em. Kilawee's Tree House which nut you want? This is Mr. Kilawee's personal secretary, how can I help you?"

After re-brushing his teeth Kurt, sunk back under the rain shower. He heard the phone ringing every five seconds making his head explode like an atomic bomb. Jeremy explained to the callers. "No he isn't a homosexual, no he does not date guys and girls, no he's not gay, no he's not available to make a comment, no, no, no," echoed throughout the apartment. Kurt wanted to crawl under a rock and die. He was ruined. And it was all her fault. He consoled himself with lies.

But the truth was this was *entirely* his fault for not being truthful about his attraction to her when he first laid eyes on her wavy brown hair, her sparkling icy-blue eyes, her infectious warm smile, and the way she giggled or got giddy over a new assignment. The graceful impeccable way she asked hard questions that weren't the nice kind. The kind of questions no one wanted to answer. She refused compromise; she desired the truth so adamantly that she repudiated anything less than the whole truth.

Unsure about the truth or how he was going to back paddle his way into his affluent life again, he was clueless. He was trapped. And it was his doing. Digging into destroying people's lives was ruining his. But he couldn't stop–he was addicted. He had to clean up this disaster and get back into the swell of his prestigious life. Thank God, for good friends like Jeremy.

Jeremy rapped on the bathroom door and hollered, "Dude, you need to get ready. I laid your clothes out on your bed. Get your butt in gear – time to face the music maestro."

Kurt dried off–still feeling like shit. He hadn't had a hangover of this magnitude in years; guess he deserved this one,–big time. Wrapped in a towel at the waist he nearly bowled Jeremy down in the hallway.

Jeremy was pissed. Arms folded with a black leather-bound notebook in one hand and a rubber-banded stack of cash in the other. "Man, we got to talk about this shit."

Kurt strutted by him. "No, not now, I've got to get ready. You said so yourself."

Jeremy followed him into the bedroom.

Kurt looked over his shoulder ready to drop his towel, "Hey, do you mind?"

"You don't have anything I haven't seen before–times ten. Besides you're too damn skinny to be my type." Jeremy turned away.

"Yeah, well I like to show my wares to women." Kurt dropped his towel and slipped into his work clothes. "What do you mean I'm not your type? You plan on sharing that with the smut papers for an extra spoof on 'The Tragic Demise of Anchorman Kurt Kilawee'?"

"Okay drama queen; just get your skinny ass covered. I have a bone to pick with you." Jeremy threw the leather notebook and money on the bed in front of Kurt. "What is that shit? Are you dealing?"

"That's for me to know and you not to find out." Kurt tucked his shirt in, buttoned his pants, and zipped his fly, giving Jeremy the silent treatment. Not that he didn't want him to know, he just didn't have the time to explain.

"So aren't you going to tell me? I think I have a right to know."

"Not now. I have to get through this fucking day first. And if I live, then we will sit down and discuss it. This conversation is over! Is the car ready?"

Jeremy puffed-up haughtily, "Yes, of course. I run things efficiently." He followed Kurt's longer than usual stride out the door, grabbing the tabloids and coffee he picked up earlier while Kurt was sleeping off his drunk.

The queasiness returned in the pit of Kurt's stomach, it didn't do well on the silent ride to the Empire State Building. He was glad for one thing that the ride was short and Jeremy left him to his thoughts. The tabloid he reviewed was filled with lurid libel trash. Plastered across his drunken stupor photo were the words, "OUT OF THE CLOSET". He muttered. "At least they could have used a better shot, did I really look that bad? Christ the photo of Antonio makes him look like fucking model."

Jeremy gave him a solemn look of betrayal. "Well, maybe if you weren't doing or dealing drugs you'd look better too." He said through a clenched jaw.

Kurt shot him a glare and shouted, "I am not dealing or doing drugs. And if I was it would be posted in the *New York Times* or the *Washington Post*. Now drop it!" He returned to reading about the sleazy lifestyle he supposedly led. They had all sorts of photos of him with models, sex-pots, starlets, and some great shots of him and Amanda together at several black-tie affairs. His weight loss was documented thoroughly by the series of snapshots going back about three years since he left Chicago.

"OH SHIT!"

Jeremy and the driver cringed. Kurt looked at Jeremy and continued. "Did my real mother call this morning?"

Jeremy's big eyes grew larger and shifted away. He gulped his coffee and squeezed out a squeaky, "Yes."

Kurt slouched back, covered his face with the tabloid paper, "Just–Fucking–Great! My father is going to shit. I will never hear the end of this from my brothers. Damn it! Damn it!" He pounded the door armrest.

"I'm sorry man." The whine remained in Jeremy's voice, "I just answered the phone. When I tried to calm her, she kept crying and asking me if I spent the night every night or was I just a fling. I explained that we were just friends and I only stayed the night because you were too drunk to be trusted alone..."

Kurt flung the papers, "Just shut-up, just shut-up! We will fix this. I don't know how, but somehow I am going to wake-up from this damn nightmare. My life is a fucking nightmare! It can't get any worse!"

Jeremy looked out the tinted windows as they approached the Empire State building, "Oh, yes it can... uh-huh. Oh, yes it can. Man–look out the window." The paparazzi and news reporters from all the major stations swarmed the town car. "Remember you wanted to be on the major networks–well here's your chance or death wish–you pick."

Everyone crowded in chattering, asking absurd questions, casting out slanderous statements, and banging on the tinted windows waiting for Kurt to face his public.

Familiar with the back entrance, Kurt instructed the driver to circle around to an underground parking area. The plan was to circumvent his not so adoring new fan club.

"Jeremy you stay in the car. Detour them by getting out at the front. That should give me enough time to use the service elevators and make my way to the news room. I'm sure Rich has secured the building on our floor." Just before Kurt was about to exit he turned to Jeremy, and said. "Hey, I owe you man, real big. One more thing, promise me if anything happens to me in the near future–that stuff in my dresser, the notebooks– make sure you get them to my dad, even if you have to drive them to Chicago. Remember he's the Commissioner of the Chicago Police Department," a serious dark storm brewed in Kurt's eyes. "You got that? Tell me you understand– no one but him. Promise me?"

Jeremy gave him a halfhearted smile. "Ya sure man, it's all cool. Wow your old man is the Commissioner? You're scaring the shit out of me. Good luck."

"Thanks, I don't think Hell has 'good' luck. See you at the office."

Kurt reached Rich's office, just so Rich could ream him. Rich's screaming and swearing was muffled to the NYCB employees. Ironically Kurt felt safe; yet exposed. His co-workers had a ringside view. No one was safe to leave because of the chaos his ordeal created. And if the humility he suffered wasn't bad enough, he felt the full brunt of guilt having Amanda's name dragged through the sludge of society's biased judgment. Rich shamed him profusely.

At Rich's desk, Kurt sat in front of five trash tabloids plastered with degrading headlines, "Anchor Comes Out of the Closet!" "Does News Anchor have AIDS?" The more he read the sicker he became.

Rich ranted, "You've ruined NYCB's creditability!" Shamefacedly, Kurt cowered like a dog being punished for crapping on the carpet.

In a charging stance Rich planted fisted knuckles on the desk, "Well, what have you got to say for yourself Mr. Kilawee?"

Dwarfed by his boss's disdainful presence, nauseated, morose, and perplexed he was unable to save his soul from damnation. Defensively, he conjured, "Well, I am not gay."

"Oh, that's a fucking a newsflash! Do you want me to call a press conference? What do you propose that we do to fix this mess? And if you say file libel suits, I will throw you out this thirtieth floor window." Rich slammed his palm on the window, probably to avoid strangling Kurt. "Do you realize the pain you've put Mandy through? She's devastated; she came in bombarded by the paparazzi. They're asking her if you've given her AIDS."

Feeling a little reprieve from his nausea, Kurt stood. "Well then by all means, call a fucking press conference. That would be a miracle! She won't let me touch her. You read my reports–if she's not getting attention and expensive gifts from you, she's with her boyfriend the bartender. So if she has sexual diseases they didn't come from me. Maybe you might want to check yourself or Antonio." Kurt's face flushed red as his necktie. "Did you have sex with her?" The pang of the green-eyed monster blinded him with thoughts of Rich intimately touching Amanda.

Rich's face turned grave, "Don't you dare accuse me of harming her. Hell you spend more waking hours with her than I do."

"Thanks to you for forcing me, I wouldn't be standing here defending myself against hearsay and libel. Last night wouldn't have happened if you would have let me live my life. All I do is drink and lose sleep over Mandy, Mandy, Mandy! And hell she won't even let me call her Mandy! Oh no, you're not pinning all the blame on me. I didn't ruin her life. You did!" Desperation curded inside him, he wanted to go find Mandy to defend his actions. But first he wanted to vent his loathing for what Rich forced him into. With his fists balled, he moved closer, prepared to strike if Rich lifted a finger.

Rich studied the vast skyline of concrete and glass buildings surrounding them. "These buildings are a powerful reminder that New York City is a force to be reckoned with. Its glamour and prestige can lure unsuspecting young women, to powerful men with personal conquests."

Angst wrenched Kurt's gut.

"What personal conquests? I didn't hire Amanda under false pretenses just to wine and dine her while my wife gets plastic surgery in Europe trying recapture her youth to keep my happy ass at home–we know that wasn't me. Better bring Sarah and Mandy in here. Let's tell the dirty rotten truth. You baited a young, innocent, vibrant, amazing woman to the Big Apple just so you could chew her up and spit her out. When you're finished what is she going to do with the pieces? Huh? Then what?"

Rich exposed a sinister grin.

"Damn you Rich. You leveraged my position against my better judgment. I can't sleep. I survive on alcohol and coffee. Day and night all I see is her blue eyes, while her scent arouses every nerve in my body. And it doesn't matter if she's cross with me or laughing at my expense, as long as I hear her voice, I think it's all good. Her competitive edge and her witty personifications push me to do my job better. Her drive for the truth is second to none. I thought it was second to my own, but she surpasses anything I do. She does it with grace, agility, and the energy of an innocent child. I deserve some of this bullshit that you dished out, but she doesn't." His words were humbly honest.

Calmly Rich turned, his hand pulling down his face, he tried to establish clarity. Looking at him was a sick damaged man he had helped create. He saw passion burning in his younger counterpart that he used to possess, "Do you know what your absolute problem is?"

Kurt sighed, his stomach clenched. "No, why don't you enlighten me. I am tired of solving everyone's problems, so why don't you solve mine."

Rich rested his hand on Kurt's shoulder; the one Amanda attacked with the '*fuck-me*' shoe. Kurt winced.

"Kurt my boy," Rich said fatherly.

"I'm not a boy, especially not yours, so don't patronize me." He shoved Rich's hand off his bruised shoulder.

Interlocking his fingers behind his neck, Rich continued, "Kurt your problem is, besides the fact that you're and egotistical son-of-a-bitch. You're in love with Mandy."

No comeback or defense plan, Kurt's mouth dropped. He needed a container and he needed it– NOW.

He rushed back to the desk where a trashcan awaited his attack. Without warning he proceeded to vomit. Jeremy and Amanda pounded the glass door. Rich quickly obliged letting them enter.

"Jeremy take him out of here. Mandy stay." Rich held her back, as Jeremy struggled to get Kurt and the trashcan out the door.

Chapter 8

Aids – Epidemic in New York City – Fact or Fiction?

The controversial documentary was not canceled as the NYCB staff had secretly wished and debated its demise. Instead, Sarah Underwood arrived for an emergency meeting of the board of directors. The board agreed it was perfect timing based upon what had just transpired.

Having Kurt and Amanda discuss the AIDS epidemic openly and frankly would allow them to utilize the bad publicity to launch the cutting edge NYCB network back into a positive spotlight.

"No such thing as bad publicity," was an intricate part of NYCB's mission statement. No other major or minor network was broaching the AIDS subject, but Amanda Lindas and Kurt Kilawee were about to take reporting to an explosive level.

They had conducted several prior serious interviews with doctors and patients that were struggling with the cure and the disease. Amanda had convinced HIV positive persons to allow NYCB to film them using shadow effects thereby camouflaging their identities. They gave the public the truth that people with AIDS were not monsters to be feared, but real people who deserved love, respect, and compassion.

Kurt came up with the shock element that guaranteed them national news recognition. He and Amanda had agreed to take the HIV blood test. They both felt confident in their newsworthy decision. At the end of the show the results would be revealed. Neither of them knew the results. Originally the plan was to tape the whole show. They agreed it would be the safest route to avoid adulterated controversy from the public forum; they were breaking in on virgin territory.

In the interim, Kurt rested to regain his bearings peacefully in his office, but when Jeremy, Rich, and Amanda checked on him, he wasn't faring well. Rich took extra precaution and called the paramedics. The paparazzi fed the public frenzied fanatic false stories. Kurt viewed a small TV brought in so he could monitor what the networks were dishing out about him. They chewed him up like piranhas on fresh meat.

Sarah snuck in to razz him. "Sure, all the women in New York are taking diet pills and paying millions to fat farms and all we need is to follow your regiment of booze and caffeine. And I am supposing wild nighttime escapades. Live hard you'll die young." She patted his pale cheek as he rested on the gurney brought in by the paramedics.

The saline potassium drip inserted intravenously helped bring color back to his face.

"Kurt, I appreciate what you've done for me. I don't know what you did or said to Rich, but it worked. I have never seen him so attentive. And just so you know the Board and I have filed libel suits against the five trash tabloids. You will be in for a hefty sum once we're through with them."

Kurt smiled languidly, he had no clue why Rich made amends with Sarah, but he was relieved. He would feel even better if he could placate Amanda, but her intransigent attitude kept him at a loss to ask her for forgiveness. He wasn't sure what man-woman relationship laws he broke, probably all of them in her law books. She paid him a pity visit laced with "you should've known better" written in her cool eyes.

Just as Sarah was stepping out she turned, "Hey just so you know, we've decided to do the last segment of tonight's show live. The sooner your name is cleared the better. So wear a happy-camper face and give our audience that intrepid charisma they desire. Use that *happy-talk*; I'm paying you big bucks for. Give our public something *real edgy* to talk about. At least try to lighten our listeners' load on this serious subject. Be a lighthearted good example and try to be a good sport."

"Yeah right, just send the paramedics back in and hook me up to some happy-juice." Kurt said mildly caustic.

"Well, about your drinking, Jeremy filled me in; you might want to stop abusing alcohol." Her demeanor went from playful to serious.

"See, everyone has that wrong. I don't abuse alcohol. It abuses me. You don't see my empty bottle of whiskey laying here getting treatment do you?" He cracked a shit-eaten grin.

"Well then maybe instead of mixing caffeine with booze you might try mixing some food into that liquid diet."

He brushed her away with his hand, "Oh hell, food is way overrated–I eat to live, not live to eat."

"Well, I want to talk to you before I leave tomorrow. Let's meet at *The Tavern on the Green* around eleven, so I can make sure you eat."

"Yes mother, hell between you and Jeremy I'll never be an orphan. How about a less conspicuous place? That place gives me bad vibes and heartburn." He pounded a fist on his sternum, "Besides I've been eighty-sixed out of better joints than that. I just can't eat there."

"Why does it make you eat your heart out?" Sarah laughed suggesting she knew more than she was saying. "Get out there Kurt, and kick some ass. You can do it. You have my seal of approval." Her warm motherly charm wooed him.

DESIRE FOR TRUTH

####

Later that evening, Kurt had recovered from his hangover, but not from his personal and public embarrassment. The makeup artist had her work cut out for the TV spot, Kurt was still ghostly pale.

Amanda stayed away from him, secretly reading the garbage tabloids on his past escapades with other women. The public was waiting for what could possibly be the last 'Golden Couple' TV moment. This televised portion could make or break their careers. The moment of truth was upon them. Every eye in the studio and probably half of New York City was tuned in.

The pre-taped portion of the program aired, Amanda and Kurt were wired up and ready to shoot the last segment live. It was time to reveal to the New York audience and to each other the results of their HIV tests. Envelopes in hand–Rich and Sarah knew what was about to transpire, but Kurt and Amanda were left clueless.

Could NYCB's Golden Couple handle the pressure of real news happening to real people, like themselves?

Kurt was the lead in, "Can we have a drum roll please?" One of the sound stage guys piped a prerecorded drum roll over the studio speakers. Kurt placed the envelope to his forehead. "And the winner is?"

"Wow, Kurt you seem so sure of yourself, would you care to elaborate?" Amanda asked critical of his intolerable sophomoric tactics.

"Well Amanda, I am positive that the results of this report are negative in my favor?"

"And why are you so phenomenally self-assured? Share with our audience on how they can be as positive as you that those results are negative."

"Ms. Lindas are you pushing the envelope with me? Or is the humid weather making you more petulant than usual?" His emerald eyes glowed merrily. He did happy-talk poking fun at her while choking inside about something so deadly serious.

"Oh, you know who makes me petulant." She smirked.

Okay, maybe he was pushing the envelope along with her buttons. Hell anyone could make a mistake. And in years past he had participated in unprotected sex. But with his mother harping on him and his brothers he knew the chorus to: *Don't play in the rain without your raincoat.* He shook himself from his barbed thoughts.

This was news in the making and Amanda wasn't going to rope his goat, not for free at least. Kurt turned the table.

"So ladies first, right? Let's have some call-ins, should the *lady* go first?" He cracked a smile. "Ladies always come first, with me." He tapped the legal envelope on the news desk.

Rich and Sarah caught the innuendo in the sound booth they shared in a laugh. "There's the Kurt we all know and love."Sarah commented.

Amanda blushed as it crossed her mind what Kurt was referencing; but she was quick on her comeback. "You heard it here ladies– *The New Edge on Truth*. Do we have any call-ins on Mr. Kilawee's promises or bragging?" Her smile was a right-back-at-ya smile.

In the sound booth Sarah commented, "You're right Rich, she's damn good. They're good together. Their chemistry is remarkable."

Kurt appeared flustered, but regained his composure in a millisecond. "Let's get this edgy party started–drum roll please. Amanda, ladies first, that includes you too. So show me yours and I'll show you mine. That's what our audience wants–giv'em what they want."

Confident that her report was good; she tore the envelope open with exceptional self-assurance. But her face dropped when she removed the paper.

Kurt wavered on her concerned expression. Instinctively he knew something was amiss. One thing he had learned about her was she had no poker-face; she wasn't good at hiding the truth. "Well, don't keep our audience waiting what's the score?" He smiled unsettled.

Desperately she wanted to break for a commercial, but time was limited. So the best thing she could offer was diversion. Nervous she cleared her throat and swallowed an imaginary frog. Her eyes bulged, "Well it shows... *your* middle name is Allen. And, I... *ass-umed* it started with an A–but Allen wasn't my first choice." Her eyes glittered with merriment at his expense. The close-up camera faded from her amused face to terror on Kurt's.

Kurt tugged at his collar as if something or someone was choking him. He sipped water from his mug and cleared his throat, "Well, Honey it appears our envelopes have been mysteriously, perhaps purposely switched. But..." he released a whoosh of air. "The show must go on." His eyes turned cool and serious, his head jerked a nod towards her, "Go ahead Amanda– Baby. Make some noise–let our audience know the truth. That's why we're here–for the new edge on truth."

Solemnly, yet miffed at his flippancy and pet names, Amanda turned the paper over to see his results. She closed her eyes grimacing like getting a Tetanus shot. In a weird alien way, her heart pounded to a nervous beat. With a deep breath she announced, "Well, Ladies and *Gentlemen,*–you will be surprised to know–Mr. Kilawee has," she paused, glanced at her opponent, then raised her eyebrows, "a clean bill of physical health. But, the jury is still out on his mental health issues." She added a reserved, "Congratulations, Mr. Kilawee you are negative. I'll bet you never thought you'd be celebrating something so negative. Tell us Kurt, how do you do it? Tell the viewing audience what is your secret?"

Relief and mischief spread on his handsome face, "Well first off– the Gentlemen can disregard the announcement. Let me put some fictitious rumors to rest," he flashed a look of indignation at her. "I am definitely and strictly a Ladies' man. I am proud to say I am a safe-sex advocate. In fact I like to practice safe-sex as much as I can. How does that grab you Ms. Lindas? Does that satisfy you… and your questions? Or should I be more graphic about the safe-sex positions I like to practice." He could barely contain his jovial laughter. Part relief, part instigative, and of course flirtatiousness stirred his playful sparring.

Rich chatted in his ear piece, "Alright cowboy, give it a rest–you've made your point–good job. Open her envelope we're running out of air time."

Kurt snapped to attention, he didn't want the viewers or himself to miss the rest of the story. He was relieved so far with his contribution to their newsworthy cause. Unfortunately his mother wasn't going to be as happy as Rich and he was at his newsworthy antics. But, he envisioned his phone ringing in offers from other safe-sex practitioners.

It just couldn't get better than this.

"Okay *Ladies* and Gentlemen–" he tore the small end of the envelope.

Amanda jumped and fumbled, "Only Gentlemen need to reply."

"Is that apply or reply? What are we doing now personal ads Ms. Lindas?" His antagonistic style was shining through his bright infectious grin.

Blowing the envelope open, slowly with bated breath he pulled the crisp sheet of white paper out. He studied it as if he was doing research. His poker-face intact, he persisted in prolonging her agony.

Gracefully and tactfully, Amanda inquired with her signature velvety coo, "Well, Kurt do you need help reading the material or would you care to share your findings with the rest of the class?"

"Well, it states here that you're a female." He scanned her once over, "Whew, they got that right," he chuckled. "Also you received an A-minus on your blood test. I thought I read somewhere that you were a straight 'A' student. Well, I guess that proves you can't believe everything you read. Can you?"

His flippancy triggered her animosity. "Okay this is a serious matter, just get to the results." She drummed her fingers and tapped her pen.

"Well, everyone can breathe a sigh of relief your middle name starts with an F. And all this time, I could have sworn it started with a B." He caught her sneering. "Oh–and by the way,–you tested negative." A huge smile smeared his face. On his game, he went for the kill, "So, we've discussed my sex life; would you care to elaborate on how you've managed such a negative sexual record Amanda? What's your chilling secret?"

Muffled laughter pervaded in the wings; everyone waited for her reply.

"Well Kurt, I'm with you that safe-sex is the best sex, but for our younger audience I believe my tried and true *truth* is– 'No' is a good answer. How does that grab you?" Verbally she nailed him; physically she interlocked her fingers to prevent herself from flipping him off, or reaching over to strangle him.

Kurt refused to be outwitted. They needed to create hype and controversy for news to enlighten. "To our viewers, we at NYCB– *The New Edge on Truth* suggest everyone get tested and practice safe-sex. Remember together, Kurt Kilawee and Amanda Lindas practice good safe-sex."

"It's a wrap!" Rich's voice echoed through the station.

Kurt stood unclipping his microphone and removing his earpiece when Amanda got in his face. Her mike still attached and on, "You jerk, you just implied to all of New York that we practice safe-sex together!" Her chest heaved.

"True, I may have implied that. But I'd like to think that I've allowed our viewers to infer that my statement, although technically not the exact truth, was derived and presented to them based upon a conclusion of evidence given. So therefore, I assisted New Yorkers to *infer* that you and I are practicing good safe-sex together. If you care to make my statement credible then look me up, I'm in the book. And I sincerely do like to practice. Remember–hearsay becomes fact when it is recorded or printed as a part of history. Right? We've just made legendary History. Oh, in the future, don't *imply* that I am swayed towards gentlemen. I enjoy the physical company of *real* ladies, and you have my permission to quote that as fact." He slipped his jacket off, swung it over his shoulder, and loosened his tie. "Is there anything else I can conclude, imply, or help infer to further your career Ms. Lindas?"

"Damn you! In front of everyone in New York, including my boyfriend, you have the audacity to make viewers think we are a sexually active couple."

"The news is supposed to make people think. I'm not sure how this war got started Mandy. But what I am damn sure of is I'm secure in my sexual preferences. I don't know about your sexuality, but mine doesn't need hearsay." His glowing angry eyes narrowed. "And furthermore, I didn't appreciate waking up to all the bullshit because of the malicious intent of your bartender boyfriend!"

Sarah and Rich sat perfectly still in the sound booth listening in on the heated sexually charged private confrontation.

"Oh, so now you have an aversion to bartenders? Funny you seem quite complacent at keeping them in business."

Kurt gathered his cool, "*Au contraire*, I happen to like bartenders. Bartenders are the friends we all wish we had. They bring us drinks that make us feel like super-heroes, and they tell us the lies we want to hear about ourselves. In fact you can tell my favorite bartender, Antonio Casali; he'll be hearing from my lawyers and NYCB's lawyers. It appears he likes to screw with the wrong type of men."

Bitterness boiled beneath Kurt's pinked skin. The things he didn't like about Antonio weren't his bartending skills, but his shady background and the fact; Mandy was already in love with him.

Something instantly changed in her cool eyes; she placed her hands on his chest automatically transposing his and her demeanor. "Please Kurt don't bring Tony into this. He tried to help because I asked him. I saw you and Jeremy arguing. You know I hate it when you two fight." Tears welled in her eyes, *real tears*; she released an exhausted sigh, "Don't bring Tony into our fight, he's innocent. Can't we come to a peaceful agreement? Tony is my chance for a good relationship. Just because you don't want love doesn't mean the rest of us can live without it." Her tears wet her cheeks.

The sting of her words caused a burning sensation in his eyes. *What was she saying about him not wanting love? Everybody wants love. Don't they?* He felt like such a dirt-bag. He was too late; she *was really* in love with Tony.

Each time he admitted it, his heart broke a little more. Her confession was killing him. His chest tingled from her gentle touch. Slowly he removed a tissue from his pants pocket and dabbed her tears. Brushing aside a wavy strand of hair from her face, he studied her. Her breathing labored in rhythm with his. His eyes blurred, he froze, trapped by her pleading blue eyes. Softly he whispered. "Amanda."

"Yes, Kurt," her voice barely audible, she took the tissue from his trembling hand.

"Ah,–I have to go..." He shrugged forcing a smile, "Just for the record, I am sorry." Gently he kissed her forehead.

Rich and Sarah sat dumbfounded spying on the passionate scene that should have ended with an electrifying passionate kiss.

Kurt rushed from the studio, sprinted to his office, picked up his soiled shirt, and swiped his shoulder harness from his lower desk drawer. He checked his revolver, safety on, *check*, and bullets in the chamber, *check*. Just as he slipped on the harness, Jeremy barged into his office.

"Didn't your mother teach you to knock Lionel?" Kurt said eyeing Jeremy's new guise. Intentionally deferring the questions written all over Jeremy's face; Kurt asked his own desultory questions, "What's with you going all Ralph Lauren on me? What's with the Kelly-green polo shirt and the yellow sweater wrapped around your neck? Please tell me you're returning those yellow Big Bird pants? Wait, are you seriously wearing boat shoes without socks?"

"Are you finished attacking my attire? If someone, we won't mention initials like, KK, didn't vomit on his shirt, he wouldn't be wearing the shirt I wore this morning. How soon we forget?"

Kurt sidestepped Jeremy and rushed out as if he were competing in a 50 yard dash.

Jeremy jogged alongside him trying to keep up, "Where's the fire and why are you packing heat?" He spoke in a hushed tone keeping the one-sided conversation private as they headed into the crowded elevator. "Kurt answer me!"

"No."

Outside the Empire State Building, Kurt stopped at a convenient news stand and snatched the slanderous tabloids just to catch up on his new life. "Hey Joe, grab me a pack of Marlboros." Kurt patted his pockets realizing he had left his money clip at his apartment that morning in all the chaos. "Hey Lionel, pay the man."

Flustered, Jeremy reached into his own pockets, "Here Sam," he plopped the money on the counter and turned to reprimand Kurt. "Why are you wasting my hard earned cash on trash?" He pointed to the papers in Kurt's hand. "And the man's name here is Sam, not Joe." He scolded as Kurt fumbled to light a cigarette. "And when did you take up smoking and carrying a piece?"

Jeremy snatched the matches from Kurt's shaking hands, "Here let me help with your slow death wish. Why the hell are you shaking? For someone as cool and brilliant as you were today, you are acting like a basket case. You know what I think?" He followed along as Kurt bypassed the town car giving the leftover paparazzi the slip.

Kurt puffed his cigarette, choking now and again; he hadn't quite mastered his new addiction. "Sure, now that I'm back on my game, I'm not so newsworthy. But fuck up again and I'll be depicted as an infamous jackass again. Damn magazine reporters are so fickle." He mumbled to himself, yet audible enough that Jeremy and passersby could hear him. "Yeah, Jeremy, I'm brilliant. Just call me Mr. Sagacious–Pugnacious. I'm one fucked up profoundly wise hard-ass. What is brilliant about making her cry, embarrassing her in public, and pushing her into some dirt-bag bartender's arms? Tell me that Sherlock? And if I'm so fucking brilliant then why do I feel like shit? Huh Einstein?" Disgusted Kurt took a long drag off his new pacifier weaving into a crowd of New Yorkers.

Jeremy stepped sideways to confront him nudging people out of the way. But the only thing that caught Kurt's attention was almost getting sideswiped by a taxi. He promptly gave the driver the finger and flicked his half-smoked cigarette at him in retaliation.

"Do you want to know what I think?" Jeremy interrupted.

"No, but I'm sure you're going to babble some bullshit, and you won't shut-up until you speak your piece." Kurt stopped at the crosswalk light.

Jeremy put one hand on his hip holding his chin with the other, "Hmmm... damn man, you made me forget what I was going to say."

"Let's keep walking. I have a meeting with some face-cards tonight." Kurt unconsciously patted his pistol concealed beneath his lightweight Member's Only jacket.

"Oh, I remember now," Jeremy interjected, "I think you need to go see a shrink! You're off the deep end."

"Great, you and the rest of the nut balls think alike." Kurt skimmed one of the tabloids trying to change the subject. "Hey, it says here that you're leaving me for a golf-pro. Is that true?" He eyed Jeremy's new duds. "Are you cheating on me man?" Kurt feigned disappointment. "Now, I get it. You're on the bandwagon using my fifteen minutes of fame for your own advantage. You sly dog, and I'm considered the sleaze?"

Jeremy cringed sheepishly, "Well, I answered your phone and he called asking for me." His demeanor was jubilant yet shy. They walked to East 33rd down to Lexington.

Approaching Kurt's place they stood out front starring at the sturdy redbrick building accented with white faux shutters and wrought-iron scrolled railings on the concrete stoop. New York's Gramercy Park and Kips Bay was full of buildings similar to the one Kurt called home. Bursting with character, it held the history and secrets of people who came and went. It had an interesting past and possibly a great future. The type of building that could weather any storm and stand firm. It was like an old friend comfortable, reliable, a true safe haven.

"Hey Lionel," Kurt scanned his home.

"Yeah man."

"I'm happy for you. Have fun with that golf-pro. Get yourself a little action, but remember to practice…"

"Yeah I know, practice safe-sex. What are you my mother?" Jeremy shoved his hands in his pockets looking at the ground.

"Yeah, I guess so," Kurt grinned at the thought. "I have a Shrink, you know?"

"Really? How come?" Jeremy's focused switched upward at the welcoming building.

"My real mother, and my other mother, Sarah suggested it. And that prick Rich demanded it. Besides my Shrink is one of my informants."

"For the black leather binders, man that is some deep shit you've fallen into."

"Yeah, I stumbled into it. I have to find the truth before I can do anything with the information. That's why I am packing heat. Sometimes truth is a dangerous thing. But remember what I told you this morning, it is imperative that you take the journals, you know, just in case something happens. I'm counting on you man." He patted Jeremy's shoulder.

"Yeah okay, but why ruin your life for a story? Why don't you hand them over to NYPD?"

"Well, it's not that easy. A lot of innocent people will be part of the fallout. I believe Rich is a part of it, but I need more information. I agreed to see the Shrink to get reinstated to carry a weapon."

"What did the Shrink tell you?"

"What I already suspected." Kurt sat on the cement stoop.

"Like what for example?" Jeremy followed Kurt's lead and sat.

"I am an egotistical, women user, alcohol abuser, sex advocate with addictive personality Type-A. In other words, I'm a fucked-up shithead. No wonder Amanda hates me."

"I told you man, she doesn't hate you. She loves you–she just doesn't know it, yet. Give her time. Women like her are like me. We need time to trust ourselves. When the right one comes along it takes us a little more time to warm-up to the idea that someone can love us as much as we love them."

"God Jeremy, for being a guy, your womanly nonsense makes sense."

"Yeah, it's a mystery and a curse with me."

The evening sky turned a midnight blue as the streetlights flickered on. The night air was stifling, but they stayed on the steps waiting for Jeremy's date to arrive. Content with each other's company, they waited.

"Dude, you aren't going out tonight are you?" Jeremy said concerned.

"Well, I have a face-card meeting and technically I'm still on Mandy duty." Kurt said taking a drag off a newly lit cigarette. "I just can't watch anymore. I feel like I'm watching someone steal my candy. Is that weird?"

"Yeah, man, that's weird. Like someone ripping your heart out–I know how much you like candy." They laughed. "Hey, tell you what, I'll do Mandy-Candy duty tonight. Lionel and I will watch out for her."

"Really the dude's name is Lionel? Hmm... imagine that. Life sure can throw a wicked curveball. Just when I think I'm on top of my game, and ready to pitch a no-hitter; I get smacked by a line drive right to my heart. Now I am playing second fiddle to a college student/bartender. What am I going to do Jeremy?"

"I don't know man. I guess you better start learning to play the game and the fiddle better. I know she's attracted to you 'cause she's always mentioning–" Jeremy attempted to mimic her cooing. "You remember Jeremy when Kurt did that? You remember when Kurt said that? It's a game we play in the van on the way to our interviews. I call it the 'Remember How Cute Kurt is Game'."

"How come you never told me this before?"

"I don't know, maybe I was jealous you two found each other and I was just a liaison–a third wheel or more like a flat-tire. You never liked anyone better than me at work, and then along comes Mandy-Candy and I got put in leftfield in the dark. Like, game over–fool. You know."

"No I didn't know, but I am sorry. You are my best friend Jeremy. And not in the lovey-dovey sense, but like real friends? And that's the truth. Really." Kurt sucked in a deep breath of stagnant summer air. "God, I can't wait for fall to come, this has been the hottest longest summer of my life."

"You really mean that I'm your very best friend in the whole wide world?" Jeremy contemplated. "Like, you would take me back to Chicago to meet your mom and dad? And your brothers? They'd meet me as your best friend and you wouldn't be ashamed of who and what I am?"

"What man? You're the best. Besides, they know you're gay. Don't you read the papers?"Kurt punched him lightly in the arm and chuckled.

"Oh, I wasn't referring to that–I was referring to the fact that I am of the darker skin disposition."

Kurt ruffled Jeremy's short afro and pushed the papers into his lap. "Dude wake-up! Didn't you see our *color* photos? Christ Jeremy, you amaze me. And I mean that in a good way."

"You amaze me too. In more ways than you'll ever know. You're like the big brother that I've always wanted."

"I thought you had a big brother."

"I do. But I don't want his happy-ass around me. You, I can tolerate. Him, he's a real piece of work."

"Yeah, I hear you; my brothers are real assholes. Big frickin' Chicago cops. Busting my chops all my life because I'm the 'mama's boy' or 'pretty boy'."

"They got that right."

"Thanks, I didn't ask to be good looking and the youngest. Hey, I thought you were on my side."

"I am, but dude, you have to face the truth. Your mama has got your balls in a vice grip. That's why you're so wild with the chicks. I can see that."

"Wow, you could have saved the company a shitload of money based on that analysis." Kurt raked his hand through his sweat laden hair, "That's what my shrink alluded to. And I have some obsessive addictive behavioral issues." He lit another cigarette.

Annoyed, Jeremy grabbed the cigarette from Kurt's mouth and crushed it with his shoe. "What's with the smoking bit? Damn that's nasty, Mandy won't like that shit." An epiphany flashed. "That's it! That's it. You're attracted to her because she fits the mother image, except you can have sex with her and you can't with your mother. That's that 'Oedipus Rex' syndrome thing. High-five me man." Jeremy raised his hand waiting for a high-five.

Kurt refused him the glory.

"Great! Just great, now I know I'm screwed up. There's no way in hell I want to be married to my mother." Kurt put his head in hands. "Damn, that is just sick. I need a drink." He stood, "You coming in with me yellow pants guy?"

A rush of fear hit Jeremy. "Hey check my pants out." He stood and pushed his tush towards Kurt.

Kurt glanced down and instantly looked away. "Dude, I told you and the rest of the world, I don't check men's asses out. Leave me alone."

"I know that doofus, I mean is my ass black?" Jeremy rolled his eyes at Kurt's distorted face.

"Dude, we already establish that, if your face is of the darker persuasion then so is the rest of you. Now stop, you're killing me. You look fine, no dirt. Okay? Ya happy now?"

They walked into the cool apartment; Kurt went to the refrigerator and pulled out two Heinekens, "Beer okay for you? I'm knocking off the hard-shit for awhile."

"Yeah, what brought you to that conclusion? Man you should have seen Rich's face when you barfed into his executive trash bucket. I thought he was going to have a cow or crap his pants. Or was it puking your guts up in front of Mandy-Candy? Not to mention the rest of our co-workers."

Kurt took a long swallow to gulp down his embarrassment. "Hey, don't refer to my future wife that way. Only I call her Mandy-Candy, I like that nickname for her." He said removing his jacket he unlatched his pistol harness laying it gently on the granite counter. He unbuttoned his shirt.

Jeremy took a long swallow, "Did you just say–my future wife?"

Kurt slipped off his shirt exposing his muscular, but thin white torso. He was ripped, but about twenty pounds shy if his regular weight. "No, I didn't say wife, did I? I meant my future girlfriend–not wife," he shook his head a few times erasing the thought of having a wife.

"Yeah whatever, you just did one of those Freudian-slip mumbo-jumbo things. Like you think something but you don't mean to say it, yet you say it 'cause it's what your subconscious wants you to say, 'cause it's the truth. And you know it is. Can I be your best man?"

"Sure, if we ever make it that far. It doesn't look too promising after what I did today."

They were interrupted by a short blast of a horn.

Kurt looked at Jeremy, "Sounds like your date is here. Pretty rude, I should go out and coach him about first-date etiquette. A gentleman always parks the car and comes to the door to greet his date and the parents." Kurt toasted his beer to his best friend; his smile brimmed ear to ear. "Go knock'em dead."

Jeremy tentatively stared at the pistol on the counter.

Kurt caught him. He read Jeremy's mind, "Hey no worries the Doc says I'm not the suicidal type, but I may have underlying latent tendencies towards being homicidal." He pushed Jeremy to the door, "So go–shoo–get out before I have a relapse, an outburst, or an episode, or whatever they call it."

Jeremy unleashed his nervousness about Kurt's state of mind. "You're not just pissing on my shoes and calling it rain are you? Tell me the truth, man."

"Now stop, besides the truth is relative. It is whatever you perceive it to be. Now go, or I'll go and straighten out that horn blowing new guy." Kurt cajoled an empty threat.

Jeremy swung open the door, "You'd better stay in or go to an all night fake-n-bake. Get yourself some color, Belinda told me Mandy-Candy likes her men like her coffee; strong, hot, and tan or was it sweet? You need to work on the tan part. You're a ghostly poster child for anorexia."

"Get out of here, before I really do shoot you."

"Why can't you handle a dose of the truth?" Jeremy smiled. "Go cover-up I don't want the neighborhood going to pot. I will call to check on you." His eyes flashed a warning.

Kurt finished off the rest of his beer in a chug. "Get out of here. I'll see you tomorrow, if you're lucky."

"Well, just remember, I don't want Mandy to be a widow before she's a bride."

"I gotcha, I'm staying home and I won't shoot myself. I promise. Are you happy?"

Jeremy smiled. "Yes I am, bye man." He strutted down the hall out the wooden front doors to his new love adventure.

Chapter 9

Kurt ignored Jeremy's advice about staying home. Yet, he did consider the fake-n-bake over shooting himself. But, as in all decisions made in haste, he'd wished he hadn't opted for a nude tanning session.

He thought he knew what he wanted. Regretfully, his vain ego won, by argumentatively refusing to adhere to the time limit suggested by the Oompa-Loompa salesgirl.

The defenseless salesgirl gave into the demands of a lunatic who claimed to be more intelligent. Seriously, how could she be smarter than him at any given moment? So subsequently he paid the price for not listening to the knowledgeable tan clerk. His ghostly appearance had advanced to a shameful shade of lobster red. And although baring his ass in public wasn't an option, no tan lines were optimal in his mind. Thank God, he had the acumen to cover his man parts.

This proved in some instances one can be equally as stupid as they are intelligent. Kurt realized he hadn't been in the sun for most of the squelching summer. Keeping up his celebrity appearance was difficult. Honestly, he was too busy making money watching Mandy.

Whoever said– "money doesn't make you happy" was right. Of course, he wasn't unhappy with a six figure bank account and income, yet he couldn't buy Mandy's love or repair her devastation. The freakish desire to protect her from her future played havoc within him. Hers was the typical case, as he saw it with his sagacity, *what you don't know can hurt you*. But how could he reveal what he had discovered in his diligent investigation of Antonio?

Restless he reviewed the late night telecast of the now famous, NYCB–Aids Documentary. Aggravated and ashamed, he shifted on his tender burnt ass.

He empathized with Mandy's embarrassment. Not only did he destroy her journalistic innocence, he also ruined her private and professional reputation. On an intimate level, his self-serving actions crushed him. How could he honestly pretend he was promoting the truth when he unabashedly twisted words to fulfill his version of truth? Adding lies does not enhance the truth, in fact it lessens it.

Next to his burnt feet on his luxurious Emperador Dark marble coffee table was his typed masterpiece: "The Elusive Truth".

The most extreme exposure story he had ever written. Painstakingly he masked his sources with pseudonyms to protect them and him.

Earlier that evening, his fingertips flashed across his electric typewriter keys like fire across a dry prairie. He succumbed to the creative force that drives all successful writers. Ill-at-ease he could not control the inner passion shooting through him igniting an electric pulse. Possessed and poisoned by the force, only one other had the disease worse than he did: Amanda Lindas.

Reading over his meticulous words, he hoped for redemption for the untruths he had told; by exposing those who seemingly escape the consequences of their lies and crimes.

He reviewed his opening statements:

"I promise to tell the truth, the whole truth, and nothing but the truth, so help me God."

"We hold these truths to be self-evident, that all men are created equal, that they are endowed by their creator with certain inalienable rights; that among these are life, liberty, and the pursuit of happiness…"

"Ye shall know the truth, and the truth shall make you free. - John 8:32"

What part of the truth sets a man free? If one man tells his truth can it send another man to his death? If another tells his truth can it save a life and imprison another?

How does society arrive at the truth? Does truth change with the times and fluctuate like the weather? One can be the victor or the victim of truth.

Is it true that in the long run only the strong will survive? Or shall the meek truly inherit the Earth?

These universal questions are not easily answered; I believe we, as a society, are at risk of insanity. We focus on and believe "reality" is external. We believe material things make us happy and reflect our success. We compete against each other creating greed, envy, and jealousy. These three attitudes evolve with power into corruption.

Can we stop the corruption that takes place every day in government posing as our savior against big business tactics and mob mentality? Do we blindly accept the politicians' world views and refuse to search for truth to save ourselves? When you learn the truth, will you choose to accept it whether it frees you or imprisons you?" Can we keep closing our eyes to the "mob corruption" in our cities?

This article compares and exposes uninformed lackadaisical voters with those who are born into, or marry into a crime family. All are blinded by love putting false hope in a euphoria lifestyle in Utopia.

DESIRE FOR TRUTH

The Mob possesses the means and mentality to inflict limitless suffering on innocents as do many governments. Most innocents believe joining a family or cult is safe. They willfully join for freedom only to discover they have committed the ultimate betrayal against themselves. Enticed into believing that loyalty guarantees freedom, but in reality they receive a false promise of protection–similar to governments that lure low income people into slavery with handouts. Feed the masses and control the vote. It is the comparative of selling their souls to the devil. Fear is so intense that some are unable to live with their choices. Death becomes more desirable than life.

Later as enlightenment ensues; in order to produce freedom for their families they convey the *real* truth to an outsider. I am that outsider…

He tossed the manuscript to the table. He called Mandy, attempting a pathetic apology. No answer again.

Restless he picked the report and thumbed through it.

Earnestly I believe that reality and truth are mobile. They exist differently in each of us–hence one man's loss is another man's triumph. As individuals we choose to believe and follow the idealisms of a controlling party like our families, religions, or political parties.

And therefore we become victims of our own truths and choices. The reality of life is– We are the masters of our fates, successes, and failures.

Expressing that reality, Kurt was confident he had captured the truth in black and white. A news report can control and guide how the masses think and feel. Further into his report he explained his views:

The defining moment is when the news media feeds the masses negativity and fear; it works because the majority refuses to think or use common sense. They believe the world is a rotten place filled with death, disease, and destruction. Fear sells, creates chaos, and leads to militant government or mob control.

Fear is the medication they desire; inactive people want someone or something to blame for their lack of action to obtain success. The same news propaganda requires the public to accept that there are shortages of gas, oil, jobs, and opportunities. The controlling government gears people to believe that the truth relies on the opinion of the masses, in the disguise of government protection, and not in the individual's creative self.

Ultimately, Kurt preferred to present news that promoted hope and freedom of choice. Unfortunately society was already poisoned to desire the biased truth, a twisted version of hopelessness.

The public is shamefully led to believe that a magic pill will be invented for them to obtain perfect weight, perfect emotional balance, and perfect health. Instead of living their lives and owing up to their actions or non-actions they would rather blame the government, or focus on the crippled lives of Hollywood pop-stars, or live vicariously through the accomplishments of athletes and sports team. They believe the success of their team is a real part of their own success.

Admittedly he had become one of them. A product of the late fifties early sixties, he was born into a world that brainwashed him into believing success was money and fame. It was not his parent's fault that he bought into it. They weren't the type to believe in all the hype. His mother focused on helping the less fortunate and his father put criminals behind bars. Both lived their lives protecting victims.

We must ask the question—who are the real victims of society? Is it the disciplined taxpayer who works hard to create a successful lifestyle or those who wait for the government to give them an entitlement handout eliminating their desire to create better lives?

Imprisoned by his own hurtful truth, he called Mandy several more times, begging her forgiveness. Forgiveness is always the hardest thing to ask for; especially when you know you don't deserve it. In his life, he had never had to beg a woman for anything.

Each babbling message he left on her answering machine became progressively pathetic with his heartfelt apology. And yet he wouldn't confess why her forgiveness was the only thing that could exonerate him.

The raw truth was he had no idea how he staggered into this crazy roadblock in his life. How could one person change your whole life? Was love really that strong? Was he experimenting with real love? Could love be the most powerful tool of truth? Could love conquer a multitude of lies, badgering, and hateful spiteful actions? God, he sure hoped so... or he was screwed.

Distraught in the darkened world of her apartment, Amanda's phone rang nonstop. She refused to answer it. Her mother, her father, Antonio, and especially Kurt were relentless in trying to draw her attention away from the evening news and the cable networks telecasting her devastating demise in the public eye. Her reputation as a serious credible news reporter and journalist was ruined because she allowed Kurt to destroy her perfect professional image with cruel sexual connotations.

And it didn't stop with ten million New Yorkers–no that would have been sufficiently tragic. No, her demise went national. How could one person destroy everything she had worked so hard at perfecting? And how could that same person knowing what he did continue to beg for her forgiveness? Like her forgiving him for destroying her life was going to change anything other than allowing him to live guilt free.

Not going to happen, Asshole.

Resolute she would be redeemed by the report that sat on her desk waiting to be delivered to Rich's desk in the morning. Realistically she could receive great reviews and beat Kurt at his own deceptive game.

Her ultimate goal was to be the best reporter and give the public what they deserved–the truth. Unfortunately, their popular telecast, humoristic as it may have appeared to others, she viewed it as a critical personal and public disaster. Could she defer the bad publicity and channel the energy into her election awareness article? Venturing over to her desk by the dim glow of her small TV, she picked up her article "The Political Cesspool".

An election year promotes stirring up the crap on the bottom of the barrel providing sludge for the political personal arena to throw around blinding the public from the real issues. This year is proving to be no different except for a proud moment for women's rights. The private sector has accepted Geraldine Ferraro as Walter Mondale's running mate.

We ask the public question– Is the world ready for a woman to control the second most powerful position in the world? The world seems to have stumbled out of the dark ages of human rights. Is this the beginning of allowing minorities to have a clear powerful voice?

Unfortunately she had encountered the disgruntled uprising of a few oppressed minorities whose ancestors were victimized for years. Being made equal wasn't enough, they felt entitlement. A "truth" they sincerely believed they were now deserving of more rights, and exclusive treatment above the majority which had controlled "truth" for hundreds of years.

Her story addressed and analyzed the corruption of the so called "good" rulers of society up against the organization and loyalty of the "bad" rulers of the underground.

It was peculiar to her that the Mafia was strangely accepted as loyal money makers, businessmen, family men, and even devoted church attendees. They were epitomized and glamorized in a weird case of endearment by many in society just like some politicians.

She reviewed her copy further:

We want to believe that our leaders have our best interests and society's best interests in their grasps.

We all know in our hearts- Politicians do not pay millions, or accept questionable donations for a position that pays minimal in comparison just to help the masses. Once in office they obtain power that they have no intention of surrendering.

During an election year-can we trust our leaders to keep our world prosperous and safe?

Was she crazy to believe her quest for delivering the truth would inspire the public to take responsibility for their choices and accept the consequences? Could her article spur the public to the polls and vote their conscience?

Now that she was the laughing stock of the free world who would take her article serious?

To settle her nerves, she took another contemplative bite of rocky road ice-cream. Somehow she had to regain credibility as a reliable news reporter/journalist, but how? Where would her next big break come from? Her thoughts were interrupted again by the telephone and the answering machine.

"Hey you've reached Amanda. I am not available, so please leave a message after the beep..." Beep.

"Hello Mandy, this is Mom. Listen dear your father has gotten wind of your telecast. Let me say, we are pleased that you don't have HIV, but why would you want the whole world to know about your sexual activity? Call me. Let's talk. My editor is pressuring me for a story on my wayward New York City daughter and her hot new lover. By the way, he's quite the looker. I never thought I would have to do a slop celebrity story on my baby girl. Please call me. Love you, Mandy."

Great now my mother wants to make money off my fifteen minutes of fame–my overnight success–yea!

Nothing that another scoop of ice-cream wouldn't solve, she shuffled in her fluffy bunny slippers over to the freezer for another scoop of encouragement.

The phone rang again. Same boring message repeated. Beep.

"Hey Amanda..." a soft sincere male voice wavered. "Mandy please pick up, this is Kurt. Please pick up, I know you're home. And I know you've seen the national news... call me. I know you're angry with me and you have every right. Please let me apologize in person... please forgive me."

An unfamiliar whine, a sign of desperation rose in his tone. She enjoyed his pain. It meant he suffered remorse, but it didn't erase her contempt or repair her pride. This time his actions cut her so deep that she wasn't just bleeding pride– this time she had allowed him to pierce her spirit.

Part of her wanted to attack him publicly and prove she was the better journalist. But another part cried, "It just doesn't matter. I'm just gonna go eat worms." She fought the little girl inside who wanted to run to her parents for protection. Even though she despised her father's lifestyle and what he did to her mother, she desperately wanted his strong arms around her now.

The incessant ringing phone had no mercy. Its piercing irritating beep made her want to throw it out her eleventh story apartment window.

With vengeance, she threw her ice-cream laden spoon at it. "Damn phone–damn Alexander Graham Bell, how irresponsible of you to die and leave society with your stupid invention!"

"Hey Sweetness, this is Tony. I saw the news. Hey, we need to talk, meet me tomorrow in Central Park by Bethesda Fountain around noon. If you need me call me. I'm home studying. Bye."

Tears rolled down her cheeks. He was so kind not to breakup with her over the phone. What a gentleman. She released a sullen sigh of defeat. Twenty-six years old ruined professionally and personally, how could it get any worse? How could one day ruin her whole life? The phone rang again. She sank into her cozy cocoon of blankets and pillows swaddled in her Joe Montana jersey she was prepared to hibernate.

"Amanda, this is Dad, answer the phone. Pack your things; I'm stopping payment on your apartment. Why would you discuss your love life on national TV? Didn't your mother and I teach you better? You know better than to air your dirty laundry in public– I love you honey, but we need to talk. Call me back."

"Talk, talk, talk–" she mumbled. "Yeah, we need to talk. More like you need to vent." She ascertained, "Didn't your mother and I teach you better?" was strictly rhetorical.

"No Dad you didn't teach me better. You taught me not to trust men. And damn you're right!"

In her fractured mind, Kurt was just like her father–a real jerk – a real ladies man– a real pain in the ass! She hated them.

"Yeah, Dad you taught me– *talk is cheap* and *actions speak louder than words*!" She tossed a few sofa pillows at the menacing phone.

Just when she had cried herself to sleep, the phone rang again.

"Hey this is Amanda–" BEEEEEP.

"Amanda, me again, listen to me. I am sorry for my unprofessional and trenchant actions. Please let me make it up to you. Please, you have to forgive me... I – I can't stand that I hurt you. Call me back Babe." Click.

In a fury, she threw her last pillow at the phone and screamed, "Babe? Call me back Babe! What? I am not your Babe. Dammit Kurt, because of you I'm not anyone's Babe!" She jumped out of her blanket cocoon and stomped the floor in her bunny slippers like a crazed lunatic when Belinda barged in with a large knife.

They *Banshee* screamed simultaneously.

"What are you doing with a knife?" Amanda finally choked.

"Don't ever do that!" Belinda's free hand held her own heaving chest, "You scared the B-Jesus out of me!" Catching her breath she eyed the disarray in the dim apartment. "What the hell happened here? Where's Kurt? I heard his voice and you screaming at him. I rushed over to help."

"Really Belinda? With a knife? Which one of us did you plan to stab first or should I say *saw* first?"

Belinda lowered the serrated bread knife clutched in her hand. "Well, I grabbed the closest thing." A puzzled look returned to her face. "So where is he?"

Amanda picked up the answering machine and slammed it on the counter top, "Here! He's here! Driving me crazy! Begging me to forgive him for screwing up my life. And I can't–I can't forgive him!" Amanda flopped like a rag doll to the kitchen floor. Sobbing so hard her frail body shook.

Immediately Belinda dropped the knife to hover over her shrunken distraught friend. She held Mandy and cried with her.

"Hey don't cry, I saw the show. It wasn't that bad, really. You'll bounce back. You're too tough on yourself. Come on let's get to the sofa. You want a glass of wine?"

Amanda sniffled wiping her tears with the back of her hands. "Yes, I need wine. Wine always helps. Will you stay with me?"

Belinda guided her to the sofa, "Sure, anything you want. Now sit and I'll get wine. You can tell me anything." She handed Amanda a glass of wine and a napkin for her tears. She sat close hugging Amanda. "Do you want me to call him?"

Amanda wiped her eyes and blew her nose, "Call who?"

"Who else? Kurt the flirt. I'll give him a piece of my mind and a chunk of yours too." Belinda smiled.

Amanda reciprocated with a small smile, "Yeah I know you could, but I won't let him think that I can't fight my own battles. You should listen to all his messages that damn phone rang constantly. The other one is Tony."

"Wow, I forgot about him. What did he say?"

"He said we need to talk." Her head flung backwards to the sofa. The cool wine soothed her dry raw throat. The crying and screaming left her desiccated.

"Oh, the–I'm going to dump you talk." Belinda shuddered. "I hate that talk, even if it is me dishing it. I'm so sorry, but in a weird way I don't blame Kurt for defending himself, that was a sick trick Tony played in front of the paparazzi the other night."

"Oh great! Kurt gets your sympathy too. Great, now I have no career, no boyfriend, and no new best friend, and I think my mother is on his side too. I'm sure my father would take his side; if given the chance. Where did I go wrong? Where was I when all this shit was piling up on me? God, I pride myself on seeing details and deciphering facts and relaying the truth. Just listen to the answer machine before I throw it out the window."

Belinda sprung up almost too anxious to hear the tape. She listened intently. "Man, you two have it bad. You're train wrecks. You smacked right into each other. Bam!" She pounded her fists together. "I feel bad for you both. You should have told him the truth."

Amanda sat up, her eyes wide, "What? Don't you dare feel sorry for him–this is entirely his fault. He didn't have to ruin our serious telecast by mentioning he likes to practice safe-sex, and that he likes to do it often, or imply he and I practice safe-sex together. He could have kept his mouth shut. He could have been professional not sophomoric."

Belinda's nose scrunched up. "Sophomoric? Should I know that?"

Frustrated Amanda stood up and stomped her floppy slipper feet, "Childish, immature, you know."

"Yeah, that's his stud signature–his public expects it. That's who he was until you came along. It's something you do to him that makes him crazier than usual. Sorry, but that's the truth. I see how he looks at you. He's tried to tell you, but you just don't give a rat's ass about him. You're so into yourself and what you crave that you don't see how wacked out you make him. Hell, he doesn't know where or what or who he is around you. If you want my take–I think he's totally in love with you. Like hopeless. And he despises himself for it."

Amanda stood shocked at her friend's exposé of the truth.

"No way, he can't love me. He intentionally ruined my career putting his own career and fame in the forefront, such a selfish rogue. If Tony breaks up with me, I am so going to rip Kurt to shreds." Amanda went on a reckless tirade.

Belinda quietly watched and started to giggle.

Amanda stopped. "What is so funny?"

"Duh you. You should see yourself. That's the biggest hissy fit I've ever seen. You're spazzing to the max, very entertaining. Way out of character for a prim-proper control freak. So you are human like the rest of us. You need to chill."

The phone rang. Belinda shot up to answer it.

Amanda jumped between Belinda and the telephone shaking her head she clamped her hand on the receiver. The answer machine beeped.

"Mandy? Come on, I know you're there, just talk to me. We still have to work together; I want us to settle our differences beforehand. I have to meet with Sarah tomorrow morning. Please talk to me. Meet me in Central Park around noon at the fountain."

Amanda's jaw dropped as if Kurt was privy to Tony's message.

Belinda tried to push her away from the phone. "Answer him Amanda–how can you be so cruel? Cruel is not who you are?"

Just so Belinda couldn't persuade her to cower to Kurt's pleas, Amanda hurled the phone crashing it to pieces, "Look at the new me!"

The answering machine took on a life all its own. Kurt's pleading voice filled the room, "If I don't see you there tomorrow, I will come to your apartment. You can't avoid me forever. We need to talk." Click.

The girls stared blankly at each other.

"See, I told you." Belinda laughed first. "He's hopeless. There's power in knowing you've got him where you want him." Belinda popped the tape out of the recorder. "Here save this for back up."

"Yeah thanks, but what am I going to do with him now?" Amanda was clueless.

####

The next day, around eleven, Kurt met Sarah at *The Tavern on Green*. He didn't dare go to the office for fear he would meet immediate defeat in Amanda's eyes. He decided she needed space on their common ground or battlefield depending upon how one viewed it.

He was in no condition for battle. And much to his relief Antonio was not on duty.

Hopefully Amanda would be at the fountain and accept his explanation and apology. Maybe Sarah could help him phrase his apology?

The early business luncheon was just strictly that; other than Sarah razzing him about his new sunburned look which he blamed unabashedly on Jeremy's suggestion.

Kurt shared his opinion on what he believed the next step was in launching NYCB into the pie chart of the top five broadcasters in New York. His resolute focus was on the upcoming Yacht Charity event scheduled at the beginning of October. The charity function was a last ditch effort for political figures, judges and unions to gain much needed funding. Everyone that was anyone would be invited. Big stories breed at spectacular star-studded parties like germs in a Petri dish.

Problem was he didn't get the company invite. He was privy that Rich kept it, and was plotting to take Amanda. He refrained from revealing it to Sarah, but his gut intuition told him she already knew.

They left the restaurant only after Sarah was satisfied that he had eaten enough to hold him over for the next week. She paid the tab even at his adamant protest.

Sarah stopped at her town car and pulled out a manila envelope. "Here this is for you." She handed it to him. "You'll be happy to see, I finagled you an invite for the Charity Event in October." She smiled at his boyish grin signaling to her his deepest appreciation. "Let's take a stroll, shall we? I love Central Park in the fall. And since I leave for France soon, I'd like to see the beginning of the splendid colors." She interlocked her arm with his and tugged him along.

Autumn in Central Park emits a splendor second to none for those who love warm colors. The seasonal array of oranges, yellows, and reds were in the beginning stages inviting New Yorkers and tourists to gather in the shadows of the Maples, Oaks, and powerful Elms.

They strolled silently. The peaceful park set the stage for an intervention. Kurt felt it coming.

"So what really happened yesterday?" Sarah's large made-up eyes fluttered at his astonished face. "Don't look so surprised. Rich and I were in the sound booth. We saw the aftermath. Why the hell didn't you kiss her?"

He cleared his throat, fumbling for words that escaped him. "What? What the hell does everyone expect of me? I didn't because she would have written me off the page. She doesn't want me. She wants someone that doesn't exist. Like a fairytale prince that doesn't ever upset the apple cart. The type perfect guy that doesn't have a shady past; I'm not him. She deserves better than me." He sighed. "Don't get me wrong, God knows–I want to be him." He spilled his guts because he knew the truth would leave on the next flight to Paris. He trusted Sarah like an older sister he never had.

Sarah laughed. "What do you mean you're not him? Oh you are him. If not, you're certainly first in line. If you could have witnessed the scene as Rich and I did you'd think and act much differently."

"Yeah well; it is easier to enjoy the ambiance of a fire so long as you're not standing in the middle of it. I didn't witness it; I was too close to know the next move. I get flustered around her. I've tried to get her to talk to me. I've sent flowers, went to night clubs, bought her drinks," his eye glazed over as he gazed upward at the stately Elms. "I've done everything I can think of to get her to..." He stopped talking. He wasn't sure what it was he wanted from Amanda.

They continued to walk up West Dr. passed the Sheep Meadow and then twisted down towards The Mall of Statues. They stopped to admire the grand promenade. The bronze Indian Hunter shadowed their path.

Sarah prodded, "What do you want from her?"

Such a simple question should invoke a simple answer. Kurt contemplated what it was he wanted. "I guess I want more than I'm willing to give." He smiled at his intimate thoughts. He knew physically what he wanted to give to her, but why couldn't he get her to that point? She was mysterious and elusive. Just when he thought he had her she'd slip through his hands like water.

"Well don't keep those thoughts to yourself. Get her alone and tell her the truth. Be honest with yourself. She's not your typical type. Not the type you use as a casual affair. I think you've met your match. You're thirty, it's about time you started thinking about what sort of legacy you're leaving to this world."

They continued on past Columbus, Shakespeare, and Sir Walter Scott, self-made men in their own rights, who had left monumental legacies.

Kurt wasn't surprised at Sarah's intruding observations. He needed the voice of reason to help clear his mind. "I don't know what my intentions are, but I know I am not the same person I was before she came to NYCB. And I'm holding you and Rich liable for whatever happens." He patted her hand and grinned.

"Oh no you don't. Whatever you've gotten yourself into you will have to figure out how to get her, or get over her. We aren't claiming any responsibility. We were looking for someone to counter your professional style. We had no idea that you'd be looking for a personal lifestyle change."

Just then they approached East 72nd Street, the impressive wide stairway opened up before them. The tripled-tiered neoclassical Bethesda Fountain–*the winged angel of the waters*– beckoned them to embrace her beauty. Close to noon, they crossed over and stood by the ornately carved sandstone balustrade. Down the huge descending staircase sitting right in front of the fountain sat Amanda. Kurt caught his breath and leaned into Sarah for support. His jaw dropped.

Sarah held his arm like a vice grip preventing him from running down to the fountain's edge. She saw what he saw. Amanda was not alone. She was lip locked with Antonio Casali.

If you could hear someone's heart break Kurt swore Sarah heard his heart shatter. "Are you okay Kurt?"

He slumped onto the stone railing, forgetting about his burnt ass. He winced as his hand covered his shocked face. "No Sarah, honestly, I'm not okay."

After a few deep breaths, he looked again. How could Amanda show up at noon with Antonio? What sort of cheap prank was she playing?

Sarah placed her hands firmly on his shoulders, "Get a grip. What do you want to do? I don't think she saw us."

Kurt's eyes shifted to his nemesis and back to Sarah. Biting his lower lip he shook his head. "She's looking right at us. What do I want to do? Hmm... Exactly what are my choices? Any that won't land my burnt ass in jail? Nothing. The hardest thing for anyone to do is–nothing. You know me; I like the hard way."

"Kurt, be real. This is your chance. This is the alpha-male time for triumph. Go fight for her. No woman wants the man she loves to surrender. Go face your demons, but be nice."

Kurt stood and interlocked Sarah's arm with his. Slowly and precisely he descended into the pit of emotional Hell. He was already there; he might as well get an inside burn. It was a beautiful autumn day and he was resolved that no one was going to ruin it, not Amanda or Antonio.

Amanda kept a deadly stare locked on Kurt's eyes. The closer he came the more surreal she felt. He saw her, but at what point? And why was Sarah Underwood still with him? Tony had spotted them first. He filled Amanda in about Kurt and Sarah's past; with what he knew from their secret dinners and lunches at *The Tavern*; just enough to trigger the little green screaming monster inside her.

Kurt stopped. He shadowed her. Tony stood. Kurt didn't budge. He didn't speak. He just stared. Not an evil stare. But the type of stare that pried deep into a person's soul. As if he possessed the power to read Amanda's inner most thoughts.

Sarah tried to tug him away.

Tony clenched his jaw and balled his fists.

Kurt ignored the physical challenge. He spoke slow and low.

"Hello Amanda. Fancy meeting you here? I wanted to talk with you privately, but since you brought your Italian friend here, I guess we can clear the air." His eyes stable. Hers frozen. "Mr. Casali you have nothing to worry about. Your pretty girlfriend and I are not in a relationship physical or otherwise. We are just work associates, right Sarah?"

Sarah squirmed.

Kurt held her arm tighter, "Right Sarah?"

"Yeah, right. Just work associates."

His piercing stare demanded the truth from Amanda. "Right Amanda?"

She didn't accept or reject his efforts.

Tony took her listless hand. "Come on Mandy, I have to work. I'll get you a taxi."

Kurt cracked a smile. "No, you go to work. Mandy can ride to the studio with us, like one big happy family."

Sarah chimed in, "Yes my car is just around the corner. Leroy's waiting to take me to the airport and Kurt back to work. Why don't you join us Amanda?"

Amanda stood. Kurt shadowed her. It appeared that he was glued to the concrete sidewalk. She looked at Tony and back at Kurt. The earlier kiss was a gesture of goodwill not a making up kiss. They had decided to slow their relationship until after his mid-terms. The separation would give Amanda time to get her career back on track. Tony had voiced he felt she had feelings for Kurt. He suspected that Kurt had feelings for her; a person would have to be blind not to see it.

But Kurt and Sarah didn't know the truth–their perception was twisted by what they thought they saw.

Amanda released Tony's hand and kissed his cheek.

Just then, her beeper and Kurt's beeper went off; they gazed down at the little black boxes attached to their belts.

URGENT flashed with Rich's phone number. Sarah's beeper went off too. They all looked at one another. It was time to get back to work somewhere something newsworthy and urgent was taking place in New York City. Maybe someone else's heart was breaking.

Tony gave Amanda a quick hug, "I will talk to you later, Sweetness."

Kurt immediately guided Amanda away from Tony taking her by her elbow, "Yeah let's get going Sweetness." He gave Tony his best alpha-male glare, expressing, *I win this time.*

Leroy sped out East 72nd Street a direct route east to York Ave. then took a left up to 74th and over to FDR drive. It seemed like a lifetime to Amanda. Sarah conveniently sat in front making a radio call to Rich for directions and the news scoop. Amanda had to fend for herself in the back seat with Kurt's unnerving stare. She was curious as to why his face was sunburned. She exposed a smirk; internally enjoying his pain.

"What are you smirking at?" Kurt opened the floor for discussion. His hands clasped his knees creating wrinkles on his gray-silver dress slacks.

"Oh, nothing, just wondering, what happened to your pretty face?"

DESIRE FOR TRUTH

Kurt wanted to share. *The same thing that happened to my ass,* but he figured this was not the time or the place to share his embarrassment. "Why who wants to know?"

"Me silly, seriously would I ask, if I didn't want to know?" She spotted the white small ovals around his eyes as her first clue. "You know you should cover your face with the towel they give you, or did you protect something more important?" Her smirk evolved into a smile.

He smiled. She was good at details. But, neither spoke about the white elephant that rode between them.

"Yes, I guess you could say I was protecting something that is very important to me."

"Hmm…more important than your face–the face of NYCB?" She mused.

"Touché. In the heat of the moment, I made the best decision for protecting my best interest." He pointed to his eyelids, "These are nothing that cosmetics can't fix."

"Humph– your best interest or most interesting part? I suppose you're right. Too bad there's no makeup to fix your words once you blurt them out on national news and ruin another's career and reputation." She snipped.

Kurt rolled his eyes, "Oh, here we go–shoot that damn white elephant. I said I was sorry and if you'd had the decency to pick up your phone last night," he grimaced as he shifted from one burnt cheek to the other, "none of this would have happened." He pointed again to his slightly charred face.

"Oh so now it's my fault, you burned your face, and I gather your ass based on the pain that riddles your face."

"How kind and observant you are?"

"Yeah, well it's too bad you aren't more like me."

He chuckled. "We are like two peas in a rotten pea pod. So, tell me how *sweet* Antonio felt sorry for you, and how you kissed and made-up. Go ahead tell me the exclusive inside story." Truthfully he hated the thought of her with someone else, but that was his exclusive.

She expelled an aggravated sigh; her hands fidgeted adjusting her skirt; as she considered a revelation. Instead she changed the subject, "You know you should use aloe on that burn."

Mischief whirled in his eyes, "Are you offering to apply it?"

"Oh don't you just wish."

He scooted closer, butt pain or not, "Yes, that is one of my wishes. Will you grant me two more?"

"Still presumptuous–I didn't agree to grant the first one."

"Oh, I can see in your eyes that it has some appeal."

"There you go seeing things, creating your own false truth."

"Are you ever going to forgive me? I'd love to make it up to you."

Sarah interrupted, "NYPD just pulled two bodies out of the East River just past 125th Street right in the middle of East Harlem. Unfortunately New York has an unglamorous side. You two okay?"

Before Amanda had a chance to reply they reached the site. She didn't have an answer anyway, so it was better left unaddressed.

Rich popped Kurt side of the door open first.

"Oh shit, what happened to your face? Someone get over here with makeup! Amanda you're on first. Jeremy set up where they're bringing the bodies up–away from the direct sun." Rich barked orders while assisting Sarah out of the front seat. He greeted her with a peck on the cheek and raced over to help Amanda maneuver the rough terrain in heels.

Jeremy gaped at Kurt bewildered.

"Shut-up Jeremy, this is your fault."

Put-off Jeremy shifted his hips and bobbled his head in objection, "I told you to stay home. I suggested you get a tan, not a burn. What else did you do without my permission?"

The makeup artist gently applied the foundation to counterattack the redness while Kurt counterattacked Jeremy. "If you're asking if I went to meet the face-cards the answer is no, they didn't contact me."

"Jeremy get your ass over here! We want to be the first to get this live." Rich screamed.

In the forefront, Amanda was prepped with her earpiece and a gentle touch of makeup. She stood relieved her back was to the gruesome scene.

Unfortunately everyone else, including Kurt, didn't have the same advantage. Jeremy kept his camera steady on Amanda as two bloated, blue, bloody bodies were reeled up and out of the murky green East River.

"This is Amanda Lindas reporting live for NYCB– *The New Edge on Truth*. Two bodies were discovered in the East River. No identities are confirmed, but our sources believe they are the men listed earlier on NYPD's missing persons report…"

Kurt moved in closer as Rich signaled for camera two to zoom in on him. "This is Kurt Kilawee reporting for NYCB– *The New Edge on Truth*. …" his voice tapered off and his eyes widened. Immediately he recognized the men as they were placed into black body bags.

"Dammit Kurt say something!" Rich jolted him from his stupor.

"Our thoughts and prayers go out to the families of these unfortunate men. These men were beaten and shot execution style, a bullet in the center of the forehead. NYCB will keep you posted on their identities when the information is released. Now back to you Amanda." Kurt cut out quickly from the camera. The expensive lunch Sarah had forced him to eat earlier, became fertilizer. It was unlike him to be squeamish. He blamed it on his chaotic life, the animosity between him and Amanda, and his stupid ass-burn. Not the fact that the two dead men were his informants.

Rich had Amanda wrap up the story. The news crew stood watching Kurt heave. Rich approached and gave him a jovial slap on the ass.

Kurt shot straight up, clutched his behind, and spewed every obscenity he knew.

Amanda interjected, "Wow, Mr. Kilawee that's an extensive expletive vulgar vocabulary–real professional."

Kurt wiped his mouth with his handkerchief, ready to retort her goading.

Rich stepped between them, "Okay back to your corners. I think you two need a break from each other."

"She started it." Kurt blurted.

"Did not." Amanda played into his prattle.

"Did too."

They sandwiched Rich.

"Did not."

"Did too."

"What the fuck childish game are you two playing now?" Rich pushed them apart. "Kurt take a few days off and get that burn healed. Amanda just keep away from him when he's in his volatile moods."

Jeremy grabbed Kurt before he earned himself more than just a couple of days off.

Separation was just a band-aid, not the cure to the cancerous bitterness that claimed their professional and emotional lives.

Chapter 10

"What are you doing here?" Amanda spun around aghast, after Kurt traced his index finger down her backbone through her sheer blouse. She was engrossed in taking mental notes of the guests attending the posh Yacht Charity event. His gentle touch startled and triggered her into a defensive mode. His prying presence made her jumpy like getting her hand caught in the cookie jar only much worse. More like getting your hand caught in a blender and someone turns it on. Her hot story was possibly life altering.

Nonchalant Kurt swaggered from behind a white resin column, one of several that supported a myriad of clear garden lights encircling the helicopter pad turned dance floor. The lights crisscrossed the pool and Jacuzzi area on the 480 foot mega yacht rumored to be the largest in the world; supposedly belonging to a Saudi Arabian Royal Family.

Cool and collect decked out in a befitting tuxedo; Kurt exuded the picturesque James Bond sort of ruggedness. Enough to make any normal warm-blooded woman swoon; and Amanda realized grudgingly how she fit so stereotypically into that swooning subgroup.

It made her sick to think her intellectual premise wasn't stronger than her basic sexual instincts when it came to him. Why was he always making her lose her focus? She had a very attractive attentive beau, so why she was even remotely attracted to Kurt evaded her practical no nonsense mind. In a whisper she seethed, "Don't bother trying to exploit me, I wasn't born yesterday."

His black fedora tipped back allowing her to see his blazing emerald eyes. Leaning forward within earshot distance, he said, "It is obvious you weren't born yesterday," he eyed her bluntly from head to toe slowly returning to her icy stare. "For your information, Ms. Lindas I did not come to exploit you in any way, shape, or form. I'm working. And by the way, I am an invited guest, not just a guest of a guest–unlike some eye-candy. This assignment is mine even more so than yours."

Mortified she waited with bated breath, had he busted her? Secretly she was taping a slanderous conversation between two unsuspecting guests, while she waited for Rich to return with drinks.

"Your 'Lover' put me on the lurch too. Our ratings are shaky, and I am here to fix them. By the way, I must say your form looks divine." He pushed his hat forward shadowing the evident mockery in his eyes.

"Rich is not my Lover! How dare you?" Amanda fretted about what almost became a career disaster. Flashbacks of private lunches pinked her face. *But how would Kurt have known? How did he suspect them as being an item?* Her heart beat incessantly, her breathing rapidly increased. Trying not to let him shake the ground she walked on, her posture stiffened. Her chest heaved slowly; she noticed his eyes drifted to her breast. Realizing her nipples were hardening beneath her camisole under her white chiffon blouse she crossed her arms over her chest for protection against his leer.

"Woo– I guess you do care. Very intriguing Ms. Lindas, I can see my presence and tenaciousness is causing a rise in you. It makes me enjoy this yacht party all the more."

Perturbed and embarrassed, Amanda strutted off in her black glittery five-inch stilettos; she headed towards the first available bar to console herself with a fine glass of champagne. She refused to allow him to ruin a magical evening only written about in urban fairytales. This evening, her goal was to enjoy celebrity status while acquiring accidental truths on the next big headline.

The yacht swarmed with "the toast of the town" New Yorkers, Hollywood types, and of course, buzzed with the "who's who" of the political scene. Just the main deck alone was covered with enough scandal to write a juicy tell-all book. But which scandals were the best headliners? Keeping ample distance from Kurt should be easy on a yacht large enough to accommodate well over a hundred guests. Or could it?

In a small lounge, she found solace, entertained by a five piece orchestra. It was touching and intimate; a welcome relief from the loud rock music on the upper deck. Entertainers such as Hall & Oats, Survivor, Air Supply, and other up-and-coming bands were the headline performers.

She amused herself by reviewing the events of the night. Earlier she had spotted Belinda rockin' out with some of the rock stars wearing a sexy cocktail uniform. That night, Belinda was her Fairy Rockin' Godmother; she convinced Amanda to wear the '*fuck-me*' shoes after teaching her to strut in them adding a sexy sway to her hips.

The cocktail gig came about when Rich called asking if she knew anyone who could fill-in last minute. He sent a town car with champagne and chocolates. The night was destined to be a success. Her diligent stiletto practice in the hall of her apartment building paid off well. She learned to strut like it was nobody's business. That combined with her elegant fitted formal black skirt with a thigh-high slit up the side, topped with a Coco Chanel white chiffon long-sleeved blouse; made her a dressed to kill contender. She had felt divine, prior to Mr. Sauvé's entrance. Confidentially she was pleased that he noticed her.

Earlier, Rich had introduced her around the yacht to several of New York's finest news personalities. Perhaps, so she could squeeze some tidbits of fresh news from their tight lips.

The New York news teams where better than exceptional, how could she compete? Time would tell. Rich disappeared several times leaving her to her own devices. Not one to squander opportunity she made good use of her time alone observing celebrities mixing and matching among themselves. Not only were they not faithful to their original dates; some stowed away to the lower staterooms pairing with same sex partners. She deduced they were more open with their sexual preferences among friends, but what about possible foes?

Friend or foe a journalist job is to report the truth. Facts and truth were her only allies. The secret VIP staterooms were an item of concern and inspiration as she lurked into the shadows. Seriously taking notes on who went in where and with whom? Some came out with the white powder sniffles or reeked with the telltale signs of fine Marijuana.

She had Belinda out on the sly too. One could never have too many informants. It was Belinda who spotted dateless Kurt upon his arrival giving Amanda the upper hand in the avoidance game. Much to Amanda's surprise, Kurt had also meandered in and out of the VIP staterooms.

Of course, she only dared herself to venture near. Just because she was a Midwestern Cheese-head at heart, didn't mean she was naïve to the goings on of high society. To her there were two scenarios– *the cream always raises to the top,* and so does the scum that should be skimmed.

During her observations she noted enviously that Kurt seemed awfully friendly with the New York State's Attorney, Rudolph Giuliani. She was a great fan of Mr. Giuliani and his work. They hovered close with the New York judges seeking reelection. Side by side they perched in the limelight of the top deck near the helm like static birds on an electric wire, possibly "a good-ol'-boys club".

On one of her trips to the ladies room, she spied Rich and Kurt in the cavernous lower decks entertained by New York's infamous shady characters. A lineup of "too close for comfort pals", like Anthony "Fat Tony" Salerno, Anthony "Tony Ducks" Corallo, and Salvatore Santoro, all were noted in the mob underworld.

Stealthily, she used her small tape recorder to record conversations that she would piece together later.

Decidedly bored with her own company, she ventured back to the rocker's deck, just in time to hear Hall & Oats sing their most recent hit; "Private Eyes".

The crowd was heavily into the party synergy. The alcohol infused dancing fools were jammed together looking like a large centipede or a deformed multi-armed octopus. Safe on the outskirts of the rambunctious crowd; she bobbed and swayed to the music. A strong hand slipped around her slender waist; warm whispers sang the chorus into her ear. She blamed her shivers on the chilly October air, until she realized the eerie warm breath and soothing voice belonged to Kurt.

"I'm watching you…" he sang, while his hand smoothed her hip feeling her sway. She hesitated to turn towards him; rubbing her neck and ear she attempted to erase his words.

She pulled away. She had to. He raised his glass to her. His hazy eyes indicated he was toasted, probably stoned. But if the truth be told she was well over her limit too.

"Did you know Ms. Lindas that is one of my favorite songs?" Kurt toasted her and sipped. "Did I tell you look lovely tonight? I think expensive stilettos and yacht parties become you." He flirted overtly.

"Yes, you did mention something rather roguish earlier. What do you want now? Aren't you supposed to be getting information on some big news breaking story?" She backed away slapping his hand that rested too comfortably on her hip.

His hands lifted high still toting his half-filled glass. "Don't shoot, don't shoot! I'm just the messenger. To answer your first question, I want the same thing now as I did earlier. And second, yes, you're correct–I came for a big story and I'm celebrating it. Now would you care to have a celebratory drink with me?" His long legs resiliently kept him steady as the dance floor swayed. "I have my story, so what's your story? What's a hot looking babe dating a guy who is almost old enough to be her father or her boss?" He placed his arm around her shoulders. Then he placed his free index finger on her lips, "Nope, no… don't tell me, let me guess. He *is* your boss and he plans on getting you out of this lovely skirt you're almost wearing."

His finger skipped from her lips directly down to drawing an invisible line from her knee to the upper edge of her thigh. Where the slit abruptly stopped, so did he. Seriously studying her eyes, he exhaled a whiskey laden breath, quirked his brow, and smiled. "I have wanted to say and do that all night. Babe, you've got the look. Care to dance? They're playing our song."

The gifted Hall & Oats began the song, "One on One". As the duo sang couples gathered closer. He put his whiskey on a tall cocktail table and folded her into his arms without waiting for a definite "no".

Kurt didn't give her the chance to protest even though it was written all over her face. Pulling her close, one arm wrapped her waist and the other hand interlocked with her smooth hand, he guided her into following his lead. It wasn't an easy feat, but he managed. Inhaling her fresh scented perfume he said, "I know you're thinking we don't have a song– but 'One on One' should be our song. Isn't this better than arguing? You have to agree we make a stylish couple. You fit perfectly in my arms and God knows our bodies were designed for one another," his cheek pressed against hers. He sang "One on One" in tune with the band.

His sweet heartfelt words weakened her resistance. She thought him uncharacteristically clingy. But even intoxicated, he was a debonair dancer; a perfectly harmless friendly drunk. Maybe?

When the song ended, a DJ took over the music. Kurt was relentless at keeping her as his partner. Other men tried to break in, but he swayed her away coveting her like a prize. He claimed every song was one of his favorites.

Amanda became quite suspicious that the DJ and Kurt were in cahoots with one another. But, she had to admit she wasn't bored. Rich had disappeared again. Anyways, Kurt did have some redeeming qualities like his dancing skill, taste in music and clothing. He was impeccably charming when he wanted to be. She kept her thoughts to herself refusing to feed his vanity.

Every waiter was at his beckon call bringing fresh drinks between song breaks. He abandoned his good manners as the evening advanced. Frustrated she gently removed his greedy fingers, hands, and arms like returning separate unwanted items, not trying to offend him, but also unwilling to encourage him.

Nobody's fool, her interest was in his revelation of the "BIG" story. Maybe in his drunken stupor, she could persuade him to divulge details. Perhaps his "BIG" story would mesh with her *little* stories. She was onto something, she suspected Rich as a key player in a racketeering scheme, but she needed more evidence. Was Kurt the missing link?

Against her better judgment, for the sake of exposing the truth, she continued her charade.

"Kurt, exactly what are we celebrating?" She cooed interlocking her arm with his escorting him from the din of the crowd to a dimly lit private bar in the center of the yacht. No one would suspect her of coercing. "Let's have another drink, shall we?" her tone surreptitiously blithe.

The bar had subtle contemporary track lighting spotlighting scattered cocktail tables topped with lit candles adding a romantic ambiance to their cozy *tete-a-tete*. Kurt was in his usual talkative state; dispensing more alcohol could push him into an exodus of the truth; which she earnestly desired. She wittingly poured on her charm, "Bartender, a glass of Dom Perignon for me, and your best Irish whiskey for him." she smiled.

In high spirits Kurt chimed in, "Yep, nothing but the best for me. On the rocks please. I like it rough and rocky." He taunted her with his quirky grin and squeezed her shoulders further tantalizing her. His sandy hair tousled across his brow. He was the epitome of smug.

Amanda took the drinks and assumed control. Kurt followed like a puppy vying for a treat. At an empty table they could safely continue their private chat. Placing his drink opposite of hers, she coaxed him to sit, his back towards the crowd, so he wasn't easily distracted. This was a prime opportunity to get inside that mercenary mind of his. His "Big Story" teased her like a starving fish trying to bite a worm without getting hooked.

"Salute!" she said raising her sparkling fluted glass in his honor. "So tell me, what are we celebrating?"

He reciprocated, but became instantly suspicious of her recompense. Inclining towards her, he sucked in a breath, "Now listen and listen carefully, although I may be slightly inebriated, I assure you that I am in total control and my perspicacity is intact. There is a lot going on here that doesn't add up to Headlines, more in the order of *Deadlines*." He slowly exhaled blowing the wind out of her sail. "I hope you're not just being nice to me to get my story, you'll ruin the perfect image I have of you and your integrity, remember the tango is meant for two. So humor me and act like you're my date."

Just as she opened her mouth to respond, he swigged down half his whiskey with a grimace. He glanced over his shoulder and said, "Excuse me; I need to say a quick hello." He stood, fastened his tuxedo jacket, and rifled through his hair, feathering it back into place leaving his fedora.

Before Amanda could defend herself, he was up shaking hands with Ronald and Eva Crown, New York Real Estate moguls. Ronald jovially mussed Kurt's hair and playfully ducked when Kurt tried to return the gesture.

Was there anyone that Kurt didn't know? And what about Deadlines? While babysitting his hat and drink, she sipped hers pondering his next move. He was flighty and so unpredictable tonight.

To her delight, he chauffeured Ronald over to her, "This is my g-girl– good friend and business associate, Ms. Amanda Lindas."

Amanda extended her hand and attempted to stand to greet the prodigious businessman. "Pleasure to meet you, Mr. Crown."

In taking her hand he kindly helped her to her wobbly stiletto trapped feet. "The pleasure is mine." He glanced at Kurt with an agreeable smile. "Any friend of Kurt's, especially his very attractive friends, are my pleasure to meet."

They chatted about the real estate market and Ronald's 68-story Crown Tower on Fifth Avenue off East 56th near Tiffany's flagship store, until Eva reeled Ronald in another direction.

With their exit Kurt picked up his drink and interlocked Amanda's arm around his.

She deduced that Rich had not introduced her earlier because of their aversion to Rich. Rich could be repressive, yet charming. Amanda discovered as Kurt sauntered her through the crowd that he was stopped by nearly everyone. Kurt was the likable popular face of NYCB.

It dawned on her that NYCB needed Kurt. He didn't need NYCB. Enlightenment often comes when one least expects it.

Her enlightenment didn't prevent her from pointing out his introduction faux pas, "Listen, Mr. Kilawee you need not introduce me as your good friend. We both know we are *not* good friends."

He patted her hand and proceeded, "One could only hope that we could be." His smile was gracious, but his tone was sarcastically tainted.

"Hey Harry, how's it hanging? This is my associate Mandy." He stressed the informal nickname obviously fishing for a rise from her. "Mandy, this is Harry Hansen of *Pleasures* magazine."

"Hello, Mr. Hansen, Amanda Lindas, with NYCB news," she said extending her hand.

While shaking her hand, Harry winked at Kurt. "Hey Kurt, great work on your super article. You received excellent reviews." He turned to Amanda still holding her hand. "You better watch this guy, he is up-and-coming. The next big story is his for the taking."

Amanda nodded, smiled, and remained cordial. Thinking, *yeah, I'm just a lost puppy hanging onto every word waiting for him to throw me a bone. The impetuous things a girl must do to catch a big story.*

Earlier that same day Kurt had placed the exploitive magazine on her desk, with a few of the rave reviews. She promptly tossed them in the trash without as much as reading one sentence. He was better than that. When he questioned her later, she simply denounced them as, "Trash belongs in the trash." Somehow she thought he would make her regret her actions and words.

At each introduction, Kurt took presumptuous liberties introducing her as his associate, his assistant, his pimp, his personal hygienist, his secretary. The more people she met the more jobs and personalities he created for her. He was amused as were his friendly acquaintances.

"Hey Clint, this is my little sister Amanda."

Incredulity flashed on her face.

"Sis this is Clint Howard with *Players International* magazine."

Clint smiled warmly and said, "Nice taste in little sisters. I thought you only had brothers Kurt?"

A quirky Elvis grin washed Kurt's face, "Yeah, well I've always wanted a little sister."

"We are always looking for fresh new ladies." Clint boldly stated to Amanda and then looked at Kurt. "Hey great article in *Pleasures*, just remember you owe me a better story. Take good care of your 'little' sister."

"I plan on it." Kurt smiled escorting her away.

Shuffling through the crowd, it seemed as the sky darkened the shady characters and weirdoes multiplied.

Touching her chin with his fingers, "Hey is that a genuine smile I see spreading across your beautiful face? Glad to see you're finally enjoying yourself."

"Well really, your little sister? Is that the best you can do?" She couldn't deny her amusement of his wry introductions, Kurt was truly funny. They strolled away from the pandemonium across the upper private deck spider webbed under glowing lights.

His fingers lingered on her chin, his face shadowed hers.

Shivers gathered on her spine, unsure if it was from the cool night air or his touch, she crossed her arms over her chest. Her downcast eyes skittered away from the romance she spotted in his. The warmth in his handsome face stopped her cold. His lips quivered slightly as he leaned in for the kill.

Was he nervous; this self-assured gigolo, Mr. Suave? She realized in a split second. Instantly a thought raced into her romance muddled brainwaves, she pulled away just as his lips barely brushed hers.

He wasn't ever going to share his story with her; he was putting the make on her.

"Oh, hell no! Damn you Kurt!"

Breaking his spell, she escaped down the outside stairs forgetting she wore five-inch heels. She stumbled, but caught herself at the bottom grasping the slick lacquered wood railing.

"Damn it Amanda! Why are you running from me?" He trailed after her with his swift long gait his jaunt to the bottom steps was within seconds of her.

She stood her ground, "You tricked me! You were supposed to tell me about your 'Big' story! You led me on." She stomped her foot. A blinding pain shot up her leg from her crushed throbbing toes. Three hours too long in her Cinderella stilettos, she had been trapped making believe she belonged in the jet-setter celebrity crowd.

For hours she dwelled in the magical urban fairyland, hours past reality and humility. And he played along, Mr. Prince Charming and all his royal friends. His patronizing actions infuriated her. Four drinks above of her limit, a paroxysm of her foolishness turned into tears. Flustered she headed straight towards the gangway exit. Just about midnight, the city Cinderella just wanted a yellow pumpkin coach and her Frickin' Fairy Punk-rocker Godmother, Belinda. With her purse clutched under her arm she wobbled across the gangway that chartered her back to reality.

A uniformed attendant flagged a taxi. Beyond humiliated, Amanda slipped into the yellow carriage. Releasing a disgusted sigh, she shamed herself for leaving Belinda. A shoulder to cry on would be a big help, she wiped her tears. *Oh well, if Belinda could handle the wild clubs, she could handle the yacht scene too.* An adept party girl, she was way smarter than Amanda.

In reality–she was unprepared for the role she was playing.

"Driver, take me to 35th and 8th." She barely articulated the directions when much to her chagrin she saw Kurt running alongside the taxi.

"Stop!" he yelled.

The driver wasn't going fast enough, Kurt opened the door and slip safely into her taxi. Slamming the door, he flashed a disgruntled look at her, and then slipped the driver a twenty. "Thanks Bob."

His triumph left bitter defeat torturing her mind.

The driver looked over his shoulder, "Hey no problem Kurt, a little girl trouble huh?"

Kurt took his angry eyes off Amanda for a second to address the taxi driver. "Yeah, I guess you could say that Bob, how's it going for you man?"

"Great! Good to see you. Where to? The usual?" Bob faced forward.

"Yeah, sure Bob," Kurt said exhausted.

Amanda was appalled. *What did he mean by the usual? And of course how the hell did Kurt know Bob personally?* Her arms fastened across her chest.

Kurt sunk back. When he regained his composure, he addressed her, "Well ex-cu-uu-se me! Okay, I'm sorry, I find you physically attractive and I tried to kiss you, so sue me." He wanted to add, *you're driving me frickin' crazy*, but he refrained.

She sat silent. *Great, so now, he's apologizing for finding me attractive.* She just couldn't win. He was driving her insane.

Out of breath, he continued his rant, slouching in the far corner of the dingy cab, "I thought we were having good time. And you–" his tone accusing. "You emitted flirting signals of more than just friends."

The cab driver drove off in the opposite direction heading north on 12th Avenue towards the park.

"You are sadly mistaken. You're the flirt, not me." She corrected.

He flicked his hair stirred by her anger, "Oh I see, so it's okay for you to wear these '*fuck-me*' stilettos and I'm the flirt." He seized her ankle awkwardly lifting it up so the taxi driver could get a good look, "Tell me Bob? Are these '*fuck-me*' shoes or what?" As swiftly as he gripped her ankle, he released it. "Yeah, this game is not rocket science is it? What does a woman expect of the common man?"

Her eyes shot poison; if looks could kill she would have wiped him off the face of the Earth.

He knew it.

And Bob knew it.

Men were damned if they did, and damned if they didn't. Kurt was headed for Hell and damnation. Around her, he felt possessed by some voodoo priestess. For all he knew it could be that Joan-Jett imp Belinda, or maybe the bartender at *The Tavern on the Green*. All he could mumble was, "I'm sorry. God, am I sorry." He rubbed his aching temples.

Out of his misery an epiphany struck him.

"Wait, this is not about me and you!" He glared at her, "This is about your boyfriend the bartender." He winced, "Oh my God. You're serious with him." Now humiliation tripped him. He tapped the cabbie on the shoulder, "Hey Bob this is not the *usual,* take her to 35th and 8th." The fact was– Amanda was the most unusual woman he had ever met. She was slowly killing his self-confidence. "Take her home, and then take me home." He was resolved to defeat.

He became docile as the cabbie turned around at 52nd Street to head South on 12th Avenue.

Without warning, Kurt sat up and broached the subject again. "You're afraid he'll find out you were on a date with me, or should I say with our boss."

"Don't flatter yourself that was not a date. Jealousy will get you nowhere. Why don't you keep your pathetic ideas to yourself?" She shifted to her corner of the way too small taxi.

"Whoa, are you sure about that? We danced, we drank, we laughed, and I introduced you to all my wonderful friends. We got our pictures taken together. You acted like you were having a splendid time and now you're sharing my cab with me. That's a real date. Honey, just look me in the eyes and tell me you didn't have a good time?" He eyed her full length.

She couldn't look him in the eyes. Lying was not her forte. She did have a good time. And if she looked into his dreamy emerald eyes, he would know. *God, why was this ride taking so long. Whatever happened to everything happening in a New York minute?*

She huffed noticing he continued to stare at her exposed leg. Desperately she wanted to cover it, so he wouldn't get any ideas of running his finger up the slit again. The thought of his actions choked her as the rush of unrequited desire flooded her senses.

"What's the matter? Can't lie to me can you Mandy?"

"Oh, bite me!" She said shocking herself and him. Just a little slang she had picked up from Belinda. She turned her back towards him.

"Wow where did that come from? And where would you like me to bite you?" Kurt chortled. Maybe she wasn't Miss Prim-n-proper. He placed his hand on her shoulder. "Maybe a little nip here, I promise I won't leave a love-bite for Mr. Casali to see." She shrugged his grasp. Her icy eyes gave him instant chills.

"Why do you care if we are seeing each other again? You have enough floozy euro-trash models to date. What is it with you?" A fierce inferno burned within her, "What the hell do you know about relationships anyway? And what makes you think you're such a catch?" She rattled questions not allowing him to answer or herself to breathe. Finally she gulped for air giving him time to retaliate.

"I don't know why I care, I just do! And yes, I could have stayed behind with my floozy euro-trash, but I didn't! And only God knows why! Bob take me back to the yacht." he rubbed his lips. "All I wanted to do was show you I am not the jerk you think I am. I wanted to celebrate my success story with you, but you tried to take advantage of my inebriated state. And don't lie because you're not good at it!" His arms crossed keeping his anger and tender emotions intact as he blindly glared out his window.

Bob gazed into his rearview mirror, made a U-turn, and turned up the radio as Phil Collins sang, "You Can't Hurry Love."

"Bob don't turn this cab around, take me home!" Amanda shouted. "I am not going to listen to accusations. I merely went to the party because Rich invited me." She pleaded her case. Her peripheral vision caught Kurt's rebuttal emerging. "Obviously, you can't handle your alcohol, so you should quit drinking. You're not good at it." Her face flamed hot.

A nervous laugh emanated from Kurt's throat as his hands brushed through his hair, "Listen honey, I can handle my liquor, and my women. I may have had a few too many, but I can still perform. I'm good at that." He smirked victoriously. "In fact, Clint offered me a couple of his House Honeys, so there. How's that grab you?"

No longer a misunderstanding–the situation became a competition of the wits.

"That just proves you like sloppy seconds, someone else's leftovers," she quipped.

He slapped knees, "Well, you're nominated for tonight's Smart-ass award. Where's the 'thank you Mr. Kilawee for introducing me to societies rich and famous?' And speaking of sloppy leftovers, where's your married date, Mr. Rich Underwood? Does Tony baby know you date our boss? Is Tony meeting you at the club later?" If she wanted shock therapy, he could jolt her.

Aghast Amanda's eyes widen and her mouth dropped. Her words were held captive in her throat. "What do you know about anything? It is not any of your business what I do. You're not my keeper!"

Pointing his finger at her, "I will tell you this–you don't know half of what I know. And who I know it about. I know more about what you don't know, mixed with what you think you know. You're getting too involved. You should keep silent. You're too close for your own good."

"Oh, what are you my self-appointed bodyguard or big brother? Huh? And I thought you were so cute about introducing me as your little sister. All you want is to control me, so I don't get the story out first on what was really going on at that so called charitable event. Well don't get in my way. I have out reported you for the last three months and I will get the copy to Rich before you do! Bob stop the cab I want out!"

The cabbie screeched the taxi to an abrupt halt. Amanda swung open her door almost hitting a car in the next lane. Kurt seized her with his long arms yanking her to his side. Opening the door on his side he dragged her to the sidewalk. "Oh no, you don't. I was instructed to get you home safely. And if I have to carry you home over my back like a sack of potatoes I will!" His fury overwhelmed him.

Her fury resulted in stomping her foot hard to the concrete sidewalk, nearly crippling her. She wished right after she did it that she hadn't. First of all–it hurt, and second–it was an outward display of childish rebellion. It reminded her of fights with her father. She struggled to keep her composure. "What do you mean–you were instructed?" Her face inches from his. Heated passion sweltered across her mind.

His face close to hers, his breath hot and whiskey sweet–he asked. "You want the truth?" The truth was he wanted to take her in his arms and home to his bed.

Amanda jerked a nod.

"Well, I will fill you in this much." his thumb and index finger spread about an inch. His voice grave and cool, "I was instructed by our employer to make sure you had a good time and to make sure you got home safely because our employer's wife came home early. Someone informed Sarah that her henpecked, oversexed husband was entertaining a certain overwhelmingly beautiful, smart, charming young lady, while she traveled. Our employer was prepared to offer a penthouse suite at the prestigious Trump Tower to that young lady with all expenses paid. And a new Mercedes Benz, which by the way, I selected and had it painted the icy-blue color of her eyes. This time her bonuses come with strings attached. Believe me, I am not a fan of our asshole boss who trusts me as his closest confidant. And as far as your Italian boy-toy bartender there is plenty about him you don't know. My advice is be careful who you trust. Most things are not what they appear. Now, please get into the cab and let's try to act civil." He gripped her arm guiding her back to the taxi.

Shell-shocked by his revelations, Amanda swallowed hard. Was Kurt telling the truth? Was he trying to protect her or con her? *Wow, a Mercedes the color of her eyes?* Her mind wandered as she obeyed him and slipped into the taxi forgoing her usual rebuttal about him calling her Mandy. He did say she was beautiful, smart, and charming. But "be careful" and "things are not what they appear" eerily engulfed her like Alice falling down the Rabbit's abyss. Loaded questions swirled in her mind giving her an instant headache. Feeling faint she flopped back against the worn leather seat.

Kurt couldn't look at her. He saw traces of fright in her face, scaring her was not his intention. Clearing his dry throat, he said, "Bob, take her to 35th and 8th."

He needed time to sort his jumbled thoughts. His headline story needed to be completed and on Rich's desk in the morning. He didn't want Amanda in the middle of the biggest scandal to hit New York; his big break. Unfortunately or fortunately he had held his story back, ever since the two face-cards he was supposed to meet were dragged from the East River. They had inconveniently disappeared. He was lucky; he ended up with an ass-burn that night. It could have been him that day with the decorative hole pierced in his head wearing the black bag attire.

At the solemn red-bricked apartment building, woozy from her close to fainting episode, Amanda allowed Kurt to assist her to the door. Pummeled by her pride, she couldn't fault him for illuminating the truth. Gently he guided her to the entrance on 35th. The large wood door shadowed by dim lights indicated a welcoming embrace. In the diffused light he lifted her chin; she gazed at his emerald eyes and mute lips. His eyes shifted searching hers for something deeper.

His pink lips parted. "Are you going to be alright?" his voice barely audible. "I'm sorry, please believe me, I had no intention of harming you. Your perception of me is distorted. What you believe about me as truth has been projected and twisted by the reputations others have painted. Mandy when I'm near you, you bring me to the edge."

She nodded mechanically. "I know, I'm sorry Kurt, but..." Her eyes filled with anguished tears.

Before she could say anything more he covered her quivering lips with his wanton kiss. It was tender and warm. So deeply passionate she couldn't help but give into him willingly and fully allowing him to explore her mouth with his. His kisses traveled to the tears on her cheeks and then to her chin and down her sultry soft neck. When she tried to pull back he covered her lips again. His arms cradled her. He pulled her close to the warmth of his firm chest.

In that moment she felt safe. Safer than she'd ever felt in any man's arms. How could she have let this happen? Reluctantly she pulled away. Her eyes and body said yes, betraying her mind.

"Mandy, please stop pushing me away..." he pleaded barely breathing fearful the moment wasn't real. Had she really let him kiss her?

She touched her fingertips to his lips. He placed his firm hand over hers and kissed each tip, sending electric shivers down her arm to her back causing her heart to quake.

"I have to go, Kurt. I need time to think. I promise we'll talk."

"I want more than just words, Mandy."

"I know," her eyes lowered away from his dominating stare. She shoved her key into the lock and opened the door allowing only enough room for her to slip in. This was going to be the longest night of her life.

Chapter 11

Passed out on her sofa, Amanda was awakened in the dead of sleep by her incessant ringing phone. In a sleep driven fog, she squinted at the clock deducing that it was 3:15 a.m. She struggled to get her footing and collect her bearings. By the second set of rings she was a little less than comatose. Brushing her tangled waves from her face, she put the phone to her ear upside-down and muttered, "Hello? Hello? Who's there?"

"Mandy? This is Rich, we have a breaking story!" she flipped the receiver, Rich continued, "I'm sending Jeremy over to your place now. Get yourself together, be outside. He'll be there in about fifteen. See you at the scene."

"What's happened?" Still dazed with the phone lodged in the crook of her ear and shoulder, she stumbled into her bedroom to get dressed. "What's the weather?" Rushed she tried hopping into a pair of midnight-blue slacks, falling to her knees, *shit, ouch!* She rolled to her side, kicked her legs to shimmy into her slacks.

With grim undertones Rich explained, "There's been another execution murder. It's a cold drizzle out here, dress warm we'll have umbrellas and a tent. I haven't been able to contact Kurt. Didn't he take you home?"

A cold chill ran rampant through her, standing to put her heels on she slipped and fell backwards into her small closet, smashing her head against her shoe rack. "Ouch! Yes, Kurt dropped me off just after midnight. He's okay, right?"

"Oh he didn't stay? Never mind, just be ready. Let me worry about him." Rich's voice didn't project his typical self-assured tone.

More than ready, dressed in a midnight-blue wool pantsuit and white button down blouse, Amanda paced in front of her apartment building. The drizzling rain reaped havoc with her hair. With her hairbrush in hand she frantically brushed her wavy mane into a ponytail, borderline presentable.

The van squealed to a stop, Jeremy leaned over and flung open the passenger door. "Jump in. We need to get to Central Park like now."

His head twitched as his fingers drummed the steering wheel. The wipers squeaked whipping faster than the rain fell.

"Have you heard from Kurt?" She asked deathly afraid.

The whites of his eyes were bright saucers, "Well, not exactly. I've been busy. The last I heard from him was a message on my answer machine after midnight. He was giddy about someone who finally kissed him. Hmm– wonder who that was girlfriend?" His nervous smile said he was withholding information.

"And? What else did he say? Come clean, I know there's more. Stop wrestling with your thoughts and talk." She felt her heart stop; she crushed her fist to her chest. "Did he allude to anything? Damn him! Damn it I knew I should have invited him in! Oh, how could I have been so stupid? You know he had way too much to drink."

Jeremy drove erratic, he passed through red lights and swerved to miss the early morning delivery trucks that lined Hell's Kitchen on 8th Ave. "He ah, said he was going to investigate a lead, but he was going to have a celebration drink first. Girl you got him so messed up." Jeremy's voice reduced to a squeak, "He said–he was going to *The Tavern on the Green*."

"Oh no, he didn't! Tony worked the late shift. They were having a closed party for some politicians. Kurt wouldn't dare gloat to Tony. Would he?" The rain splattered harder on the windshield as Jeremy careened around taxis and other commuters.

His eyes cut to her. "Oh yes he would. Missy you don't know the alpha-male you're dealing with. You kissing him secured his bragging rights. He's been waiting months for the mouth to mouth with you. Damn girl, you're like heroin to him. Like catnip to a cat, like alcohol to an alcoholic, he's a crack-head over you."

"Okay, Okay, I get it. Damn I wished he'd let me tell Tony. Oh my God–I am an awful girlfriend." Her hands covered her face.

Finally they reached Columbus Circle. The CB radio blared with Rich telling them to get to 66th Street to the police barriers. They could enter with their press passes. His crackled directions continued... adding to their already tense drama. "The set up area is in the children's park across from *The Tavern* off 67th."

Jeremy and Amanda shuddered.

Just as they passed through the police barricade, Jeremy spotted a familiar tall man donning a tan trench coat wearing a black fedora. Even at a distance Jeremy immediately recognized the gait. There was no mistaking it was his best friend. The relief that washed across Jeremy flowed directly to her. "Amanda look!" ecstatic he pointed out the obvious.

Under a black umbrella dripping with rain, Kurt was getting fitted with an earpiece. An angelic glow beamed life into Amanda's eyes. The smile on her face reflected pure relief.

DESIRE FOR TRUTH

The scene was total chaos under the temporary, yet stable NYCB tent. They were the first news station on the scene, set up with cables, cameras, wires, and mikes.

The police sirens whirred. Flashing blue and red lights whirled around them as they jumped from the NYCB van into ankle deep mud puddles.

Kurt stopped testing his mike as soon as Amanda approached. Their eyes connected like magnets, Rich intercepted and started coaching her through the crime scene rules. Her body shook chilled from the eerie scene and the cold October morning. It didn't help that she hadn't slept. The relentless rain raged on the tent like a thousand drummers drumming. She hovered close to hear Rich's instructions over the racket. Her freezing bones made her teeth chatter.

The next thing she felt was Kurt's oversized trench coat gently wrapped around her shoulders. He held her close wrapping his arms around from behind giving her extra warmth from his body as his chin rested on her wet head. She welcomed his warmth, too tired to fight his overt unprofessional hugging. Rich's eyes narrowed immediately in disapproval of Kurt's forwardness.

Jeremy saw it and tapped Kurt out of the arena. "Come on let's do the lead in…"

Reluctantly Kurt left Mandy's side. "Stay here, keep warm," he instructed. "Come on Rich let's get this show rolling. Some of us haven't slept yet." He hollered and flagged the camera crews closer to the yellow crime scene tape that wrapped the playground still swarming with New York City's finest C.S.I unit. His good friend the lead investigator, Agent Tom McCarthy had promised him first right of refusal on top controversy crime investigations.

Just outside the yellow tape Kurt stood holding a black umbrella. Still dressed in his tuxedo from the prior night's gala affair; he hoped the rain would subside so they wouldn't have to do voice-overs.

"Reporting live in New York City this is Kurt Kilawee with NYCB– *The New Edge on Truth…*" He motioned to Amanda to step into the scene. A personal assistant slipped the warm protective trench coat from her shoulders. Amanda stepped under the protective covering of Kurt's umbrella.

"Good morning early New York, this is Amanda Lindas with NYCB." She turned toward Kurt, "We are in Central Park reporting another macabre execution style murder. Kurt you've been on the scene since two this morning. Are there any details you can share?"

Kurt paused. In his earpiece the chief investigator, McCarthy, spoke slowly, "Kurt this is bad. We have a certified ID on the body."

"Amanda I am getting feedback from NYPD–they have identified the victim. We are waiting on the formalities of contacting the family before we can release the name. Our hearts and prayers are extended to the victim's family. At this moment we know the victim is a Caucasian male, twenty-five to thirty, with dark hair, approximately five-foot ten inches tall. The victim according to authorities was shot and killed at close range with a single bullet wound to the forehead. It is believed this incident could be related to the two earlier murders of two men found in the East River by East Harlem." The feedback continued. Tom urged Kurt to bow out of the telecast and meet him behind the crime scene tape.

Rich stood behind Jeremy motioning to Kurt and Amanda to wrap it up and sign off.

"Well, Amanda it appears they cannot release the victim's name at this time. As soon as we have verification and a reprieve in the weather, we will be back on the air to review the facts of this unfortunate gruesome murder."

"You heard it first from– *The New Edge on Truth... An Execution Murder at the Playground in Central Park*, this is Amanda Lindas reporting live with Kurt Kilawee for NYCB."

Their eyes locked and spoke volumes, yet neither said a word.

Kurt handed her the umbrella, making an effort to wrap his large warm hand around her chilled fingers before Rich escorted her back under the news headquarter tent. Assistants brought chairs, hot coffee, and donuts while they waited for the rain to subside. Amanda sat clutching a hot coffee laden with cream, she accepted Kurt's jacket as her personal shroud. Jeremy stayed close drying off the camera equipment with the rest of the blue jacketed crew members.

With his hot black coffee and a lit cigarette in hand, Kurt stepped away. He entered under the crime tape with his buddy Tom and other C.S.I. agents. The large surrounding trees canopying the park area diminished the down pour to a slight, yet constant drizzle. The body was covered with a protective white plastic sheeting to contain and secure the evidence.

"You ready for this?" McCarthy asked somberly as he took a long drag off Kurt's cigarette. "Just warning you, I think you know the guy."

Kurt took a long drag off the cigarette. His heart sank thinking about the men dragged from the East River. Tom lifted the white plastic sheeting revealing a lifeless ghostly blue man and a bloody mass. Kurt turned away quickly. Shocked he shook his head first, and then nodded, confirming he recognized the victim. "Give me a moment Tom," his voice trembled, his eyes welled with tears. "Holy Christ almighty, how the hell does this shit happen?" He pressed his fingers to his eyes.

"So is it him? The same guy you bitched and moaned about, so many nights in your drunken stupors? It's him huh? Jesus Christ, Kurt."

"How did you confirm his ID?" Worry attacked Kurt's senses while nausea pried at his stomach like a crowbar forcing open the manhole cover on his locked emotions.

Tom flipped open his black report booklet, "Right here near the body we found his wallet, Victim: Antonio Carmine Casali, twenty-six years old, a student at Columbia University, and part-time bartender at *The Tavern on the Green*. We called Gus, the manager, for the family contact number. Antonio's an only child, still lives with his mother. Mother: Anna Marie Casali, a wealthy widow, she lives on the Upper West side. We are waiting her okay to release his name and details. There's something else..." Tom placed his hand on Kurt's shoulder, "I hate to ask, but where were you from midnight until one-thirty this morning? Gus said you came into the bar during a private party, around twelve-thirty, pretty tanked. He also said you and Antonio exchanged heated words–about a woman."

"I see, so you think I'm capable of this atrocity..." Kurt shook his head in disbelief. He took a gulp of hot strong coffee, something he shouldn't have. It came back up full force splattering his shoes and Tom's. His vomit reeked of alcohol.

Tom laughed uneasy, "Great, thanks man; you still don't have the stomach for this job. Wait until I call your brothers and the old man." With a dead serious grovel in his voice, "Look at me. – Tell me, I don't have to tell them I had to book you on suspicion of premeditated first degree murder?" He slapped Kurt roughly on the back to help him stop gagging.

Kneeling on one knee, with his forearm supported across his thigh, Kurt wiped his face with his handkerchief. "I can't believe you're asking me. I'm crazy about her, but I am not a murderer. God, I know I've done some crazy shit in the last couple of months, but I'm not insane. I can still get women the old fashioned way. I don't need to knock off their boyfriends to get their attention. Christ Tom, do you think that I've finally lost my fucking mind?"

Tom squatted next to him. "Kurt, what I think doesn't matter. Our job is to get at the truth, the facts, not emotionally involved. It was all over the tabloids how he almost ruined your career, and now the night of his murder you have an argument because you're so plastered you had the audacity to gloat about getting his girlfriend. Man you've got to look at the evidence. You need a lawyer. I have to confiscate your gun for ballistics."

Kurt's eyes widened. "Are you arresting me for the murder of Antonio Casali?" Just as the words of reality slipped out of his mouth he saw Rich prepping Amanda for the next interview with the Chief of Police.

Kurt stood and adjusted his disheveled tux jacket, slicked his wet hair back, replaced his fedora afterwards. From his shoulder holster he handed Tom his gun. He looked at Tom and said, "I may be a lot of things, but I assure you I am not a murderer. If being in love with Amanda Lindas is a crime then I am guilty as all hell. I would die for her and her love, but I wouldn't kill for it. Do me a favor don't cuff me in front of her." He slipped his badge from his jacket chest pocket and willfully surrendered it to his long time pal and confidant.

Rich witnessed the exchange from the other side of the tape. He lifted his palms up and mouthed– *What the fuck?*

Kurt shook his head at Rich and pointed to Amanda. His actions clearly told Rich not to put her on. But Rich never listened before why would he start now. That moment an incisive enlightenment of tidal wave proportions came to Kurt overwhelming him.

Rich knew. That bastard Rich knew all along that Tony was the dead man. The seething anger of an erupting volcano welled up inside him. His breathing labored, his chest heaved with intensity of a bull ready to charge. His vision blurred, distorted realism became surreal. The realm of spiritual truth and injustice encapsulated him.

Meanwhile under a NYCB umbrella Amanda interviewed Police Commissioner Benjamin Ward. Jeremy nervously manned the camera. Not only was he a fan of NYPD's first black Commissioner; he had had the opportunity to be present when Mayor Koch appointed him into office. But the real jitters set in when he saw Kurt's face and body language expressing severe distress.

The rain had ceased to be a deterrent. Rich directed Amanda to start without Kurt. He didn't explain he just kept her back to the scene of Kurt's detainment.

"Hello New York this is Amanda Lindas back on the scene of *the playground murder in Central Park* reporting live with the Honorable Commissioner Ward. Thank you for joining us. This is an unusual privilege to have you with us at four a.m. Chief Ward. We now know that the victim's name and identity has been released by the family. Can you share with the public the breaking news?" She lifted the microphone.

"Yes, we have received the confirmation from the family. Our victim is Antonio Casali, a twenty-six year old Caucasian-Italian male…"

Amanda trembled choking, she pulled back the mike, "Excuse me, did you just say Antonio Casali?"

Her blue eyes bugged out in disbelief. Inside, her college professor's words badgered her, "*Keep your emotions out of it. Report the news.*" She forced the mike to the Chief for affirmation of the incomprehensible truth.

"Yes, Antonio Casali was a Columbia University student studying for his masters in business and he worked as a bartender at *The Tavern on the Green,* across the street from this playground."

Wavering insecurity fought to come out, she forced it back. *Report the news. Get the facts.* Mechanically numb she asked, "Who would commit such a heinous crime? Do you have any suspects at this time?"

"Yes, we have an alleged suspect in custody at this time, but we are not ruling out possible mob involvement. NYPD Organized Crime Control Bureau will be conducting a thorough investigation. We are thoroughly reviewing all the evidence that we have gathered from reliable witnesses."

"Chief can you share the name of your alleged suspect?"

The Chief hesitated a moment. He glanced back at Agent Tom McCarthy double checking what he was about to report was the truth as they knew it. Agent McCarthy nodded.

"The alleged suspect for the murder of Antonio Casali is Kurt Kilawee. He is detained in police custody."

Kurt was within forty feet of the news cameras, not just NYCB cameras, but all the national news media moguls.

Photographers came out of the woods, jumping fences, and crossing police barriers to take a picture of the suspect. Bulbs flashed, people shoved to get closer, and uniformed police officers apprehended the violators while Tom and the other agents formed a human barrier around Kurt until the chaos settled.

A fog of tiny sparkling firefly like lights swarmed around Amanda. Her emotions quaked to the surface; she had quit breathing at the mention of Kurt's name. And with the camera still rolling she dropped to the wet ground.

In shock, Jeremy dropped his camera; unsure of whether to run to Kurt's aid, pick up Mandy, or faint.

Rich screamed for another NYCB camera man. He got more than he bargained for when the other news stations hovered around Mandy and Commissioner Ward. The Commissioner shouted orders to the police officers. "Get the paramedics. Give the lady some room. Everyone get back!" He scooped Amanda's listless body up in his arms and carried her to a waiting ambulance where the paramedics treated her for exhaustion. Jeremy followed his hero.

In the heated moment of dire chaos, Kurt managed to overcome his human shield.

Like a speared bull he charged past the news seekers and clutched the lapels of Rich's trench coat, "You-son-of-a-bitch! You knew. You knew it was Tony all along! What kind of a sick bastard are you bringing her here to report her boyfriend's murder! Damn you, Rich this is the lowest thing you've ever done! You put her at the crime scene when you knew damn well she was involved with the victim." He double palmed Rich's chest hard. Rich shifted backwards, but regained his footing quickly. Their fists flew. Heavy strong punches landed before the agents could separate them. Kurt released one last right hook clipping Rich squarely on his left jaw.

CRACK! Everyone within earshot distance heard Rich's jaw snap. He tumbled like a tree crashing in a forest.

Tom yanked Kurt's arms behind him, low and brisk he said, "Good God Kurt, really man. Now, I have to cuff you, I have no choice." He slammed the cuffs around Kurt's wrists. He read Kurt his Miranda rights. "You are under arrest for the murder of Antonio Casali. You have the right to remain silent. Anything you say can and will be used against you in a court of law. You have the right to an attorney. If you cannot afford an attorney, one will be provided for you. Do you understand the rights I have just read to you? With these rights in mind, do you wish to speak to me?"

With his wet head lowered, his hair dripping in his face Kurt kept silent as Tom guided him to the police cars lined up at the 67th Street entrance. In passing, they approached the ambulance where Amanda was receiving treatment.

Kurt begged, "Tom, let me talk to her, give me a minute, please." Tom took pity; he brushed Kurt's wet bangs from his eyes. Kurt pleaded, "Amanda, you know I didn't do this. I would never do anything to hurt you. You have to believe me. Rich did this."

Still in shock she sat erect and glared incisively at him. "Did you gloat to Tony, that I kissed you?" His not so innocent eyes shifted away. "Why would you do that? Damn it Kurt I hate you!" She twisted away from his gaze.

Her words like a warrior's lance pierced him. "What? You hate me? But Mandy, I didn't..." Flabbergasted he vented, "Well fine hate me, I hope you enjoy standing in a long line of about twenty-million people. Thanks to NBC, ABC, CBS, and NYCB and every other news station everyone hates me–probably even my own mother. McCarthy, take me to the station."

Hours later Kurt was still at the police station in the detainment room. He waited impatiently for his release and his lawyer. He drank bitter old coffee. And against the rules, he smoked like a chimney. Hung-over suffering from the lack of sleep, water, and food, he looked haggard.

McCarthy allowed Sarah Underwood in to visit.

"Hey handsome you're looking roguish, nice bruises and dried blood on your face and knuckles. I've arranged for your father fly in from Chicago on the company jet to help obtain your release."

He didn't lift his head to acknowledge Sarah or her words.

For three years he rode the wave of ultimate success as an Anchorman/investigator. And at the pinnacle he was finally going to prove his adroit abilities to the world, someone trips him. Facing his father's disappointment was nothing compared to unrequited love kicking his gut.

"Well are you just going to sulk or are you ready to talk?" She picked up his cigarette pack and slipped one out, "Do you mind?" She put it to her mouth. Robotically he struck a match and lit it; she inhaled deep and blew the smoke out slowly between her red lips.

The same shade of red that encircled his eyes from the lack of sleep and his earlier sobbing breakdown. He felt like shit and he knew he looked it too. He refused to speak anymore with anyone at the station, even Tom. He surmised it was Tom who called his father or his father contacted the police station when his arrest was plastered on national news.

The price of infamy had taken its toll. Jeremy was a basket case and Mandy had refused his petitions. His only desire was to tell them the truth.

Now Sarah was sitting on the end of the interrogation table trying to goad him into doing a tell-all story. What was there to tell? He had already given his side of a lopsided story. It appeared on all accounts that he was the guilty party, but they had no hard evidence to convict him. Ballistics hadn't come back with the testing on his 9mm Glock. He knew it would pass. It hadn't been fired in the last two weeks. The last time he used it, Tom was with him at the NYPD target range. He had cleaned it right afterwards as he always did. That's when he shot off his big mouth about Mandy-Candy and her Italian stallion beau. God, why didn't he just keep his mouth shut? Sometimes he was his own worst enemy. He knew Tom believed him, but he wasn't in love with Tom. It was Mandy's faith in him that was shattered.

"So, aren't you going to ask me about Rich?" Sarah prodded.

Kurt sat back and stretched long legs onto the table crossing them at the ankles. His bruised and gauzed wrapped hands were clasped below his waistline, "So, how is that Son-of-a-bitch?"

"Whoa, I'm sensing animosity?"

"Yeah, you bet. That Bastard set me up. He forced me to take Amanda home after the Yacht party. And he set up the meeting with the anonymous informant at *The Tavern*, so I don't have a fucking alibi or a chance in Hell of being released, so I can find the guy. My luck they'll drag his ass out of the Hudson River. So, if that sounds like animosity then you're damn right."

"Well then," she said and paced behind him. With her long thin hands she did a deep pressure massage on his tired tense shoulders. Kurt leaned into it. His carnal senses enjoyed a woman's touch when he was stressed. He cracked his neck, then tightened and released his shoulders. "Relax and listen up," Sarah whispered into his ear, not helping by rekindling his neediness for sex.

A hard neediness he felt ever since Amanda returned his ardent kisses at her door, but refused him. Before he got too involved with Sarah, he plopped his feet down and leaned forward resting his head in his hands. "Sarah stop!"

"Kurt, listen to me, Rich is out cold. His jaw is wired shut, so even if he wanted to disclose the informant to the police, he is in no condition. So, you'll have to sit tight until things clear; if in fact they do. If you would have just gone home and slept off your drunk instead of boasting your conquest to Amanda's boyfriend maybe you wouldn't be in this situation. Maybe if you had listened to me about quitting the booze or at least tapering off, you'd be in a better situation with Amanda and not here for first degree murder."

"Thanks mom for that rendition of 'I told you so'." Kurt's sarcasm swelled, he lifted his head. "Better yet, since we're telling half-truths and fairytales, maybe if you and Rich didn't hire Mandy, I wouldn't have fallen for her. And Antonio and I could have been best friends. I liked Antonio. I wouldn't do anything to hurt him even though he almost ruined my career. He met Amanda at the right place and right time. Those things happened, and I happened to be in the wrong place at the wrong time." He slammed his hand on the table. "Fuck me. If Mandy would have just let me spend the night, none of this would have happened–end of story."

"Wow, I'm impressed. You did pursue her after all."

His fidgeting hands raked his wayward hair. "Did you think I wouldn't?"

"No I guess not, I forget you're not the type to take no for an answer or succumb to a challenge. Anyway your father will be here soon. How do you feel about that?"

"Numb, I don't feel a damn thing," he confessed. "I'm thirty years old and my life is over because of your rapacious husband. My so called friend, that bastard set me up."

"Kurt, listen to yourself, why would Rich do that? The only thing he wanted to do was increase our ratings."

"What? Ruin my life to increase the ratings. I think that's a bit vindictive. And didn't you look at the photos I sent you? He's had a thing for Mandy ever since he hired her. He has motive too. Damn, I've heard love is blind, but for crying out loud is it stupid too."

"Oh, look who's talking Mr. Loverboy, have you forgotten why you went to boast to the bartender after midnight." She puffed her cigarette agitated by his verbal abuse.

"Well, love is a contagious sickness. And I loathe sick people, so leave me alone." He sunk his head on top of his folded arms hiding his face.

She patted his back. "Kurt this is just a bad day. Things will get better. It could be worse you could be in the hospital with your mouth wired shut."

Not lifting his head his words were muffled, "Yeah, I've been trapped in a fucking bad day for the last five months." Sitting back he slouched in his chair, "You're seriously telling me being in the hospital with a broken jaw is worse than going to prison for life. Hmm... somehow I'm not buying that. I'm tired. I need a leave of absence from my life. I need a fucking vacation, so I can drown in self-pity."

Just as Kurt finished his sulking spiel, his father, bolted through the door. The Chicago Commissioner Keith Kilawee stride was long and sure, he hugged Sarah first, and then pulled Kurt to his feet. The tall sturdy man, built larger than Kurt, folded Kurt into his protective arms.

Kurt felt like a little boy again. He felt tears sting his dry eyes. They were desiccated after tears shed for Antonio and Amanda.

He had never seen his father so torn. Flooded with emotion father and son clutched each other. It was almost six months since they'd last seen each other. Kurt had visited Chicago for his Mother's birthday. A lot had happened in the time spent a part.

Sarah slipped out quietly allowing them privacy.

Kurt's voice trembled, he held back man tears. "Dad, I'm sorry I've made a mess of things. But I didn't kill anyone. I swear I would never do that. You do believe me, Dad? I would never harm anyone. Not like that– not murder."

"Your mom and I know you wouldn't commit such a heinous crime, but a crime of passion doesn't look promising. Knocking your boss out and breaking his jaw on national TV didn't help." He pulled away to look Kurt in the eyes. The same similar watery emerald eyes and the same crooked grin challenged him. "You look like hell. It's a good thing I left your mother at home. I spoke at length with Tom. He said you don't have an alibi, and you have a strong motive–the love of a woman? It's that Midwestern Anchorwoman–right?"

Kurt rubbed his head and gave a sheepish grin, "Yeah, Amanda Lindas. I suppose I'm pretty transparent when it comes to her, but I wouldn't shoot her boyfriend and think I could have her too. I am halfway sane. At least I think I am. I'm ashamed to bring you into this, but you have to talk to Jeremy for me." Kurt's eyes widened signaling to his father it was impertinent that he go see Jeremy.

Just as his father was about to question him, Tom McCarthy walked in. His uncapped flaming orange hair and bright blue eyes reminded Kurt of when they were younger and going through the academy together. He tossed Kurt's fedora to him.

Tom did the half-hug handshake with Kurt's father, "Hey Commish, flight okay? So what do you think of your wayward pretty boy?" he chortled to ease the tension in the holding room.

A relieved Keith Kilawee patted Kurt's shoulder, "Well, he's not so pretty right now, but they tell me he still cleans up pretty, for the ladies. You have good news I hope?" Slight traces of worry lingered on Tom's face.

Kurt perked up hoping for a slice of good news and maybe the promise of food that he declined earlier while he felt the gut ripping turmoil of dry heaves. "Well, are the ballistic tests complete?"

"Yes, and of course you didn't use your own weapon. That's all it proves, unfortunately. Your love triangle motive is still the hot topic. Kind of funny you always the ladies man and never fall for one woman and here you sit. I figured if you ever got bit by the love-bug it would be fatal. Did she talk to you?" Tom fought back a snicker.

"Ha ha ha, at least someone is enjoying my shitty life. Did you see her? Was she here?" Kurt went from hopeful to helpless instantly.

Tom cleared his throat, "Umm... yeah she was brought in for questioning about you and her and the victim. I thought for sure she'd stop to see you."

Nervous all over again, Kurt paced, "Yeah, I'm sure she came by and looked through the fucking looking glass, like I am a crazed monkey in a cage. Or a fucking lunatic." He slammed his opened palms on the two-way glass mirror. As soon as he did, he knew he had crossed the line of police etiquette. His father and Tom immediately took hold of each arm. In a stronghold they escorted him to the chair that kept him company for the last six hours.

"Come on Kurt we don't like this anymore than you do, knock it off or I'll be forced to cuff you again." Tom reprimanded.

"Again, cuffed again?" Keith yelled and smacked Kurt on the shoulder with an open hand. "Really? What part of obeying the law don't you understand son? It seems–I've failed with you."

Kurt retracted gripping his sore shoulder, "Really Dad? Police brutality?" He looked to McCarthy for sympathy, and received a smirk. "My life is not your failure–it's all mine. I'm thirty years old, not a teenager. You don't have to treat me like a punk kid."

Rage peaked; Keith slammed a tight fist on the table, "Then act like a man and start taking this seriously. You're a trained detective. If you were any good you'd be figuring a way to prove your innocence instead of worrying about what some woman thinks you look like."

Humiliated and humbled, Kurt rubbed his face, "I know, I know, God, I know… This has never happened to me before. Go speak to Jeremy, first, and then go to the hospital. As soon as Rich is coherent make him write down the informant's name. That's my alibi; get him to clear my name. Get me out of this fucking joint. I'm tired, I'm hungry, and I need a shower." Kurt buried his face into his crossed arms on the table again, totally conceding.

The heavy emotional strain between father and son was mortifying to witness. Tom left leaving them to mend their fences.

Keith put his hand on Kurt's shoulder, "I'm sorry son. I'll get the information. We'll have you out soon, I promise."

Chapter 12

A week and a half later Amanda dressed in a slimming Coco Chanel black sheath dress covered with a sheer duster. The October rain drizzled down the dusty pane of her apartment window adding gloom to her already dreadful day. The inevitable was happening today.

Today was Antonio's funeral.

She waited patiently for Belinda to come across the hall to announce Jeremy's arrival. They were riding together to St. Paul's Chapel at Columbia University. A place where she had spent many afternoons sharing Antonio Casali's life, now she was obligated to share in his death.

Via a carrier, she received the memorial card, hand delivered and hand written requesting her attendance. Grief and guilt inundated her, not only towards Antonio, but also towards Kurt.

She had refused Kurt's invasive calls; even after he sent a beautiful bouquet of white roses, a Hall & Oats tape with a note of apology. A note filled with sincere remorse for his irrevocable actions. On the bottom he wrote "One on One"– *Love Kurt.*

Love Kurt, Love Kurt– LOVE KURT!! That was ridiculous. What the hell–she couldn't love him! She hated him! Not that she blamed him for Tony's death. But if spirits carry memories to the next world, then Tony's last memory was she willingly kissed his arch enemy. How could she ever live that down in this lifetime or the next?

Knowing Kurt he put a little more detail and flamboyance into his boastful confession, as he habitually did in his news stories. It was his intrinsic nature to twist the truth; a leitmotif of his writing and reporting style.

The other disturbing incidents that rocked her core were that Kurt made front page news when he was accused of the murder, and then again when he was acquitted and released with the help of his super-hero father, the Chicago Police Commissioner. Antonio's story not fully disclosed or properly told was second and third page news. Antonio deserved better. Amanda was resolved to find the truth about his untimely cruel death.

But first she had to get through today.

Her mother had called everyday begging to visit. She suggested she would take a leave of absence for an extended period to help her daughter grieve. Besides that, she was sick of Chicago's Society drama. New York would be a welcomed change of scenery. Amanda remained adamant about coping with this tragedy with her New York family. Having her meddling mother intervene between her and Kurt was not going to happen. She wasn't sure if there would ever be a Kurt and Amanda anyway.

Belinda arrived decked out in black lace leggings, black leather mini, and a slashed up black lace top, with all the bling of a true-to-herself rocker. Amanda clutched her black trench coat slung over the red sofa. Arm in arm they tottered in their heels somberly to the elevator.

At St. Paul's Chapel on Columbia University campus, Jeremy parked the van in the procession line for the gravesite– Trinity Church Cemetery off Broadway and Riverside. The same churchyard, James John Audubon was laid to rest on his old Estate. She knew of the history because Antonio had taken her on extensive West Side tours, Washington Heights, and Harlem. Yet he never took her home to meet his mom at The Apthorp. A prestigious complex on Broadway sandwiched between 78th and 79th Streets where his mother still lived. Antonio loved New York and its history. He had plans to be a part of New York's future. What a merciless thing fate can be. But was it fate or just rotten luck?

At the chapel, she spied Kurt in a black trench coat and his signature black fedora. His hands shoved deep in his pockets and his head hung low. He walked behind Rich and Sarah. She and Belinda flanked Jeremy as he encouraged them to lean on him. He posed as a pillar of strength escorting them into St. Paul's Chapel.

The chapel was styled in Northern Italian Renaissance Architecture adapted by the architect Stokes. Its façade clad in redbrick and limestone complemented the other campus buildings. Amanda stopped momentarily to breathe deep as she gazed up at the green ceramic tiled dome appropriately crowned with a terracotta lantern–a welcoming beacon.

The columned portico of the visitor's entrance was familiar. She and Tony had attended the mediation services on several Tuesday afternoons. Her memory flashed back to the first time she was captured by the beauty of the carved cherubs atop the columns. Tony explained with the excitement of a scholarly boy how he discovered that they were sculpted by Gutzon Borglum. The famed sculptor had sculpted the faces of Mount Rushmore. She marveled at the marble inlaid floors and the salmon colored roman bricks intricately designed in a herringbone pattern on the vaulted ceiling and dome. Somehow it all seemed so surreal, like maybe Tony's love for this place and its Italian splendor was ominous of his departure.

DESIRE FOR TRUTH

With a simple nod of acknowledgment; Jeremy shuffled them past Kurt. Amanda held them back under the Columbia motto carved above the central entrance laced by ornamental grape vines. She whispered the motto to Belinda and Jeremy, "*In Lumine Tuo Videbimus Lumen*," she paused. "In Thy light shall we see light. Antonio believed that. It was an intricate part of his philosophy; his love and addiction to knowledge was infectious and pure..." Very much like her addiction to truth. Tears rolled softly down her cheeks, knowing she would never hear his voice again.

They proceeded down the aisle between the dark wood chairs; there were no pews typical of other churches. The chairs were filled with a myriad of mourners. With the exception of the front row reserved for the immediate family. Much to her bewilderment, they remained empty. She caught sight of the closed mahogany and silver coffin centered under the ninety-one foot dome. A closed casket ceremony was essential. Her throat tightened causing her to gasp when she realized the casket was covered with a splendid array of white roses. Roses too similar to the ones Kurt had sent to her.

Jeremy wrapped his arm around her shoulders giving her more support. Her instructions from the carrier's note asked that she sit in the second row reserved for his closest and dearest friends.

She lowered the lace veil of her pillbox hat to cover her face in honor, but also in shame. She was masquerading as a trusted girlfriend. Sorrowful shadows filled the chapel; the sixteen arched windows that circled the dome exposed dreary drizzle as if the angels were shedding tears.

Kurt positioned himself a safe distance across the center aisle to the right and back two rows to capture a view of Amanda, the "would be" widow. That's how he saw her, had he not meddled in their relationship she wouldn't have been just a stand in widow–she could have easily become Antonio's bride. Her face covered demurely with a lace veil; of course she looked stylish elegantly dressed in a sheer coverlet. His amorous mind drifted to the memory of her provocative slit skirt exposing her upper thigh and tapering down to the five-inch *F*me* shoes. A passionate heat rushed to his cheeks.

Oh shit, sorry God, he thought brushing his feathered bangs from his eyes. He tried to brush away his pithy thoughts.

Leave it to him to shame his Irish-Catholic ancestors in front of God. But God knew this wasn't his first time committing sacrilege. After his carnal desire subsided, he thanked God no one could read his mind.

With Rich and Sarah sitting next to him; he fidgeted with his hair, his hat, trying unsuccessfully to obtain a comfortable seating position for his lanky form on the hard chair. His escorts were along primarily to keep him under surveillance, rather than supporting Amanda's tragic loss.

God, how he wanted to sit close to her, to hold her soft hand, and kiss her salty sultry tears to help alleviate her sorrow. Admittedly Jeremy was an excellent proxy. Jeremy was his rock during his incarceration and the buffer between his father and him while his innocence was arduously proven. Although, he was released from the guilt of murder by the physical facts, he was haunted with emotional guilt of his actions and his last gloating words to Antonio. That moment of joy was ephemeral. Unabashedly he cherish every second of that night with her.

Now, he gazed upon her with pangs of remorse and spasms of hopeful redemption. His focus switched from Mandy to the front row of empty chairs. Where was Antonio Casali's mother, Anna Marie Casali? Was she afraid of retaliation from his killers? Did she know who had executed her only son? His brain hurt trying to remember where Tom said she lived. Maybe he could redeem his guilty soul by giving her the satisfaction of bringing her son's murderer to justice. Where was Anna now?

The priest called out, "peace be with you."

And along with the other mourners Kurt chanted, "And also with you." He rang true to his Catholic roots, but the last time he had graced the inside of a church was last Easter around his mother's birthday. He was tempted to relieve his guilt by attending a confession, but he knew a priest would have to take a year sabbatical after reproaching him on his sin filled life. *Hell*, he risked getting slapped through the wooden confessional mesh for all the sins he had committed since his last confession. *Heck,* he'd be saying the "Hail Marys" and "Our Fathers" into his next life.

The magnificent ethereal music from the impressive pipe organ filtered ghostly through the somber chapel with an Italian love song. The priest began the mass reminding Amanda of the last funeral she had attended at Easter, her grandmother on her mother's side. It was the embodiment of grandeur, but also an appropriate display of her grandmother's altruism. Her grandmother embraced spirituality in life as did Antonio. Amanda couldn't help but shed fresh tears for her too.

As the Father sang the last verse of a beautiful farewell blessing the bronze bell knelled to the University and community that the service had come to an end. Amanda wept. She remembered Tony saying the bronze bell was inscribed with: *"To Ring Out Through the Ages for Truth, Justice, and Liberty"*.

The words convicted her. In dedication to his memory, she would search for truth and find the man or men responsible for his malicious murder. He deserved justice, so his soul could have peace and liberty.

She would right the wrongs that were printed about Antonio Casali's involvement in the Mafia.

Amanda refused to believe that he had any connection to the mob. Kurt was released based upon Rich's forced testimony, and the murder weapon was found with a history connecting it to the mob "made men" whose bodies were pulled from the East River. Suspects were aplenty, but no names were released. The culprits wouldn't be brought before a judge for almost a year, or more. This was the only closure she would get. Guilt and shame still imprisoned her heart and mind.

After the church service she and Jeremy followed behind the rest of the NYCB news crew. Belinda stayed behind with some of Tony's college buddies. The congregation was asked to exit to the right side of the Chapel–that request relayed by the Priest from Anna Marie Casali.

The rain had subsided, but the chill of the day still lingered. Amanda wrapped herself tighter in her black trench coat, trying to squeeze the shivers out of her body. Today was her first day outside in over a week; she shunned Rich and Kurt.

Many of the mourners stopped to express their condolences in front of Rodin's magnificent bronze sculpture– *The Thinker* positioned in a courtyard just past a small grove of Chestnut trees.

Many questioned how a beautiful person filled with promise, love, and knowledge was senselessly gunned down in the prime of his life.

Several cars lined Amsterdam Avenue, directly behind the stately black hearse. Rich's metallic-gray Cadillac was one of many. It was rarely outside of his parking garage. Amanda was puzzled by Sarah and Rich's attendance. A bartender's funeral doesn't qualify as a work event. Or did it? Was Rich really that attached to his favorite bartender?

Something peculiar stirred her emotions towards Rich. In a conundrum she noted he was unnaturally detached since the incident. She was relieved Rich and Sarah insisted that Kurt ride with them to the gravesite. And what was Kurt's deal? Why was he so interested in the outcome now? His father cleared his name and made him into a martyr–a special human interest story. "The Super-Hero to the Rescue."

It was obvious who Kurt had inherited his edgy good looks from and his Super-Hero complex– "I'm God worship me" attitude. Supreme ruggedness exuded from his father. The opportunity to witness their relationship came when she was brought in for questioning. She felt pity for Kurt in his disheveled state, but not for Rich and his bruised swollen face. Something about Rich and Kurt just peeved her. They were back to being buddies after Kurt shattered Rich's jaw and blatantly accused him of depravity. Her inquisitive mind wouldn't let her grieve in peace.

Jeremy touched her gently on the shoulder, "Hey, you doing okay? You know no one could blame you if you decided not to attend the burial. We could just go on to *The Tavern*."

Amanda turned her eyes from *The Thinker* and responded. "I'm fine. I want to go. Tony..." her voice cracked. "Tony would want me there. I have to... to say goodbye." Her eyes glistened with tears.

"Okay, I just want you to know, we are here for you."

She believed his sincerity. She even let herself believe that the travesty of Kurt's attendance wasn't about him getting ahead of her on a story. What story? She had no leads. Did he?

The NYCB van was parked several cars behind the Cadillac. Jeremy sat upright and uptight in the driver seat. They followed close on Amsterdam Ave. all the way to West 153rd taking a left towards Broadway. They turned right onto Broadway and entered the Trinity Church Cemetery. The gravesite was located just behind the grand Gothic Tudor styled Episcopal Church. Amanda marveled at it. It looked like something out of a frightening fairytale.

No sooner had Rich parked his car, when Kurt jumped out. Even before Jeremy had the van in park, Kurt was at her passenger side door. He reached in for her hand, slipped it through the crook of his arm and escorted her to the gravesite naturally as if he were her guardian or husband. He was awfully clingy in a suspicious way. Was he trying to help or just getting his picture in the tabloids?

The paparazzi cameramen were everywhere. Kurt immediately folded her into his hard chest keeping her face hidden from the flashes using his coat as a shield. Tired of playing the tough-girl, she welcomed his protection. Without words Kurt pushed the whoremonger photographers away with one outstretched arm.

The priest stood at the gravesite as the pallbearers placed the mahogany coffin gently on the accordion rack and rolled it into place. Other mourners gathered sporadically around in small hovering groups. Some whom she had met were Antonio's college friends. Others loomed eerily as dark silhouetted strangers. She scanned the churchyard searching for Anna Casali, even though they had never met. Perhaps one of the many strangers was Antonio's father, whom he had never known.

Kurt steadied her from behind keeping her warm; his towering height blocked the loathsome scandal paper photographers from getting more pictures. None of them stood out more than the others.

The priest began, "Our Father who art in Heaven," his words drizzled like the soft rain. Kurt pulled a small black umbrella from his side pocket to cover them. It was then that she observed a slender tall woman with a man under a large red-leafed maple tree. The man dressed in a chauffeur's uniform popped open an umbrella protecting the woman. The sleek woman wore a long black wool jacket and a large brimmed veiled hat. Under the veil her black gloved hands blotted her eyes with a handkerchief. It seemed odd that they stood nearly twenty yards away, yet attentive to the funeral service.

There was a refined elegance about the woman, melancholy dwelled as she leaned into her escort. Frail, but not elderly like a grandmother, she must be Antonio's mother or possibly an aunt.

He rarely spoke of family. Even after months of dating, she had met a few of his closest friends. Did his extended family even know? They must have, the funeral was more than average. Although she knew he was Catholic, they never discussed his connection or conviction to the Church. The Father spoke kindly, but not familiar of him. No specific details of his life were shared.

"Dust to dust, ashes to ashes..." The priest finished the ceremony as the rain increased to a frantic downpour. The pallbearers were quick to cover the coffin with a blue tarp.

That was it. No one shared his life story or his accomplishments. He deserved more. Her chest cinched with sadness. What if Antonio was her soul mate and now he was gone forever? What could she say? What does anyone really know about another person? A life struck down at a tender age should have a kind eulogy from a loved one, what a shame.

"Peace be with you." The father shouted over the pounding rain.

Kurt murmured, "And also with you." He switched the umbrella to his left hand to sign the cross with his right, and then he hugged her.

Too emotionally distressed to shrug him, Amanda stiffened, her stilettos sunk into the soft ground. Temporarily stuck, Kurt posing as her human shield, held her shoulders tighter, and plucked her up and away from the muddy gravesite. She remained mesmerized by the slender woman being escorted to a black Lincoln. With clouded eyes she strained to see the license through the blur of pouring rain. The tenacious truth seeker in her knew to memorize the numbers.

Needy for the truth, she instinctively discerned that the mysterious woman could shed light on Antonio Casali's life and tragic death. In her mind she pieced together what she had to do for peace.

She wanted vengeance. She vowed to tell Antonio's real story. She would not be at peace until the truth was told.

Kurt shuffled her towards Rich's car. Jeremy and Sarah tried to dissuade him, but he was inflexible. His gait was sturdy and swift, his arm wrapped her waist nearly lifting her off her feet. Jeremy looked at Kurt dumbfounded.

Opening the back passenger door closest to the curb, Kurt directed Amanda into the seat. Quickly he went to the street side door and regained his place by her side. Sarah and Rich got in. No one spoke on the drive to Central Park West and 67th Street.

Kurt coddled her like a baby. Amanda felt secure in his arms, but wondered why so protective–so fatherly. She gazed admiringly up at him trying to understand his actions. It was all so awkwardly intimate.

They arrived at *The Tavern on the Green*, her emotional wall burst. The flashback of the gruesome murder, Kurt shackled, and Rich laid out cold. "Oh no," she sobbed.

Kurt hugged her, "Rich, Sarah, give us a moment." They obligingly got out. He smoothed her face with his gloved hand. "You don't have to go in. It's been a long hard week and I know you're emotionally exhausted. I'll take you home. We can talk about everything." Sincerity reflected deep in his serious emerald eyes.

Tears seeped from the corners of her eyes. She sniffled. Her heart beat like a frightened bird in a cage. She recognized his desperate wanting. He was trying so hard, but she couldn't give him the satisfaction. "We cannot start where we left off on that horrid night."

With gloved fingertips, he brushed her tears. At that moment he wanted her warm trembling lips on his. He wanted to take the pain from her heart, but her icy eyes said–don't. He retracted. Shaking internally, he stringently controlled every ounce of his strength not to crush her to his heart.

Rich rapped on the tinted window.

Jeremy went further and opened her door, "Come on Mandy, I'll take you in, and I'll get you home safe." He shook his head at Kurt disciplining with his stern eyes as only a best friend could. "Let's go." Jeremy helped her out slowly.

She overheard Rich reprimand Kurt. With his jaw wired he sounded like a dog growling.

Once inside the tavern, the atmosphere switched up to lighthearted jovial conversations, just like it was when Tony tended bar. A celebration of life party was exactly what he would have wanted. Gus had a marvelous display of food and drink in the crystal room. It was magical. Amanda examined the crowd looking for the slender woman.

Kurt was behind her in a second, scoping the room intently as he removed his damp coat and helped by removing hers. He took it without a word like a personal valet and checked them with his fedora at the coat check. Then he brought her a chilled glass of Chardonnay. All the while, Jeremy and Belinda hovered close with suspicion.

Amanda accepted the wine cordially, but sincerely wanted him to stop catering to her like she was royalty. Or acting like a mother duck gathering her lost duckling, he was rigorous.

After a few sips of wine, she finally spoke, "Kurt, what are you doing? Why are you being so attentive? You're making a scene and making me nervous." She said noticing he wasn't drinking. Seriously something was awry.

Mute, he collected his thoughts.

"I'm sorry. I just want to help…" he choked on his words. "I am so sorry for everything."

"I know. As you should be, but... I need my space right now. Okay?" She stated matter-of-factly. "What has happened will not undo itself overnight."

He scratched his head; thinking of how he could stay close to her. Crossing his arms over his chest, he relented, "Okay, I am going over there," he pointed towards Jeremy. "But if you need me, I won't be far."

His hesitation to leave her side was creepy. She nodded slowly releasing him.

He backed away scanning the room like a cop looking for a suspect.

"What is your problem man?" Jeremy scolded, "You're acting like a slightly retarded cat chasing an invisible mouse. Cool it, stop scaring Mandy. And me."

Kurt fidgeted putting his hands in his front pockets, he jingled his change. He shifted from foot to foot then leaned over and whispered into Jeremy's ear, "Something is not right. I feel we're being watched. As soon as we left the chapel, I felt it. I don't think we're safe."

"Dude you're just being paranoid. Why don't you have a drink in your hand? What's up with you? You're making me nervous."

Kurt continued to survey the crowd. Amanda was less than twenty paces away, but she was awfully friendly with Tony's college buddies making Kurt all the more anxious; for his heart. What he didn't want was her to start dating any of them. He saw her wine glass half empty, so he went to the portable bar and picked up another for her and a club soda with lime for himself. He slipped in behind her close enough to inhale her sweet perfume.

Without a formal introduction he interrupted the conversation with a low tone, "Hi Sweetheart," he bent slightly and placed a firm territorial kiss on her cheek. "Here's a fresh drink. Did you get anything to eat? I see you're wasting away to nothing and we can't have that–can we?" He exchanged her half empty glass with a full one.

Shock written clearly on her face, Amanda flashed a disgruntled look at Jeremy. The other men backed away giving Kurt the space his presence demanded. His height, stature, and persona exuded undeniable alpha-male dominance. He extended his right hand and shook hands while expressing sincere sympathy for their loss.

She flagged Jeremy over to yank Kurt away.

Jeremy and Belinda joined the group with the intent of getting the attention off Kurt and onto Belinda.

"Come with me, you look hungry." Jeremy clasped and tugged Kurt's elbow splashing his tightfisted club soda.

Kurt wrapped his arm around Amanda pulling her with leaving Belinda behind to entertain the black suits. "She looks hungry too, she's coming with us."

"What are you doing Kurt? That was so rude." Amanda twisted out of his clutches. Nonchalant he sipped his club soda. "And what are you drinking?"

He grinned and toasted, "Just club soda with lime, honey."

Jeremy and Amanda both reached for the glass refusing to believe him. He lifted it to their noses individually allowing them to sniff.

"See, you two need to start trusting me. I haven't had a drink since," he gulped. "Since that night," he squelched his emotion that traveled from his gut to his face by drinking his club soda dry. He furrowed his hair to avoid eye contact with them.

"Wow, man, I'm sorry, but you're acting weird even for you. Are you sure you're not on something?" Jeremy inquired seriously.

Kurt's hands fastened to his hips, "I can't believe you just said that. Were you not with me the last couple of days? What the hell do I have to do to prove to you both that I am not the ass you think I am? I do have feelings, just in case you're interested." Visibly upset, his glare shifted between them.

Amanda sipped her wine. Dumbfounded by his declaration, she didn't have a response. This man was not the Kurt Kilawee she knew.

Jeremy cast his eyes to the floor, then up again. "Well, you must be going through withdrawals, 'cause you're a spazz." He eyed Kurt, "Let me see, maybe it's the painkillers they gave you for your busted hand from hitting Rich?" Then he spanned the room, "Speaking of which, where is our tight jawed boss?"

In a quandary on the couple's whereabouts, they all checked the room, thinking it strange that Rich or Sarah had not spoken to them.

Kurt put a hand on Jeremy's shoulder and the other on Mandy's, "You two get something to eat and start thinking of good things to say to me, try words that sound like an apology. I'm going outside to have a cigarette.

Save me some shrimp and salad." He gave Amanda another peck on the cheek.

"A cigarette?" Jeremy and Mandy said in unison.

"Come on, cut me some slack. I've given up drinking, clubs, and women. I've got to be bad in some area of my life, or people will follow me expecting me to feed the masses with fish and bread. Damn you two are tough." With extra drama he flicked his hair and sauntered out the front entrance hoping for insight to appease the intuition eating his gut.

Outside he slipped from under the red awning and took cover near a large tree wrapped in white twinkle lights. In the shadow of dusk, he lit a cigarette and panned the area. The horse drawn carriages were still doing the tourists' rounds giving him more camouflage. *Where did that bastard go?* The Cadillac was still parked where they left it earlier. Why would Sarah not hang inside? Oh, she could be in the ladies room. He took a long drag off his cigarette when he noticed three men and a female walking toward *The Tavern* from the right. His gut was spot on.

It was Rich and Sarah, but who were the two men? And why have a meeting after a high profile funeral? Kurt leaned back on the tree contemplating his next move. He waited to see if the men were mourners or just informants that Rich stirred from the bottom of the cesspool. Lately Rich had a bad habit of doing things out of the norm.

Kurt squinted to make out the facial features to see if he knew them from other encounters. One was close to a head taller than Rich which made him six-three to six-five. The other slightly shorter one, probably five-eight, he had an obvious scar on his upper left cheek. Both were Caucasian, he gathered from the glowing light that fused through the glass enclosed garden room.

Kurt finished his cigarette wishing he could have a drink and a woman instead, but he had to be on his game and those vices were off limits until he solved this case. Then he could reward himself with a stiff drink and a fine woman. And Amanda Lindas was first on his list of things to do. He smiled to himself at her compliance of allowing him to hold her and kiss her in public.

Rich opened the Cadillac trunk handing a package to the linebacker sized thug. Sarah was timidly standing watch. What were they up too? It looked like a payoff, but for what? Kurt waited on the sly.

Just as Rich and Sarah moved under the red canopy entrance, the men disappeared like vapor.

With his long stride Kurt easily caught up to Rich and Sarah; he stole his way between them. "Hey, I've been looking for you two. I wanted to let you know I will be getting a ride home from Jeremy. Where have you been? We've missed you." One arm around Rich's shoulders the other stronghold on Sarah's. "Come let's share the good news with Jeremy and Mandy." He brought them straight to the crystal dining area where a NYCB group had gathered.

"Hey look what the slightly retarded cat just dragged in." Kurt said and patted them on the back like good sports. He shared his best boyish grin, without rumination. "So Jeremy, I just told Rich and Sarah that I will be getting a ride home with you tonight."

Jeremy stood to protest until he saw Kurt's dire look. "Oh sure thing," he said and picked up a chair. "Here Sarah, you don't look so good, you okay?"

Her trembling hand touched her perspiring forehead, "Ah yeah, I guess, I don't feel well. It's been a long day. Kurt will you be a dear and get me a scotch on the rocks." She displayed a faint smile and a knowing look in her eyes.

"Sure, can I get anyone else a drink?" he slapped Rich on the back hard, "How about you old man? I'll bring you a drink with a straw. How's that grab you?"

Rich sneered at him. Then through his teeth he drawled, "No. Thanks."

The tension stretched like a taut rubber band on the verge of snapping.

Kurt strutted like the master of ceremony–the toastmaster, he cheerfully added his natural pizzazz, "Here's to celebrating a man, I truly admired." *Especially his taste in women.*

Later that evening, after they dropped Amanda and Belinda home, Kurt felt apprehensive about their safety. "Jeremy, do you think we should go back and stay with them?"

Jeremy laughed. "You just don't quit. You haven't given up on all chicks; you still have the hots for Mandy. You aren't fooling anyone but yourself."

"No, I mean, yes I still got it going on for her. But something just feels wrong. There were two thugs with Rich and Sarah, and someone was burning a hole through us at the Trinity Church, I feel something, but I can't decipher it."

"Man you have your bloodhound instinct back. Maybe you turning into a Saint convinced God to give your gift back. I saw you doing your Catholic thing at the funeral. You're still spooked because maybe that bullet was meant for you?"

"I told you, not to say that out loud." Kurt stewed with his emotions. "Turn around, we have to go back and get the girls. I'd feel better if they stayed at my apartment."

Jeremy took the first U-turn he could, "Yeah, I'll bet you'd feel all warm and cozy with Mandy in your apartment. Don't you mean bed?" a snicker fled his full lips. "She won't fall for it. And besides, you need your sleep or did you forget you're still the face of NYCB? I hear you snagged a big bonus for all your front page news."

"Damn, I forgot. Mandy won't be back for another couple of days. Shit! How am I going to protect her and work too? They have to come with us, it's not an option."

"That attitude ain't gonna fly with her. When are you going to realize that?"

"I know, but I can't help but feel responsible for her. Let's just check on them."

They took the shaky elevator to the eleventh floor. Once they stepped off they heard screams. Something hard slammed Kurt's shoulder. Jeremy hit the floor. Kurt tucked, rolled, and popped up quick to his feet. He pulled his Glock from the harness under his coat.

Both girls screamed again and dropped the empty wine bottles they had used as lethal weapons.

Kurt shouted, "Stop! What the fuck?" He winced at the pain shooting through his right shoulder. "What are you two doing?"

Jeremy rubbed his bloody head, he propped up on one elbow trying to stay coherent.

The girls ran and hugged Kurt's waist. He released his shooting stance to wrap his arms around their trembling bodies. "Okay, we're here now. Or at least I'm here. I think you gave Jeremy a concussion. Now what happened? And don't talk over each other." Kurt warned as he walked them towards Amanda's apartment.

He pried the girls off to scrutinize the door. The wood doorjamb had the markings of a crowbar or large screwdriver used to pry open the deadbolt.

Up against the wall, Amanda and Belinda panted heavily. At another time he might have been quite turned on by their fright, but something was seriously awry. Whoever did this knew where Amanda lived and she was their obvious target. "Mandy," his voice stern, "were you both inside your apartment?"

Amanda wheezed, "Yes, we were inside," fearful tears washed her face; she pushed tighter to the wall trying desperately not to faint. With her next breath, she explained, "It happened right after you left. We felt like someone was following us, so we decided to stay together."

"That's good, power in numbers. And?" Kurt prodded.

Belinda chimed in, "Then we locked the door and barricaded it with a chair propped up against the knob."

"Good girls, I'm impressed, you've been watching *Magnum PI?* Did you get a look at them?" The elevator vibrated. Both girls stayed plastered to the wall terrified. Kurt kept his Glock drawn and searched the hall.

"Well, someone answer me." He squatted to check Jeremy lying in a considerable amount of blood. Jeremy was coherent and breathing on his own.

Amanda piped up, "No, when they couldn't get in, they ran."

"Do know for sure how many? I need details not speculations. Did you call the police?" Kurt talked loud as he searched the other side hall.

"Not sure, we went out after we heard them run. It sounded like more than one person." Belinda offered,

"Why didn't you call the police first?" anger fed his words.

"We wanted to see them, so we would have something to tell the police." Amanda said defending their actions.

"Oh, so when we came up the elevator, you thought we were the guys?" He picked up one of the empty wine bottles, "Whose bright idea was this? Don't answer that. Too many cop shows–I gather."

He did a short come-hither wave. "Come here watch Jeremy, stay together, I will call some plain clothes officers and an ambulance. Don't panic, I will leave the door open. Amanda is your phone portable?" She nodded.

Kurt stepped into her apartment the lights were all on–he flicked them off after he found the portable receiver. He figured the men were just a deterrent to scare Amanda off someone's trail. Perhaps she was onto a story and someone was onto her. If they wanted her dead, she would be.

Damn what a close call. Kurt shuddered at the thought of losing her before he had time to admit his feelings for her. If it was love–it sure complicated life.

He finished making the calls by the door. The girls shivered in the cold hallway. Clad with only short shorts and T-shirts, Kurt couldn't help but notice they were perky where most men, including him, fancied it. "You two get covered. I can see you're chilled." His eyes flickered to their breasts. Both girls immediately covered themselves and turned on their heels to their respective apartments. He called after them, "Keep the lights off and hurry up." He squatted to help Jeremy.

Amanda peeked out her door, "Who coronated you the King?"

Kurt stood and stepped into her space-bubble, nearly breathing down her neck, "Now listen, do you have a gun?" Amanda shook her head. He stepped closer. Her eyes strained upwards to meet his fixed stare. "Do you have a badge?" he asked. She shook her head again.

He took her hand and placed it on his flexed bicep and squeezed it into his forearm muscle. "Are your muscles as developed as mine?"

Her angry gaze turned into a humbled eyelash flutter. His chest cinched and his breath hinged at her flirtatiousness. Still controlled he blew out a slow whoosh of air. "Then I suggest you get your pretty ass covered before anyone else gets a gander of it. Do we understand each other?" Willfully she moved backwards, unwilling to expose her behind to his gander again.

The undercover cops arrived, took their stories, and photos of the damages. Jeremy refused the paramedics suggestion to go to the hospital, they warned him if he started vomiting to get to a hospital. Before leaving they instructed them to keep him awake a few hours just in case. The night was still young.

The detectives suggested the girls to stay at a friend's house. Kurt, of course, offered his place and protection. And with the same breath he asked the police to investigate his place eliminating any possibility of undesirables lurking there.

The plain clothes cops left and reported back–all clear.

Kurt instructed, "Girls go get your toiletries and a change of clothes. Keep the lights off!" This time, there was no rebuttal against his authority.

Chapter 13

Relieved that his place was secured, Kurt drove his unexpected guests in the NYCB van to his apartment off Lexington and East 33rd. He had not driven in a long time other than the new Mercedes that Rich had him select and store for an eventual mistress gift to Amanda. That thought still turned his stomach.

Yes, everything in his life was borderline insane like him driving a van in Manhattan traffic. In a gruesome weird way Antonio's murder created a needed separation from work, women, drinking, and clubs. While under house arrest, he bonded with Jeremy decorating his bachelor pad and working out in the basement gym. Fate can give you a break you didn't know you needed or even deserved.

Still on the side of caution the men huddled Amanda and Belinda between their protective body shields as they walked up the cement steps to Kurt's place. Secretly Amanda was amused like acting in a scary crime movie, but also petrified because this was real. Anxious to finally see Kurt's place, she wished it was under better circumstances. The added benefits were safety and escaping her dreary apartment.

Kurt unlocked the door, turning only the dimmer on; he revealed a modern, yet slightly traditional bachelor pad. Her eyes expanded with unexpected delight. It was no surprise his pad reflected him. Bold blacks, rich browns with accents of tan and splashes of red, amazingly well put together with the dark wood trim and exposed redbrick walls. The floor plan was an enlarged version of her place.

"So who's your decorator?" she said drawing a finger across the black granite breakfast bar.

"I had some expert help from my pal, Jeremy." Kurt palmed Jeremy's shoulder.

Jeremy sheepishly grinned. "It's a gift and a curse."

Kurt removed his jacket and motioned to Amanda and Belinda to do the same. Both were still dressed in skimpy PJs. He wanted to say something derogatory about their hearing abilities and lack of following instructions. But he refrained, hung their jackets in the hall closet, and immediately became the thoughtful host. "Anyone hungry? How about something to drink? Sorry no alcohol, you can thank my father and Jeremy for that inconvenience." He rolled his eyes at Jeremy and proceeded to take them on the nickel tour of the living area, den, and kitchen nook.

Belinda's mouth gaped at the luxury, "Wow, for being a dweeb, sometimes, you've got it going on–this place is really bad. It makes mine and Amanda's places look like the projects."

"Coming from you Belinda, I will consider that as a compliment." Kurt said popping open a can of Diet-Coke. He handed it to Amanda knowing it was her favorite, she accepted it exchanging a small smile.

Jeremy looked put out, his empty hand extended expecting Kurt to hand him a soda, but Kurt busied himself with Belinda's soda first.

"Yeah well," Jeremy said, "if you think this is 'bad' wait. The tour includes an ostentatious master bedroom and bath. You ain't seen nothin' yet." He reached into the refrigerator securing his own soda, and shut it before Kurt could grab one. Jeremy's nostrils flared as he glowered.

Kurt elbowed him over, "Ladies first, Lionel. Speaking of which what's going on with your love match?"

Jeremy frowned, "What do you care? It's been all about you these past weeks. I haven't had any time for myself."

Under his breath, his soda covered his lips, Kurt retorted, "Well, it isn't like I planned on getting arrested for murder." He sipped and glanced at the kitchen clock. "Well, it's almost eight, getting late ladies. Let's finish the tour because some of us have to work." Setting his soda down, he habitually pulled out his shirt and proceeded to unbutton it. Casually he removed it as they followed him down the dim hall to his master bedroom. His upper muscular body naturally flexed with his sauntering steps.

Belinda socked Amanda's arm and mouthed *wow*.

Kurt flicked the bedroom light on and then dimmed it. Keeping the apartment dark was primarily for safety since he lived on street level. He tossed his shirt into a basket in his overly organized walk-in closet.

Belinda and Amanda stood astonished by his huge bedroom. They admired the California King waterbed centered against the redbrick wall surrounded by a massive headboard containing a shit load of books, VHS tapes, cassettes, and speakers. They not only gawked at his bed, but were equally mesmerized by his physique as he walked to the headboard turning on the recessed lights and romantic music.

A mind-boggling fantasy thing occurred while he stood next to the bed, half dressed. Both women bit their lower lips. The soft lighting cast a warm glow highlighting his masculine planes.

Amanda's mouth went dry. A familiar twinge fluttered inside, an electric urgency swept through her. More than she had expected. No longer was he thin and pale as she had remembered from his time spent on the gurney at work. Now he was transformed into a tanned Adonis. In her peripheral vision, she realized Belinda had discovered the same proverbial golden calf. Jeremy had left the room unnoticed.

While Kurt demonstrated all the electronic gadgets thinking his knowledge was making an impression on them, he realized they were sizing him up like lionesses salivating at a rare steak.

A loud thump and crash came from the other room. The girls quickly ran and clung to his sides. In all honesty he jumped too. Three hearts racing at paces that could shame a racehorse.

He reached into a small cabinet in the headboard, and slipped out his .38 Special, realizing his dire mistake of leaving the Glock on the kitchen counter top. Amanda and Belinda stayed glued to him.

Amanda felt her heart exploding in her chest. She swore she felt his heart thumping beneath her hand strategically placed on his firm pectoral. Unsure if she was going to faint from fright or melt into a puddle of sexual fantasies, she realized Belinda was exploring further down his six-pack abs. Out of unforeseen jealous instinct, she slapped Belinda's roving hand. Belinda snapped a sharp tap back.

Comprehending the sensual effect he was causing, Kurt attempted to separate them. It had been months since he had the opportunity to be undressed in the company of a woman. Jeremy barged through the door just as Kurt removed the riled grasping nymphs.

Peeved and shirtless, his hands on his hips, Jeremy flexed his bronzy-brown pectorals, and said. "What is going on in here? Does anyone care what happened to Concussion Man in the kitchen?" he rubbed his wounded head.

They all turned various shades of red.

Amanda offered, "Ah, Kurt was just showing us his…"

"I bet he was." Jeremy cut her off.

Kurt remained flustered. This was one occasion that he was innocent.

"Hey, we haven't seen the bathroom, yet." Belinda said trying to unglue their sticky situation.

Jeremy's eyes rolled, "Yeah well, that won't clean this mess up."

Kurt strolled out of his lavish suite leading the way. More puffed up than when his tour began. He had no idea that showing a condo could be so invigorating. No wonder real estate is such a growing prestigious field. He swung the mahogany door open to matching cabinets in the majestic marble clad bath fit for a king and his followers.

Amanda didn't know where to look first. The tall custom cabinets made perfect design sense based on Kurt's height. The rich chocolate marble slab vanities contrasted with the cream and brown checkered accents bordering the shower and wainscots. The bath was certainly befitting a king's taste, but invariably must have cost a king's ransom too. One could not help but feel they were being enchanted by royalty, and hugely underpaid. Mirrors encircled the room reflecting the glamorous Hollywood vanity lights keeping in sync with Kurt's flashy personality.

Amanda swore that if she looked up ostentatious fantasy in the Dictionary or Encyclopedia Kurt Kilawee's bathroom photo would be inserted. Two perfect male specimens half-dressed reflected a maze of men in the mirrors across the bath– brazenly arousing and irresistible to either sex. She suspected an orgasm would ripple through her if she didn't leave the erotic room. Her raw emotions released her animal instincts from their inner prison. It took great effort to sequester them.

"Holy shit Kurt!" Belinda said stepping into the large glassed shower with wall jets, dual shower heads and rain showers. "Damn how many orgies have you had in this contraption?" She turned on the built-in custom wall radio. Marvin Gaye's "Sexual Healing" piped out, she licked her lips and swayed hungrily exuding a neediness that peaked in them all.

Kurt turned away crossing his arms over his broad chest just naturally flexing more of his desirable manly characteristics in the mirrors. Amanda sucked in a sharp breath. He couldn't have planned this erotica on this day in this way. She was unprepared for this vision–biting her fist of knuckles she tried not to notice how snug his pinstriped black slacks fit his firm buttocks and masculine front. She thought to back out of the room, but she couldn't for the sheer reason, she wanted to feast with her eyes on his skin.

Jeremy stepped into the shower gyrating around and twirling Belinda.

"Okay, okay– The tour is over." Kurt flicked off the radio cutting the explicit entanglement like a guillotine, his words precise, "Party's over– time to stop!"

When he raised his voice, Amanda slipped out into the hall. The image of his rippling tan muscles and his taut well fit slacks made her feminine wiles heat up and boil over. Separating herself from him, she squeezed her hands between her inner thighs trying to calm her innate sensual arousal. The vibration of his voice and visions of his half-naked hard body sent her sexually charged urges reeling; silently she panted through a quick self-induced orgasm. How the hell was she going to work with him on a daily basis again? This intense feeling was not going to disappear anytime soon.

"Time to decide sleeping arrangements." Kurt said directing traffic out of the bathroom back into the kitchen.

Yeah, so not the subject to bring up in a room full of estrogen and testosterone; she released an edgy sigh.

Jeremy looked at Kurt, "Looks like instead of building a bathroom fit for a palace, maybe a bed for the second bedroom would have come to your mind?"

"Hey, we all claim to be adults here. I'm sure we can be civil and agree to platonic sleeping arrangements." Kurt argued.

"Yeah like you and the word platonic or bed were ever used in the same sentence–ever." Jeremy grumbled.

Amanda and Belinda sat quietly on the leather sofa with their legs and arms crossed.

"Okay enough English lessons Jeremy, the girls can have the sofa bed and you can sleep on the far side of my bed. Everyone can sacrifice one awkward night for the sake of safety." Kurt asserted.

Belinda raised her hand, "Hey, what if the goons come through the door." She pointed out the close proximity of the door to the sofa. "Who is going to protect us, if you studs are in the other room?" Her lascivious eyes danced alternating her gaze giving each man equal time.

Amanda bobbed her head in agreement still unable to make eye contact with Kurt for fear her inner pleasure would pulse into action again.

"Yeah Genius," Jeremy challenged. "How's that sleeping arrangement going to save them? And I am tired of sleeping on that sofa bed. How about you and Belinda sleep out here, and Amanda and I take the big bed?"

Kurt scratched his head. Belinda perked up. Amanda inadvertently kicked Belinda, as if her foot had a mind of its own.

"Ouch, what was that for?" Belinda curled her legs under her.

"Some people are having a hard time concentrating with all the skin exposure." Amanda said pointing an accusing finger at Belinda, who apparently hadn't been laid in a long time.

Kurt laughed at their predicament because he wasn't willing to give up his new heated baffled waterbed. Exhausted; he needed a good night's sleep. And the clock was now inching towards nine.

"I agreed the girls need to cover up. New idea, follow me," Kurt said misunderstanding the girls' request; he flagged them to his oversized bedroom closet. "Amanda here's a stack of my T-shirts pick one and go change out of those short pajamas. Belinda select one from Jeremy's folded stack, they'll fit you better. That should help." The girls left to the bathroom. Kurt slipped out of his dress slacks into sweatpants. Jeremy followed suit.

"You ladies covered now?" he inquired.

They innocently walked out. Kurt's eyes committed treason. His X-large T-shirt covered more, but still revealed a portion of Amanda's thighs, and clung lightly to her chest exposing the slight peaks of her perky nipples.

Jeremy elbowed him, "Earth to Kurt."

Kurt jostled back to reality; rubbing his tired eyes he cleared his throat, "So here's the deal."

They all stood at the foot of the oversized bed.

"Given that I handle a gun with the most expertise, and the nice guy that I am–I'll sacrifice sleeping on the right closest to the door. Although I prefer the middle of *my* bed," he looked for gratitude in their faces. "Well okay, which one of you has the next level of firearm expertise? Jeremy what is your experience with a pistol?" Kurt caught Belinda and Amanda smirking. "I am warning you now–the first one that uses any of this as a sexual innuendo will sleep in the basement with the rats. Or risk being shot by me. So answer my questions truthfully or suffer the consequences. Jeremy?" Kurt rubbed his forehead in dread.

Jeremy massaged his own temples trying to extract answers from his memory. "Man, my experience was this past week at the shooting range with you and your dad."

Kurt winced, "Did you have to remind me? Okay, Belinda, in short detail and preferably in English, what is your experience with firearms?"

Belinda twisted her bobbed hair at the base of her ear, and chewed her lower lip, "Well hot shot, once I shot an ex-boyfriend in the foot with a Midnight Special, purely by accident." Her big eyes suggested innocence.

"Wow, ah okay... No guns for you." His patience was borderline fatigued. "Okay, Amanda what do you have for me?" he shot a derisive look at Belinda and Jeremy sniggering.

"Umm...well. I can shoot a BB gun rifle."

"Oh yeah," a glimmer of hope reflected in his face and tone. "You're a Midwest girl, right? And you must have practiced target shooting, right?"

A nervous giggle escaped, "Well technically my best shooting was at a moving target." She caught everyone's interest. Kurt was at the forefront.

"Really, I'm impressed. Like hunting rabbits or pheasants?"

The instant giggles seized Belinda, Amanda had shared her experience at one of their "We hate men" late night powwows.

Unfortunately Kurt wasn't in a humorous mood. "Belinda stop. Amanda, what was the moving target?"

"Jeez, Kurt you're such a downer." Belinda complained.

Amanda confessed, "The target was my high school boyfriend, I caught him cheating. I shot him from the front porch." A film of embarrassment flashed across her face. "I hit him five times."

Belinda cracked a wicked smile and scrunched her nose at Kurt.

He mimicked her nose scrunch back at her. "Okay Amanda, remind me to never teach you to shoot a handgun or a high powered rifle."

They were getting nowhere fast.

"Great," Kurt said exasperated, "how in the hell did I end up with Huey, Dewy, and Louie?"

Jeremy retaliated, sleep deprivation was setting in, with his minor concussion, "Well, as long as we're profiling, maybe it's because you act like Mr. McScrooge McDuck. Damn man, my head hurts can we just come to a decision here?"

"Alright, I'm going out on a limb here. Jeremy you take the left by the window." Kurt placed the .38 Special on the left built-in sideboard. "Amanda you sleep closest to me on the right." He cut off the verbal dissension in the troops. "Shut-up Jeremy, I don't want to hear it. She sleeps closest to me, because I for one know how to use a 9mm, and two, they are after her."

Jeremy mumbled, "Yeah, they aren't the only ones after her."

"Belinda you sleep in the middle with Amanda. There it's settled." Before he could leave the room, Belinda raised her hand apprehensively.

He raked his hair. "Now what?"

Belinda gazed at her bare feet, "Well, that all sounds hunky-dory, but honestly, I can't be trusted in that crib with you guys half-naked. Hell, I'm having a hard time just standing here. I think you dudes should cover up too."

A wave of relief washed through the room; at least one of them was honest enough to admit the truth. Amanda stood by trying to imagine how she was going to sleep next to Kurt without touching him. Emotionally and physically fatigued, she was out of her common sense wits. Kurt had to put a shirt on or she wouldn't sleep a wink.

Kurt glared at Belinda, "What? We are all adults here."

Jeremy paced at his side of the bed, "That's the problem. It's because we are adults. If we were kids this would be a no-brainer like an innocent slumber party. Belinda you won't have problems sleeping next to me. You're cute and all, but not my type."

"Well, hate to blow your mind. But I'm being honest about how my mind works. I can't be trusted in that bed unless you two put on more clothes."

Both men relented and went into the closet. They returned donning T-shirts and sweats.

Kurt surprised them all by kissing Amanda on the cheek, "Sleep tight," he said and immediately excused himself.

Before going to his den to do journaling, he grabbed his Glock from the kitchen, doubled checked the door locks, and peered out the front window. All appeared secure and to his liking. He sat at his writing desk turning on his green shaded Banker's desktop brass lamp. The one item, he and Jeremy had argued most about. Kurt won.

He liked it. And he always got what he liked.

Quickly he penned the day's events. A heat wave engulfed him, as he flashed back to Mandy standing clad in his T-shirt. He removed his shirt, vowing he'd put it back on when he retired to bed. He wrote down every detail of Rich's thug friends and Anna Marie Casali. Tired he glanced at his TAG Heuer wristwatch, it was nearly ten.

He rubbed his eyes and tried to recall where he put the scratch paper Tom had given him with Anna's address and phone number. With all the funeral commotion, the Rich and Sarah escapade, and getting attacked by the girls, he had to rack his brain.

Then it came to him. In the dark he went to the hall closet and rifled through a trench coat he thought was his. But instead of Tom's note he found the hand written invite requesting Amanda to sit in the second row.

It struck a chord on how they had gotten to this point; he reread the scripted note. Life was unfair– finally Amanda was unattached, in his apartment–nearly naked in his bed–but also in danger.

Luck had not totally abandoned him; Anna Marie Casali's address was on the stationary header. He confiscated it, folding it into his sweatpants pocket. Then he went through his coat and found Tom's chicken scratch note. Good thing he found Amanda's note, at least the address was legible. He returned to the dimly lit den and wrote down the information and discarded Tom's note into the trash.

Tomorrow after work he would pay Anna a visit. Just as he was about to turn out the light, he heard soft footsteps approaching the den. He swiveled in his leather office chair to see dewy eyed Amanda staring at him. Perhaps she had been crying over the day's events.

They gazed lazily at each other.

Kurt attempted to stand, but Amanda shuffled to him placing her cool slender hands on his bare shoulders, she turned his chair to the desk.

"No. Don't get up. I was just checking to see when you would be coming to bed." Her cooing words carried an awkward sexy hint.

Oh how he wished to hear those words from her over and over, he thought, forgetting to close his journal.

In the interim, Amanda brushed her breasts against him to see over his shoulder. Hearing his breath catch, she leaned closer. His neck pulse raced at her fingertips as he sunk into her caress, he closed his eyes. The pause allowed her time to read his last entry about Anna.

Her eyes strained, as she committed to memory the phone number. She wanted to read more, so to delay him further she massaged his neck muscles with her thumbs delicately rotating up to the base of his skull.

Kurt leaned his heavy head back falling prey to her sly sleight of hand movements.

"What is taking you so long?" She asked. His eyes remained closed as she skimmed his detailed report.

"I was journaling. That's what a good professional journalist does." He teased.

Amanda tapped him sharply on the forehead for being a smartass.

He opened his eyes just quick enough to see her studying his journal. With one swoop of his hand he slammed the journal shut–startling her. She squeezed his bruised shoulder caused by her empty wine bottle hit.

He winced, gripped her wrists and quickly swiveled his chair. She landed on his lap. "Oh, so you're wondering when I was coming to bed huh?" His eye flashed contempt. "Come and rub my aching shoulders huh?" He squeezed her wrists tighter watching her wince. "Wondering what I'm writing huh? Did you get enough or should I read you a bedtime story?"

She hadn't meant to stir his anger. But by sitting on his lap she realized she had stirred something more than intended. In vain she struggled to be released.

But he refused, even though his carnal body was reacting to their accidental entanglement. His voice thickened as his needy arousal made no mistake of his interest in her. "Well? Now what Ms. Lindas? What do you propose we do now?"

She forced a swallow. Her tender lips opened than pressed shut, the rolling turmoil in her sex emerged making her dither. All that came to mind was his masculine bathroom with multiple reflections of his Adonis body. If he released her wrists, she knew their encounter would elevate to the point of no return. She wanted him now, like no other man in her life. How did she allow her desire for truth get this far? Her desire for the truth put her on the threshold of his desire. His pectorals flexed hard holding her as his privates permeated a perpetual throbbing current.

He did the unthinkable. While holding her thin wrists high with one strong hand, he slipped his other under her borrowed shirt gently cupping her warm breasts. His fingers stroked her taut nipples causing her to press tighter into his erection. He was hard and ready. His gentle caresses pulled her to the edge of climax.

Still keeping his stronghold on her wrists, his eyes intently searched hers. Her eyes shadowed to telltale bedroom eyes, acknowledging him to go further. His arm circled her waist crushing her to his bare chest as his lips pecked kisses up her tender smooth neck giving her more reasons to quiver.

The heat of his breath increased her need; her eyes closed waning to ecstasy. A whimper of pleasure escaped her throat.

He conquered her mouth with his, muffling her whimpers back into her interior. The more he kissed her the more she released. Just his kisses sent her into an orgasmic comma.

Her body shuddered when he released her wrists allowing her to explore his soft hair, hard shoulders, and broad chest as his hands explored her curves.

His mouth covered a firm nipple wetting it through the thin T-shirt while his hand reached between her thighs into her hot moist sex. His large firm fingers sent her into a rapturous plea.

"Kurt, Kurt, oh… yes, yes," she panted trying to quiet herself. He continued to pleasure her above her expectations. It felt so good; she just allowed herself to slip into an erotic paradise. It was no wonder women swooned to him.

He knew his moves well, and having her trembling to climax from his tender strokes confirmed it. He clutched her hips pressing down on his hard manhood. He wanted to be in her hot center. But the need to regain self-control was essential before he made the mistake of taking her all the way. He wanted her, but not on the rebound. He wasn't prepared to take a back seat to Antonio Casali's memory. No clue as to how intimate she and Tony had been, he surmised last week's events mixed with grief and fear had brought her to him tonight.

Anyone can have a moment of weakness after such tragedy. She played perfectly into his hands, but she wasn't ready to be his for the right reasons. No doubt he wanted to ravage her, but his ambiguousness and pride refused. Getting her to whimper and shudder in ecstasy in his arms was enough for him–now. When did he grow a conscience?

A wave of self-assurance flooded him; he hadn't lost his touch to bring a woman over the edge. Slowly he released her, using breathing techniques he controlled the torrent undercurrent in his groin.

Slow and low he said, "We should stop. You should go back to bed." He couldn't believe after all these months he finally had her right where he wanted her, and now he was asking her to leave. He had to.

He just had to.

"Okay Babe, I'm going to lift you up. Can you stand?" He felt warm tears falling on his shoulder. "No tears. It's okay. Let's just get separated for now. We'll talk about everything later. You do remember we were supposed to talk."

Amanda sobbed, "I'm sorry."

"No, no, there's no reason to be sorry." He cupped tear stained face with his hands, his thumbs rubbed her tears away, "Come on, Babe no tears, we're okay." He smiled. "I really *need* you to leave the room - now." He wanted to claim her, but every ounce of his integrity reverberated that the timing wasn't right.

Besides that, Jeremy would bust down the door any minute and shoot him with his own .38.

With his strong arms he hoisted her to standing, he stood behind her. Intentionally he turned her away keeping her at a safe comfortable distance. She stood with her arms crossed and her head hung low. He slipped his hands under her soft hair, toying with the lengthy spirals he seriously thought to bury his face in it softness. "Amanda?" he whispered.

"Yes, Kurt?"

"I don't want you to think that, I don't want you. I do." His voice breathless and quiet, "I need you… to promise me."

She went to turn towards him, but he dropped her hair and gripped her shoulders preventing her from moving.

"No, we can't. Just promise me tomorrow you won't leave this apartment. Give me a chance to find the thugs. I have to work." His grip tightened on her shoulders, "I need to know you're safe. Belinda needs to stay too. We've pulled innocent people into our chaos; give me a chance to unravel it. Promise me?"

Amanda kept her face forward. "Kurt, it's not fair for you to take this all on yourself. I want to help. It's my story. It's my life." In an instance she looked over her shoulder, fluttered her long wet lashes, and darted her icy eyes, "Antonio was my boyfriend."

Instantly she deflated his ego and his libido. How dare she bring that up? She came willingly to him. The audacity of her words and actions; pissed him off, he wanted to shake her. It burned him instantly like striking a match. "Amanda that's not fair. I can't change what happened!" He shouted clamping down on her shoulders. "Promise me you will stay here tomorrow. Let me get you into protective custody."

Amanda squirmed out of his grip just as Jeremy plowed through the door with the .38 drawn.

Kurt automatically raised his hands. Amanda pushed by Jeremy and ran to the bathroom.

"Put that damn gun down!" Kurt blew up and skirted around Jeremy.

At the locked bathroom door, Kurt pounded. "Amanda, you had better not leave this apartment until I have a chance to protect you." his opened palm slammed the door, shaking the pictures on adjacent wall. "Damn it, Mandy!"

She slammed her palms on the door with full force, "Don't call me Mandy! Don't tell me what to do. It's my story! You take me to work with you."

"No, you're staying here where I know you'll be safe. I don't trust Rich."

"My safety is not your business. I can take care of myself!" She screamed back and turned to lean on door. That was a bold faced lie; she didn't have a clue on how to protect herself.

Kurt slammed on the door again, harder.

Jeremy and Belinda stood sentry.

Kurt glared. "What the hell do you two want?"

Jeremy crossed his arms propping the gun on his bicep. "Maybe we'd like a little peace and quiet, so we can get some sleep, or maybe we want to use the restroom?"

"You hear that Amanda? Some people like peace and quiet in their lives." He slammed on the door again. "You're pushing me over the edge again!" His emotions were flying everywhere.

Bypassing Jeremy and Belinda, he strutted to his bedroom, snatched a pillow with a light blanket, and returned to the den for his Glock. He placed the 9mm on the coffee table, plopped down on the sofa, covered up, and socked his pillow a couple of extra times. He was resolved that he was going to get some sleep. He'd deal with that damn stubborn woman in the morning.

Chapter 14

Kurt was the first to wake. The morning sun sliced through the dark-chocolate living room draperies dancing on the red-bricked wall. Squinting at his watch, he discovered it was before five, plenty of time to put his stringent plan into action. He'd be damned if Mandy would get the best of their situation. He had plans to detain her.

First thing he had to do was shower and shave before his detainee charges came to life. Tiptoeing down the wood planked hall, as well as a six-foot three man could, he peered into his bedroom at the threesome slumber party. He cringed.

There they were all snuggled together with Jeremy in the center. Sometimes he wondered if Jeremy was all *that* gay. Whatever, it put him in a quandary on how to get Jeremy's attention without waking the girls. He selected his work clothes and gathered the girls' clothing. The premise was–no clothing–no going outside.

Late October in New York was a chilly force to be reckoned with and so was he. He figured his clothing would be too large for them to go out in public, but he confiscated Jeremy's just in case, along with their purses.

No money, no IDs, meant no taxis or buses. He felt like the Grinch stealing Christmas, taking anything that might add to hindering Amanda's escape. The thought of her researching Antonio's death on her own made him shudder. He had to delay her until he could get protection for her.

After his shower, Kurt dressed in one of his finest suits; he took the first load of loot to the van. He remembered to seize their coats too.

As luck would have it Jeremy, was beginning to stir on his own. The girls rolled over to the edges of the bed.

Angels when they sleep, Kurt mused.

He tugged on Jeremy's big toe. Jeremy shot up. Fright plastered across his face, too much to speak. Kurt hushed him laying his finger to his lips he waved Jeremy forward.

"Come on, we need to go." Kurt whispered harshly.

"Okay keep your pants on." Jeremy scolded back.

"Just go get your pants on."

Jeremy entered the half dismantled closet. "What the hell, a bomb go off in here? Where are my clothes?"

"Oh, on the couch. We have to take them out to the van." Kurt explained while locking the .38 into the sideboard cabinet that contained his journals and other personal incidentals he'd rather his temporary hostage-guests didn't dig through. He went to his den and snatched the journal with the information he needed for his after work project. An exclusive interview with Anna Casali was pertinent for getting his story and solving Antonio's murder.

"Oh, so now you're kicking me out. What did I do? You decided to sleep on the sofa not me."

Still whispering not to rouse the girls, Kurt corrected and commanded, "No, that's not it, but you did piss me off last night." Kurt stewed with his conscience. "Just get dressed, I need to get to work and go over our assignments with Rich. Plus I need to get some undercover agents over here."

Jeremy grudgingly selected his work attire and slipped into the shower. In no time, they were off, with the van full of confiscated spoils of war.

Amanda and Belinda exhausted from the night before stayed in the warm waterbed until almost eight which was late by Amanda's standards. Kurt's apartment had a quiet eeriness about it. She had to admit that was the best night's rest she had had since she moved to New York five months ago, it seemed like ages.

Maybe it was the first time in a long time that she had felt secure, knowing a man was protecting her. She shrugged the feeling off, it only dredged up memories of her father before he screwed around on her mother.

Belinda stirred some, but then she returned to La-La-Land.

In search of coffee, she gave into her childish urge to snoop through his things. After all; she'd be a discredit to her journalism career if she didn't do a little investigation on her house host or was that–prison warden–she hadn't quite decided which one Kurt was.

For starters, she opened all of the kitchen cupboards. She couldn't do her best probing without a jolt of java. His new fangled coffee pot on the top shelf looked unused. Luckily he had Folgers, her favorite coffee.

Now, how the heck was she supposed to use the new pot? Hers was an old fashion electric perk. Well, if she had to stay captive then she had to have coffee, so why not bother Mr. Bossy Anchorman at work? She flicked on the new remote control television to see his morning live reports.

Yep, sure enough his handsome face was projected larger than life as he covered the local elections. Televising live from the anchor desk he explained, "In other news, the commotion brought about by the murder of Antonio Casali has Amanda Lindas taking a short sabbatical from NYCB and the public forum. We at NYCB wish her well and also extend our condolences to the Casali family..."

"Oh why don't you tell the truth? Amanda Lindas can't be with us today because I am holding her captive in my luxury bachelor pad, making her sick with envy."

Belinda stumbled sleepily down the hall. With a huge yawn and a stretch of her petite arms she spoke, "Hey, who you talking to?" She rubbed her raccoon makeup eyes.

"Oh, the TV," Amanda said pushing the NYCB anchor desk phone number figuring Kurt was ready to be unhooked and leave for assignments. Impatiently she waited for him to answer. She watched as Belinda rummaged the drawers and the closets. A real pro-snooper, she was pulling out some pretty provocative items, women's panties, lingerie pieces, and plenty of packaged condoms.

"Who you calling?" Belinda inquired looking at the dismantled coffee pot. She found the coffee filters in the pantry and acted like she was a scavenger hunt winner. "Yahoo! Score!"

"Hello Kurt, this is Amanda," she hushed Belinda.

"Hey Amanda, how was your night? Nice bed huh?"

"Oh yeah, probably the best sleep I've had in months, but I didn't call to chitchat about sleeping in your bed."

"You sure it was *just* my bed? So, how can I please you today?" More sarcasm rippled through.

"Belinda and I want coffee, but unfortunately we don't have the newest and grandest of coffeemakers at our apartments, so you'll have to give us a quickie lesson, so we won't blow up your place."

He laughed and gave her directions; she relayed them to her quick study assistant. As he coolly spoke, she became suspicious, nosed around in the hall closet and then traveled to his closet with his state-of-the-art handheld phone. Much to her dismay she discovered something was not kosher and she wasn't Jewish.

"Hey before I let you go. Where the hell is our clothing and our purses?"

"Good observation. They're safe with me. You won't need them because you need to stay put, make yourself at home. If you're hungry there's plenty of healthy food. Or you can order out on my accounts, there's a coffee shop, a deli, an Italian place, and Chinese on 33rd. You will find menus in the kitchen drawer by the answer machine. Have it delivered. Don't leave the premises." his tone was edgy and stern.

"What? You took our clothes?" Her throat tightened emitting a shrill.

167

"Yep, and your shoes too," a snicker slipped past his lips.

"Kurt Kilawee, you can't hold us hostage. I need to get to my apartment. I have things to do."

"Not today you don't. I have to go, see you this afternoon. If you need anything call the office. I promise you, I will be checking up on you. Bye Sweetheart."

"Don't you call me that!"

He had already hung up.

She tore through his apartment looking for clothing that she could wear outside. Belinda started the coffee and joined in her quest.

"That Bastard! He took Jeremy's clothing too. We could have adjusted them to fit halfway decent." Amanda vented.

Belinda stacked her findings of odds and ends on the counter. Scissors, needles, thread, jewelry, and handfuls of condoms, "Damn this guy has got this place totally childproof." She threw the condoms like confetti, "I mean literally–childproof."

Amanda had to laugh at their dire predicament. She tossed a few condoms at Belinda, "Where are you finding these?"

"Well in the side drawers of the bed, duh? And then in that fancy box thingy on the coffee table–looks like a 1930's or 50's cigarette box, and even in his desk drawer, and of course in the orgy bathroom. Imagine great sex in there." Belinda laughed until she snorted.

Amanda poured two cups of coffee. They needed a plan. And she couldn't contrive evil plans without a jolt of caffeine. "Well, he was telling the truth about practicing safe-sex." Her mind recalled their private escapade in the den. She sipped her coffee preoccupied momentarily in the flow of the bygone ecstasy.

Belinda tossed a few condoms at her breaking the spell, "Say, did you do the nasty in the den last night? You've got that far away look. Care to share?"

Amanda straightened erect, and began closing the kitchen cabinets. "No, we did not do the 'nasty', but damn girl," a wide smile spread across her face, "he's got magical hands if you know what I mean." She cleared her throat. "Enough about him, we need clothes and shoes. Oh wait," like a cat emergency, she darted to the den. Rustling through his papers on his desk and bookshelves, she searched for his notebook. *But of course, who was she dealing with–Mr. Thinks of Everything, damn him!*

She plopped down into the huge leather chair–the ecstasy chair–she mused. As she leaned back she spied a crumpled piece of paper in the trash. Curious she retrieved it finding Anna Casali's name, address, and a telephone number scribbled on it. If her photographic memory served her right it was the number Kurt had written in his journal. He was planning a meeting with Mrs. Casali. Amanda knew in a split second she needed to contact Anna Casali before Kurt. Surely Anna would speak to her over the acquitted accused killer of her son.

"Belinda–Belinda!" Amanda ran down the hall, "I've found her number! I'll call Anna Casali and meet with her before Kurt. You need to stay here just in case Kurt calls. Don't tell him where I am, stall him, say I'm taking a long shower in his erotic bathroom, or I'm napping in his woman trap exotic bed– anything, but don't tell him I've left." She was all out of breath when she found Belinda decked out in one of Kurt's white Armani dress shirts. Belinda took one of his leather belts and punched extra holes in it so it hung slightly crooked across her hip. The collar turned up Elvis style; the sleeves rolled up to her wrists and scrunched to her elbows. She had his bright aqua T-shirt under her new boyfriend style shirt dress. It was too large on her, but it looked hip like a shirt dress on steroids.

Elated she almost hugged the life out of Belinda, "Damn girl you're brilliant. That's perfect! Put something together for me, I'm going to shower. Boy, Kurt is going to be pissed, us wearing his expensive shirts as dresses. Serves him right, he took our clothes, so we'll take his."

Belinda transformed one of Kurt's blushing pink dress shirts layered over a solid black T-shirt, an adjusted a black silk tie wrapped at Amanda's waist. With the collar turned up Amanda donned his prize Armani black blazer rolling the sleeves together and scrunching them to her elbows. Her shirt dress fit perfect with modest length at her mid-thigh. She thought if Kurt liked her in his T-shirt wouldn't he just die to see her dressed in his suave guise. A woman's touch was all it took. They posed in the bathroom admiring their new duds in front of the Hollywood mirrors.

"Now we need shoes. And transportation."

Belinda responded, "Not me, I'm staying right here and living in luxury for as long as I can. Hey, I found a few subway tokens. And some odds and ends of makeup, earrings, and a big ass bottle of Chanel No.5." She placed all her new found treasures on the dark chocolate marble vanity.

They experimented with her finds, and broke the seal on the expensive perfume. Amanda surmised it was the token gift Kurt had offered her in apology for his first transgression towards her at the night club.

She kept quiet about it for fear Belinda would disown her for not accepting gifts from guys who were sorry jerks.

"Belinda go ask Kurt's neighbors if they have women's shoes or boots, size seven, okay. And I'll call Mrs. Casali."

Belinda went on the scavenger hunt, she decided to ask for safety pins and other essentials she thought they may need for wardrobe alterations.

Amanda started to punch in Anna's number when the phone rang. Startled she answered on the first ring. "Hello, Kurt Kilawee's residence…"

"Well, hello Sweetheart." Her nemesis said.

"Oh, it's you," her demeanor switched from pleasant to borderline bitch.

"Wow is that a way to treat your benefactor? I was going to compliment you on your phone skills. How's everything? You and Belinda being good girls, I hope, not destroying my place are you?" he sounded concerned.

"Oh, you know women. We just do what women do."

"Yeah, I was afraid of that."

"We found your childproofing equipment." She let loose a malevolent snicker.

Dumbfounded he asked, "What childproof equipment?" Then it dawned on him. He went from quizzical to defensive. "Oh, never mind, I catch your drift. I told you the truth. I like to practice."

"That's beguiling. You told that truth to the whole flippin' nation. Is that why you stocked up, for all your safe-sex partner offers? Yeah, Kurt, I'm not enthralled. Why did you call?"

"Well, this conversation is taking a dive. I have a few assignments nearby, and I was going to bring you ladies lunch."

"Don't bother we're not invalids, we know how to cook, clean, do laundry, sew clothing, and burp babies." He brought out her contemptuous nature.

"Yep, we are going off the deep end here. Just sit tight. It won't be long."

"Oh, aren't you the man with the fancy clichés'? I'll bet you wish I'd sit tight in more ways than one." The cynical route was all she had left. She wanted him to hang up so she could leave. It was around ten; her time was running out along with her patience.

"Yeah," he snickered to himself, but loud enough for her ears to twitch. "You are so right about that." The snicker turned into mocking laughter.

"Bye Kurt, have fun, I have to go. I have things to do, places to go, and people to see." She hung up before he could retort her decision.

Belinda ran in with black knee-high boots–a bit nineteen-seventyish, but who cared. "Mandy the boots are size eight, but we can use a pair of Kurt's angora socks to make them fit."

They did their happy dance. Belinda got busy searching for money or more subway tokens while Amanda called Mrs. Casali.

"Hello, Mrs. Casali, this is Amanda Lindas."

"Pronto, Amanda, my Antonio spoke so well of you. How are you?"

Amanda's vocal cords strained while tears welled in her eyes, shame returned just hearing Antonio's mother's somber Italian accent. Amanda wept, for the one woman who deserved his love. "I'm well, thank you." She bit her lower lip choking back remorseful sobs. "Is there a way I can meet you somewhere today so we can talk?" Amanda trembled. Belinda came to her side and stroked her back.

"Of course, Amanda, why do you cry? You must believe as I do that my son is with God. He is better off than us. I think that it would be lovely for us to meet. I enjoy talking with Antonio's friends they rekindle his spirit. Will you come to my home?"

"Oh, maybe somewhere Antonio loved to go. I don't wish to intrude. I just want to understand more about his life. We only dated for a short while, but I have always wanted to meet you."

"Then let's meet at Clinton Castle and take the ferry to Liberty Island. Antonio loved New York and our Lady Liberty was one of his favorites. Let's meet for lunch, say around noon?"

"Yes, yes that would be wonderful. See you then."

Belinda gave her a tissue for her tears. "Wow, you did it, now we just need to get you transportation. Here are Mr. Bossman's expensive socks."

Amanda slipped on the socks and boots while Belinda continued to search the place for more money. She went back to the bedroom closet and started rifling thoroughly through Kurt's pockets.

"Jackpot!" Belinda screamed. "God hears even the smallest whisper from your heart," she quoted her Norwegian grandmother. She ran into Amanda in the hall. "Look, look," she screamed excited as a kid who just discovered all-you-can-eat ice cream. In her little hands a shiny object dangled accompanied by a money clip stuffed with cash.

Amanda held Belinda's hand to seize the shiny dangle–two keys on a Mercedes Benz key ring with an extra tag that had D11 written on it. Keys to a car and a parking tag. Jackpot!

Belinda unrolled the money from the monogram money clip K.A.K. on one side and *To Kurt With Love*" scripted on the reverse. Shoving a pile of condoms aside, she counted the hundred dollar bills first on the kitchen counter top, "One, two, three, four, five hundreds, two fifties, and three twenties, yes! Wow six hundred and sixty bucks." Elated, she suddenly stopped. Amanda was examining the money clip. "What? Why aren't you cheering with me? Don't tell me that 'with love' crap is bothering you. I thought you didn't care about him. Say, I wonder where he keeps his car? I wonder what color it is."

Amanda admired the keys in her hand. The argument that ensued in the taxi ride home came back to her crystal clear. "These keys are not to his car. And the car is the color of my eyes. These belong to my car."

Belinda's jaw dropped. "Okay girlfriend, you've lost your frickin' mind. You don't own a car. Are you wigging-out on me? Fill me in."

"Follow me, there must be a parking garage close by or attached to this building." Amanda clutched the keys and snatched half the money off the counter with the money clip. She figured Belinda deserved half for a finder's fee.

Ready to leave at the door, the phone rang. They waited for the answering machine, Kurt's recorded debonair voice, "Hey this is Kurt Kilawee, I'm not in but I'd love to call you back, you know what to do after the beep..."

Beep. Even on the answering machine he exuded sexy.

"Hey Kurt, this is Shannel, I was hoping you'd call me back, I think I left my black hooped earrings on your bed stand, the last time we ah–got together. Give me a call; I'd loved to get together with you soon. Ciao Baby."

Amanda put her finger in her open mouth feigning to gag. "Come on Belinda help me find my car and then you can come back just in case 'Ciao Baby' calls."

"She's a new one, should I call Shannel back and thank her for her donation?" Belinda tapped the black hooped earrings dangling from Amanda's earlobes. "And then maybe I'll call and thank Jessica, Sami, and Tami for their contributions too. Oldest trick in the book leaving an article behind just to hook up again, how majorly wicked. I love it."

Belinda understood wicked, she and Mandy had listened to all Kurt's messages while they had their second cup of coffee and munched on dry cereal.

"Yeah, call them and thank them for me." Stirring his girlfriend harem pot gave Amanda incentive to follow through on her mission.

They headed out and down a back stairwell which led them into a musty old basement garage. It reeked of mildew and urine.

"Eeewe, nasty, I can't believe Kurt would store my car here." They kept walking almost at a jog holding their noses while trying desperately not to gag. Then they spotted another door which led them away from the stench into a showroom style garage with fluorescent lights lined up across the ceiling. The new paint smell reeked of chemical residue, although strong, it was pleasant compared to the other garage. This garage was nearly full. Some of the cars were gated in large cages. The girls approached D11 and of course, Kurt had the prized car covered with canvas and securely locked behind a white iron-gate.

"Not to worry," Belinda produced another key ring with a plethora of keys. "It's got to be one of these. This lock is some major security."

Astonished at her partner in crime, Amanda commented, "Where did you find those?"

Belinda deftly tried each key in the lock concentrating on not repeating, to save time. "Oh, in his dress shoes' box, I hide shit in my shoe boxes all the time.

Finally after trying ten keys, she had success. The iron-gate lock clanged opened sending an echo through the garage.

They separated one on each side of the car to pull the canvas cover off their prize. With a deep breath of anticipation they unveiled the gleaming showroom condition icy-blue, 500 SEC 2-door Mercedes coupe. The flashy chrome front grill displayed the famous divided circle emblem. The vehicle exuded sharp angular manly lines. A sleek body styled with tailored navy-blue leather interiors. The dash and the door panels were accented with chrome and burl wood grain. It was breathtaking.

They ran their nimble fingers from front to back, and then back to front.

"Wow, this car is mint." Belinda released an orgasmic sigh.

"Yeah, if Kurt was a car, this would be him." Amanda exclaimed. The car was a total personification of perfection, luxury, and ostentatious. She loved every inch of it. "Well, time for me to fly." She sat behind the wheel and realized she didn't know the directions to the Liberty Island ferry. She looked to Belinda. "You don't happen to know the directions, do you?"

Belinda drew an imaginary map in the air racking her memory envisioning the route. She was used to the buses and subway, so it took her awhile to come up with a viable route.

Amanda waited patiently, admiring Kurt's taste in cars. She leaned over to the glove compartment and opened it. Inside was a small leather binder with the bill of sale, "Oh my Gawd."

Belinda ducked her head into the driver's side window curious.

"It says here that he paid fifty-six thousand dollars for this car. Quite the bonus present for me." She skimmed the title page it was in Kurt's name and hers. "That's weird; why didn't he put it in Rich's name?" A quizzical look washed her face. Money laundering came to mind.

Belinda snatched the papers, "Yes, very strange why would it have your name and Kurt's? You aren't married or even living together."

Amanda took the papers and put them back into the leather binder. She slipped in the key and revved the engine. "Okay what's my plan of action?"

"It's real easy. Exit the garage on 33rd; go left on Lexington, take Lex down to Gramercy Park, go right on east 21st then you should come to the huge intersection at Park Avenue. Then take a left, go down to about 14th near Union Square veer left onto Broadway. Stay on Broadway all the way to State Street, Battery Park should be right there. You'll find it. You're smart."

Wide eyed, Amanda said. "Wow, how do you do that? She reached back into the glove compartment and found a pen and paper and scribbled the directions down. "Wish me luck girlfriend."

Belinda shook her head, "Oh hell no, I'm not wishing you luck. You've got too much of it already. A new man, a new car, and me for a best friend, uh-uh you don't need good luck. You need to share what you have with me." Belinda smiled and patted Mandy on the shoulder. "Be careful. I will try to hold off the wild man for you."

"Thanks Belinda. I owe you big time."

"Just remember that when you get back."

On her drive through lower Manhattan, Amanda shook behind the wheel after she pissed off a few cabbies. Thankfully she made it safely to the Liberty Island ferry. She parked her beautiful coupe and paid the parking attendant extra to secure the car's safety. She felt like she was leaving a newborn baby with a total stranger. She had to.

No other options, but to get the truth from Anna Casali.

They met inside of Clinton Castle terminal. Anna was dressed in a mourning black wool suit with a pill box hat covering part of her blonde bobbed hair in classic Jackie Kennedy style; reminding Amanda of her own mother's hair style. They greeted each other with warm hugs.

A rush of fresh emotional tears filled Amanda's eyes. She blotted her eyes with the handkerchief she had confiscated from Kurt's dresser.

Once they boarded the nearly empty ferry on gangway five, the breeze off the murky Hudson sent chills through her. Pulling the Armani jacket tightly to her chest, Amanda withstood the cold as the wind tousled her hair. They received VIP status to enter the warm chamber near the Captain. The loud engine churned and chugged while they managed to have a private chat.

Seated on a slotted green wood bench, Anna started the conversation making Amanda feel at ease. "You know my Antonio loved New York. It is the only home he has ever known. I came here in the autumn of 1957. I was already pregnant." Her brown eyes sparkled with intense warmth and love.

Curiosity peaked Amanda, "What about Antonio's father? Where is he? Where was he while Antonio was growing up?" Amanda instantly cowered apologetically. Had she crossed personal boundaries? "Oh, I'm sorry it's just the reporter in me."

174

Anna smiled, taking her gloved hand she patted Amanda's knee. "Don't worry. I want to share our history with you. I believe you can help solve our tragic mystery. Antonio's father stayed in Italy. My husband, Carmine Lucchesi, unfortunately was involved with the Italian Mafia in Naples. He felt I was not safe there, so when I turned twenty he sent me to America on an ocean liner. I remember being seasick for most of the voyage. He had my papers changed from Lucchesi to Casali, his mother's maiden name. He was not aware that I was with child. Antonio was born in the spring of 1958; Carmine made contact through the bank and a selection of shady messengers. Financially we were well taken care of; I know he loved me, but controlled love doesn't make a marriage. I was not allowed to return to Italy, nor have any contact with my family. It broke my mother's heart. There was bad blood between my father and Carmine. Carmine was my father's friend as I was growing up, he took a fancy to me which angered my father. I thought I was in love with the neighbor boy in the orchard next to ours. His name is Giovanni Maggiore. Unfortunately my father owed Carmine a huge sum of money, and I was used to erase the debt. Carmine asked for my hand in marriage as soon as I turned eighteen, but my father held off until I was closer to twenty. I cared very deeply for Carmine, he was always good to me, but Giovanni was furious." Tears welled in Anna's eyes.

Amanda felt her own heart ache. She offered Kurt's handkerchief to dry Anna's tears. The ferry rocked across the thick white capped waves shifting them closer.

"But why would your mother and father have you marry a man old enough to be your father? How did Giovanni handle your acceptance of the marriage?"

"He handled it like many men who think they've been wronged, by taking refuge in another woman's arms. I agreed to the marriage as did my parents because I am the oldest of seven children and they needed my father alive. Do you understand?" her hands trembled. "I did care deeply for Carmine."

Amanda was shocked by the reference that Carmine would kill Anna's father for an unpaid debt. She decided to focus on Giovanni and his trespass. "Who was the woman that Giovanni betrayed you with?"

"Well, books and movies are written about this kind of betrayal, the other woman was my best friend Tessa Branacci. Tessa was available, a very beautiful voluptuous woman. I hated them. Hate is an awful poison to harbor. It poisons the person that holds on to it, not those it is directed at. I was happy Carmine sent me away. I never forgave them until much later. Later, I didn't blame either of them for finding the love that I chose to throw away. I lived without the love of a man, but I had my little man, Antonio. He filled my life with eternal blessings and joy."

"How did you find out about Giovanni and Tessa?"

"A woman in love finds ways to conquer difficulties and separation. Years later my parents sent my sister to New York to find me. We had a very special time together, and she informed me of their marriage and that they had three daughters at that time. She said Giovanni stayed on his father's land outside of Naples. A lovely sprawling home on an olive orchard, Tessa always wanted that lifestyle, it was not for me. I love New York with all its splendor and high energy. I remember when I first brought Antonio to Lady Liberty; he thought we were related to her." The sides of Anna's eyes wrinkled when she smiled. "Let's go outside and welcome her."

The ferry approached Liberty Island; Amanda interlocked arms with Anna to stroll through the blast of freezing air swirling on the outside balcony. The patina Lady Liberty stood towering tall with her torch-less hand held high. Unfortunately she was covered with scaffolding undergoing major repairs. The noon sun provided little warmth as they stood in reverence to the omnipotent Lady who appeared jailed behind metal bars, still representing freedom to the masses.

Of course, it would have be a woman to greet the masses what man would have the patience to stand there, Amanda mused. She hadn't seen the invincible Lady up close until now because of the construction. She felt a kindred spirit to Lady Liberty and to Anna. A day of supreme adventure, she was delighted to share it with Anna. "This is my first time to Liberty Island."

Anna held her close, "I love sharing first moments with people in New York. It's a magical mystical place meant to be awed, but painfully this concrete city also demands respect." Anna's demeanor was that of resolution as if pain and sacrifice was her life's mission.

Amanda wanted to change that and offer Anna new hope.

Hopefully she could spend more time to unravel the past to revive Anna's broken spirit. Just being near Anna made Tony's spirit flourish; nothing mattered but them connecting.

Exiting the ferry they walked the grounds, Anna reminisced about endearing moments that she and Antonio had shared visiting the Statue of Liberty. To get out of the wind; Anna bribed the security guard to allow them into the pedestal. They came upon the bronze plaque inscription written by Emma Lazarus.

Amanda read the last portion aloud like a news proclamation:

DESIRE FOR TRUTH

"... 'Give me your tired, your poor. Your huddled masses yearning to breathe free. The wretched refuse of your teeming shore. Send these, the homeless tempest-tost, to me: I lift my lamp beside the golden door!'"

Overwhelming emotions cinched her insides when she realized what America represents to those who have no freedom. Immigrants come to fall in love with a land that embraces liberty and makes impossible dreams reality. It saddened her think that Antonio's mother sought that freedom for him only to have his life brutally taken.

Anna's sacrifices were all in vain, if Amanda could not help right this wrong, even if it meant her turning her life and career upside-down. She couldn't think about Kurt, or even her own family; she was determined to make a difference. They toured around the lower museum of the massive statue sucking in her historical grandeur and marking time with Anna's memories of her only son before the workers returned from lunch.

The return ferry arrived; Amanda and Anna quickly sought shelter from the wicked October wind.

"Anna I would love to do an exclusive story on Antonio. I believe we can show New York and maybe the world how precious and awesome one life is. Will you allow me to do his story?"

Anna's bold brown eyes smiled as she nodded yes, "I was waiting for you to offer. Will you stay with me awhile? I have many photos, more stories, and a special favor to ask of you. My Antonio believed in you. He was in love with you, but he felt you were not ready. He was so patient. I must admit he didn't care for that Anchorman. But I told him—jealousy destroys love; it is a dangerous tool. I believe the Anchorman is innocent, and if given the chance he and Antonio would have made good friends. They are very passionate men; you are very privilege to be loved by both. As I was loved by Carmine and Giovanni, don't forget to give love a chance." The gleam in her eyes gave way to her wisdom.

Anna's observation about love took Amanda awhile to absorb.

They agreed it would be beneficial for Amanda to stay at Anna's residence to put the story together, and keep her protected within the wrought-iron gates of The Apthorp.

Amanda explained her dire situation and why she was wearing Kurt's clothing.

Anna laughed jovially at her predicament. "You are a woman of great wisdom and resourcefulness."

At the pier their laughter turned into concern. Two squad cars flashed their blue and red lights near the parking area surrounding her new Mercedes. *Damn, Kurt was fast.*

Amanda observed the area spotting Tom McCarthy, holding the radio receiver of a police car. His unmarked car blocked the entrance, she didn't dare approach. Anna held her back and suggested they retreat into her waiting Lincoln. They stood momentarily sizing up the scene deciding when they should make their exit.

Meanwhile Tom voiced his concern to Kurt over the police radio to the CB radio in the NYCB van.

Earlier Kurt had followed his gut intuition. An uneasy feeling rode his conscience. He stopped at home. That was the beginning of his disastrous day.

Jeremy laughed at the disaster the girls had created in Kurt's pad. He stated they should have Mayor Koch declare it a national disaster area.

In Amanda's absence, Belinda had taken liberties and ordered food from all the menus stowed in the kitchen. Styrofoam food containers and condoms littered every inch of the kitchen counter.

"Tell me where Amanda went and how she was able to leave without clothing, money, or shoes?" Kurt shouted.

Belinda stalled him with fashion fodder using her normal slang terminology slowly creating a massive fuming cloud in his psyche.

"Get to the point Belinda, and speak English damn it!" his blood pressure rose to dangerous levels. Red faced with anger and determination he shouted, "I don't have all fucking day! Where did she meet Anna Casali and what transportation did she use?" He slammed his hand on the semicircle entry table scattering more condemns to the floor.

Belinda jumped; her eyes widened, and dread spread over her face. "Well, you see I found these keys and a money clip..."

The floor rumbled beneath her feet. Kurt stormed up to her. He lifted her off the floor crushing her small arms to her sides, "You what? She didn't? The Mercedes?" he dropped her to her feet.

Jeremy tried to calm him. "Man you got to chill. It is Amanda's car too. You said so yourself. You left her name on it."

Gripping his own hair; Kurt shook his head. "I can't fucking believe her!"

A locked up chuckle, released from Jeremy. "Yeah, she kicked your ass, Dude." He then flashed a knowing smile towards Belinda.

Belinda let a smirk cover her initial shock to Kurt picking her up like a rag doll, "Yeah she burned you bad."

"Well, I'm glad you two are enjoying my pain." Kurt huffed. "Jeremy go contact Tom on the CB, ask him to send an APB out on a stolen 1984 icy blue 2-door 500SEC Mercedes coupe. Have her arrested for theft. She'll be safe in jail."

Immediately Jeremy bolted out the door as quick as Belinda ran to lock herself in the erotic bathroom.

Kurt headed her off pushing his body weight against the solid mahogany door, "Oh no you don't. I'm not through with you. Where is she? And what is she wearing?"

Belinda tried hard to shut the door, but his brute strength was that of five men her size. To control an angry man she decided smooth talking was her only device. "Okay, okay I will tell you, but you got to chill out. You're a crazy ass fool." She stepped away.

Kurt burst through the door almost landing in the shower, "Alright, you're right." Exhausted he bent over grasping his knees, his hair fell into his face, "I am crazy right now, but you don't understand the danger she may be in. What was she wearing and where did she go?"

Just as Belinda was about to confess, Jeremy came running into the apartment. "Kurt, come on. Tom found her. You aren't going to like what she's wearing."

Kurt glared at Belinda, shifted gears and headed for the door. He turned to see Belinda running after him, he shouted, "Is she wearing my clothes like you?"

Belinda nodded and spewed, "It's not like you gave us any choice. You know dumbass this shit is entirely your fault!"

"Well smartass, you're damn lucky she isn't wearing a black zippered bag." Kurt scolded and dodged out the door slamming it as hard as he could leaving Belinda scared and bewildered.

On the radio Tom harassed Kurt, "Hey she's looking pretty cute in your Armani pink shirt, but why the hell did you let her wear your black Armani suit jacket? Hell you wouldn't even let me try it on? I'm hurt man." Tom laughed. "I hope you get credit for creating a new fad in women wearing men's evening clothes to visit the Statue of Liberty."

Kurt blurted back over the receiver, "Oh very funny man, I didn't *let* her do anything. Do me a favor–detain her until I get there. We're on our way."

"Are you doing a special report on 'How to Dress Your Girlfriend' or 'How to Steal a Mercedes' I've done so many favors for you–you'll have to let me name your first born child."

"Save the jokes McCarthy. Get the blue suits to impound the car, and don't scratch it." Kurt's fury escalated with his heart rate. Jeremy couldn't drive fast enough even if the van had a jet engine.

"Hey, you're talking to one of NYPD's finest. What are the charges? I can't arrest her on grand theft. I'm looking at the title and registration and it has her name on it. Boy did she kick your ass." Tom's laugh was boisterous.

"Impound that car, damn it! It's half mine!"

Jeremy grabbed the radio receiver. "Yeah Tom, she did good! Looks like our friend is getting his fair share of karma. I get to name their second child."

Kurt shoved Jeremy, "Hey, how about a little sympathy here?"

Jeremy squawked over the radio, "Tom he wants sympathy."

Tom's Irish mocking laughter vibrated in the van, "Best I can do is let you know she's safe and getting into a Lincoln now. We ran the plates... but I think you know the score on that one."

Kurt pounded his fists on the van dash.

Chapter 15

The stately wrought-iron gates of The Apthorp on Broadway welcomed Amanda and Anna into a safe haven. Here Amanda was sure to co-create the exclusive story she desired to exonerate Antonio.

The Renaissance Revival limestone buildings epitomized the high class living of New York's privileged. The iconic setting commanded the entire city block between West 78th and 79th Streets. It evoked envy of those in the selective group who had obtained rent stabilization, of which Anna Casali was a fortunate member and soon to be an owner.

Once inside the massive gates they passed under the coffered vaulted tunnel entrance, grander than any wonderland that Amanda could imagine. The chauffeur circled around the brick paved drive containing a picturesque central courtyard, a fountain, and park benches. At building C he stopped and escorted them into the New York palatial gem. Surreal and dreamlike; she swore Antonio's spirit was guiding Anna and her together in total agreement. They agreed Max, the chauffeur, would escort Amanda to her apartment for clothing and personal items when it was deemed safe and problem free.

The problem was Kurt.

No sooner did they enter the spacious three bedroom third floor apartment when the phone rang echoing off the creamy plaster walls accented with white trim, matching paneled doors, and wainscot. Even with multihued antique wool rugs placed at the dining and living areas over herringbone cherry wood floors, the ringing phone seemed cacophonic. The apartment was large enough to comfortably fit her apartment and Kurt's collectively inside with room to spare.

Anna answered her ivory and brass Empire Princess phone while Amanda eavesdropped and strolled through the elegant living area. She admired the solid cream sofa, pink floral pillows, and striped draperies. But what she admired most were the large verdant Italian countryside tapestries dotted with villas and farmhouses.

Immediately her ears twitched recognizing the angry voice on the phone as Kurt's. She had grown accustom to the fluctuations in his tone and attitude. He was not happy. But most of it was his own doing; he shouldn't try to control her. It wasn't good for his blood pressure.

Anna pulled the receiver from her ear and hand covered the mouthpiece. Amanda studied her face; it reflected amusement, not anger.

"Ms. Lindas, I have an anxious young suitor who wishes to speak with you, and furthermore he has made demands that I return you to his company. How do you wish to proceed?"

Amanda stalled with her dilemma. Should she or shouldn't she speak with him? Returning to his company was definitely not an option; however she felt she owed him some appeasement; if only to prevent him from torturing Jeremy and Belinda with his tumultuous fits. A definite clue he was the last born in the family birthright order. He was so demanding.

"Please be patient Mr. Kilawee. I believe she is contemplating whether you can be cordial. Although you may have the right to be upset, you don't have the right to bully her or me." She raised her eyebrows inquiring Amanda's intention. "Well, Amanda do you wish to speak in private with Mr. Kilawee or shall I tell him to call back at a more convenient time? Perhaps when he is calm," Anna's warm smile hinted she thought him rather humorous.

Amanda smiled back and agreed with a nod to speak to him.

"There is a phone in the guestroom just to the right of the den." Anna instructed, "It is your room for as long as you like." She added for Kurt's burning ears.

Amanda walked into the spacious Victorian styled bedroom. With apprehension she picked up the brass and ivory receiver, "Hello." She said sitting on the scrolled white and brass queen bed, covered with a white bedspread sprinkled with pink rosebuds. She listened to Kurt inhale and exhale heavily.

"Be nice Kurt!" Jeremy uttered a warning in the background.

"Hello," Amanda repeated, "are you trying to tease me with your heavy breathing or is there a point to your interruption of my exclusive interview with Mrs. Casali?"

"Amanda, I can't fucking believe what you did!" his manners were lost to oblivion. "Your actions were uncalled for and irresponsible."

"So much for being nice," Jeremy hollered.

"What I did? Drive *my* car? Dig in your trash for information you carelessly threw away in a moment of passion? What did you expect from me? Huh? Who the hell do you think you are? You took my clothing and my purse. What the hell did you expect from me? Do you even know who you're dealing with?"

Befuddled and humiliated unable to lash back, Kurt fumed silently.

"Well?" she prodded.

He responded with a nervous laugh, "You're right. How stupid of me to try to protect you, and I..." his voice thinned to silence.

"And you what? You wanted to get the exclusive story by trapping me in your apartment? I am not a child. And I use my resources to the best of my ability."

"Yeah, you sure do," his voice was grave. "Let me come see you. Come back and we'll work things out." His confusion was high and his self-control was low. "Come on," he begged, "at least give me my clothes back."

"You'll get them when I get mine, and not until."

"Okay, fair enough. When?" He refused to let up, he had to see her.

She hesitated. They really needed more cooling off time.

"Well? What's it going to be Princess?" he reverted to his suave disposition. "We can meet in my den and finish what we started." His voice deepened with romantic need.

"Don't sweet-talk me, besides I did finish."

She waited for his refute.

"Well Kurt? No comment? Okay, how about this, you go and secure my apartment. Then I will go pack my suitcases and leave your precious freshly dry-cleaned clothing for you to pickup after I leave?"

"No deal. I want to see you."

"Kurt, I don't think we should see each other under the circumstances. I can't trust you."

His voice cut through the phone, "You can't trust me? What the hell did I do, but try to protect you... and remember I helped you finish? And I am not the one who committed grand theft."

"Oh, so kidnapping is *not* a felony in New York? You tried to prevent me from getting this story. You intended to meet with Anna, so you could boost your career, and mitigate your actions towards Tony and me."

"You really think that? I give up! I can't get you to believe the truth. Jeremy, you talk to her, I'm done. Just get my fucking clothes and my money clip back, she can protect herself. I'm going out for a drink, Belinda you coming with me?" Kurt threw the phone to Jeremy.

"Amanda? This is Jeremy."

"What is he doing?" Concern replaced her anger.

"He went to his room," Jeremy whispered like a pro-golf commentator, "he's coming back–he changed his shirt. And now he has Belinda by the elbow scooting her to the door."

Kurt shouted, "Come on Belinda honey, let's go get you some new clothes, so you won't have to run around town in mine. My treat. Then we'll go have a drink or two."

He did it again. His antics triggered the green monster in Amanda's inner being. "Jeremy put him on the phone!"

"Hey Kurt, she wants to deal now." Jeremy handed Kurt the phone.

"Oh, now you want to talk?" Derision filled the cavern between them. "What changed your mind?"

"Just stop it! You're driving me to drink. We can meet, but in public."

"Now you're making some sense. Where? And when?"

"How about Zabar's tomorrow? It's on Broadway and 80th."

"Do you know who you're talking to? I'm a seasoned New Yorker. I know where Zabar's is. What time?"

Yeah, I know who I am talking to, a hotheaded mental case. Amanda thought, stopping herself, she answered his latter question. "How about around three, that will give me time to get my clothes and have yours dry-cleaned."

"You're not going to that apartment without my protection. And that's not a question."

They were at a stalemate.

Amanda folded. "Fine control freak, I'll borrow clothes from Anna, but you have to bring Jeremy and Belinda with you. No funny business."

"You sure you don't want to join us for dinner and drinks tonight? I'm taking Belinda shopping." He pushed her buttons knowing he won this battle, but their war was far from over.

"Good-bye Asshole!" Amanda slammed down the receiver.

####

The next day at three, Amanda, Anna, and passersby were wooed by the blaze orange Zabar's signs centered under redbrick arches. The aroma of fresh roasted, freshly brewed coffee, and homemade pastries tempted them to enter. Amanda succumbed to the multilevel gourmet grocery store wearing a well-fitted aubergine wool pantsuit Anna gave her for the adversary meeting.

Anna had insisted on walking to 80th with Amanda, but as an extra precaution the chauffeur followed them with the Lincoln.

Inside Zabar's they wandered around selecting delectable French and Italian cheeses, lamb chops, roasted chicken, Nova smoked salmon, and the specialty D'Artagnan Medallion Duck *Foie gras* as a celebration meal for joining forces.

Zabar's was packed as usual. Amanda stood in line enticed by the bakery selections displayed under glass. A familiar reflection of a tall undeniably handsome man approached her from behind placing his strong hands firmly on her hips. She stiffened to his touch.

Kurt leaned down taking liberty he kissed her neck gently. "Hmm, is that your sweet fragrance that entices me or the apple-cinnamon strudel?

Don't make a scene, I'm just happy to see you–alive." His words strangely lulled her into a haze. "Now where can we go to talk–alone?"

Looking over her left shoulder she caught a glimpse of his calming green eyes, "Pretty presumptuous aren't you? We–don't go anywhere alone. You require a chaperon. Where's your entourage? I need to talk to Belinda."

A thick Brooklyn accent broke their intense bond, "Yo next in line, say what'll yous guys like today?" the white uniformed baker asked.

Kurt selected several strudels, bagels, and pastries. A quizzical look scrunched on Amanda's face.

"What? I think Belinda has a tapeworm. I have to take out a loan to keep feeding her. She's like a stray cat, once you start feeding them, they don't go away." Amanda smiled, his mission accomplished.

Past the pastries they met up with Jeremy and Belinda at the antipastos and salad counter. Each had their individual lists in hand, apparently stocking up for a cold winter or a nuclear holocaust. They stopped ordering long enough to hug their wayward friend.

"Say nice duds, you look great Mandy." Belinda said and twirled for Mandy to envy her new stylish Donna Karan black pantsuit; compliments of Kurt.

The outfit was true Kurt style– elegant, sensible, and fitted. A bit overly studious for Belinda's style, Amanda feared the worse. Was Belinda brainwashed and sleeping with the enemy? The latter thought made her stomach squirm.

"Thank you Belinda. Well, don't you look well suited and rested? Care to join me for an outside chat?" Amanda squinted at Kurt.

Immediately tension filled their cramped aisle. Kurt handed Jeremy his basket of pastries, placed his hands on her shoulders, and caressed them. "Amanda pull in your claws, nothing has happened to cat-fight about. Although, I like a cat-fight now and again, this is not the place or the time." He turned her to face him. They were squished together on all sides by the early afternoon rush of mothers, wailing children, and harried maids gathering last minute gastronomical fantasy foods for dinner.

He pulled her close, "Now, I know you're mad at me because you think I was trying to pinch Anna's story. But my main objective is your safety and now Belinda has to be protected too. Jeremy, I, and some plainclothes agents went to your apartments. They were ransacked. Someone is looking for something you have, or information you've documented. Come clean with me. This isn't a competition. This is serious life and death shit here, understand?" His hands cupped her face and searched her eyes. "No apartment–without me. Do you understand?"

"Okay fine, just give me a moment with Belinda, and then... we need to get my things. Do you have my purse?" At that moment, she couldn't think of anything else except how secure he made her feel and how much she wanted him to kiss her.

She broke away and rushed Belinda outside.

Fatigued Kurt and Jeremy stood in the long confining lines, but ultimately they knew it was well worth the wait. Zabar's reputation for the best gastro pleasures was surpassed by no other Upper West Side food venue. Kurt kept his eyes steady on the girls.

Outside, Amanda diligently sought answers, "First off, did you go with to our apartments?"

Belinda eyes bulged like Marty Feldman's, "Oh Mandy they destroyed everything. Our sofas, chairs, and mattresses were slashed and shredded. Your bookcase, desk, and dressers all chopped to pieces along with mine. We have nothing left, but clothes and shoes."

Amanda shook Belinda's shoulders, "But what about under the bottom shelves in our cabinets, did they get my journals and tapes?"

Belinda covered her opened mouth, "So that's what they wanted. Oh my Gawd, Kurt kept asking me, but I was in such a funk, I totally spaced them."

"Good girl," Amanda hugged her, "Now we need to get them, but the guys can't help. They can guard the apartment outside while we gather my journals. The journals will be safe with Anna. Don't you dare tell Kurt—even if he promises to buy you a suite at The Plaza! Do you understand?"

"Yes, I promise, but what will we hide them in?"

"Umm, suitcases, I need clothes, to stay with Anna. Don't tell me they shredded them too?" Panic rose in Amanda.

"I don't think so? I don't remember. It looked like a dumpsite after a tornado."

Kurt, Jeremy, Anna, and the chauffeur were heading out the door laden with white and orange signature shopping bags and pastry boxes.

"One last thing Belinda, tell me the truth. Did you sleep with Kurt?"

Shock covered Belinda's already blushing face. "I'm no fool; I know how much you think you don't like him. Shoot, I know enough not to score with another chick's dude. Besides he sleeps on the couch when he's not pacing around pouting about you. He's not all bad, just a little crazy. You should give him a chance. Damn girl, was he pissed at us. He had the car impounded too."

"Yeah, I saw that. I'm sorry for thinking you and him, well you know? I guess he's got me thinking crazy too. Anyway, shush they're coming."

Kurt exchanged pleasantries with Anna and openly gave her his card. "I'll take Amanda to her apartment."

Amanda stepped into their private *tete-a-tete*, "Oh no, I ride with Anna. I just need a couple of suitcases full of clothes, Belinda can help me. You and Jeremy can play lookout. That's the deal or no deal." Her eyes iced.

With a clenched jaw, he gritted his rebuttal. "Fine. We'll follow you. No funny business!" He mimicked her warning from the prior night.

Before the chauffeur finished putting their purchases in the trunk, Kurt opened the Lincoln passenger back door. Anna entered first giving him an opportune chance to love-tap Amanda's bottom. He couldn't resist, in return he received a brutal sneer from her lovely face.

At their building on 35th, Amanda and Belinda entered her apartment first. Belinda's description wasn't far from the truth. All the wood furniture was kindling scattered amongst her family photos.

Violated. Amanda clutched photos to her aching heart. How stupid was she thinking she could protect herself from the unknown? She wiped away tears. "Belinda, I'm sorry I got you involved, I'll replace everything they damaged of yours. I'm so glad they didn't harm you."

They hugged for a tight moment.

In the bedroom they found two useable suitcases out of four. Back in the kitchen they pried up the bottom shelves where the pots and pans were stored. With relief they discovered her journals and cassette tapes intact. The thing she needed most was her passport which was hidden with her journals. Quickly they wrapped the journals with her clothing. Forced to leave things behind, Amanda selected multiple coordinating outfits. She layered herself with jackets, and had Belinda do the same. They packed shoes and hygiene items, and headed across the hall to remove the bottom shelves in Belinda's kitchen.

"Oh Belinda, I'm so sorry," Amanda repeated, devastated. "We could have been killed if Kurt hadn't insisted we stay with him." They worked hastily securing the journals, zipping the suitcases just in time.

"Come on ladies, no time for picnics, let's get out of here. I will hire someone to clean up the rest." Kurt said. "You have what you need Amanda? Are you okay?" His concern was genuine.

She nodded. He gripped the suitcases, bewildered he asked. "What the hell did you pack, bricks and the kitchen sink?"

The girls exchanged winks and laughed.

"You know women, we never pack light. You're a strapping man, you can handle it." Amanda squeezed his taut bicep. "Come on Super-hero, I have dinner plans with my new hostess."

Kurt scowled and lugged the suitcases to the elevator.

On the elevator ride down, they all stood silent as if they were strangers. The familiar buzzing of the elevator and squealing cables left the girls wondering if they'd ever return. Desolation hung in the air.

Finally they hit bottom and exited on Kurt's command, "Let's go ladies. No dawdling, say your good-byes." He hoisted the overweight suitcases into the town car trunk and asked Max if he needed any assistance once he got to The Apthorp. The chauffeur assured him there was no need of further assistance.

Amanda collected her purse and extra jackets from Belinda while Kurt addressed Anna.

"Mrs. Casali thank you for your hospitality towards Amanda, please call me if there is anything I can do. Private agents will be watching your area. Please be careful. I am doing everything I can to flush out your son's killer. I am sincerely sorry for your loss. I hope Amanda will bring you the comfort you deserve. She's awesome, but don't tell her I said so." Kurt smiled as Amanda approached the other side of the vehicle; he excused himself and strutted over to open her door.

Amanda quickly faced him avoiding his hand contact with her rear. "Oh no, not this time," she said sharing a genuine smile keeping eye contact.

Uninhibited and debonair he spontaneously pulled her close effortlessly he hugged her, "Maybe not this time, but sometime soon. Be careful, I will call you."

"Well, if it makes you feel better." She hugged him quick, released eye contact, and handed him his dry-cleaned clothes. "Your *with love* money clip is in the jacket pocket." Hastily she slipped into her seat, fearful she'd confess about the journals and her arrangement with Anna. She sensed he'd be distraught and royally pissed if he knew her plans.

####

Two weeks later at NYCB, Rich summoned Kurt to his office. Rich's jaw was still wired shut. Four weeks had passed since the incident. It still pained Rich to speak, eat, or even look at Kurt.

Kurt entered on a sarcastic note, "Hey Rich, You're looking good. Have you lost about thirty pounds? Tell me—what is your secret?"

Rich sneered and grunted, "Amanda called, says she wants to extend her leave. She may not come back."

"What? She never mentioned a damn thing about taking more leave. Why can't she come back to work? Why does she insist on hiding things from me?" Kurt fumed.

They had spoken daily over the phone sharing their morning coffee apart, but together. He thought they had reached a common ground and progressed towards a trusting relationship. Now, his hopes were dashed.

Rich pulled a travel document from his desk drawer and handed it to Kurt. "That's not all she's hiding from you."

Bewildered Kurt reviewed the documents which contained a flight ticket to Rome and a train ticket to Naples, Italy. "What's this for?"

"She's going to Italy; on that same flight." Rich relayed through gritted teeth, "Sarah's friend works in that travel agency. Amanda asked me not to tell you that Anna Casali has personal business in Naples; she wants Amanda to handle it for her. I think you should follow Amanda, for her safety, of course." He grinned with a grimace.

Kurt knitted his throbbing brow. "Okay, but what about my spots and interviews?"

"Damn Kurt is your work your life? We'll fill spots with pre-taped shit until you return. It's only a week. You'll be back, she'll be back, and we'll be one sick dysfunctional family again. Go get packed, I'll have Jeremy drop you off at JFK. Don't let her see you."

Kurt reached the airport midday, receiving special VIP security clearance, allowing him to board the plane early and with his gun. The Alitalia flight to Rome's *Fiumicino Leonardo Da Vinci* airport was about nine hours. It seemed impossible to think he could keep himself hidden from her in a small secluded area. Questions flooded his mind. Why didn't she tell him? And why would Anna ask her houseguest to fly to another country as a favor?

He spotted Amanda as soon as she boarded the plane. Her seat was in *Magnifica* business class; hopefully guaranteeing that she'd use the restrooms to the front and not wander back. It was an overnight flight, so the lights were off for the in-flight movie.

Against his better judgment, he ordered a couple small bottles of scotch hoping he'd fall into a drunken sleep. He wasn't keen on long flights.

As the flight proceeded, Kurt wished he would have upgraded to first class. The cramping in his legs forced him to get up mid-flight to stretch. He ordered two more scotches on the rocks. His other option was having his lower legs amputated. He stood in the back chatting with two cute stewardesses, probably his first mistake.

His joking style and charming anecdotes gathered a few fans who recognized him from the cable network. Unfortunately in an enclosed airplane news travels faster than on land, this he discovered firsthand.

After a few more drinks, Kurt had forgotten himself and his mission. He leaned his elbow nonchalantly on a ledge holding his drink in the same hand. While he flirted untying a flight attendant's apron he hadn't a care in the world, until Amanda's icy stare met his.

"Well, Mr. Kilawee, I see you're up to your old tricks." She said folding her arms across her chest. The stewardesses cleared away.

Kurt jerked up, spilled his drink while simultaneously hitting his shoulder on the sharp metal upper cabinet. He winced then blushed when she eyed his gaping shirt exposing his chest to his female audience. He fumbled single-handedly trying to button a few buttons. Awkwardly his effort to be presentable was futile. All he really wanted was to crawl beneath a seat like a compact suitcase.

"Well Mandy, you know what they say–you can't trick an old dog with a new teacher." He fumbled his words, more from getting caught than from consuming alcohol. He was busted. Without an escape route.

The tension between their locked eyes pushed the other hens out of the sacred henhouse.

Amanda broke the silence like ice cracking across a barren pond. Kurt crossed his arms guarded against the inevitable verbal blows he was about to receive.

"Having fun? Did I interrupt your pleasure flight?" Her chest heaved. "You have about," she glanced at her wrist realizing she still had not found her Gucci watch. "Hmm... about four hours to explain why you're on my flight?" Her foot tapped the metal threshold.

Oh how he wanted to vaporize at that insane moment. Some fellow flight patrons pushed into the area seeking restroom privileges. They succeeded in shoving them closer. Kurt used the tight opportunity to extend his long arms over her shoulders. He drew her closer, to eliminate any reason for shouting.

"I'm waiting," she huffed shrugging his arms off her shoulders.

Unable to think straight, he was unsure if Amanda's foot tapped Morse code for S.O.S or if it was his heartbeat. Her disappointment disturbed his natural ability to dig himself out of a hole.

"Thank you for being patient, I'm thinking of a lame excuse that you're not going to like or believe." He quirked his boyish grin and rubbed her tight shoulders hoping physical attention would drive the insanely fractious look off her face.

"Kurt, I'm not in the mood for your antics or lies. If you don't tell me now, I promise you that the fire Marshall on this plane will have to take me into custody for going ballistic on you. Tell me now!" She flicked his hands from her tense shoulders.

His eyes roved the small compartment; he felt claustrophobic and motion sickness. "I found out, from Belinda."

Her sharp fingernail poked into his chest, "Liar! You did not because she doesn't know."

"Ouch! You don't have to get violent. I had PIs tracking you and a snitch at the travel agency." She poked him again even harder.

"Don't lie to me, you're out of practice. Anna and I paid off your men." She jabbed him again.

In defense his hands splayed on his chest. "Hey don't poke the messenger. I'm sorry I lied. You paid off my guys? Wait until I get back to them."

"I'm warning you, don't change the subject! Answer me. Who put you up to this?"

"Alright, alright if I promise to tell the truth will you sit with me? I'd love to join the mile high club with you."

"Kurt, get your mind out of the gutter. For the last time tell me." Her face flared red as her eyes darted icy blue shards.

"How can you seriously consider a mile high as the gutter?"

"I'm won't justify that comment with a response. I'm through with your bullshit–tell me now, or I will never speak to you again!"

His repertoire was bankrupt.

"Fine, Rich sent me to cover you and your story. He said you asked for an extended leave of absence."

Amanda's face went from hot red to a pasty gray. Her eyes did an awful backward rotation to white and she dropped. She flopped forward to his finger bruised chest; he caught her before she hit the floor. An attendant was at his side assisting him with blankets and pillows. "What happen?" she asked.

"I don't know, one moment I'm telling her the truth, and the next moment she's falling on me."

"Yeah, well perhaps you should tell the truth more often, so it isn't such a shock." Another attendant handed the original attendant some smelling salts and snickered at her derogatory comment.

Kurt recognized them as his former fan club members, "Great a couple of comedians. Well, don't quit your day or night jobs, let's just get her off the floor."

One arm under Amanda's legs, the other under her back, he hefted her with one powerful upward thrust, leaving the flight attendants awestruck at his strength. "Okay shows over folks, everyone return to your seats. She just fainted, she's okay."

Kurt sat her in the empty chair next to his, her head wobbled like a bobble-head. He held her chin to steady her. "Hey ladies, bring the smelling salts, how about some water and a scotch?" They marched to his orders.

"Mandy, Mandy," he whispered waving the smelling salt under her nose. "Come on look at me?"

She responded, touching her head she gazed around. "Where am I? What happened?"

"Well, you're on a flight to Rome. I was telling you the truth and you fainted. Care to share with me why?"

"I guess because you rarely tell the truth." She smirked.

"Alright enough already, when's the last time you ate or drank?"

"What are you my personal physician now?"

He grinned and said, "Why do you want to play doctor with me?"

"No, go away, leave me alone." she pushed him.

He was solid as Superman.

"I'm not leaving you alone—ever. Why would you faint?"

Then it occurred to him, why do many women faint? Was she pregnant with Antonio's kid? Suddenly, he felt like he was going to faint. He stood up, took the scotch he requested, and shot it down. If he was going to hear the daunting truth he wanted to be half wasted.

Uneasy, he squatted close and whispered so softly he could barely hear himself speak. "Tell me the truth, are you pregnant? Is that why you and Anna got so close—so quickly?" he swore his heart stopped beating waiting for her answer.

Waking up half of coach, she screamed, "What? You Ass! How could you even think that? Me pregnant?"

Kurt covered his face with his hand.

She continued ranting, "I would have had to had sex first, and unprotected sex for that matter to conceive a child, which for your information and ego I had neither with Antonio. What part of national news did you participate in?"

Their audience grew. A few lewd comments and whispers identified them as NYCB's 'Golden Couple'.

One guy shouted, "Say your line Kilawee, you know the very last one."

Kurt stood and looked around, a little embarrassed, but strangely relieved their private conversation had turned into public ridicule and adoration. He clutched her hand and raised it high. "Yes, folks this is Kurt Kilawee and Amanda Lindas from 'The New Edge on Truth' – together we believe in practicing good safe-sex."

The audience applauded and cheered, Kurt did a grandeur bow. Unfortunately Amanda wasn't feeling the love.

She tugged her hand back and scornfully said. "You can sit down now Dr. Kilawee."

The flight attendant asked, "Miss Lindas can I get you anything?"

"Yes, please bring me two Chardonnays."

"Would you like them brought together or separate?"

"By all means together," Amanda glared at Kurt.

"Oh, so now you're going to be a two-fisted drinker, just to prove a point." Kurt bantered.

"Oh no, you've underestimated me as usual, I plan on sharing."

The attendant brought the wine in separate plastic tumblers, Amanda stood to receive them. One she chugged so fast it would have made a wino proud. The other she splashed on him, "Here, have a drink!"

He jumped up, his face dripping and his shirt soaked with wine. A huddle of flight attendants brought towels to dry him. Wiping his face, he maintained a grin allowing them to touch him. Apparently Amanda was not as entertained, so he up the ante and removed his shirt keeping eye contact with her. He won the wow factor he wanted by flexing his muscles.

"There's no such thing as bad attention or bad publicity, right Ms. Lindas?"

Abashed Amanda strutted to her original seat.

Kurt paid the passenger next to her to exchange seats with him. He kept his shirt off insisting it wasn't dry. She feigned sleeping, dodging his ploy to kiss and makeup.

Using a last-ditch effort, he whispered, "So, we won't be joining the mile high club?" A quick sharp slap to his cheek was her answer.

The head attendant escorted him back to his original seat for the duration of the flight to the *Fiumicino Leonardo Da Vinci* airport in Rome.

Apologetic and sluggish Kurt gathered their luggage at the crowded baggage claim. The crowd in customs acted like wild elephants charging the Serengeti, fatigued, yet he refused to hire a porter. "Amanda slow down! We have plenty of time to catch the train to Naples. Tell me why you fainted?" He trailed her closely. "And don't sell me the bogus song and dance about my telling you the truth. Why did you ask Rich for an extended leave?"

Astounded she stopped and turned to face her exhausted unwanted volunteer porter, "You're insane. I'll bet your parents were never really married."

Sweat trickled down his face, he dropped the heavy suitcases, "What? Why would you assume that? On what grounds are you basing your illusion? You don't even know my parents."

"No, but I know their son. And he acts like a Bastard!"

"Oh, very funny, maybe you and the flight attendants can develop an act on your extended leave. You think you can just leave and expect your cushy Anchor position to be waiting for your fashionable late return? Get real–high profile careers take tenacity, professionalism, and perseverance to reach perfection."

"Well, you ought to know–Mr. Perfect. But I know what you don't know. In fact I've forgotten more about what you don't know of what I do know–sound vaguely familiar? For your information, I didn't put in for a leave. I never called Rich and I never entered that travel agency. But what I did do was turn over several journals and tape recordings to the FBI and the NYPD to indict Rich on charges of racketeering, money laundering, and hiring a hit man. Rich Underwood would be last in line behind two other men that I'd never call if I needed help." Angry tears played havoc with her mascara. Kurt took his handkerchief to wipe her face. She slapped his hand away.

"Well, who are they?"

"You and my father!" she spun on her heels racing to nowhere. Her eyes blinded by resentful tears.

He clutched the suitcases and jogged after her, "Amanda! Stop, you don't even know where the hell you're going."

She stood speechless looking around the terminal trying to get her bearings. It was a good thing the signs were written in English and Italian because she knew very little Italian. Trembling she patted the side pocket of her trench coat double checking that she hadn't lost the documents Anna had given her.

Now what was she going to do with him tagging along? How did Rich know she was leaving the country? She knew one thing that Kurt was too smart not to have turned Rich over to the authorities. So, why didn't he?

Kurt hollered, "Go to the right. The train to Naples departs there."

"Stop being so bossy!" She said following his directions.

"Why didn't you confide in me about Rich?" he huffed alongside her.

"I didn't know which side you were on."

"Great! Great impression I've left on you. How do you know which side I'm on now Miss Smart-ass?"

"Seriously you don't get it Mr. I-Know-Everything? Rich sent you here to get you out of his way. He knows you following me buys time to get his affairs in order. You're not on his side or you wouldn't be here."

"Very good reporting and thanks for inducing my point of motivation, now can we start working together?"

After showing their passports and tickets to the train attendant, they boarded the train. Amanda plopped down in a window seat, interlocking her hands on her lap.

Kurt stowed their luggage to the front exit area, placed his small carry-on into the overhead bin, and sat in the plush seat next to hers, "Well, are we going to be partners?"

"No partners. You and me– we are not 'a we'."

"You and I…" Kurt corrected, "could be 'a we', if you'd say yes."

"Yes to what? Are you proposing marriage?"

Kurt's jaw dropped.

"That's what I thought. You can't even say the 'M-word', can you?"

"What brought that on? You just said I was one of the last three men in the world that you'd turn to. I guess given the evidence, I'd be the 'M' material seeing as one is your father and the other is old enough to be your father. And let's not forget you've just turned him in on three felony charges, so I win by default. Lucky me."

He folded his arms and slouched back into the primo-class seats. The flight and the luggage workout started taking its toll, not to mention the energy it took to argue effectively with Mandy. With one eye opened in her direction he warned, "I suggest you get some sleep and don't attempt some super-heroine escape. Two men dressed in black have followed us since we disembarked the plane. If they don't catch you–I will. And I can promise you the 'M-word' won't be the one you want to hear. Besides that, we still have to have our little talk especially about what happened in my den."

"Oh please, give it a rest. Just because you give a woman an orgasm doesn't give you the right to stalk or badger her." Amanda rose to look towards the back.

Quick reflexes, he yanked her down by her forearm. "Don't make me handcuff you." He glowered into her placid eyes, "I might like it. So what rights do I get?"

"What? An orgasm doesn't come with rights." She sat grudgingly, "Oh you're incorrigible, despicable, and deplorable."

"I know, but I'm also loveable, adorable, and stronger than you, so I suggest you start working on the 'we' part in your brain. You know, you owe me one back."

"Keeping score are we?"Amanda scooted closer to the window to watch the Eternal City flash by her. She had never been to Italy, one of the most romantic places in the world, and now she was forced to tolerate it with Mr. Playboy and two odious thugs.

"Yes–sort of tit for tat," he said and elaborated. "If someone gives you an orgasm then you should be cordial and return the favor."

"Seriously Kurt, do you even listen to the crap that escapes your mouth?"

"So you're saying you didn't enjoy the orgasm?"

"Ugh! I don't know anyone that doesn't enjoy orgasms." She curled into a fetal position choosing sleep over bickering. Naples was at least a two hour ride.

"Me either, so just to be clear–we agree you owe me one." He cuddled up to her placing his hand on her butt. She slapped his hand hard. "Ouch, I just want you know there's plenty more available."

"No thanks, I think I can handle the rest of them on my own. You've been a big help. Keep your paws to yourself, Mr. Kilawee."

He retracted momentarily. "Speaking of big–I don't want you to miss out on my other talents. Did you enjoy our time in my den?" he whispered.

His perseverance earned him a swift kick. Her heel landed squarely on his upper thigh just missing his groin area. "Okay, I'll take that as a maybe." He retreated rubbing his thigh writhing in pain, "One of these days, you will regret how nasty you're treating me now."

"I doubt it, but feel free to keep lying to yourself."

They rested uneasy. It's hard to sleep when you're being watched. The trick was when the train stopped; Kurt rushed her to the front exit and lowered the suitcases to her. They successfully avoided the drowsy thugs dressed in typical black suits and dark turtlenecks. The weather in Naples was light jacket weather not tight turtlenecks.

Together Kurt and Amanda hid behind a pillar, slipped their trench coats off while deciding their next move.

Kurt lit a cigarette. Amanda double-checked her deep coat pockets.

He offered her a cigarette.

"How can you condone that nasty habit?"

"How can you constantly condone that bitchy attitude–it's just as nasty!" He dropped the half smoked cigarette squelching it. "At least I can quit buying cigarettes."

"And what, start licking ashtrays? Shut up, what are we suppose to do now? I have my room booked at the *Hotel Potenza* on *Piazza Giuseppe Garibaldi*. It's supposed to be fifty meters away. Where are you staying?"

He interlocked her arm with his, "With you of course."

"Oh no you're not, you can't be trusted."

"Oh, I can be trusted." He raised his eyebrows. "The truth is–it's you that can't trust yourself with me. That's why you stayed at Anna's apartment, especially now that I know you're not pregnant. Thanks for that tidbit of reassuring information." Over his shoulder he spotted the thugs searching the railway station. To give them the slip, he ushered Amanda forward through the thick crowds and across the piazza.

Secretly Amanda appreciated having him carry her luggage. He was a God send. So strong and attentive, that the Bell desk attendant assumed they were a couple.

"So will it be a queen bed or two twins pushed together Mr. and Mrs. Lindas?" Kurt looked confused, but Amanda instantly demanded separate rooms which set off bickering fireworks.

"Honey, we should be together, at least we should share a private bath and a connecting room." Kurt insisted.

"Don't call me Honey, and no, we are not sharing a bath. You are not invited to stay with me."

"*Signore*, we have private baths in our rooms." The manager said interrupting their heated discussion.

"I will call you anything I want. We are staying together for your protection. Besides that, who will carry your luggage dear?" Kurt questioned and then addressed the Manager, "We'll take a room with the twins together that will equal a king. I like sharing a bath with her."

The manager frowned, "Are you two married?"

Kurt laughed and clutched her to his side, "No, but there is still hope for her pre-honeymoon jitters." He winked to get his point across.

"*Signore*, we run a safe establishment, if the lady insists on a separate room then we will honor her request."

Amanda pushed away from Kurt, "The lady insists."

Kurt took a wad of folded bills from his pocket and paid for both rooms without any further comment.

She was stunned speechless at his compliance and his gallant gesture of paying the bill.

Kurt and the other gentlemen savored the peace and quiet.

Like a pack mule, he hefted their luggage up *Hotel Potenza's* six decorative blue, white, yellow *fleur di lis* risers, passing a small bar and pizzeria just to encounter several more flights of stairs.

"What no lift?" he grumbled while she led the way. At least with this workout he got the added benefit of her agreeable behind. The best part of his trip so far.

Once settled in their rooms they finally agreed to go eat at the little *tratorria* connected to the *Pensione*.

Kurt ordered the *prix fixe* Italian pastas and a bottle of red wine for them. The small restaurant was dark and smoky, Amanda sat vulnerable, she slipped into fatigue from all the mayhem. Like a candle flickering in a breeze her thoughts swayed on accepting his assistance or going out on her own.

He reached across the small table còvering her hand with his, "Come on, let me help you. What are you here to do?"

"I'm here to deliver two envelopes for Anna."

"Allow me go with you, as your assistant, or bodyguard. You're in a foreign country and you don't speak the language well. You also have gangsters following you. My guess is they're keeping their distance because I'm with you…"

Suddenly, before he finished his spiel, they heard gunshots fired from outside, bullets punctured the wall just above Amanda's head. Chunks of plaster fell; Kurt immediately flipped the table and shielded her with his body. "Stay down and stay here."Crouched low he pulled his Glock from under his suit coat. "Everyone stay down!" Kurt hollered as he waddled to the opened iron-gate entrance. Another shot popped the outside chalkboard menu, just missing his shoulder by inches.

He shifted back into the bar kicking one of the double doors closed. Of course, Amanda hugged to his side, "Really Amanda? Now you want to get close? What part of the word–stay–don't you comprehend?" Exasperated he pushed her back behind the table.

"I'm afraid."

"So getting shot will make you less scared?" He raised his eyebrows questioning her logic. "I'm going out there, you stay here. If you follow me, I swear I'll shoot you myself."

Amanda clutched her sides and leaned against the cool brick wall. Uncertainty and fear plagued her. Had she gone too far for the truth? Was this Rich's doing, Carmine's or Giovanni's? Who wanted her dead? And how did she pull Kurt into this dismal affair?

She obeyed him, but cringed at each gunshot she heard from the alley behind the *Piazza Giuseppe Garibaldi*. The police sirens whirred surrounding the *Hotel Potenza*. Many heavy footsteps drummed the cobbled pavement and raced past the entrance. Kurt burst through the back door of the small kitchen, his gun still drawn; his eyes riveted, spotting Amanda they softened. She was safe where he had left her.

The Italian police had infiltrated and surrounded the area. They questioned everyone in the *tratorria*. Kurt, their major witness, provided concrete details. He had wounded one thug in the shoulder, so hopefully a blood trail would lead the police to the lout.

They took Kurt's statement, checked his gun, and his badge. As they checked out his background, Amanda stayed glued to his side. He was still perturbed with her for not staying when he had instructed her. But he kept his arm around her trembling shoulders to calm her.

After the commotion died down, Kurt escorted Amanda to their rooms. He asked somberly, "Do you want me to stay in your room?"

"You scared me. I thought you'd be shot and not come back for me. You shouldn't be involved. You shouldn't have followed me." Her voice quaked and tears fell.

"And if I didn't follow you, would you have returned to me alive?" He turned quick and crossed the hall. The thought of her dying sent sharp pains to his chest. An ache he had never experienced before. He needed time alone. "I'm here, if you need me," he said glancing over his shoulder wounded by her empty stare. His desire was to make her feel safe not scared.

Alone in her room Amanda sobbed. Kurt leaving her behind brought to light her deep seeded resentment of when her father left her mother. Fear opened a wound that time had not healed. Isn't love supposed to make you feel safe? With every bit of her soul she wanted to believe that Kurt's benevolent actions were heartfelt actions of love. How could she open herself up to trust him?

An hour later, a knock came at her door, she stiffened in her bed. "Who's there?"

"Room service from Mr. Kilawee."

She recognized the bell attendant's voice; she crept across the quaint room from her double bed. The room barely fit the bed, a rustic dresser, and a round side table. She opened the door; the bellman held a tray with cheeses, crusty rolls, fruit, and a bottle of red wine. A hand written note: *Mandy, I'm here to help you. Love Kurt.*

In tune to her hunger and her desire, how could she refuse? He risked his life and threw that "love" word around carelessly.

The long restless night threatened her sanity. She prayed for a better tomorrow.

Tomorrow could be the cornerstone of their enigmatic future.

Chapter 16

Before noon, the next day their taxi driver, a 'wanna-be' Mario Andretti, dropped Kurt and Amanda outside of *Camaldoli di Napoli*, at the mouth of an extensive undulating dirt drive. Amanda visibly shaken stumbled out of the backseat. Her persistent companion paid the amateur racecar driver a generous tip.

Presumably Kurt enjoyed the rollercoaster fright plastered across her face as the driver took unnecessary wild turns at eighty plus. A malevolent glee sparkled in Kurt's eyes. His mood was mischievously childlike after their distraught night. He acted as if he had resolved a gnawing issue or came to terms with their dismal situation. During the rambunctious ride, Amanda had involuntarily shifted to his side several times, but he didn't make a pass.

Anxious Amanda continued her journey up the drive on foot. The landscape matched her imagination based upon Anna's description. Anna informed her that Giovanni had inherited the moderate sized farmland with olive trees, lemon groves, and small vineyard from his parents. It took some asking around that morning in the *Piazza Giuseppe Garibaldi* to get the scoop on the exact location.

An alliance was formed with Kurt after much remonstration on her part. They agreed to handle their earlier investigations separately. Primarily to avert attention from either being singled out by asking too many questions. In any city too many questions could alert people to jump to conclusions creating a venue for trouble. They believed their discretion worked in their favor.

Kurt caught up easily using his long stride while she wobbled in high heeled boots; something she already regretted. But she couldn't go back and change even if she wanted. Wrapped in her trench coat, she tapped the side pocket; Anna's envelopes were still safe.

Her promise was to deliver two: one addressed to Giovanni Maggiore and the other to Carmine Lucchesi. They remained sealed. As a trusted messenger; she left them sealed, unfortunately for safety she was forced to share her mission with Kurt.

Together they tromped up the hill passing an olive tree orchard on the left and rows of organized grapevines to the right.

"Hey, where's the fire?" Kurt huffed as they ascended the hillcrest. "It is midmorning in southern Italy not midday in New York. We don't have a list of interviews lined up. Can't you relax and enjoy the scenery?" He asked knowing *relax* wasn't in her vocabulary.

Regretful that he had snuck downstairs the night before, it left him out of sorts today. But he couldn't sleep, not with her across the hall. He drank a bottle of Chianti with the bartender and collected information on Giovanni and Carmine. Giovanni was noted as a hardworking local farmer. Carmine on the other hand was not someone you'd want to tangle with on a good day, let alone trying to protect a hardheaded woman on a wine hangover day.

Amanda turned and smiled, "I told you that smoking habit was going to slow you down."

He wanted to banter back; *no it's the lack of sex and too much wine.* But he kept quiet to keep the peace.

Amanda reached the top only to discover their destination continued further down another snaking gravel roadway. Dismayed she wanted to scream; *why did I wear my expensive leather boots?*

On the hilltop she had a splendid view of the property. About five or more football fields away sat an elaborate cream-colored stucco estate with a red-tiled roof. The landscape afforded her panoramic eye pleasure with the autumn foliage in reds, oranges, faded greens and lavender layered to the horizon. The villa might as well have been a five mile gait. *Where was a strapping football player like Joe Montana when a girl needed one?* When Kurt finally joined her she eyed his stature.

"What? Why are you looking at me like that?"

"Oh nothing, just thinking," she refocused to the picturesque vista. She had assumed it would be a rundown country house with ragged landscaping.

"Looks like time ages homes in Italy to perfection unlike some desolate farmhouses back in the states," he said, pausing momentarily. He took her hand and sighed. "Well, let's get a move on, Sweetheart, that villa won't come to us."

When he smiled the morning sun lit his face accenting the small crinkles outside the corners of his luminous eyes. Really quite handsome in a quirky way, Amanda thought. His warm gentle grip caught her off guard.

With his fingers interlocking hers she struggled to release her hand. She had agreed to let him assist her, but not as a companion–business only and nothing more.

Reluctantly he released her hand, shoved his rejected hand into his coat pocket, pulled out his mirrored aviator sunglasses, he covered his dissatisfaction.

They strode alongside each other quietly. The late October morning melody consisted of birds chirping merrily, wind whistling through the orchard leaves, and dogs barking in the distance.

"Did you know Ms Lindas *Campania* means 'fertile countryside'? This area is noted for its agricultural vegetation, nuts, and fruit trees." Kurt spoke his thoughts, "And... St. Peter and St. Paul supposedly preached here near Naples?" His effort to coax her into a nonconfrontational conversation seemed futile.

Amanda was too preoccupied with her aching burning feet to add to his gibberish or play his trivia game, or whatever his ploy was. This was one time she wished she had the nerve to ask for a piggyback ride. Internally she laughed at the grandiose image of her straddling his back with their Dick Tracy trench coats flapping in the wind. Her laughter bubbled out. It aided in easing the painful gnawing on the balls of her feet.

"What's so funny?" He angled his fedora; lifted his sunglasses to fixate his eyes on hers. "Do you want to share it with the rest of the class Ms Lindas?" He chuckled blithely. Her laughter was rare, yet very infectious.

A little embarrassed she shrugged, "Oh, I was just envisioning—" she stopped her explanation short. Squinting into the sun, she tried to see if anyone was rousing about the perimeter of the idyllic villa.

"What? You can tell me. Hell, we are past the awkward first date stage, aren't we?" he thought about his note. She had thanked him for the food and wine, but failed to mention his note.

Amanda kept walking. She pondered his statement "awkward first date stage". She quelled the memory of their first passionate kiss; the very thing that inflicted her life with much grief. And then the amazing physical encounter in his apartment.

Shunning her thoughts, she shaded her eyes with her hand. In the distance she spotted a black and white herd dog and an orange speck of a female figure by the multilevel house. "Never mind," she said. "We are not dating, so we won't have awkward date moments. This is business, not a friendly vacation between lovers."

He stepped close to her, removed his sunglasses barrier, and brushed aside a spiral curl of her hair, "Well it could be. Want me to carry you the rest of the way? Bet I can."

She cracked up laughing somehow he had read her mind. "You just never give up do you?"

"No, it doesn't fit with my effulgent virtuous personality. I bet that I can carry you. Those stilettos must be torture. Wish you'd let go and have a little fun."

The truth was her boots *were* killing her feet. And just how harmful could one innocent piggyback ride be?

"SSSoooo, how do you want me to carry you?" he persisted. "We can do threshold, piggyback or chicken fight style?"

The vision of chicken fight style sent her into hysterics. What would Giovanni and his wife, Tessa, think of them? Her sitting atop of Kurt's shoulders–made her think of the stilt wearing circus clowns. He sure had a deft way of making her laugh.

"Come on–you know you want me..." his brow rose a couple times, "just pick a position. I can do any position you prefer." He adjusted his coat resting it squarely on his shoulders.

Her index finger tapped on her lips, seriously she contemplated his offer. It definitely had to be piggyback; it was the least intimate *position* as he so unequivocally referred it to. "Okay, piggyback works for me."

Kurt turned and crouched with his arms curled back to catch her as she took aim and jumped on.

"Come on, hike up and don't choke my neck, hold my shoulders." He shifted her up cupping his arms around her thighs. "Feels better already huh?"

Suddenly the position impeded her comfort zone going against her intimacy distance rules. The fragrance of his hair and cologne whiffed across her unsuspecting nose. *But, God did her feet feel better instantly*. A subtle rush of ecstasy traveled from her nose to her toes.

At her new elevation, her view of the tri-level villa circled by cypress trees was better. Steadily Kurt plodded like a parading Clydesdale. Perfect even strides, she hoped he didn't mind her weight; she wasn't exactly a twig model. His breath labored very little as if he were accustomed to caring a woman on his back or otherwise.

Desperately she tried not to focus on his muscular shoulders as they flexed beneath her clutching hands. "Are you okay?" she asked hoping he'd say yes. She wasn't crazy about the gravel digging into her tender feet again.

"I'll let you know when I am tired. You just sit tight, Honey."

"Hey, I have a name–use it."

"Yes, but I prefer Honey or Sweetheart over Amanda. In Latin Amanda means– 'being loved or loveable'. So, change your disposition towards me or do you *want me*... to call you Mandy?" He stressed the *want me* while raising his head pushing his hat into her face.

Quickly she caught his falling hat which nearly sent them both tumbling to the rough gravel. She placed his hat on her head and gripped his shoulder. "Wow that was close."

Kurt staggered slightly, "That's an understatement–good thing your ride is a stable strong man. Don't avoid my question. Do you prefer Honey,

Sweetheart, Babe, or can I call you Mandy Baby?" He sang a snippet of Barry Manilow's popular song "Mandy".

"No, no not that, all through Jr. and Sr. High, I suffered deep anguish. I prefer Amanda." Her arms adjusted a little tighter around his broad shoulders. "Are you implying that Amanda is an inappropriate name for my lovable personality?" She purposely blew the words in his ear.

"Okay, Sweetheart be careful, I'm only human, and of the male species."

"Oh that's right, I forgot, I'm the alien bitch. What is with your name calling?"

"I like pet names. I give people names that suit them better, like Jeremy; tell me he doesn't look like a Lionel. And Leroy he's a very astute chauffeur, so I call him James like in classic movies. I don't call names out of spite or meanness. They're endearments. I give pet names to people I like and care about."

She kept quiet thinking about her first day when he had asked to call her Mandy. And then later when she had pushed him to frustration and he called her a bitch.

In silence they passed the grove of lemon trees.

"So, Mandy… did you know that Johann Wolfgang von Goethe wrote about the magnificent lemon trees of Sorrento? And that Sorrento is where the liquor *Limoncello* was invented?"

"Aren't you just a well of trivia today? Where did you learn that?"

"In college I studied Italy as an independent study elective for my undergraduate degree."

"Oh, I assumed 'women's studies' was your elective of special interest. Besides I think Goethe was better known for his literary work '*Faust*'"

"Yes, but Goethe was also known for the novel '*The Sorrows of Young Werther*' which was considered his autobiography. You should read it. It is about an obsessive man driven to despair and destruction by his unrequited love for a woman. The main character commits suicide over unrequited love. Even Napoleon Bonaparte considered it one of the greatest works in European Literature." He stopped a moment to readjust her.

"So, you are telling me this–why?" she giggled. "Oh, because you feel you're being unfairly treated. First and foremost, you're not the type to commit suicide."

"How do you know that? I've never suffered this much for unrequited love before."

"Seriously quit whining. You know as well as I do when someone loves himself like you do he will figure a way out of his dire situation. I still think '*Faust*' is Goethe's greatest contribution to the world along with his in-depth study of color theory. I went to college too."

"Okay, then you must believe the message of '*Faust*' is true. A man who strives on, and lives to strive, he can earn redemption."

"Oh you are good. Twist it back to you. Alright, if you know that you must know the German word '*gretchenfrage*' means Gretchen's question when she insisted that Faust explain his religious status. Now, '*gretchenfrage*' is used to aim at the core of an issue forcing the answering person to make a solicited confession or a difficult decision to tell the truth. Which leads me to ask—why are you really here in Italy with me?"

Kurt stopped again. The pure irony of this truth telling journey was that he needed to get 'a monkey off his back', but she was holding on tight. "You know Gretchen was condemned for killing her illegitimate child?"

"Don't change the subject. You're worse than the audience who forced Goethe to change the ending from 'she shall be saved' to 'she's condemned'. Come clean and confess your sin." She kicked him as best she could from her awkward position.

He plodded on. "No,–you're not a priest, so no confessions from me." He grinned. They just had their first real conversation about nothing and about everything. "Besides, an unsatisfied man is the ultimate conclusion of any tragedy."

"Well, I won't argue with your scholarly abilities. But frankly you owe me an explanation."

"Yeah well, remember you owe me something more physical." With her left hand Amanda smacked his chest. "Ouch! Not quite what I was thinking."

"Well, stay out of the gutter–you're getting dirty."

He squeezed her thighs, "Don't get me started."

Closer to the house, she spotted the female and the dog again. They were in clear sight. The urge to drop down emerged, so as not to appear uncouth. "Hey, do you see the woman over there by the table?"

"Yeah, do you think she's Tessa or a housekeeper?"

"Well, I'm not sure, but do you think she can see us?"

"Yes... unless she's blind."

Amanda shifted up straight and kicked to get down. "Put me down, let me down, I don't want her to think..."

"What do you care what she thinks? You will never see her again in this lifetime? You should care more about not kicking your ride." He said and lowered down trying to release her without dropping her on her head.

"I'm a frightful mess," Amanda unruffled her clothing, primped her hair after Kurt plucked his fedora off her head.

The woman staggered towards them in classic orange pumps, wearing a snug orange V-neck sweater with even tighter blue jeans. Curiosity was written on her face.

She bore an uncanny resemblance to Sophia Loren, and acted as if she hadn't seen people in a long time. She drew closer and set her full glass of white wine on the rustic wood table under the loggia. Amanda knew in a minute she was Tessa, Anna-Marie's best friend, the traitor.

A distorted disgusted look inflated on Amanda's face as if Tessa was her rival.

Kurt tapped Amanda's shoulder and shook his head like a father warning a child, his hushed words rushed. "Hey, use your poker-face Miss Journalist-of-the-Year, – change your attitude."

Amanda quickly adjusted her face to reflect – I need a favor from you, so I'll be nice. "*Buongiorno Signora Maggiore. Mi chiamo* Amanda Lindas," her right hand extended to the air.

Sophia Loren's twin flashed Kurt a flirtatious smile.

It spurred a twinge of unexpected jealousy in Amanda's gut. Although Kurt wasn't her property, he was her guest at this strange party.

Kurt stood behind Amanda like her bodyguard.

The curvaceous vixen hostess sauntered past and went straight in for the kill. "*Buon giorno Signore*," she smiled fluttering her thick mascara eyelashes, indisputably making another pass.

Amanda watched him squirm. Unnaturally his face flushed like a schoolboy getting his first taste of flirting. *Sure Kurt, – Mr. Journalist-of-the-Year, where's your poker-face?*

Kurt cleared his throat, "Uh-um... *Signora, parla inglese?*"

Yep, self-assured he steered straight to the answers. That was his all too familiar interview style.

"*Si*, but love is spoken in all languages–you agree–*capice?*" her wide, pretty smile was way too encouraging. Although she was older, she embodied the sex appeal that European women seemed to emanate naturally. Tessa didn't miss a beat. Amanda perturbed by her flawlessness and forwardness pondered whether it was good European etiquette to trip a hostess.

Feeling like a third party intruder, she fidgeted from one foot to the other wanting desperately to slip into one of the chairs that flanked the table. Uneasy she brushed imaginary dirt off her coat, feeling the envelopes, which created instant motivation to circumvent the trollop.

"*Excusi*, may I speak with *Signore* Giovanni Maggiore?"

Tessa stopped undressing Kurt with her eyes and pawing at his chest.

The sultry woman snapped and hollered towards the arched door, "Giovanni, Giovanni your guests have arrived– *Andiamo!*"

Immediately her attention reverted back to the hunk of meat in front of her. She slipped his coat from his body like a pickpocket stealing a wallet. Gently she caressed his shoulders.

Amanda blushed remembering how good they felt on her piggyback ride. She gave Kurt a contemptuous glare.

Innocently Kurt mouthed– *What?* His hands extended open and away.

Just as Tessa was getting a little more touchy-feely nearly frisking him – they were all saved or caught by Giovanni Maggiore.

Shock immediately spread on each face–all for different reasons.

Kurt's eyes swelled like green saucers. Automatically he backed away from his sexy attacker as if he was the pursuer.

Tessa still in overdrive turned her mislead affection onto her husband as if she was only toying.

Giovanni stood stiff in weathered jeans and a white dress shirt. He scanned his intruders, while rolling his sleeves to his elbows. His strong tan arm wrapped Tessa's waist. He squeezed her tenderly, smiled, and said, "Tessa, have you offered our guests drinks and food?" He kissed her cheek, unraveled her from his arm, and lovingly tapped her rounded rump. "Please be hospitable–bring food and wine."

Tessa took another roving gander at Kurt, and spoke directly to Amanda, "You keep him happy or someone else will…" She left them staring at each other.

Shocked, into believing she was seeing an apparition. Amanda swallowed hard, as if a clump of dirt had lodged in her throat. So dry she gulped down Tessa's wine. Were her eyes and ears deceiving her? She blinked several times; her heart throbbed uncontrollably she started to hyperventilate. Dizzy, she collapsed.

Immediately Kurt scooped her up into his arms.

"Down for the count," he said, knowing exactly what had transpired in her mind. Giovanni Maggiore was undeniably Antonio's father. This interwoven dark secret was not on her agenda, it could be her undoing?

Every bit of Giovanni's facial features and mannerisms were exactly like the son he presumably never knew existed. Kurt felt Amanda's painful shock. Unfortunately she had to deliver the good and bad news.

Giovanni held a chair. Kurt sat her down then fanned her with the envelope she had dropped.

Slowly she came back; reality checks can really suck. Her duty was to expose the truth no matter the consequences.

"Sweetheart, are you okay?" Kurt continued to fan her.

With the back of her hand, she wiped perspiration from her forehead, "Please call me Amanda." Even in distress she wouldn't relinquish him any slack for endearments. She was quick to notice the manila envelope fanning her back from Never-Never Land.

"*Signorina*, are you okay?" Giovanni's tender voice was reminiscent of Antonio's. They were clones. The eyes, the nose, stature and smile were beyond any shadow of any doubt–no DNA testing needed. The jury was not a hung jury. *God sure liked that model.* Why didn't Anna-Marie disclose that Giovanni was obviously Antonio's father?

When she returned to New York, Amanda was going to reprimand Anna for leaving out the facts. *What else was a lie in this twisted story?*

The truth was mind-blowing. Amanda felt remorseful to pry further. But as a professional journalist, she renounced her personal feelings and pushed forward. She clutched Kurt's wrist and snatched the envelope. "I'm fine, now. Thank you." With her courage gathered, she stood.

"Bravo, let's sit and *mangiare, mangiare*." Giovanni spread his arms pulling chairs out inviting them. "Sit–we were expecting you – eat and drink with us."

Amanda looked astonished. "But how did you know?"

"Strangers–questions, news travels fast in Campania's air. You and your man friend," Giovanni took her left hand and rubbed her ring finger, "you ask too many questions. Why is it so important for you to find me?" His brown eyes turned from warm sparkles to dark pits.

Her mouth dropped. Obviously neither she nor Kurt would win the best undercover investigative reporter award, if one even existed.

Flirty Tessa returned with a picnic basket; she set the table with four wineglasses, two bottles of red wine, a tray of delectable antipastos, cheeses, prosciutto ham and Italian bread. Apparently they were staying longer than Amanda had anticipated.

Kurt sat, nibbled and drank while Tessa rubbed his neck and shoulders–like a pro.

His face livened with anguish and pleasure while Giovanni didn't seem to notice, or didn't care. Or worse yet, maybe he put Tessa up to it so he could focus on Amanda.

Amanda fiddled with the envelope and juggled her thoughts to organize the truth. She looked to Kurt for words, but Tessa had him in another time zone.

"*Signore* Giovanni, we are here because I have a message for you from Anna-Marie..." she didn't get the last name out before Giovanni and Tessa turned white as the sheets hanging on the clothesline.

Giovanni began coughing; unable to speak he motioned to Tessa for a drink. Tessa grasped Kurt's arm and pulled him to his feet, she dragged him like a reluctant puppy on a short leash into the house. Amanda and Kurt exchanged quizzical looks.

In a flash, Tessa returned with a glass of water, and without her obedient puppy, Kurt. Giovanni drank the water. When Giovanni returned to the living, Tessa returned to the villa.

The tears in his eyes, made a wave of deep tenderness flow from him to Amanda. Like a floodgate opening after a heavy rainfall, questions poured from his mouth. "How is Anna? Is she well? Is she with you? Can I see her? What does she have to say to me?"

The time for truth was now. Covered in self-loathing, she handed Giovanni the envelope scripted with his name in perfect penmanship. "Anna-Marie, asked me to deliver this to you, she is not well enough to travel" Amanda choked back tears. Giovanni was going to learn the cold devastating truth.

Tentatively he took the envelope and opened it. It contained several photos mostly black and white snapshots of Antonio as a child. With trembling hands he unfolded the enclosed letter and fumbled photos to the tiled patio.

Amanda busied herself picking them up and laying them on the table. Her mouth was so dry that words would not flow. Maybe it was just as well, she grabbed another glass of wine. Giovanni began sobbing at the letter's contents.

It was written in Italian, so she was unable to read it.

Between heart wrenching sobs he mumbled, "A son...our son–oh my God! That murdering son-of-a-bitch Carmine...how could he?" Giovanni's sad tears turned into tears of anger. He balled his fists and pounded the table sending food and wine airborne.

Amanda wanted to comfort him, but not knowing the extent of his anger, she saved the wine before it drained onto the table.

Tessa came running from the villa with Kurt in close second place.

Tessa leaned on Giovanni's shoulder and skimmed the letter. She swallowed hard, her chest heaved, her tears dripped on Giovanni's white dress shirt. "Oh my God, we've killed her. Oh Giovanni... we've killed her. He was your son. I knew it, I knew it. Carmine must have found out and murdered him, to punish us." Tessa wailed in broken Italian and English burying her face in his shoulder.

Amanda looked at Kurt, his face mirrored her remorse.

"What is she saying Kurt? They killed Anna? I don't understand?"

Kurt's Italian wasn't great when people were having calm conversations, let alone hysterics. Time spent living in Little Italy had helped him. With his hands on Amanda's shoulders, he explained, "She's saying Anna-Marie is dead..." his voice cracked, "her weak broken heart."

The world was shrinking around her; Amanda sank deeper into the small chair. Kurt reached for the letter from Giovanni's shaking hand. At the bottom he read aloud:

"Giovanni when you read my words I will be with our son, Antonio. I lived my whole life with lies and without your love. I lived because I had our son to love. His whole life reminded me that true love never dies. I cannot live without his love and laughter. My Giovanni, I go to my grave loving you and I go to be with our son. I believe Carmine knows his killer, but I cannot face the truth that it is because of my love for you that my son was murdered.

All my love– Anna Marie"

Tears ran freely down Kurt's face. True love to him was elusive, yet he understood unconditional love of a mother. He forgave his mother for her overbearing love. The doting love a mother has for her children is surpassed only by God's love. The urgency to call his mother and tell her how much he loved her overwhelmed him. The next best thing was he pulled Amanda up from the chair and wrapped her in his arms. He held her and they wept for Anna and Antonio.

Waves of guilt shuddered through him. He hid the truth about the other part of the letter. Amanda wasn't going to like it, but he just couldn't bring himself to reveal what he had already suspected.

Anna's words explained that Antonio was in love with the young lady delivering the message and that he was planning to ask Amanda to marry him at Christmas. Antonio's life ended before he was able to confess his love.

Kurt would profess that truth to Amanda,–later, much later. He felt ashamed using Antonio's misfortune for his gain. But, he knew she desired truth over anything.

And the truth was– he was in love with Amanda.

Never again would he allow anyone or anything to come between them. She fit so perfectly in his arms. Gently he lifted her face to his, wiping her tears softly with his thumb, he said. "Hey Babe, we need to call New York, maybe Anna is still alive."

Amanda sniffled. A huge sigh rushed from her chest, "You're right, maybe Anna didn't take her own life. Maybe Jeremy or Belinda can go check on her."

A deep breath of false hope gave her strength to turn to Giovanni and Tessa. Never in her life had she seen anyone age so quickly. The news reflected in their gaunt faces.

"I am so sorry, I didn't know. Anna led me to believe that Antonio was Carmine's son, but you can see by the photos, he was your son. I am so sorry." Tears burst from her again. Kurt steadied her caressing her arms.

Giovanni pulled away from Tessa. He put his arms around Amanda. "No, I am sorry. You did nothing but love my son and Anna says he loved you. You are my daughter like my own daughters. You are innocent, but you are in grave danger. You search too hard for the truth. Sometimes the truth sets us free, but truth can harm you and those you love. Come stay with us, until I find Carmine."

"You know Carmine?" Amanda thought about the other letter she promised to deliver. "Where is he?"

Worry creased Giovanni's forehead. He looked up at Kurt. "You have to protect her. Do you understand?" Acute rigor controlled his voice. "Carmine is not someone you want to cross."

Kurt nodded acknowledging the serious threat. If Carmine had ordered Antonio's murder, who he thought was his son; he would have no apprehension to kill them. "Giovanni, I understand, but talking sense into a stubborn woman is impossible."

"Sure throw me under the bus." Amanda snapped.

Kurt raised his hands up, "Now Honey, I'm relaying the truth. You don't listen to reason, and now we're both going to get hung out to dry."

She socked his arm, "Don't Honey me– who invited you? Remember you followed me. I didn't ask for your protection."

They bickered about who was right and wrong while their startled hosts watched.

Out of sheer desperation, Kurt apprehended her arms like a criminal and twisted her to face their audience. Locking one arm across her neck and shoulder, he placed his other hand gently over her mouth. Just long enough to get her to quiet, "Now, politely ask our hosts if we can use their telephone to call New York." He removed his hand before she had the initiative to bite him.

She settled and asked to use the telephone.

Tessa guided her into the centuries old, yet very chic villa. Decorated in warm harvest colors, splashes of vibrant cobalt blue, and lively accents of sunny yellows, it was a happy house. No less than four young ladies scurried behind the scrolled iron railing on the tiled staircase in the far corner of the large living area. Amanda guessed their ages twelve to twenty. Her heart sank; as it occurred to her that the young girls were Antonio's half-sisters. Sisters, he had never known. Unfortunately she brought the horrible sad truth to this happy abode.

Tessa handed her the phone and watched her with intent.

"No, no, no... Belinda say it isn't true." Amanda sobbed and slipped to her knees on the cold hard floor.

Belinda had confirmed that the police found Anna-Marie's lifeless body on the park bench next to Antonio's grave that morning.

Tessa instructed the girls to go get the handsome man.

Kurt raced to Amanda cradling her; he took the receiver from her clenched fist. "Hello–who is this?"

Belinda cried and repeated the tragic information.

"Hey Belinda are you and Jeremy okay?" Kurt's intuition flared.

"Well, early this morning some assholes came to your door, they threatened to kill you and Amanda, if you don't stop digging into their dirt–you know what I mean?"

"Yeah, did you get a good look at them?"

"Just through the peephole, I'm not down with torture. I'm a pushover when it comes to pain."

"Okay, get on with a description." His patience wore thin. His knees ached planted on the tile floor. He rocked Amanda in his strong arms.

"Oh, I'm bad at this. One was your height, but skinny not muscular like you..."

"Thanks, I never thought you noticed. What ethnicity are they?"

"What? What do you mean by that?"

"Jesus, Belinda, what race? What color?" Kurt shifted Amanda to his lap as he sat on the freezing tile; he caught an instant chill, "Shit."

"What? I'm doing my best."

"Not directed at you– go on."

"Like Brooklyn bred bruisers, you know the type. The other dude was like Amanda's height."

"With or without heels?" Kurt blurted impatiently still dealing with comforting Amanda and his cold ass.

"Dude settle, like five-seven and beefy. They wore matching black leather jackets, jeans, and biker boots. The beefy guy is a scar face."

"Good girl, identifying marks are important. Anything else?"

"Ah, yeah skinny has a machete tattoo on his right forearm. I saw part of it."

"Tell Jeremy to get the plain clothes detectives on them."

"Oh I almost spaced it. Anna-Marie left a large envelope for Amanda. The cops found it on her. I opened it because the cops told me too."

"What was in it?" His concern was that it contained more secrets.

"Well, she wrote that she may have forgotten to take her heart medicine, and if Mandy was reading the letter then it meant that she came back safely. And..." Belinda took a lengthy pause.

"And... what? I don't have all day."

"She left everything to Mandy, the whole shebang, the apartment on the Upper West Side, her bankroll, life insurance– everything, clothing, furs, furniture– everything! Damn Mandy sure is lucky, in a weird sort of way."

"Yeah, very weird, let's hope our luck holds," he said somberly. Anna's generosity was overwhelming, but maybe Mandy was going to earn it the hard way. "We'll call you when we sort out this mess."

213

Kurt had Tessa take Amanda to a bedroom to rest. Giovanni insisted they stay the night, just until he could get the authorities to flesh out Carmine and confirm if the men following them worked for Carmine or another Mafia Don. Word travels quickly underground, with so many rats to relay messages.

In the office adjacent to the bedroom where Amanda rested Kurt paced. Leery he petitioned, "Loan me a car Giovanni, I know Amanda and I will be safer in Rome. We need to go to the American Embassy. Tell me how you know Carmine so well?"

"I thought you and your beautiful companion already knew. Isn't it why you came to me first?"

Kurt shook his head, "No, we came to you first because we were able to find you first. I don't know the connection, she might know."

"Carmine is my uncle, many years older. Anna-Marie and I were sweethearts, well obviously more. But she accepted Carmine's proposal over mine. She wanted travel and big city excitement, all I had to offer was my parents' farm and love. Carmine provoked Anna-Marie into marriage because her father owed him money. Carmine loves the ladies and he is very cunning. He enticed my Anna, but she always loved me." Giovanni lifted her letter. "Sounds petty now, but I was fit to be tied when she agreed to marry him. Spiteful I was unfaithful with Tessa, so Anna left with him. Whatever you do, don't lie to yourself. Go after love with all your heart."

Kurt intended to do just that. But first he had to get Amanda to safety and then he'd use the 'L-word' and 'M-word'.

Chapter 17

They stayed until noon the next day with Giovanni's family before traveling the Mediterranean seaside roads to Rome. Their route added four extra scenic hours to their emotionally strained trip. By twilight they arrived at the stately palatial Excelsior Hotel on *Via Veneto*, adjacent to the American Embassy.

Amanda expected the city area to be a derangement of pop culture as it was portrayed in *La Dolce Vita*. But her expectations were eradicated standing in front of the prestigious Beaux-Arts landmark. The castle like hotel embraced neoclassical meets modernism. An aura of deep lavender mist surrounded the white exterior with golden illumination radiating through the draped windows of the cupola centered in the corner of the hotel.

Inside the Empire décor was equally impressive, Amanda stood mute allowing Kurt to check them into a junior suite. His protection was a must until she came up with another viable plan.

In rigid silence they passed the marbled grand entrance and took the lift to their suite. Still royally pissed at Kurt for his intrusion in her mission, she was thankful for his sincere, yet placating attitude.

Upon entering the suite, the white frame moldings jumped out from around the gold striped fabric walls. Symmetrical and perfect together they contrasted in the enchanted room, not unlike her and Kurt. The main attraction was a bit nerve racking and intriguing. A crystal chandelier centered above a sprawling king-sized bed covered with a white spread laced with swirls of delicate green vines scattered with innocent red rosebuds. Thankfully the décor was warm and inviting, emitting a strange romantic calmness. She had never stayed in a room that exuded so much romance. The suite encroached on her senses titillating her like a forbidden fantasyland.

Both stood statuesque captivated by its distinct character and ambiance, one could not help but fall in love with its charm.

Kurt organized his clothing and personal items, then he approached her, "Do you want me... to help you unpack?"

His words were the first kind words spoken between them since she awoke to discover that he and Giovanni had rifled through the contents of Carmine Lucchesi's private envelope from Anna.

Giovanni's advice to Kurt repeated in Amanda's mind, "A moving target is hard to hit, but two moving targets are more difficult–getting lost in Rome was better than getting killed in Naples."

Mute and motionless she stood; like a marble masterpiece draped in cream wool slacks and a cream chiffon top over a camisole that hugged her curves. He knew she was alive by the subtle rise and fall of her chest. Taking charge he placed her suitcase on the foldout rack to the right of their bed. Neither had slept well since their treacherous night on the plane. His mind plotted to devise an anecdote to get her to respond. Crossing the line of confidentiality, he had committed the crime of the century, according to her.

Worried by her silence, although desirable in some respects, he felt emotionally threatened. Secretly he prayed that God would grant him the right of passage into her thoughts. She had him emotionally, mentally, and physically on a raw indecisive edge. A passionate place no woman had ever taken him before. A place he could be the victor or victim. His desire was to capture her mind, body, and soul. The one real talent he possessed was his amorous way with women. But she was no ordinary woman and the Excelsior hotel wasn't just an ordinary place.

The Excelsior Hotel was an extraordinary palace and Amanda was Rome's new Cleopatra. If only he could get her to believe that nothing existed outside the walls of this paradise. They could share the ultimate slice of Heaven on Earth, if only she'd forgive him.

She walked around the room; her eyes reflected the glitter of the crystal chandelier centered over their bed. It was *their* bed– really theirs. He wasn't going to waste another night just sleeping next to her warm curves. If she was going to be his forever, he had to claim her tonight. Maybe this one night was all they had. If they were going to have a future he had to convince her to bury the past and live in the present.

The promising seeds of love were already sown, he saw them in her crystal blue eyes, inhaled them in her freshness, felt them in her clutching arms, tasted them in her passionate kisses, and he heard them in her soft sighs, and even in her disappointed words. She had given him plenty of signs over the last five months, but in the last five days she had raked him raw. On the verge of insanity, she innocently pulled him to the edge of the naked truth. He was rooted by her tantalizing nature. They'd been to the depths of hell and back. He had to have her– all of her.

Near the edge of the bed, he called to her, "Amanda, please come here."

She sauntered over gracefully like a lily wavering in the breeze, silent, but willingly. Soft and effortless, she spoke, "You know I am extremely disappointed with your actions. And..." her fingertips touched his lips, forbidding his protest, "you saying– I'm sorry again, is not enough. I want more from you tonight. You should be arrested for tampering with my evidence and my heart." Her words were cool, but her eyes were brilliant with lust and exoneration.

With equal compelling eye contact, he placed tender kisses on her fingertips; squeezing her hand with certitude, he had her rapt attention.

Under his spell, her small hands manipulated his large strong hands. Palms together at his shoulder level, she had him in a holdup stance, their fingers interlocked.

"Oh, so you want to play tough." His fingers squeezed hers, he turned her so the back of her legs were pressed against the higher than usual mattress.

"I'm not playing." Her lashes didn't flinch or flutter.

"Well, in that case I will have to read your Amanda Rights."

Her head tilted back, "Don't you mean my Miranda Rights?"

He dipped his head to meet her eyes, "No. I mean your Amanda Rights–just listen. Amanda Lindas you're under house arrest."

"On what charges?" She said squinting and frowning.

"You are under arrest for grand larceny, bribery, fraud, intimidating an officer with physical and verbal threats, and for interfering in an ongoing love investigation." His chest heaved uneasily.

"Pure speculation, stick to the facts Officer Kilawee," she raised her eyebrows. "What specifically have I done to deserve these false accusations?"

"For starters," he pulled her closer by pinching her fingers between his. "You have premeditated and plotted against me for your own personal gain. You have intimidated me with severe intent of slandering my good name. You have deliberately deceived me and led me to the brink of insanity with your insatiable desire for truth." He pulled her closer to his hard body. "All the while bribing me disguised as the most desirable woman I have ever laid eyes on, or lips on, or hands on. You've committed grand larceny for stealing my most prized possessions–my ability to reason, my sanity, my pride, and my heart."

"Really? I find that hard to believe," she said gazing into his emerald eyes reading the truth, "Tell me, what my Amanda Rights are?"

"You have the right to remain silent," he taunted her pecking kisses on her neck, "or you may whimper and scream, but anything you say or do can and will be used against you during other house arrests." His titillating journey continued down the other side of her neck to her collarbone, his interlocking grip kept her controlled.

Playful as a kitten, she nudged him back, "But what about my rights to an attorney..."

"Ms. Lindas are you resisting arrest? You do not have a right to an attorney. I don't like them, nor do I like threesomes. But you do have the rights to a handsome investigative reporter, or a daring borderline Super-hero detective, or a humbled former Superstar Anchorman."

"Hmm, I see," her lashes fluttered "and what if I can't afford a Super-hero?"

"Not to worry, one has already been appointed, free of charge. He is willing and able to assist you in any positions you wish to pursue. With these rights in mind, Amanda Lindas do you wish to make love with me?" Her breath hitched when he pressed his super-hero body intently to hers.

Flustered by his honest request her weakened knees bent causing a domino effect. They toppled onto the bed.

On top, he nuzzled his face into her flowing locks, "I'm taking that as a yes." No time wasted, he placed a series of ardent kisses on her neck. He released her hands, to explore her curves with his.

Voluntarily accepting his advances; she captured his face between her hands before his mouth reached the peaks of her tender breasts, "Yes, but there are conditions."

His lips covered her blossoming puckered lips, tasting her sweetness with a needy fervent kiss; he tried to make her conditional interruption disappear.

With physical strength she didn't realize she possessed, she forced him to rollover until she was strategically positioned on top. Pinning his shoulders to the mattress, her hands palmed his firm pecks; straddled confidently across his hips feeling the full length of his hard ridge. Her inner flower fluttered as she let her request be known, "I'm not finished with you yet."

A wash of relief spread across his face. "Good 'cause I'm just getting started." Her boldness tantalized his inner animal. Eager he anticipated her request. "Anything you say Baby." With a playful thrust of his hips he jolted her letting her feel his pleasure.

To continue his appreciation he drew her face close covering it with hot moist kisses.

In effort to delay his aggressive kisses she cupped her hand over his mouth and embedded her elbow into his chest. "Don't make me get rough with you Officer Kilawee. The conditions are–we can practice, but it must be safe-sex. And furthermore, you must honor your nationalized TV promise–that ladies go first. I assure you–I am a very demanding lady." With that said she removed her hand from his wanton mouth and replaced it with her full-lips. Feverishly she devoured him with kisses; he rolled her over closer to the nightstand. Reluctantly he pulled back from her zealous hunger.

Assuming he had control, he straddled her, "I can accommodate your first request." He extended his arm to the nightstand drawer where he had condoms stowed in hopes she'd say yes. "I never leave home without my raincoats." A wickedly cunning smile accommodated the mischief dancing in his amorous bedroom eyes as he tossed the boxes at her.

She opened the boxes and playfully tossed condoms at him, "Well you certainly came prepared and pretty self-assured–two boxes?" her naturally placid lake blue eyes sparked.

"Italy is one of the most romantic places in the world. And Rome is the eternal city of love. I thought, I should be prepared in the event I would meet a couple of hot *Signorinas*."

Her eyes widen, "Oh really? A couple of hot *Signorinas,* and not once did it cross your flirty mind that you might get lucky with a lonely, desperate, pathetic American girl?"

"Pathetic and desperate are not words that I would use to describe you." Kurt pinned her arms above her head and spread soft as petal kisses on her face. With each kiss he stated his true thoughts, "I'd say conniving, beautiful, sexy, intelligent, and detrimentally determined. And I can guarantee if you make love with me you won't be lonely and you won't regret it." His tenaciousness pulled her into sublime arousal as he nibbled across her collarbone. He forged a path of kisses down to the first button of her blouse. Deftly he unbuttoned it with his teeth, lips, and tongue.

"Wow quite the talent, I suppose it evolved from too much practice." She said suspicious.

Still holding her hands firmly above her head; he nuzzled the sheer fabric away from her firm nipples. Playfully he kissed her soft mounds and tender nipples making her squirm, he murmured, "I've wanted to do that every day since I first laid eyes on you."

"Yes I know, talk about not using your a poker-face." She arched her body into his, letting him know her true desire. He released her hands giving her freedom to run her hands through his silky hair pressing him harder to her breast.

Hungrily he tantalized her nipples encouraging her lower internal urges to release with eagerness, he returned to claim her mouth while pressing naturally on her pelvic area until she felt an inside orgasmic burst. She sighed with erotic pleasure. Her hot center pulsated with dire need.

Her heady breathless sighs were his cue to take her to the next level. Placing her hand on the zipper of his tight jeans, he said, "Time for my freedom," his whisper so slight yet so direct, "I must warn you– I'm a love virgin." He towered over her, ripped his shirt open scattering buttons around the room.

"What? You can't be serious?" She questioned unfastening his jean button. "You've never had sex?" He stripped off his shirt, exposing his tan torso glistening with fresh sweat. She unzipped his jeans and shifted his Calvin Klein's down exposing his more than ample glory. "Wow that's what I call a Super-hero."

Amused by her comment, he said, "Glad you approve, but for the record..." he guided her hands, "I didn't say make sex. I said make love– there's a difference." Ecstasy washed his face as she gave him pleasure that he hadn't had since she became his nemesis.

"Shut up and kiss me," she pulled his lips to hers.

Now, finally she was his, and he was hers. Both desired to give the other sensual healing. Clothes and inhibitions peeled away, skin on skin; face to face they explored each other like an in-depth physical interview.

From the very first meeting their sexual tension had rankled inside. Eagerly they faced the opportunity to give into the tumultuous affair they had fought to avoid. With each story they reported, each interview they took, and the constant battle vying for the camera and fans to love them was just foreplay. That foreplay had to come to this. This felt so right. They had teeter-tottered with sanity and insanity; caught in a heated rush they allowed the ultimate pleasure of bringing one another to the threshold of passionate climax.

Her body was toned, fresh, and covered with soft skin; his body taut, tan, and hard in all the best places.

Both needy they played out their fantasies taking, tasting, accepting each other, knowing this was a rare gift of fate.

Breathless, Kurt stopped and faced her. "I want to keep my national promise, but honestly I am a virgin at lovemaking. I haven't been this far in six months."

Her trusting eyes glittered like calm pools on a summer morning. "Really sticking to that virgin story? You're such a liar and a tease." She stroked his corded arms and ran her fingers down his muscular back to his firm butt, she confessed, "Well, it has been a while for me. From what I've gathered of your reputation with the ladies– Jessica, Sami, Shannel, and Tami– I'm sure I won't be disappointed," her face glowed with yearning.

"They were way before I ever laid eyes on you. Let's keep the past outside of our passion. This is our haven." His pressed urgent against her smooth abdomen; he scooped her shapely bottom into his large firm hands, "So Love, what is your pleasure–top or bottom?"

"Umm–which position do I like best?" She toyed with her decision.

He gave her time while his mouth wet her pink buds and his fingers stroked her until he created a mountain of unleashed craving.

Nearing climax, she panted, "On top, on top."

His was hot and ready, yet he taunted her further stimulating her to a whispered scream, "Now Kurt, now!" she demanded, pushing him onto his back.

"Well okay, take control," he tore a condom pack open with his teeth, "Do you do this dominant thing often?" He asked securing their protection, while she straddled him.

Their eyes steadied on each other. "I might," she confessed.

Using slow penetration they shared pure ecstasy as gratification pulsated through them. More and more she met his expectations with every exhilarating push.

She took his tenderness. The joy of being one with the man she loved delighted all her senses. To witness the same vitalizing satisfaction in his face gave her more pleasure than she had ever imagined. She leaned forward to kiss his appeased face.

"Yeah lean in, you feel so good." He went deeper causing an orgasmic tremble. He could hardly believe she was really his. "Babe..." he brushed her hair from her face witnessing ecstasy blaze on her blushing face.

She was smoldering hot. An erotic *oh my God* moment, she bit her lower lip restraining a scream.

Crushing her to his chest, he coaxed, "Let go, lose control. I want all of you." He rolled her over to missionary, giving her the full benefit of his body strength.

His ardent lovemaking gave her multiple full body orgasms. This made up for all the months they fought and went without physical contact. *Damn he was good: no he was better than good–he was great!* His power was second to none she'd ever known. His kisses captured her ankles, he caressed her toes, and extended her feet onto his shoulders, not skipping a beat; his strong hands and body released her inhibitions. They engaged in giving, taking; twisting their bodies together. They were entangled with a freshness that neither one could deny, this was real love.

"Yes..." he rasped with labored breathing, meeting his pinnacle, her pulsating ripples of pleasure overcame him. Solid together as one, she released down to the rumpled bedding, his protective body covered hers. His chest to her back, he buried his face in her soft silky hair. Inhaling her fresh scent, total bliss satiated him. Making love to her was so perfect, so real.

Amanda relished in knowing she was the only woman in his life. They shared pure truth–pure love, it was so bold, so complete. They laid together in silence; just soft rhythmic breathing. Fulfillment lulled them into a dreamy haze.

Lovingly he stroked her back and rolled onto his side. His body laden with a subtle layer of perspiration, his heart raced to catch up to his finish. Love drunk; he succumbed to it for a blissful short time.

He opened his eyes to her stare.

She smiled.

He smiled.

"Well, my beautiful Anchorwoman you're amazing–thank you."

Radiance warmed the royal room. Amanda giggled at his sincere gratitude. His face was filled with luminosity.

Snuggling down into the crook of his shoulder she laid her head on his chest listening to his peaceful breath.

He squeezed her tight, "Hey give me a couple of hours of sleep and we can go for round two."

"Oh so you're a *real* Super-hero?"

"Yeah, I thought you already knew that about me."

After a short rest they had heated shower sex taking their lovemaking to another level of total gratification. Dried off they ordered room service and fell together again relieving all the pent up stress they had harbored against one another. Finally exhausted, sleep captured them.

In the wee hours of morning, Kurt rolled over to pull her close to his warm ready body, only to hug the king-size pillow that lay in her spot. The crinkling noise of paper roused him to open his squinting sleepy eyes, still induced in a love hangover; he read her beautiful scripted note. He sighed and mused, "Everything she does is beautiful. Everything she does is magic–even her perfect penmanship turns me on." He read her note:

Hey Super-hero, I went down to the lobby to get coffee and a paper,
don't worry we'll be together soon, Love Mandy

He pressed her note to his lips; a hint of her perfume tickled his nose. He drifted back into comatose sleep knowing she'd wake him, to make love again and have their morning coffee–together. She wrote the words he needed to see, "Super-hero–coffee–Love Mandy."

An hour or so later something stirred him awake.

Mandy had not returned.

Panicked, he shot up out of bed.

Still naked he strutted around the room immediately noticing something was awry. Her suitcase was missing from the rack. His heart raced as his mind fumed into a flitting rage. He searched the room for his suitcase and his clothing– nothing.

He ran to the bathroom. On the mirror was a note written in her red lipstick, "Kurt, I'm sorry, Love A"

He slammed his fist on the white marble vanity. "Damn it Mandy! Damn it, where are you?" His words echoed to deaf walls in the majestic bath. Deranged he scowled and raked the room for clues. Immediately he spotted his money clip with a note folded into it. He seized clip and unfolded a note–out slipped a single packaged condom. The note read:

My Super-hero,

By the time you read this you will have figured out that my first note was a deterrent. I know you are furious with me and I deserve your rage. Now it's my turn to say– I'm sorry. I overheard Giovanni say it would be safer to split up to make two moving targets. Last night was the most incredible night of my life. I assure you I got more and felt more than I bargained for. I know the type of man you are lives to conquer, loves the chase, and once he has his trophy he moves on to the next conquest.

Truthfully, I need and want a man that is willing to give up one night stands with many, to have the stamina for one woman he can't live one night without.

I don't know if I am woman enough for you to want to sacrifice the rest of your nights with just me, so please don't follow me. Don't try to find me. Thank you for being you, so perfect and understanding. I do appreciate your tenacity to be my protector. I love you and I leave feeling no regrets. I will always remember our night in Rome.

Love, Amanda
P.S. Sorry about taking your clothes, but paybacks are a Bitch! Remember don't go out without your raincoat. XXXOOO's

"Oh shit!" His strangled emotions choked his ability to move. He wanted to cry, scream, and run naked through the streets. If she had planned to drive him crazy she had succeeded. With his heart ripped to shreds by the one woman that was more than enough for him, he wrapped a towel at his waist and searched the room–no ID–no airline ticket–no gun. She was as thorough as a woman could be–perfection personified. When he found her, and he would; he was going to make sure she knew she was perfect for him.

Down the grandiose hall Kurt strutted draped in a towel. He approached the concierge desk. "Did you see a beautiful woman in her mid-twenties about five-seven, with medium brown wavy hair and bright blue eyes, pass through here in the last three or four hours?" he glanced at his watch it was almost ten.

"Sir, you cannot be in the Excelsior Hotel lobby dressed in a towel."

"Well this was my best option unless you're holding a life drawing class for Michelangelo's study of the David, okay? Did you see her–she was with me last night when we checked in?"

"Sir this is Rome–we have many beautiful women." The concierge shrugged his shoulders. Seeing the crazed look on his patron's face, he offered more. "But, I believe I did see a woman with two suitcases very early this morning about seven. She asked about the American Embassy. I watched one suitcase, she left with the other, and returned empty handed."

"Okay, so did she ask for directions, did she comment on where she was going?"

"I assumed the airport; she had a ticket in her hand. And I believe an envelope."

"Is there a way I can get some clothes–now? I need to go to the American Embassy."

"Unfortunately the dry cleaners and clothier is not opened, but in an hour, you could obtain clothes from them."

"An hour is too late, how about one of those white robes you put in the rooms. That's got to be better than a towel." Kurt dreaded the thought of tramping over into the Embassy half-dressed, but he suspected Amanda was decent enough to turn his gun, badge, and identification over to the authorities. She couldn't be that vindictive, to force him to stay in Italy. Damn her, for being so spiteful. Didn't she care about him; or about their future together? Her insensitive actions wounded his heart. He had never felt such an ache with an emotional hitch. Had he lost her? What if Carmine and his men harmed her?

He would never be able to forgive himself or face his family or hers if she were killed under his protection. What was she thinking? Had he led her to believe that she was just a one night stand? Jeremy could bear witness that Kurt had never chased a woman with more vigor than her.

The prior evening he spent talking with Giovanni about their plan of action was wasted especially the part when Kurt purchased the three carat emerald and diamond ring that was originally intended for Anna as an engagement ring. Giovanni wanted to give Anna's ring to Amanda.

But Kurt insisted on buying it for the woman he refused to live without. The beautiful emerald matched the color of his eyes. Emeralds were far rarer than diamonds, like Amanda. The ring represented his eyes and love would always be centered on her.

Damn–he had every intention to propose marriage, but their lovemaking took on a life of its own. Last night he was so enthralled with her that it slipped his mind; hopefully the ring was still safe in its box hidden in one of his dress shoes in the suitcase she stole. He noted – she needed reprimanding on her theft habit.

Wearing the Excelsior robe and slippers; he walked on *Via Veneto* to the American Embassy hoping she had delivered his credentials and clothing.

Once he was admitted in to see the U.S. Consulate, he explained plenty. Out of sorts and fearful for Amanda, he babbled profusely. It was after eleven when they allowed him to call the United States to get profile information and a photo sent over. The problem was they would not do a missing person search until forty-eight hours passed.

Fearful that inaction would be too late. He badgered himself for not securing their passports and airline tickets in the room safe. He could hear his father's tirade about following the wrong head– again. Perhaps calling Jeremy was a better choice.

Jeremy would cuss him out for being an idiot putting his physical pleasure ahead of protecting a client; but he would be nicer–well maybe.

The problem was Amanda wasn't just a client; she was the woman he loved. Did he even say the words? He racked his brains to remember their conversations, but their lovemaking spoke volumes. Reviewing their night of passion just made him needy for her.

The Consulate processed a total background check on him before they would release his property. In the interim, they allowed him a personal phone call in the main reception area with people milling around him.

The phone rang several times, "Hello, who is this?" Jeremy said his voice groggy from sleep.

"Jeremy, this is Kurt, we have a problem," Kurt's chest tightened.

"No, you have a problem, it's five in the morning man, I'm going back to sleep, some of us have to work. And not touring exotic foreign countries."

"Listen man– I've lost her. She's gone." An alien whine accompanied Kurt's shameful words; he choked on his emotion.

"How? What? When? Where are you? What did you do?" The gambit of Jeremy's questions went from concern to scorn in seconds.

"I'm at the American Embassy in Rome, half-naked waiting for my clothing, badge, gun, and ID to be returned. She took everything except a towel. I need you to fax a profile and a photo of her to the embassy. They won't issue a missing person's investigation for forty-eight hours, but under the circumstances they will alert the airport security. Man, I screwed up, big time."

"Just half-naked? Hmmm, right? Why am I not surprised? I want the truth. Did you cross the line? You did. Didn't you?"

"Giovanni suggested that we were better off hiding in Rome than staying in Naples. We were shot at in Naples. We checked into the Excelsior Hotel in a suite, and for the record... she started it."

"And you were an innocent bystander? You did it–the nasty. Damn you're pathetic."

225

"Yes, I fucked up! I couldn't stop myself, she played me. Our suite was a frickin' romantic fantasy-land." He paced and tightened his robe while the office personnel eavesdropped closer.

"You broke your promise. Screw it Kurt, you never listen to your real brain when it comes to women. I knew you couldn't be trusted."

"Just help me out, fax her information. I have no leads. She was last seen alive at seven. I have to find her. There's no way I'm living without her."

"Don't talk crazy. Get your shit together. Use your rutting animal male instincts like you did last night, I'm sure you'll come up with something. Did you use protection?"

"Damn it Jeremy– yes of course I used protection. Who do you think you're talking too? She was willing." Kurt hollered acquiring more unwanted attention at the embassy.

"We talked about her vulnerability. She's been through Hell. Remember her boyfriend was executed less than four weeks ago? And she lost Anna just two days ago, she's hurting. And you took advantage. You disgust me. If anything happens to Mandy, I am holding you totally responsible."

"You're Right!" Kurt shook gripping the phone. "I'm a poor excuse for a man. But I am not sorry for spending the most perfect night of my life with her. I love her and I am going to find her and ask her to marry me– if she'll have me?"

"Did you just say the 'L-word' and 'M-word'?"

"Yes, I bought an emerald engagement ring; I was going to propose last night."

Silence transmitted back.

"Jeremy?"

"Ah, yeah–well too bad she won't know what you *were* going to do. How do you live with yourself? Why did she steal your shit?"

With an exasperated exhale, Kurt expelled, "I don't know. Who knows why women do what they do? Just fax her information to the embassy, contact Belinda in case Amanda contacts her. Leave any information at the hotel. I will check in. I believe she may contact the Mafia Don–Carmine Lucchesi, or she's running scared. She left a letter about us being separate moving targets. Maybe she'll trade our tickets in for an earlier flight. Pray, we need divine intervention. And get my plane ticket reissued"

"Why am I the one that always has to clean up your messes?" Jeremy quibbled.

"Because that's what best friends do. Thanks man, I owe you."

"You're damn straight on that. I get to go on your honeymoon."

"Sure whatever you want. Just pray that I find my runaway bride."
Hopelessness filled the abyss between them.

Chapter 18

By six a.m. Amanda had expedited and secured Kurt's personal items at the American Embassy, exceedingly careful not to leave clues behind for her sexy super sleuth.

In the last two days she had made several crucial mistakes. Too sick from fear and grief, she lost her nerve in Naples to separate from him; that was her first mistake.

The second was neither heeded Giovanni's warning to separate when they reached Rome. That mistake led them to the romantic suite in the Excelsior–making it her third. And then her fourth and last mistake was participating in the ultimate lovers' seduction.

Maybe she could live with that mistake?

But perhaps her biggest and finale mistake was professing her love *in writing* when Kurt had only jokingly implied his love. Of course, admitting his Super-hero status wasn't her favorite brain child either.

Ultimately mistakes or not, telling the truth was the only option she could live with or possibly die with on her conscience.

Everyone deserves to know when they have earned your respect and love. She had withheld the truth from Kurt and herself for far too long. If she had confessed her feelings earlier they could have been together.

Determined to make several right decisions to correct her pattern of emotionally based wrong choices, Amanda proceeded with her plans to complete her promise to Anna. She couldn't risk Kurt's life because of her desire for truth.

Step one– go to the *Stazione Termini* then transfer to *Leonardo Da Vinci* Airport. Next– luggage independence, she created a decoy by checking it onto a flight she had no intention of boarding.

The flight was scheduled to depart that evening. Her plans were to blend in, lay low, and see a few sights as a common tourist before facing Carmine and probable death.

Before nine she had completed step one and two. Plenty of time to wander she headed to a charming *Piazza* just off *Via del Corso*, harboring a world famous fountain. The fabulous, *Fontana di Trevi* designed by Nicola Salvi.

The 18th century legendary fountain known as *the fountain of lovers* was featured in two of her favorite iconic movies, *La Dolce Vita* and *Roman Holiday*.

If she had to sacrifice her life in Rome, she was going to indulge her romance and history fetishes.

The roar of splashing water merged with the early morning chatter of street merchants and tourists. Amanda daydreamed of cavorting like actress Anita Ekberg from *La Dolce Vita,* romping in the fountain baptized in its purifying water, while being showered with kisses from Kurt.

An instant reality check flashed. If Kurt caught her romping in the famous fountain, he would probably drown her. She shunned the daydream in exchange for wishful thinking.

According to legend visitors should toss a coin into the *Trevi* Fountain over a shoulder and wish to return to the Eternal City. Amanda extended her wish to return to the Excelsior Hotel alive with Kurt. She tossed several coins—some she had stolen from Kurt.

After several coin tosses she faced the central male sculpture, *Oceanus*. He held the invisible reins to the powerful winged horses. Stoically mounted on a pedestal of shells and rocks his muscular build reminded her of Kurt's powerful physical and mental endurance towards her. She made peace with herself for allowing him to conquer her physically and emotionally. There is no place better to make love than in the Eternal City– right? *Well, okay so there's always Paris.*

Thoughts of their lovemaking made her shiver. Hugging herself, she rubbed the chill off her bare arms. She put on a light cardigan and walked the small square absorbing an odd ominous feeling from the unbalanced dominance of the fountain in the small *piazza*.

It spurred a memory of when Agent McCarthy allowed her to watch Kurt with his father.

McCarthy made an off-handed comment, "You should see what you're getting yourself into."

Outside the holding tank she saw the enormous Chicago Commissioner clutch his son magnanimously, correct him, and then challenge him. It proved that Kurt was fortunate to know unconditional love and security. In her heart, she believed she and Antonio would have given anything to have a father like Kurt's. And although Kurt denied it, he was like his sagacious, dominate, over protective father. She had to admit those traits mixed well with his compassionate, loving, and sensitive nature.

Being raised by a Super-hero couldn't have been easy. And she realized dating or being married to one could prove to be equally challenging, if not impossible.

A cool morning breeze whirled about breaking her thoughts. Clutching her arms she wished she hadn't packed her coat in her luggage.

But she had to lighten her load knowing her plans to shop on *Via Condotti,* for designer clothing and expensive gifts.

Near the *Piazza di Spagna*, before indulging in a greedy shopping spree, she placed a timid call to Carmine Lucchesi. His number was scribbled on the envelope in Kurt's handwriting. She assumed the *big sneak* got it from Giovanni.

During her phone call she clearly and concisely explained her intentions and who she was to him, Anna, and Antonio.

Carmine listened. He encouraged her to come to *Casandino di Napoli*, to visit him at his sprawling villa, so they could relax and talk about *his* Anna and Antonio.

As exciting as it sounded to rendezvous inside the walls of an ancient villa, Amanda couldn't squelch the inner voices of her mother and Kurt screaming at her to meet in public. Nor could she allow Carmine's charismatic personality to coerce her, Anna had warned her.

In fact, Anna specifically instructed that the best place to meet with Carmine was in a populated Catholic Church.

St. Peter's Basilica in the Vatican City was Amanda's first and only choice. Determined and skillfully contentious she forced Carmine to agree to meet her–her choice–her timing. She felt exceptionally powerful in facing the possibility of death. Risks and demands came easier. She adopted a new motto: *If you are going to die–live large first.*

Complacent with her ability to finagle her way, her gut instincts assured her that Carmine would not kill her in St. Peter's Basilica. Even if he did, at least it was a high profile place, so Kurt and her parents would know where to collect her body.

Nothing like making national news on November first, the Italian Holiday of *Tutti i Santi Ognissnati*–All Saints Day commemorated by the closing of some monuments, museums, and small shops, but thankfully many churches remained open for the swarming public to attend mass. Today the faithful would pray for the martyrs and lost souls trapped in purgatory. She whispered, *"Grandma hear my prayer; help me from becoming a martyr."* A lump grew in her throat, her eyes swelled with tears; truth be told, dying wasn't on her list.

First of all, she hadn't resolved her issues with her parents; primarily her father. And not to dwell, but she had of slew issues with Kurt.

She missed him, but this was her story. She followed her acumen and instincts. The desire for truth filled her with false courage. To know if Carmine ordered Antonio's hit was imperative. Too many innocent people were killed in the mob families' selfish battles. The Dons needed to be exposed and brought to justice.

The day was still young and filled with insurmountable challenges. Someone had to know where she was headed on her *insane* Roman holiday. Envy fluttered inside as she dialed Kurt's home number. Belinda was still his pampered house guest.

"Hello Belinda. Hello?" The rustling of sheets transferred through the phone. Amanda envisioned petite Belinda swaddled in Kurt's oversized bed. She wrestled with the thought of her friend sleeping in the bed of the man she loved and hated. Just like Anna, she feared she was pushing the right man in the wrong direction. Too late for sagacity, her parents needed to know her whereabouts in case of mission failure. Her last story was contingent on someone knowing and telling the truth.

"Belinda, I need you to wake up!"

"Amanda? Where are you? What time is it?"

"I'm in Rome. Are you awake enough to write some information?"

"Yeah, Kurt has pencil and paper right here. Go ahead." Belinda yawned.

Yeah, Kurt was always prepared for the next big story.

Not to confound Belinda, she spoke slowly, "I left Kurt at the Excelsior Hotel. I'm meeting Carmine Lucchesi at two p.m. today, Rome time, in Saint Peter's Basilica–Rome's largest church. Did you get that?"

"Yes. But why would you leave Kurt? Mandy have you lost your mind? He goes bonkers when he's away from you."

Amanda continued as her time was fleeting.

"I know, he'll be fine. Anyway, call my mom, tell her where I am. And if I return to the States, I will contact her."

"If? What do you mean if?"

"Belinda, I'm not sure I will make it back. If I don't, tell her I love her. I have to know the truth about Antonio's murder. And don't you dare tell Kurt I called."

"Are you sure? I thought you two would hook up."

"That's yesterday's news. I don't have time to share details."

"Then tell me the juicy stuff."

"Alright, it was the most excellent night of my life. And I'm in love with him. That's all I'm going to say. Now, I need you to get me a reliable car, cash from my account, and pick up my luggage at JFK by tomorrow morning. I will call you before my flight. I'm cashing in our tickets to fly first class, but I may be put on standby. Do you understand? You cannot tell anyone– promise me."

"I promise, but I just don't understand why you would want to leave him. He's going to be pissed. Does he know you're gone yet?"

"I'm still alive aren't I? I don't think he's awake yet. I did some awful things that should slow him down. I'm hoping he thinks that I'm on my way back to New York. I don't know if he'll take the bait. Right now I'm going on a shopping spree on *Via Condotti*. I wish you were here. All the exclusive designer stores line *Via Condotti*. I'll buy you something special."

"Sure, a sign of true friendship; rub it in– a night of great sex, sightseeing *and* shopping in Italy. Just come home safe, you owe me big."

"Okay, go through my clothes and shoes, take whatever you want because where I'm going I won't need fancy work clothes or club clothes."

"Stop talking like that! You're such a downer."

"I didn't mean it the way it sounded. Just pack my photos and casual clothes into the car. I will call you for the location. I love you Belinda."

"Love you too, please be careful."

Now for a little sightseeing and shopping to kill time. Okay, poor choice of words, she thought spotting a sign in a shop window. *Gioia* Private Tours advertised– Start at the Spanish Steps and finish at the Vatican. Perfect. Amanda inquired within about the tour times; she hired an English speaking guide.

Her taking a leisurely tour would totally rile Kurt. When facing fear or danger one should use peaceful meditative activities to calm the spirit, shopping and traveling created her Yin-Yang balance.

She loved history and art, so this adventure created perfect harmony. The tour consisted of an overview of the *Colosseum*, the ancient *Roman ruins*, and would end at two in *St. Peter's Basilica* by Michelangelo's *Pieta*. The exact place she was scheduled to encounter Carmine.

Her concern was that Kurt and Giovanni would intercept Carmine first. Timing is everything; she hoped her pillow note held Kurt at bay along with confiscating his clothing. However bad she felt about her actions, she was equally content too.

The tour group met in *Piazza di Spagna* at the Spanish Steps. The steps were speckled with camera toting tourists, several couples, and souvenir peddling merchants. Their well informed tour guide started her explanation.

"These towering three-tiered terracotta limestone steps connect to the dual bell-tower palace that serves as the Spanish Embassy. On the street level here, the famous poet John Keats lived in an apartment before he died in 1821. He died in his early twenties, leaving behind a legacy of love poems."

One of Amanda's favorite poems by Keats came to her, *"Beauty is truth. Truth is beauty. And that is all you need to know."* To die young, yet grasp love and truth left her envious of Keats.

They took a short break for coffee and *dolces* at *Caffé Greco*, the oldest coffee house on *Via Condotti*. Today she'd indulge bordering on gluttony; to worry about her weight seemed futile. *Sort of The Last Breakfast scenario.*

You only live once– her macabre humor reminded her again of her dangerous quest for truth. An outsider would think her quest was to commit the seven deadly sins in a holiday weekend. Let's see, she pondered biting into a *cannoli*. Last night I committed *lust*, doing *gluttony* for breakfast, *greed* on *Via Condotti*, and I've *envied* Belinda and Keats.

Positive if she remembered the other three; she would commit them before the day was finished. *Lust*, she'd do again, if given the opportunity.

Why did being bad leave her relishing such good feelings?

With her tour companions she boarded the miniature van for a wild ride down *Via del Corso*. Totally convinced that every vehicle was driven by amateur racecar drivers vying for a Daytona 500 position, she'd be scared to death if she was in her right mind.

They arrived safely at the ancient Roman ruins. The *Ruins* were reminiscent shadows of Rome's power. Many lifetimes of creative work left in shambles. The fall of the Roman Empire was squandered power, too many conquests plundering many lands. The strong overcoming the struggling weak societies without a master plan. Her life resembled the crumbled societies; her weakness for love and pride ruined her life, not Kurt's quest to control her. Only brokenness remained. Just slabs of stone remained where Romans had gathered to share their frivolous lives. What legacy would she leave behind after her demise?

The artist renderings in her pamphlet displayed the monuments in their original glory. How could the artist envision all that glory from the rubble of partial meeting places, palaces, and fallen temples?

She oscillated between keeping her appointment with death and returning to Kurt for protection. At least in his arms she felt semblance of inner peace in the midst of her life in ruins.

Would he welcome her back into his fold of protection?

She plodded on with the tour group to the mammoth *Colosseum*. The curved rugged outside walls were once covered with beautiful *Carrara* white marble. Now, stripped to brown brick, the stacked arches tiered above with tri-level columns–Doric–Ionic–Corinthian; her Art History wicked its way to the forefront of her cluttered brain. Victoriously, she had not forgotten.

Upon entering the vast open structure, she felt the cool dampness emanate from the thick ancient walls beneath her fingers. She couldn't help but feel insignificant not only from its structural magnitude, but also its infamous powerful past. Its history boasted the slaying of innocent lives. Poor Christian martyrs displayed their fortitude of faith for the entertainment of belligerent Romans. The brutal reality of Gladiators fighting proletarian men, and wild beasts to the death for entertainment, made her cringed with nausea.

Unfortunately the male species had not evolved much in the last several centuries other than creating powerful weaponry to kill each other. Is there hope for the human species? Could women convince men to stop fighting? Could we use our intelligence to create peace? It all seemed so hopeless.

Insecurity and guilt raced through her. Had Kurt conquered her? He did use his strength and cunning manipulation to get what he wanted. He triumphed over Antonio with one boastful tale of a kiss. And she helped enhance his pillage with her note admitting he had fulfilled her desires and captured her love. Frustration, shame, and defiance ruled her heart.

Now she had to move forward with fortitude, not succumb to his control. Worse than a Christian martyr; no one would know what she sacrificed for the principle of truth.

Inner turmoil dominated her. The truth was that she enjoyed Kurt's gladiator style. She loved watching him in action. He forged a path in his career with strength, boldness, and cool self-assured tenacity. Admiration had replaced her jealousy and envy a long time ago. His quirky gladiator style was befitting. Truthfully, he fought to further his career and had not intentionally destroyed hers.

It was high time she fought for her own career; she reaffirmed her choice to meet with Carmine. *Live your dreams or die trying. Conquer or be conquered. Strive for success to overcome fear.* Too bad survival is the first essential element to accomplishing success.

The chance she was taking was no longer just about fulfilling a dream or capturing a story; it was about keeping a promise to Anna and herself. Squished back into the tin can tour van, she managed to find her courage. In less than an hour she would meet her fate.

Their next stop– *Piazza Bocca della Verita*–the mouth of truth located under the portico of the remodeled *Santa Maria in Cosmedin*, a 6th century church also stripped of its identity. Arbitrarily reconstructed and rearranged, yet it stood firm. Although scarcely a rendition of its former self it still housed superb frescos; colorful fond memories, permanently left for future generations to enjoy.

The myth of the mouth states: "bid a liar to come forth, place his hand in the mouth, tell the truth or have his hand bitten off." If Kurt was there, she'd force his hand into the marbled mask porthole, and ask, "Do you love Amanda Lindas or is she just another conquest in a long line of women?"

Of course he'd probably retaliate and coerce her do the same. She had no right pointing the accusing finger–she was equally to blame for their precarious romance. She risked dismemberment for her lies as much as he.

"*Andiamo,* time for the highlight of the tour– The Vatican City." The guide waved them to the van.

St.Peter's Basilica was the monument where truth would prevail.

Arriving at *Piazza San Pietro*, Amanda's fear-gripped imagination made her paranoid. Was she being watched? She wrapped her waist with fists filled with shopping bags; trying to squeeze the jitters out of her backbone.

The adept guide explained a Greek cross verses the elongated Latin cross, as they walked the circumference of the huge oval of St. Peter's Square. Question surfaced in her scattered fear invested brain, why was an oval referred to as a square? And what is the Italian word for oval?

"The dome was designed by Michelangelo; the portico atrium has five entrances into St. Peter's Basilica. The piazza is surrounded by a double curved Colonnade designed by Bernini. The Ionic scrolled columns are four rows deep totaling two-hundred and eighty-four columns." The guide rambled on with her endless knowledge.

The columns hid people of varied nationalities while Amanda viewed the ninety-six saints and martyrs statues lining the top. Could she be number ninety-seven? Her mind became a blurred mess as the bewitching time approached. A glance at her expensive new watch ascertained the moment of truth ticked closer.

"The far left portico is– *Porta della Morte*–Death's door."

Okay time to break up with the tour guide–she's getting too personal.

"At Death's door, the statue of St. Peter will greet us–the keeper of the golden key to the gates of Heaven." The guide elaborated.

Another quick watch check; five minutes to two, time to separate, Amanda went to the far right portico where Carmine, *her cold-blooded killer*, should be waiting by *The Pieta.*

Never keep a gangster waiting was her new creed. Was there such a thing as a warm-blooded killer?

Promptly, she entered the grandiose Basilica. Not one word or several paragraphs in her extensive vocabulary could begin to describe the majestic opulence of the white Carrara marble layered with gold leaf lettering. The urge to pay homage to the magnificent mosaics, sculptures, and Bernini's fabulous bronze canopy pulpit had her dithering. The irony was she stood amongst everlasting art and ancient tombs knowing her life was so ephemeral. A promissory mental note raced through her fear tainted mind: *on your return to Rome – tour the Vatican thoroughly, assuming you live through today.*

Her heart skipped several beats as she scanned the vast church from the barrel-vaulted gold coffered ceiling supported by eight colossal piers down to mosaic marbled floors covered by the mass attending crowds.

There were as many strangers inside as she had left outside, except one man, she recognized from Anna's photos.

A slightly older version of Carmine Lucchesi stood statuesque and debonair in the finest Italian suit she had ever seen. Even Kurt would reluctantly have to admire the man's taste in clothing. Carmine wasn't as tall or broad as Kurt, but for a man of sixty-something, he was a quite looker and radiated a demand for respect as any coldblooded killer. Could he be the man that summoned his son's death?

He stood with his hands folded in front of him, clearly mesmerized by the milky white masterpiece of Jesus lying across Mary's full fabric lap. *The Pieta* depicts the love of a mother for her son. It could not have been sculpted better or with truer emotion. The gleaming cool marble begged to be touched, if only just to comfort the poignant mother, yet touching was strictly forbidden.

With her pulse racing, Amanda reached into her Hermes bag to pull out her trendy coveted *Carrousel* silk scarf. The burgundy scarf with a gallant white horse encircled by knights on gold horses covered her shoulders and her spiral curls. To honor God, the Church doctrines of her grandmother's religion she bowed her head. Not a devote Catholic herself; yet she honored those who worshiped peacefully around her.

Flooded with emotion, she prayed that God would grant a stay of execution for her and Kurt. Today was a day to honor the dead, she prayed silently for Antonio and Anna, knowing they would not have peace until Antonio's killers were convicted.

The time was now.

She inhaled and exhaled, then stepped closer; her shopping bags rubbed up against Carmine's sleeve.

Carmine spoke first, "Michelangelo was only twenty-five when he sculpted this masterpiece. Jesus Christ was believed to be thirty-three when he was crucified. My son, Antonio was barely twenty-six when he took his last breath."

For a killer, his poignant speech was rather eloquent, she thought. By the time he finished; she had quit breathing. A whoosh of trapped air forced its way out of her lungs; if she couldn't breathe regularly soon, someone would be wiping her off the marble floor. Panting shallow breaths, her thoughts of Antonio and Anna flooded her eyes with burning tears.

Carmine turned to face her, offering the crisp white handkerchief from his breast pocket. "Please allow me," he dabbed her tears as she gazed into his watery brown eyes. She saw the stalwart tenderness that Anna had described mixed with his debonair charm.

"Please let's sit, my dear girl you're shaking." He helped her sit, packages and all, on a nearby bench.

Numb she sat as his arm folded around her shoulders. Her crippled mind tripped on the kindness of the nefarious killer. Before she could speak, trembling she handed him the tampered envelope.

"What's this?" Instant concern eroded his tan face.

"It–it's–from Anna."

"Anna?" he sighed. Slowly he filed through wedding photos and younger pictures of Antonio with him. "These are rare, I only saw Antonio a handful of times."

"Antonio appreciated that you supported them well. He really wanted to know you." Amanda offered.

Remorse and regret stared back at her.

"I cannot change the things I have or have not done. I am not proud of my choices." His focus shifted to Anna's scripted Italian words. His calm hands quivered. He covered his grief stricken face with her written words; his tears blurred the ink. "My love, my Anna is gone."

Amanda could not stop her arms from cradling him like a lost boy. The tough malevolent man whose main purpose in life was instructing others to kill wept in her comforting arms. Crushed by his treacherous actions, he was humbled by grief.

She used his handkerchief that touched her tears to wipe his. Angry at him, yet she felt compassion knowing Antonio and Anna loved him, and weirdly he reminded her of her own father. How could a person filled with such love be so hateful?

Nothing made sense. She couldn't shake the feeling of being watched. Of course Carmine had goons around; he was a notorious individual in a high profile public place.

The reporter in her demanded she ask the imperative questions. Her investigative instinct prodded her to seek the truth. *You came for the truth– damn it, Amanda open your big mouth and ask.*

Carmine regained his composure.

Amanda touched his left hand to keep their connection and hopefully suck strength from him. In doing so, she noticed his worn gold wedding band and an interesting princess cut emerald and diamond pinky ring. She swore it matched the ring she accidently, *well perhaps purposely*, discovered in Kurt's dress shoe. Carmine's ring was more masculine than the other. The large center stones were like twins. Like twins matching the deep emerald color of Kurt's eyes. Perhaps they were family heirlooms, she was immediately spooked.

A chill ran from her head down her spine to the base of her bottom. Thoughts raced to and fro in her mind– *"Ask the damn questions– if you want the answers you have to ask."* It was Kurt's voice echoing in her mind. *"Never leave an interview unfinished. Ask the damn questions that no one wants to answer, but everyone wants to know."*

"Carmine," her eyes searched his, "did you hire someone to kill Antonio?"Demanding she blurted, "I need to know the truth. Anna wanted to know."

His warm eyes turned black as unlit coals, she felt burning embers spark to the surface. He squeezed her hand hard.

"You ask very bold questions for such a young vibrant beauty."

Succinctly she pressured him. "Did you hire someone to kill your son?" She gritted her teeth so hard she thought they'd break.

She didn't even bat an eyelash.

Immediately he sat erect like a judge ready to slam his gavel, his jaw clenched, "I – did – not." Each word hammered out like nails through a coffin. Her coffin, she feared. Like the gales of a hurricane, air whooshed from his puffed broad chest. "I loved my son, even when I found out he wasn't mine. He was the last male heir to bear the Casali name. He was mine and Anna's." His hands fisted crushing Anna's letter. "I loved Anna more than Giovanni ever could. I tried to save her from his deceit and his blatant disregard for her love. He didn't deserve her love." Carmine's face raged red.

The impromptu interview continued; she had to. This risk was what she lived for, "Then who killed him? Tell me Carmine, let me bring them to justice, tell me who called for the hit?" Her icy eyes dared him. "Disclose it to me, let me vindicate him, don't let Antonio and Anna die in vain."

Carmine's eyes darted around the cathedral like a rabid dog waiting to attack, he restrained himself.

They were in God's house.

And thank God it was a big one filled with people. He wouldn't harm her in front of God and witnesses would he? Anna led her to believe that Carmine was a reasonable man, as reasonable as a strong-willed tyrant could be. But Anna didn't know Amanda had the feisty gall to ask intimate intimidating questions. "Tell me now– who did it?"

"I will bring them to justice. You should leave well enough alone. You're too damn smart and pretty to be wasted by them," his words seethed through his teeth. He reached into his breast pocket and pulled out a tabloid photo. His firm index finger landed on Kurt's image, "This man knows and he's next."

Her heart seized her throat. She began choking, a wheezy, "Why?" squeaked out.

"He knows too much. You need to stay away from him. He's crossed them and me. He knows the truth."

The betrayal she felt made her dizzy. Talk about shock and sleeping with the enemy tossed together. *He knew. Kurt knew Antonio's killers.*

He knew. All this time– he knew! And she had to hear the truth from a Mafia Don in Italy!

The one man she finally trusted with her love and life– he knew. Her eyes blinked, tears flitted onto her expensive silk scarf. In denial she voiced her opinion, "He couldn't have known. No, he would have told me." With disbelief she repeated her statements several times– *Fiction can easily become truth if it is repeated often and believed.*

Carmine squeezed her shoulders and growled, "What do you mean he doesn't know? Tell me, why would he tell you if he knew?" His eyes darted his demand, "Who are you to him?"

Amanda sucked at telling lies. But she earnestly wanted to believe in Kurt, so she confessed a half-truth, "He's my fiancé and co-anchor of NYCB news." She barely looked Carmine in the eyes for fear he would see through her lies. "We share all our information to report 'on the edge' reputable news." She stared down at her hands as if she'd grown a sixth finger. And for her lies, she believed her nose would sprout forth any minute.

Carmine curved his index finger under her chin and lifted her face to his glare, "I see why my Antonio would love and fight for you. You are a very brave young woman. My instincts tell me that you are telling the truth about this man's ignorance. For your sake, I hope he's half the man you think he is that you would risk your life for him. In my opinion there is no greater love. For his sake, I hope he lives to appreciate your beauty, compassion, and integrity. Go home, hide until this war ends." His strong hands cupped her face; he searched her clean blank stare. A perfect poker-face, as Kurt, her mentor, would have been proud to see.

Carmine held her for a moment longer rubbing her tears from her blushing cheeks, "My Antonio and Anna did not die because of what I did; they died because of what I did not do. I did not protect them and that is a husband and a father's duty to provide and protect his own. It's my duty to avenge their deaths not yours." With that he kissed her gently on each cheek. "Go hide– Rome and New York are not safe."

Amanda nodded to his loaded threatening words. She swallowed slowly; her eyes followed him as he stood.

Her tour of Rome was over.

She took cover in a small Pensione near the airport. That night she called her mother and her father. For the first time in her adult life she needed their protection and advice. Her heart broke for Kurt, had she helped or harmed him with her blatant lies? However, if Kurt really knew Antonio's killer she swore she'd hate him for the rest of this lifetime, and well into the next.

Chapter 19

Kurt's day went from blissful to shitty to apocalyptic. After his detainment and thorough background check, he was free to hurry up and wait for Jeremy's fax.

Finally by noon the Embassy received Amanda's photo and profile. Kurt used his schmooze techniques on the receptionist to obtain copies without her superior's knowledge. His mesmerizing eyes and quirky boyish grin allowed him *carte blanche* when it came to women of all ages. He still had it; chicks easily swooned to him. Too bad Amanda wasn't there to see him in action, she'd be pissed. The hardest one to win over was that wretched journalist he loved to hate. And now he feared he had lost her forever. The last thing he wanted was to find her dead.

Several hours behind, to decipher her pattern of logic movement, he had to think from the end. Lucky or unlucky for him, he had been trailing her for almost four months. But this time it wasn't for fun or money, this was their lives and future, this was Rome and not New York.

Taking his newly acquired information and clothing Kurt headed back the hotel with a map of Rome. The Eternal City was like a wicked spider web intertwined by endless roads– all roads truly do lead to Rome.

Damn it Mandy, how could you risk us for a story? He nearly paced a whole in the Excelsior junior suite's carpet before he called Jeremy again for information on her flight and his ticket.

Jeremy relayed that Amanda had checked her luggage through to New York early for the original TWA flight. Kurt asked Jeremy to call Belinda to see if Amanda had contacted her. Jeremy was steps ahead. Belinda had denied any phone calls.

"She'd better not be lying." After his ordeal Kurt had doubts if any woman could be trusted. "We won't worry Mandy's parents yet, give me time to track her. I have their information in her profile. She's a romantic freak and loves history; I suspect she's taking in the sights. She's a shopper; I wouldn't put it past her to sneak in some shopping. Rome is a busy city, but with her photo I can go down *Via Condotti*, knowing her fetish of designer clothes I may even run into her. And wring her neck."

Jeremy chuckled, "Yeah tough guy, you're screwed?"

241

"Thanks Jeremy be serious. She could be dead. I can't wait for the Italian police to move–every minute counts. We'll chat about how I fucked up later– you're not helping by chastising me. I thought you were my friend. Besides she was willing–she loves me man, she put it in writing. So, her escape act is just a glitch in our relationship." A hint of hope and sincere satisfaction infiltrated his despondent tone.

"Okay sure, talk yourself into that man. I am your best friend. It's my job to tell you when you screw up and when you're acting crazy. What time do you want your ticket?"

"I'm thinking first class on the original flight just in case she's trying to throw me off. I don't even know if I'm safe. Giovanni said his uncle will make a move. If he wants us–he'll have us. Jeremy, do me one more favor."

"Sure man, what?"

"Call my parents, tell them what's happening and I love them. This is one time I wish my dad could help. Guess it's time for me to grow up."

"I hate it when you get too serious, but I will call them. Hey man, God speed. What should I tell Rich?"

Silence hung between them.

Kurt thought about his next big career decision. He had been thinking about it for the last week, he avoided putting it into words. With the dirt he dug up this time, he managed to bury his high profile career.

"Hey, man you still there? What should I tell Rich– you are coming in on Monday right?"

"No... tell him I resign." An apprehensive sigh slipped out, "I'm in too deep this time. I need to lay low. Hope to see you tomorrow with Mandy in my arms." An unfamiliar edginess and uncertainty laced his words. "I have to go. I'll call before I board the plane. You're the best friend ever."

"Thanks, I know, back at you. You want me to pick you up?"

"I'll let you know. I'm hoping it won't be in a wooden box."

"Damn dude you're a total downer."

"No, I'm a realist."

"No, truth is– you're a pain in the ass. Be safe."

Close to one in the afternoon, Kurt checked out of the luxury hotel. He hired a town car to get around Rome. First he threw his suitcases in the trunk; he did a quick jaunt into the cafes, newsstands, and shops on *Via Veneto*. To no avail Mandy left no trail other than the newsstand merchant recognized her photo. The vendor thought she bought a booklet on *All Rome*. A popular book amongst tourists, and she asked for route maps for the metro and buses. That confirmed she was playing safe doing a little sightseeing before the night flight.

But where did she go? And would he be a few steps behind or a few strides ahead?

The city was packed with tourists and locals milling about attending masses and feasts for All Saints Day. Kurt was in tune to the hum of the city, but he remained on red alert at each pit stop. Unfortunately his best sleuthing wasn't good enough even though he had tracked her ghost steps down *Via Condotti* where she made hefty purchases in the thousands at Hermes, Versace, Bvlgari, and Mont Blanc.

Concern flashed in his mind. If they were to get married, that was after she made reparations of certain favors, and of course, an apology for what she put him through. Then – he'd sit her down and make certain she understood the word *budget*. Their combined incomes would no longer be as affluent as they had grown accustomed to.

Each store he entered he showed her photo and explained, "This is my wife was she in here? What time? Did she make any purchases?" He was pleased to see that she was remembered, of course she was unforgettable. And based upon her expensive purchases the sales people were extremely helpful; some showed him the exact products.

The Mont Blanc, Armani, and Bvlgari purchases were items he himself would have selected. *Mandy-Candy*, he mused, you *have impeccable taste*–which wouldn't matter if he didn't find her alive.

It was after one thirty when he strode out of Gucci discovering she purchased a wristwatch for herself. Sporting a devilish grin, he reached into his pants pocket and slipped out her original watch that he had taken the night on the dance floor. He claimed he carried it for a good luck charm, a part of her–like keeping her time in his hands. That same night the tabloids opened up Hell wreaking havoc on his career, his love life, and sealed Antonio's fate. Now Amanda's time was really ticking away.

Outside of Gucci he turned to go towards the Spanish Steps, when two henchmen apprehended him. The same men they had encountered in Naples. The one which he had shot in the shoulder was wearing a black sling. But it didn't inhibit the thug's ability to shove a semi-automatic gun into Kurt's unsuspecting ribs.

"Don't make a scene." He instructed with a heavy Italian accent adding another sharp jab to the ribcage, making Kurt flinch. At first instinct, Kurt went for his Glock, but he refrained hoping they wouldn't frisk him. They pushed him into his waiting town car and accompanied him for a chaotic ride down *Via del Corso*.

In silence, Kurt sat with his hands on his knees making sure he didn't make them anymore nervous than they already were. With his peripheral vision he sized them up. Linebacker– was the only word that came to mind. Both appeared to be winded, their foreheads laden with sweat alerting him that they had followed him for awhile. Eyes forward he wondered if the town car driver was one of Carmine's men too. A million questions ran rampant across his mind. Who were they? Where were they taking him? Did they already have Amanda? Was she okay? Did they put their grimy hands on her? If they did he was resolved that he would have to kill them. He rubbed his perspiring hands on his platinum-gray Armani dress slacks, and regretted it as soon as he did.

The driver took several side streets as if he were being followed. Kurt was challenged to see the street signs over the thugs' massive shoulders, but he caught a subtle glimpse of *Corso Vittorio Eman* just as they took a bridge across the *Tevere River*; the original life force of Rome.

At a loss, to break the icehouse tension, his wit waned.

"So, did either of your parents have children?" he asked chiseling the ice. Catching a small smirk from the rib poker, he continued, "Can I ask where we are going? I didn't have lunch can we stop for a bite? I hear the Italian food in Rome is to die for–."

No response from either suited idiot.

"So, is Carmine going to meet us at...?" Ignorant looks washed their faces. "So, I hear they're bringing back Gladiator training and your mother is going to try out?" That got him another metal jab to the ribs. He curled forward, "I guess you don't care for mother jokes." He didn't dare hold his side for fear his escorts would see he was packing. And he didn't dare reprimand them for their poor detainment skills. Rule number one check to see if the guy is packing heat.

They came around the *Via dei Corridori*. Kurt glanced at his watch; it was almost two, immediately he recognized the impressive *Piazza San Pietro*. "Damn guys you read my mind, I'm leaving Rome tonight, and I wanted to meet the Pope. Do we have an appointment?"

The rib poker spoke, "Yeah, he's going to read you your last rights. Now get out and don't do or say anything that will make me shoot you. Walk casual and slow like you're one of us."

Kurt wanted to say, *Yeah, lately I have been acting like an idiot, so it won't be hard to act like you two*. But at the risk of getting shot, he sequestered his defiant words.

They reached for their fedoras off the rear window panel, making Kurt feel suddenly out of place; his fedora was in the trunk. It occurred to him that he hadn't paid his driver and there again he wasn't sure the proper etiquette.

If someone kidnaps you and your driver do you still have to pay or should they split the cost? Or if your driver is one of them should you even tip at all? It was quite the conundrum, but the least he could do was ask if he could have his fedora as a cover to blend with them.

His luck Amanda would spot him and think he had switched sides. And right now that idea was a viable option as opposed to having his lasts rights read. Wouldn't his mother and father be proud– their youngest son killed at the Vatican– is that a martyr Catholic thing or not?

They stood sentry by the car as if they were waiting for a cue. Kurt feathered his hair back; the cool November breeze relieved the strain of being a prisoner. He used his right hand cautious not to expose his shoulder harness under his left arm; his gun rested just above his bruised possibly fractured ribs.

"Hey can my driver, or I should say your driver, or our driver pop the trunk, so I can get my hat? I'd feel like we were all in this together." No response from his captors, "Well then–okay."

It was an awkward situation for Kurt; not use to being ignored, jabbed, or having to ask for permission. He might as well have been having tea with his mother and the Queen; he felt so out of place.

"Come on guys it's just a hat, we'll look good going into the church together, like brothers." Kurt choked on his words thinking this could be the last time he ever thought about his brothers. These rough edged guys reminded him of them. He squeezed the bridge of his nose with his thumb and fingers just thinking about stupid shit. Like the one characteristic he had of his mother was her nose, *pretty boy with a cute nose.*

The silent thug rescinded, "Yeah let the poor bastard have his hat. He kind of reminds me of my punk kid brother."

The obliging driver popped the trunk nervous, hinting to Kurt he wasn't in on the ordeal, just along for the ride of his life. It pissed Kurt off to see another innocent life hanging in the gallows, swinging like a pendulum on a grandfather clock, as precious time ticked away.

He adjusted his fedora squarely on his head. It gave him a queer sense of power, false security, and immediate gratification that he had gotten his way–maybe his last wish. Even with criminals he could have them eating out of his hands–strictly figuratively.

Just then an impressive steel-gray Maserati Quattroporte III pulled up. The windows were too dark to reveal any passengers. Kurt saw the burning end of a cigarette or cigar. "Damn I'm *dying* to have a cigarette–oh, poor choice of words– figuratively not literally," he reprimanded himself.

Idiot number two, the nicer one, pulled a pack out and offered him one. Kurt accepted–no need to be asked twice, even though Mandy wouldn't approve. She'd understand this time. It was her fault he acquired the habit to begin with. "Thanks man, you're pretty decent." Kurt grinned with appreciation.

Unaware which thug was going to rub him out, maybe the guy was just giving him a last request.

Although if given the choice of vices, he'd pick one more night with Mandy and a good stiff drink. *Yep, well that probably falls under sacrilegious.* Standing outside the largest church in the Christian Religion, he committed idolatry with the cigarettes, booze, and lustful fornicating thoughts. Well, if he was going to Hell that day, he might as well get his last fill of Earthly pleasures.

Idiot number one, the mean bastard, shoved his gun into Kurt's sore ribs. It forced him to double over, clutching his side cautiously he kept his hand outside of his jacket. But impetuous angry words shot out.

"Dude, do you mind? If you're going to shoot me then do it. There is no rule that says you have to break my fucking ribs beforehand, damn it!"

"Yeah, well I will shoot you, but not before we see your pretty lady friend get whacked." The bastard laughed a sinister laugh, "Besides you're the son-of-a-bitch who shot me in the shoulder."

"Yeah, too bad. What can I say? I missed my target, I had a bad day."

"Just keep walking we're going into the Church, you better behave."

"Or what– you're going to call my mother?" *Shut-up Kurt,* he heard his father's voice echo in his subconscious. He cocked his hat, stood tall, and matched stride for stride with his captors and the timid driver.

Entering the cool vestibule, he was overwhelmed by the opulent beauty of the enormous church. He had seen pictures and postcards from his parent's pilgrimage a few years back prior to his father becoming commissioner. Pictures didn't do it justice. The Basilica illuminated power, wealth, a magnitude of artistry, and holy peace that filled him.

They all stood behind the first wide pier maybe twenty yards from a man he recognized as Carmine Lucchesi. Stately, self-assured, and not bad looking, if you liked tall, tanned, silver haired, debonair Italian men. Well groomed and excellent taste in suits. *What are you thinking? The man is a coldblooded killer.*

Then she walked in, his heart skipped a whole slew of beats. Her long spiral wild curls bounced to her feminine gait, with just the right sway of her behind. She was wearing heels, a short burgundy/green plaid skirt, a white sleeveless blouse, and loaded with expensive shopping bags like some fashion diva on Fifth Avenue. Her burgundy cardigan slipped from the crook of her arm.

Unconsciously he stepped toward her; he paid dearly for that step. His idiot guides shoved their hidden guns into his sides. Now frozen; he knew one dumb move on his part was going to create a bloodbath. And the sad part was most of it would be his. The odds were, he could take one of them out, but not both. Furthermore, he couldn't risk the lives of innocent worshipers. The thugs' semi-automatics under their oversized black trench coats could wipe out a small army including the Swiss Guard.

And Mandy getting shot was not on his list of things to do today. Proud he watched her cover her hair and bare shoulders with a new silk scarf. What a gracious lady. She slipped her cardigan into a bag, brought the infamous envelope out; she looked so small and demure standing next to Carmine.

A rigid tightness tormented Kurt from his throat to his groin as he witnessed her every move. Why was Carmine touching her tears with his handkerchief? Kurt blinked several times with disbelief. Was she really wiping Carmine's tears? What the hell was she doing feeling sorry for him? Coddling him? *She's lost her fucking mind!*

Carmine was the reason behind Antonio's and Anna's deaths. How could Amanda have compassion and pity for that evil bastard? Kurt had witnesses report the mob hit Carmine called up for one of New York's top bosses' son. Tony was a retaliation hit from another grief stricken killer. Watching was pure insanity, he wanted to scream.

Anxious Kurt covered his eyes when Mandy placed her arm around the sobbing mobster's broad shoulders. *Oh let's have a flippin' prayer meeting, save these bastards from themselves.*

Somewhere from within a self-defeating tortured inner demon forced him to peek through his fingers. The horrific scene unfolded. His eyes grew larger and his heart beat faster likened to watching a scary movie. You want to see the action, but you risk the rush of fear induced adrenaline when you do. Strangely enough a jealous rage erupted from the depths of his person. What the hell was Carmine doing holding her face in his hands? Was he kissing her? Kurt's spirit was having an out-of-body seizure leaving him in a cold fog.

Just then idiot one snickered and gave him another jab, "Hey looks like the boss found himself a nice piece of ass."

Kurt's head jerked towards his future second victim; Carmine was going to be first. "She's not his ass, she's mine!"

The sound of his own voice was unrecognizable; it was something from the *Exorcist*. At any moment he surmised the priests were going to come charging out and sprinkle him with holy water. With his fists clenched anger pulsated burning in his veins like hot spurts of lava. Disgruntled, disorientated, and dismayed by the tenderness between Carmine and Mandy reminded him of when she had calmed Tony at the club. Did she know Carmine? Was this a set up? Was this a new Italian mafia torture tactic? Just get a knife and cut my heart out, he thought, it would be easier and more humane. Betrayal was crippling.

The woman he wanted to spend the rest of his life with set him up. He couldn't hear their exchange of words, besides that he was trapped in a jealous fog unable to read their lips. It looked strangely enough like an affair ending, but why was she crying again. The Don was kissing her, not on the lips, but still what the fuck was she doing? What was he doing?

Kurt fanned himself with his hat believing any moment he was going to cause a scene by dropping to his knees and begging God for forgiveness of all the sins he had ever committed. How could this be happening? One day he's in Heaven loving every inch of her body and soul and the next day he's in Hell watching her comfort a killer. He'd never imagined St. Peter's to be the threshold of Hell.

Carmine was walking away with his envelope stowed under his arm. Finally no more kissing, no more back rubbing, and no more hand-holding, and thank God Mandy stayed behind alive. She was still sobbing, but not sad tears, more like angry– I hate someone tears.

Thankfully he was concealed by the white marble pillar, accented with mocking gold cherubs. He had never liked the chubby cupid type angels. And now he hated them even more.

His captors put pressure on his bruised ribs nudging him away from the elaborate sculpted altars designed to revere the dead popes. How ironic a place built to give hope to the living was jam-packed with dead people. Where's the hope in that?

They pushed him in the opposite direction of *The Pieta* to the doorway far left; Kurt vaguely remembered his mother jabbering something about "Death's Door". This wasn't a good omen.

Outside Kurt and his escorts encountered Carmine and another football player sized brute. *Damn, where did Carmine recruit? He was a better scout than Coach Ditka of the Chicago Bears.*

It took no time for Carmine and Kurt to size one another up. Alpha-male testosterone was in full rut. If it was just man to man battle– Kurt was larger and half Carmine's age, but skill and tactical wisdom danced in Carmine's corner with three gun toting thugs.

Kurt comforted himself that a physical gladiator battle would leave him the victor. On second thought, brawn to brawn would have been a discredit to their breed. A fight would ruin their very expensive suits.

In the afternoon sun, Carmine's suit was second to none that Kurt had ever seen. If he was in better humor he would have asked about his tailor. By then Kurt caught a glint of a princess cut emerald and diamond ring on Carmine's pinky, similar if not exact to the one tucked in his own breast pocket. He thought maybe he should ask about Carmine's jeweler to have a ring made. But since this wasn't a cordial visit, Kurt sneered and gritted his teeth.

Carmine studied him, then gripped Kurt's clean shaven cheeks with his thumb and fingers pinching hard making extra deep dimples. "Such a pretty boy face, It would be a shame to adjust it. I'm sure you're pretty attached to it. It's lucky for you, I believe she is telling the truth, or you'd be celebrating *All Saints Day* with my butcher." Releasing his vice grip he tapped Kurt's jaw hard, "She's a pretty little thing. I'd like to take her home with me. Treat her like a good woman should be treated." His white smile stood out against his tanned features.

Backing down would show Kurt's intelligence, but instead he clenched his fists, heaved his chest, and scowled like an angry lion ready to pounce, "Well then why didn't you? You were pretty cozy hand-holding and kissing her. Is she meeting you later? What is she your backup since you couldn't keep Anna satisfied?"

"Oh look boys; we have a live one here. All grit and no brain cells, I sure hope you're half the man she believes you are. She deserves a *real* man–the faithful, protective, good provider, and a man that knows when to leave well enough alone–*Capisce*? Antonio was that man." Carmine said delivering a sharp backhand to Kurt's cheek. His pomposity was a direct hit to Kurt's ego.

Not one to consider consequences was primarily what got Kurt into rash situations; disdainful he raised a mocking eyebrow, "For the record Amanda chose me over Antonio before he was unjustly killed. Looks like she chose me over you too."

Carmine eyes warmed, reflecting a strange fatherly compassion, "Son, there was only one woman good enough for me to fight for. Unfortunately, I didn't love her the way she deserved to be loved. My jealousy killed her love for me. And now she's gone; the one thing she wanted most I couldn't give her– real love. I suggest you don't let that happen to you." He turned to walk away, and then turned back, "Amanda deserves better than you. If I find out she lied to save your tough ass, I'll come get you– myself. Boys make sure he's on that plane back to New York. Mr. Kilawee's Roman holiday is over."

Kurt slowly unhinged his breath he couldn't believe he kept his temper in check. But knowing Amanda didn't have the natural capacity to lie; shook him to his core. She just saved their lives, but how? All he felt was grateful to her and for some queer reason to the coldblooded bastard who just slapped some sense into him.

The only other man that he ever allowed to touch or speak to him like that was his father. Of course, his father didn't have to use the brute force of semi-automatic weapons. Kurt stood shocked, holding back tears of joy, anger, and sheer exhaustion.

Why was it that a woman could calm the savage beasts with just a soft teary-eyed look, a tender touch, and a warm kiss? God cheated men.

Men had to fight, to conquer, to prove to themselves they were in control.

And then along comes tender sensual women-creatures to blow them right out of their minds. Women were the downfall of men, not the Devil.

"Come on time for you to go home–pretty boy." Idiot number one commented.

Kurt scoped the huge open square filled with crowds of worshipers, Amanda was gone. She had appeared and disappeared like a ghost. Everything was like an unfinished nightmare– she was an illusion of his vain imagination. He had no choice, but hope she was getting on a plane back to New York.

Unable to call Jeremy to share the details of his grueling embarrassing adventure, Kurt was pissed. *When was TWA international going to upgrade to the Airfone system like American Airlines?*

Nine long fucking dreaded hours, he was forced to take the flight back without knowing where Mandy had vanished. Carmine's men were infamous travel agents for getting passengers on flights. Kurt was ecstatic he wasn't stowed with the luggage. Rumor had it that others before him had crossed the mafia weren't so privileged. He knew he had come close. Was Carmine allowing him to live to lead them to his sources?

He settled into his comfortable chair–upgrading to first-class was his best decision that day. Some woman was bumped to standby. Too bad for her, he was through being a gentleman. He requested the attractive blonde stewardess to keep the scotches coming until he passed out.

Chapter 20

Clearly at comatose level Kurt opened his eyes just as the grueling flight was wavering down to the JFK runway. Much to his chagrin he was hung-over from far too many scotches. The pretty blushing blonde stewardess handed him a glass of water and palmed him a couple aspirin packs.

"Here Stud you're going to need these." The ends of her mouth curved upwards. "Whatever you do don't speak to the Captain Pilot."

A flash of embarrassment scorched his face, "Oh, sorry about my antics–I hope I didn't embarrass you."

She placed a kind hand on his shoulder, "No harm, you were quite the entertainment the first couple of hours. I was quite flattered when you sat me in your lap and asked, rather loudly, if I'd like to join the mile high club with you." She laughed. "Unfortunately my husband, the Captain, was not as entertained. But there is hope for you, if the airlines start hiring stand-up comedians, I suggest you apply."

Rubbing his beard stubble he attempted to rub off his embarrassment. He downed the aspirins and chased them with the cool water, "Sorry about that. Flirting is another bad habit I apparently have to work on getting rid of. Flying makes me crazy too."

"You and a lot of other people," she said walking away securing the cabin for landing.

Exiting the plane Kurt inched forward with his fedora covered head at half-mast, his aviator sunglasses hid his mortification. The exhausted flight attendants cooed, "Bye-byes" and halfhearted non-emotional, "Ga-byes". He tipped his fedora in apology to the concerned pilot.

His head still pounding, all he wanted was a few shots of the dog that bit him and Mandy standing at baggage claim. Before claiming his luggage he stopped in the men's room. An image of a haggard drunk man stared back–his new frustrated unrequited love guise.

After he used the facilities, he splashed his face with cold water resuscitating himself into a living breathing creature.

Still feeling like shit, he stopped at the first bar giving into temptation ignoring eventual remorse. A few shots would settle his nerves, yet upset his stomach. Life came down to choices–good with the bad.

An inexplicable bout of paranoia tapped into his psyche; he scanned the immediate area for unwanted shady characters.

Satisfied that he was solo, he headed to baggage claim hoping to obtain Amanda's luggage along with his own.

Although she hadn't boarded his plane, adding to his disappointment, her bag was checked for that flight. She'd have to get it from him, along with her other things.

Hope floated on a new brisk morning in New York City. For the life of him, he couldn't remember if it was Friday or Saturday. What did it matter now? He didn't have a job, since he had officially resigned. Why would the day or date matter to someone newly unemployed? No appointments. No intriguing interviews. No more makeup–.

See Kurt, it won't be bad to start your life over at thirty.

At baggage claim he spotted her, that dark-haired imp with the tapeworm, Belinda. She was past customs and halfway out the door with Amanda's suitcase. The baggage area was crowded; he dodged around some lethargic jet-lagged passengers. Several greeted him and laughed about his peculiar actions on the nine hour flight. Notably he was going to miss the semi-celebrity status of his Anchorman career.

Belinda disappeared by the time he managed to get outside. Greeted by a blast of November air, he clutched his suit-jacket closed warding off the biting wind. Summer was a fast paced memory, with winter already plowing into the enthralling city.

He loved New York even during the brisk biting winter it never left him cold, always charming and fascinating like new love or an old friend.

Luggage in tow, he returned to the TWA terminal. Belinda collecting the luggage meant she had lied and that Mandy arriving on the next flight was probable. He planned to wait and greet her with a smile, or perhaps not, but hopefully sober.

The monitors displayed the flights due in from Rome. Two flights were due to arrive that day. But since he wasn't next of kin, a technicality he vowed to correct; he couldn't convince the ticket bitch to tell him whether Amanda was on either.

Unimpressed by his charisma, the guest service attendant was having none of his flirtatiousness. So he planted himself on a barstool, ordered a bite to eat, and caught up on American news.

The elections were just days away, this would have been the busiest time for him. Drink after drink, he stewed and he schemed. What was he going to say and to do to her? He worked himself up and down the anger scale. His therapist had warned him to gauge his anxious anger on a scale of one to ten. By the time the second TWA plane deplaned three hundred unrecognizable faces, he topped the anger scale way over ten. More like ten times ten.

Slightly inebriated, his words slurred when he called Jeremy, "Hey man, send James-Leroy to JFK."

"Say doofus, what part of resigning don't you understand? How about the part–you no longer have fringe benefits of company cars, vans, or credit cards?" A huge reality check thumped Kurt hard. Jeremy continued his speech, "You can hire a limo, a taxi, or wait for Lionel and I to pick you up after we finish our dinner date. I have a life dude. You either wait or figure it out on your own."

"I'm tired of waiting."

"So what else is new?"

Kurt hung-up. Immediately he regretted pushing away the one person he could count on.

A few hours after he had spoken to Jeremy, Kurt stormed through his own apartment door. Like a bulldozer tearing down a condemned tenement in the projects he shoved the paraphernalia off the counter and slammed down a brown sack. It created a ruckus of clanging glass bottles startling Belinda; phone to her ear, she dropped behind the breakfast bar.

Blinded by rage like a bull he charged in and out of the rooms crashing anything in his path. "Belinda! Where are you? Where is she? I know you've been talking to her? You lied to Jeremy and me!"

Lucky for Belinda, he didn't notice her on the phone crouched in the kitchen. "Mandy the wicked beast has arrived." She kept her voice low, "The car is in the employees' lot. My friend, Jared, has the keys. He will take you to it. It's not a great car, but it should get you to wherever. Listen..." She held the receiver out for Amanda to hear Kurt ranting obscenities. "He's smashed and wigging out. What should I do?"

Kurt reached down and snatched the phone from her tiny grasp. No match for him, she let go. Instinctively he knew who she was whispering to.

"Amanda, where are you? Are you okay? Stay there I'm coming to get you." He shouted his frustration.

"No, Kurt, no," she begged.

"What? What do you mean–no? We have to talk. How could you leave me naked? You don't play fair? This isn't a fucking game. We could have been killed!" His hard chest heaved–he tried desperately to settle his temper. But to no avail, he felt his heart breaking under the pressure of her words.

"Kurt, stop, I will not talk to you if you continue to holler and pitch a fit like a three year old."

Sweat ran down his face as he paced, he flung his sunglasses and fedora on the counter in Belinda's direction making her jump. Breathing frantically, "Amanda, please. Please let me come get you."

"No Kurt, we can't. It's too dangerous. Didn't you read my letter?"

"Yes, I read it, over and over. Mandy I'm that man, give me a chance." He rubbed his forehead and raked his hair. His pace slowed transforming to calmness as if she injected him with his drug of choice–her voice.

"Kurt, I can't. We can't be together. Not now, maybe not ever." Amanda jilted him.

From his jacket breast pocket he took the note, a single packaged condom, Amanda's missing Gucci watch, and the emerald-diamond ring. Belinda reached automatically for the note, to scoop in on his babbling. He nodded giving her the okay, like he wanted to prove his sanity.

Holding a quiet sob, Kurt's voice cracked, "Baby, what about us?"

"Listen to me. There – is –no – us." Her curt words pierced his heart. He always got his way.

"What? No you listen to me! You said, you wrote... you love me. Sweetheart, you and me, make us." He snatched the letter from Belinda, reading it aloud, "My Super-hero," he listened intently for background noises then proceeded, "I know you are furious with me–. Honey that is the understatement of your career," he chortled. "You left me naked in Rome," his voice altered to a sexy whisper, "you can apologize with make-up sex."

With a tremble in her throat, she sniffled and said "Kurt I have to go."

"Mandy please come home, listen to what you wrote:

'Last night was the most incredible night of my life. I assure you I got more and felt more than I bargained for. I know the type of man you are lives to conquer, loves the chase, and once he has his trophy he moves on to the next conquest.

Truthfully, I need and want a man that is willing to give up one night stands with many, to have the stamina for one woman he can't live one night without.'

I am that man. Trust me I have stamina. Since we met, I haven't been with any woman but you, I swear. Trust me, I have only dated you, wanted you. Believe me–you're more than enough for me. Let me prove it."

"I can't, I can't." Her sobs rattled through the phone.

He heard airplanes and chatting people. She was still at JFK on an outside payphone. "Mandy are you taking another flight?"

Belinda stood silent; her arms hugged her waist, tearing up she witnessed the bittersweet lovesick couple trying to make sense of their broken lives. She knew why Mandy refused him. Should she tell Kurt the truth–did he deserve the truth?

"Amanda stay where you are!" His voice went from sexy soft to a strange fatherly sternness, "Don't leave, I know where you are. I love you."

"I'll be gone by the time you get here."

"Didn't you hear me? I love you Amanda." His vocal cords tightened with heightened emotion.

"I know. That's enough for me now."

He slammed his hand on the counter, "That's not enough for me– I want more!"

"You will always want more. I can't face losing you when you get tired of me."

"Damn it, Mandy that's not fair! You haven't given me a chance! You drive me crazy with this back and forth shit. Just stop teasing me."

He picked up his pace, throwing his dirty clothes out of his suitcase. He ran to his closet, shoved clean clothing into the emptied suitcase. "You stay put. We can go away someplace–anywhere? Let's take a vacation to the Virgin Islands, or wherever to be alone. I have something to say and I want us to be face to face. Mandy? Amanda?"

A dead silence, no sighs, no sniffles, no soft panting. The phone was dead.

Kurt looked at the phone and then at Belinda. There was a moment of rapid beeping from the receiver. Without notice, he threw the phone from the sofa against the brick wall in the kitchen shattering it.

Belinda plopped her tiny body on the sofa next to the suitcase, dutifully she folded his clean clothes placing them inside the suitcase.

The silence was deafening.

Kurt tore the brown bag open, grabbed the Irish whiskey bottle and cracked the seal. He chugged a couple of shots straight from the bottle. He eyed Belinda daring her to say something. Her big overly made-up eyes were wet with tears.

God, how he hated women and tears.

He took another swig and grimaced. With his back to her, he inhaled and exhaled. His beef wasn't with Belinda, but she lied, and had she not, he would have caught Amanda.

He wanted to vent, Belinda was sitting right there on his couch, folding his clothes, and repacking his suitcase.

Regrouping, he decided the friendly approach was pertinent to obtain what little information she might have. After all, getting people to talk was his talent. No time like the present to test his interviewing skills.

"Well, Belinda what's your take on my next move?" He turned, his hands clamped his hips, he drummed his fingers randomly–not nervous, but calculated and determined. "I won't get to the airport before she leaves."

Belinda continued packing, her eyes downcast, barely audible she mumbled, "No, you won't, even if you had a private jet."

A disheveled mess, he approached her. "I didn't hear you, what did you say?" ruthlessness coated his words, he reeked of alcohol.

She blinked at his dead stare, malevolent she repeated loudly, "No you won't! Serves you right power freak."

Kurt bit his lower lip holding his retort, "Okay, you're right, you happy now? So it's my fault Mandy is running. Where do you think she's going?" He glanced at Belinda, her high heels tucked under her legs on the sofa. He hated shoes on the furniture and she knew it. Cautiously he sat on the sofa with just his midsize suitcase between them.

She tucked her shoes under further.

"Why do you have your shoes on the sofa?" Perhaps changing the subject would alleviate his frustration.

Slowly Belinda exposed her feet. Within seconds he clutched the ankle closest, glaring at her he studied the black glittery five-inch stilettos; his grip on her ankle was tight and persistent. His eyebrows rose quizzically. "You *do* want to tell me why you're wearing *her fuck-me* shoes?" his jaw twitched.

Belinda tried to squirm free, but his hand clamped tighter. His eyes turned borderline crazy. "Ouch, you're hurting me. Ever hear of the word boundaries?"

"Answer my question and I'll let you go."

"Man you have issues. Mandy gave them to me with some of her clothes. She said she wouldn't need them."

He released her ankle, but removed the shoes from her feet.

He eyed them like prized trophies, "Tell me, what else did she leave?" Now they were getting someplace, little clues always lead to big clues. Too bad his plan to hold her valuables hostage was stymied.

"Well, like her designer work clothes and her club clothes."

"Hmm, interesting? Where would she go where she wouldn't have to work? Or not use business attire? The idea she won't be clubbing, is desirable. I know she bought some expensive things in Rome." He enunciated his thoughts, just sorting the facts.

Belinda switched her seating pose to kneeling, "Like what? What did she buy? She told me she was shopping, but she never told me what? Tell me what?" she perked up like a kid going to see Santa Claus.

"Oh and I'm the one with issues." He said shooting her an intrepid glance. "Oh no, I get my information first, then we can dither with shopping news. Where is she going?"

He watched for signs of lying– like hesitation or her eyes shifting down and left. One has to think about lying; telling the truth comes directly from the immediate short term memory.

Belinda's dour face and direct stare told him she was about to tell the truth, "No can do, don't spazz on me–I would totally tell, if I knew. You two drive Jeremy and me psycho. Your big egos are like Kirk out–beam me up; like scary how you can fit in the same room together."

Kurt sighed. Her incoherent babble wasn't the answer he wanted. He stretched out leaning into the sofa, his hands clasped together behind his head. "Okay, I suppose you'll want to elaborate on that." He was too exhausted to fight her or decipher odd comments, or maybe he needed to hear another version of the truth. Belinda could be enlightening.

"Let it rip Joanie, oops I mean, Belinda. Spill it; you still have to help me find her." He slipped up by calling her Joanie, referencing her likeness to Joan Jett.

Belinda walked to the kitchen; pulling a glass from the cupboard she poured herself a drink and balked, "Joanie? Really? Okay fine. Care for another drink–like in a glass this time?"

Kurt stayed outstretched on the couch, "Nope, I'm good. But speak English–use the new words you're learning in college." With an adopted somber mood, calmly he prepared for his next move.

"Well, you are both too much alike. You fight to be the best in everything. You try too hard to impress each other, but what you don't realize is separate you're good, but together you're great. Like dynamite."

Kurt smiled thinking about their amorous night in Rome, "Damn, you got that right."

She reached over and slapped him on his protruding elbow, "Not talking about sex right now. Like dynamite can be used for construction, or it can be used for destruction. Anyway, at work Jeremy says you both fought for attention from the camera, but then you started fighting for attention from each other. Jeremy told me stuff that you told him, but not Mandy. Why? Because you wanted him to test the raw current, take the shock, just in case she rejected you. Neither of you wanted to be rejected. Egos don't like rejection. Part of your problem is you're a spoiled rotten brat."

Kurt sat up quick in defense, "What makes you say that?"

"You must be the baby of the family always getting your own way and if it doesn't go your way then everything is shot to hell and nobody gets to have a good time. Sound familiar?"

He laid back, "Yeah, so what? What does all of this insight have to do with us getting back together? And tell me why Mandy insists that there isn't an us?" He reached into his carry-on bag and pulled out her profile.

Leaning forward he read through it searching for clues to where she would run. If he could get to her, he knew he could change her mind. "Go on."

"Well Mandy is the baby of her family too, so she understands how to throw a tantrum just as well as you."

"Yeah, you got that right. She is so damn cute when she stomps her feet, but tries not to." He reminisced. "And the way she opens and closes her mouth apprehensively before she speaks, because she wants to retaliate with sophistication. She's amazing in so many ways, but she doesn't listen to reason. When I tell her not to do something she does it anyway– her way–just to screw it up."

"Wow, you get *what* she does, but do you know *why* she does that towards you? She listens to me, to Rich, to Jeremy, but not you."

He looked up from the file, "Why? What did I ever do to her other than try to guide her career and protect her? I helped make her a celebrity."

"The problem is you remind her of someone she loves and respects, but she doesn't trust him. And he's a very important in this deal. From what she spilled to me you act too much like him and you scare her."

He looked back at the file. "Is it her father?"

"Great work Sherlock. Her father left her mother for other women. She was like nine or ten, and it stuck with her. Then you strut around with your playboy reputation when she came to town. Flashing your righteous style that you can get what you want–when you want it, and it's yours for the taking. Remember the night at the club when you were sucking face with one of those model chicks, but you made it perfectly clear you wanted something more from Mandy? Hmm?"

He threw the file onto the coffee table, and covered his face in shame, "Yeah, man was she pissed. But I tried to say I was sorry. I bought her that expensive bottle of perfume and she gave it back unopened. What a slap in the face that was. But I respected her and made a conscious effort not to do that again, she danced with me on other nights. I knew she wanted me. She sent me signals–she flirted with me." Kurt accused.

"Yeah no, you two call it flirting or dancing the rest of us call it a soft-porn exhibition, just one more way you hoard attention– ego power-tripping. You knew that Tony would show up that night, but getting caught back fired. Mandy felt ashamed. She's too faithful when it comes to relationships. And thanks to you, we have that night to share with the rest of the screwed up tabloid world."

Kurt got up and started pacing. Leaving the room for a split moment he came back with a scrapbook. He flipped to the end pages where he had laminated photos of him and Amanda at several charity functions, news interviews, and even the night of the yacht party.

He marveled over their professionally photographed relationship. "She says we never dated, but I have proof. We were on these dates as a couple. We are the 'Golden Couple', see it says it here and here and here." He pointed out the obvious.

Belinda swallowed the rest of her drink. She moved closer to admire his scrapbooking. "Yeah, the 'Golden Couple' with the enormous egos. You saw this as dating. Mandy saw it as her job, a way to advance her career, climbing the Kurt Kilawee ladder of success. Not that she didn't like going out with you, she did. But she saw you playing leading Anchorman as she played the leading Anchorwoman. Just play acting like a lot of celebrities do for the paparazzi. Mandy was going on real dates with Antonio because you didn't have the balls to ask her. Just like she said in her letter– she's not the one night stand kind of girl. She feels she can't compete with the women she suspects you want. I told her she never gave herself credit– and neither did you."

"But I told her I was sorry. That damn Rich and Sarah had me follow her. Every day and night all I saw was her. Mandy is perfect for me, I knew from the very beginning. I must have read her file and résumé a hundred times." He picked up a stiletto and stared past it. "I was so jealous, I wanted to shoot someone. Rich kept taking her away from me, and then she started seeing Tony– it shocked us. She has something no other woman has– my heart."

"Earth to Kurt, you profiled her. Before she came to work for NYCB, you profiled her into being perfect for you. Everyone I know has a mental list of what they want in a mate. And when you discovered your competition was a woman, you did your homework. You decided to conquer her. Mandy is the female version of you in a fancy smart package. She's your crack heroin. The problem is you're hooked on the pure shit. You've convinced yourself she's your cure all. You fell in love with the idea of her before you met the real her."

"But she loves me. You read the letter. She loves me. I'm her Super-hero." He packed the stilettos in his suitcase, and strutted over to collect the letter, the condom, her watch, and her ring.

"My guess is she hates herself for leaving you that letter. She is so afraid of getting hurt she won't let you inside. So even if you find her, she believes that you're like her playboy father–a player–a man who loves 'em and leaves 'em high and dry."

"But I am not like that– anymore. And it is *when* I find her, and not *if*." Anger edged his words.

"Doesn't matter, she won't let you get close enough to give you another chance. Especially after listening to all your X's on the phone. You of all people should have known to cover your romance tracks."

"I was too busy tracking her. I didn't have time to clear the messages. Look at these photos; I was love starved wasting away to nothing." He started to pace again, his blood pressure increased as their conversation centered on Amanda and their budding romance. "I have to find her." he reread the letter and focused on the ring.

It was clearly evident the Amanda drug was wearing off; he was getting needy for her. His gut instincts assured him his quest. Emotional eruptions rumbled from his inner core to the surface. "I have to find her alive."

"Alive is good," Belinda swayed the conversation. "Hey maybe you should go get cleaned up, you're a mess. And why did you pack my new shoes?"

"Those aren't your shoes. They belong to my future wife. Mandy is going to wear them again– for me." He pulled out his money clip and threw two one hundred dollar bills at her. "Here buy your own." Without further comment he followed her suggestion.

Sweeping up the pieces of the shattered phone, Belinda decided it was time to get Jeremy involved. She went to the bedroom to find the second receiver. Playing psychiatrist after only one quarter of psychology was exhausting. Kurt was an exhausting man, she pitied Mandy.

Amanda found the car in the cold dark night with Jared's help. The tin can, pee-yellow, glass bubble Pacer was a shock after driving the sleek Mercedes she and Kurt co-owned. Leave it to Belinda to find her a death trap. Well, at least Kurt wouldn't suspect her driving a get-a-way bucket of rust. Oh hell, what else was she going to do; it should get her to Philadelphia. Her sister, Dory was prepared to swap her vehicle.

Starting her new life, Amanda wondered how long someone had to hideout from the mob–like probably forever, and maybe into purgatory or the next realm of reality.

Then there was the question of Rich's indictment. She was required to leave a statement and her evidence with the state attorney; she gave her mother's information for emergency contact. Part of her debated whether she should head south to Miami to spend the Holidays under the protection of her father, but her instincts warned her about Kurt's resolute talent for finding what he wanted–when he wanted it. He did sound rather fixated on them being a couple.

Obviously he would search for her at the listed contact information, he found in her NYCB employee file.

The first day he accosted her, he creepily knew too much personal information. She found out later that it was natural as breathing for Kurt to assume and utilize any information left unprotected. "Finders keepers– Losers weepers" was his sophomoric motto.

Problem was she was at the losing end of everything in her career and life in New York City. She glance up through blurred tears into the off kilter narrow rearview mirror. The glittering lights of the concrete jungle started to shrink along with her lifetime dreams. Traveling southwest she grudgingly left behind her high hopes of the high-rise posh apartment, her icy-blue Mercedes, her designer clothes, and aspirations of making a solid six-figure income. They all faded.

The treacherous truth and future faced her through the wide cracked windshield. From a high-profile semi-celebrity lifestyle to an endless life of living underground as a blind mole she would stumble into her future.

White knuckling the shaky steering wheel she maneuvered into the black void. Intermittently alternating her driving hand to wipe her tears with the back of her hands, wishing she had Kurt's gentle thumbs to caress them away like he did at Antonio's funeral. *God my life is a fiasco.*

How did she allow three strangers, all men, screw up her twenty-six years in just six months?

Antonio's life was over, Kurt's career ruined and his life was in jeopardy. Rich's life would eventually change, a few years behind bars was drastic, not like her pathetic existence, but ruined just the same. Everyone at NYCB was at risk of losing their careers and livelihood because of one man's greed and lust.

Anger toiled in her veins, she was glad she went on a last hurrah shopping spree with the company credit card. Rich said no limit. She especially liked her selection of Mont Blanc pens for Kurt, Jeremy and herself. She also bought them dress Bvlgari watches. Kurt's was white gold with a bezel encircled with diamonds; her plan was to engrave it with "*Excelsior our paradise*".

The details about delivering the gifts had escaped her at the moment; she was too focused on her safety and praying for Kurt's.

His idea to fly to the Virgin Islands was inventive, but only delayed the inevitable. His getting tired of her and moving on. With his demanding sexual appetite; she feared it would be unrealistic for him to just have one woman.

She was a one man woman and she demanded her heart to fall for a more reasonable mate. A credit to her, at least she had the fortitude and intelligence to not sleep with the boss. Too bad she didn't adhere to the rules of not procreating with co-workers, namely Kurt.

As she drove she talked herself in and out of love with him. It would have been more disastrous had she stayed to face him every day on the set, then eventually having to watch him date other women after their affair would have surely ended.

Men like Kurt were meant to be true alpha-males, servicing many females to maintain their dominance in the herd. Her insides quivered with desire just thinking about their erotic night. Exploring and satisfying his lustful desires would take a lifetime, but she couldn't bear to share him.

Going without your addiction was better than feeding it into oblivion.

Constant beats of fear prompted her to keep checking the rearview mirror for a blue Mercedes or suspicious black sedans. Her sister's condo was approximately a hundred and ten mile drive. Rain poured on the cracked windshield obscuring her vision for the Philadelphia exit; she swerved sharply. The bald tires hydroplaned, off the road she skidded to an abrupt stop on the shoulder. Her heart pounded in her ears.

"What are you trying to do get yourself killed?" she scolded. Maybe running away was selfish and wrong.

After Philly she had another dreaded eight hundred sixty miles to her final destination. Back to her roots, deeply planted in the earthy Wisconsin drumlins, she'd be safe under Gramp's watchful eyes. His name and place not mentioned on her resume or in her profile, nor had she elaborated about it with anyone in New York. Even Belinda did not know much because Kurt had ways to make people talk. Definitely a private detective talent he must have inherited from his father.

Drowsy Amanda pulled into the parking lot at her sister's redbrick condo building located on the outskirts of Philadelphia. Exhausted from jet-lag and overwhelmed by her emotions, she locked the doors and reclined the seat. A few hours earlier than scheduled, she hoped her sister was heading home from the Philadelphia airport where she was employed as an air-traffic controller. Amanda was too tired to think or move she hoped that Kurt had passed out from his alcohol rage. His delay would give her more time. She wasn't a fool to think that he wouldn't come here first. Mixed emotions swelled inside her, but exhaustion finally won.

Hours later the morning sun reached over the top of the three-story condo building just glazing the edges of the gray shingled roof prying through the dirty Pacer windshield.

A sharp rap on the window, Amanda practically jumped through the rusted roof. Her cramped body reacted with instant fight instead of flight. She shoved the door open, forcing the culprit on the other side to jump back. With her heart racing to a heart attack she could barely see straight, but instantly recognized her sister's voice.

"Hello New York City girl– you made it safe." Dory said assisting her to a full stance.

Amanda stretched her aching body, relieved to see Dor's velvet perky eyes smiling back with love. They embraced with a forever hug.

"Do you have time to talk about what's going on?" Dor said anxious. "Or are you still being followed? How could you let yourself get into this mess? Mom and Dad are fit to be tied."

Amanda tried to smooth her hair back as if straightening her appearance she could straighten the mess she'd gotten herself into. Her big sister always tried to mother her, even though she knew it irked her. Amanda responded the best she could, "Dor I know, I'm such a screw up, I have to get to safety. This is my mess. I will get myself out of it. I just need to lay low for a few months, or years, or maybe my whole life." Tears flowed down her cheeks; she wiped them smearing her mascara to the frighten raccoon look.

Dory gave her a tissue from her purse. "Say, you sure you're up for the drive to Gramp's house? Maybe I can take some time off work and drive you. I've never seen you so worn out, come on in, take a shower, and I'll put the coffee on. We'll make a plan. You sure you want to run away from that gorgeous hunk? Mom told me all about him, and of course she had to send me copies of your telecasts. He's quite the charmer huh?"

She hugged Amanda's weary shoulders carefully maneuvering her around the chickens that nervously pecked the grounds of the condo-complex. *Seriously, who has chickens in the city?* Weirdly enough they lived there before Dory. They didn't fit with the modern, clean, an overly organized environment that reflected the controlled lifestyle Dor adhered to stringently. The landlord, Dor, and other tenants tried to remove the chickens, but some things in life were meant to drive you crazy no matter how hard you try to get rid of them. Dory shooed a few that hovered by the entrance. Stirring them, she caused a raucous of squawking and fluttering feathers of proportions that could wake the dead.

Amanda was captivated by her sister's ability to never screw up. Dory was the perfect model of the perfect in control person. No man would ever shake her world upside-down, and those who attempted paid the price. Amanda was surprised Dor had any good comments about Kurt. But that was because she hadn't met him in person.

After Amanda showered, had her coffee, she felt halfway human. She gave Dory the rundown on all the good and bad of her last six months. They had spoken several times especially after Tony's murder. Her mom and sister tried to get her to leave New York then. Hindsight said she should have listened, but Anna needed her help. Amanda cried explaining Anna's tragic end. She didn't get to attend Anna's funeral, unable to risk exposure to the mob men who wanted her dead. Belinda went in her place. Her situation was surreal–completely off her charted path.

Love wasn't part of the plan especially to a man who reminded her of her father. Through her tears, Amanda finished her story, "So now I need to hide, did you get a vehicle?"

"Yeah, Dad sent the money. He told me to buy a Ford truck. It's registered in Gramps name. Gramps will love it since he's such a Ford man. Let's get your stuff switched. I am supposing your lovesick detective will be paying me a visit shortly."

Amanda smiled and rolled her eyes, "He is quite a smooth operator, so be careful. Detain him as long as you can and be careful he can be very convincing and charming when he wants something. Or otherwise he will throw a wild tantrum. He's harmless most of the time and makes you feel sorry for him like a lost little boy. I can't believe I fell for him. He's just like Dad when it comes to women." She inhaled and exhaled trying to shake the memory of their one night of compatible erotic pleasure. "Please don't tell him where I'm hiding. I just can't face him or have him hurt because of my stupid actions."

"You can't run from love forever sis– or you'll end up like me alone with wild chickens. I'll call you if and when he makes it here. I will stall him, or better yet I'll sick him on Dad." She gave her a big bear hug and kisses.

They laughed and went to work loading Amanda's things into the new white and red striped, V-8, 4x4 Ford pickup. It sure beat the hell out of the rust trap Belinda acquired for her. Kurt would not know what she was driving now even if he was able to breakdown Belinda. In the back of her mind she figured Jeremy would detain him as a favor to her. And the fact that Kurt was drunk would slow his cunning manipulating mind down just enough for her head start. Jeremy was a true friend he understood her dilemma with Kurt.

Up behind the wheel, she felt rested and ready to take the next stretch of her backwards journey to Janesville, Wisconsin. A long drive ahead she faced her bleak future with grit, fear, and fortitude.

Chapter 21

Kurt showered, shaved, and dressed in Calvin Klein jeans with a white dress shirt, unbuttoned to his mid chest. He finished packing two suitcases with a variety of clothing, not knowing how long he'd be traveling to catch her. Instinctively he knew he'd find her, hopefully before the Mafia madmen found him.

Consciously aware he would end up in Chicago under his father's protection; he supposed living with his parents was better than the victim-witness program. An inevitable life change, he wasn't sure either was beneficial or to his liking.

After securing his reports and evidence on several mob families including records of racketeering, extortion, and money laundering businesses, he called the New York State Attorney to have the locked briefcases picked up. He was advised to be invisible, yet available. The State had to process, audit, and certify the information.

The biggest hit was directed at the Gambino Family with evidence proving the hit on Antonio Casali. Carmine had arranged a hit on a Mob boss's son which created retaliation on Carmine's hidden son. Kurt's childish antics during his drunken paparazzi incident and Amanda's interference had assisted the mob by exposing Antonio in the tabloids.

Had Kurt fought for Amanda fairly like most men do by wooing her instead of trying to steal her affection, maybe they would be living life together instead of running from death. Guilt pierced him.

Belinda appeased him by filling a garment bag with his Armani suits and his Hugo Boss suit. "Dude you might need these bad boys *if* you catch her."

"When, Joanie–the word you want is WHEN." He smirked and took a shot of whiskey.

Finally Jeremy and Lionel arrived for the intervention. Belinda happily handed the detainment torch to them. Kurt counted money for Belinda to pay his bills while he was in hiding. Generous he gave her permission to stay in his apartment. One would be foolish to lose an apartment that had a rent freeze. It was wise to keep it maintained.

With most of his informant money deposited in the Virgin Islands and in Chicago, he felt complacent. However, since he had resigned his anchor position, he contemplated confronting Rich one last time. But his face to face with Mandy took precedence.

"Jeremy meet with Rich, I'll grant you full power of attorney. Settle my contract with my lawyer. Get my severance pay transferred to my Chicago account. Don't forget the libel suits. Every minute counts for Mandy and me." He handed Belinda two thick envelopes filled with cash. "Here, this is strictly to pay the rent and utilities not for trips down Fifth Avenue, got it?" his eyes narrowed intending to frighten her. It worked.

"Fine, don't be a dweeb." She scrunched her face in retaliation. He rolled his eyes at her and grabbed his suitcases.

Jeremy intercepted him blocking the front door, "Man, you don't really want to leave tonight? You should secure your financial future in case you're unable or disabled to work. No one can protect your future better than you."

"Mandy is my future, Jeremy I have to secure her. She's out there alone risking our future." Kurt said, dropped his suitcases, and fastened his gun harness concealing it under his leather *Member's Only* jacket. He had already packed his .38 special earlier.

"Lionel please cover the door."Jeremy instructed keeping in Kurt's face. Not that Lionel and Jeremy could physically stop Kurt, but obstruction afforded them more discussion time. "You're intoxicated, sober up first. Let's get an organized plan. You can call me at certain check points. Let's map where you're going."

"I know where I'm going," Kurt retorted, "fucking crazy thinking about her, my gut tells me she's driving. My first stop will be her sister's in Philly. I know her jet-lag will slow her; she'll need to stop soon. I will find her if it is the last thing I do. I'm not living without her. And I am sure-as-hell not going into the victim-witness program without her." A pathetic whine snuck into his voice. Everything was chaotic in his perfectly planned life. It had turned upside-down when he accepted payment to watch her.

The life of a gorgeous smart single woman brought him to the edge of heartache and desire. The truth was he never let women get that close to his heart. The aching he felt was worse than any physical beating he had ever endured. Jeremy begged him to listen to reason.

Jeremy was right, he wasn't thinking straight; in fact he couldn't remember the last time he was in his right mind. "Okay, I'll stay long enough to meet with Rich tomorrow." He picked up the phone and called his lawyer. Afterwards, he sat on the sofa and passed out from the mixed cocktail of whiskey and exhaustion.

Jeremy and Lionel questioned Belinda in the den away from Kurt's earshot distance to find out Amanda's plans and whereabouts. Belinda confirmed she only knew that Mandy was driving and not flying. They wrote her parents' and sister's information to keep tabs on Kurt's travel. Their hearts were heavy for Kurt and Mandy. Love shouldn't have to be so messed up.

The next morning Kurt arrived promptly with his lawyer to Rich's office. Rich was more than furious with Kurt and Amanda and how they handled their professional careers, not that he was a prime example of how to conduct a flourishing career in TV Network News.

Kurt leisurely sat back decked out in his new navy Armani suit– dressed for the kill. He knew he'd get a huge buyout on his contract in exchange for his stock. Sarah had arranged it beforehand, and also the libel lawsuits pending against five tabloid magazines. He would have a sizable nest egg for him and his future wife. That was assuming he could find her. And convince her he was her rightful mate.

Drumming his fingers on the leather armchair, he had difficulty sitting still while his lawyer discussed the details on a conference call with NYCB's panel of lawyers. Kurt was nobody's fool when it came to astute business dealings. Sarah was on her way over, he was positive that she would to try and talk him out of resigning. It wasn't what he wanted to do, – but no other options were on life's bargaining table.

Being a public figure has its risks. The danger stemmed from his newsworthy investigations on the unions with mob connections targeted him professionally and personally. Living on borrowed time, Kurt shifted his eyes from his watch to Rich. Trusting his friend and boss of the last three and half years was a difficult task that left bitterness broiling in his esophagus.

Rich gazed out over the New York skyline, his hands set firm on his hips; keeping his back to Kurt. He addressed Kurt as their lawyers hashed out the last of the minor contract clauses.

"You're pretty damn smart aren't you?" Rich growled low, his jaw still wired.

Kurt stood, walked over, and faced the window standing adjacent to Rich with just a few feet of separation. He slid his restless hands into his front pockets, holding Mandy's watch trying not to display anxiousness, "I like to think so."

"Then where is she?" Rich said struggling to speak.

"Who?"

Kurt played along, thanking himself for breaking Rich's jaw when he did, or otherwise this whole money deal would have gone south all the way to hell. The urge to bust Rich's face again was presently rising.

Neither of them removed their eyes from the multilevel buildings facing the Empire State Building. Breathing in rhythm they matched each other's dominated male malevolence.

Rich let out a huffed laugh, "Don't play dumb Smart-ass. I know you. You got what you wanted from her didn't you?"

Kurt rocked on his heels, keeping his hands to himself, thinking about her letter in his breast pocket, "I got more than I bargained for. And I guess I have you and Sarah to thank." He smiled a pleasant thoughtful smile.

"Well?"

"Well what? You expect me to tell you where she is or kiss-n-tell? It's different this time." Kurt confessed. "I never realized that loving one woman could make me feel such intense joy and excruciating pain at the same time. Giving up everything I've worked so hard to achieve is easy as opposed to not knowing where she is." His voice cracked.

Rich turned to him–his eyes wide, "What do you mean you don't know where she is?" Anger rose, "Do you realize what can happen to her?"

Kurt pulled his hand down his worried face, "Yes, I know. But I don't think she does." He opened up feigning friendship, for extra information, "Rich, she's the only thing I care about. When the attorney general processes my information you and I both know that I am finished in this business." His breath edged out. "Her dream at reaching the top is ruined if she marries me. And I can't take no for answer." He swallowed the hard truth. "You know she followed my lead, she pushed herself to compete with me. And now her biggest story could be her last. She can't return here." Kurt knew Amanda's story would ruin Rich's life. It was just a waiting game. Breached trust is hard to rebuild.

Rich's brow knitted, "I never would have guessed any woman could cut through your protective ego shell. You owe me a finder's fee for hiring her and bringing her here to bust your balls." He slapped a firm hand on Kurt's back. "It couldn't have happened to a worse son-of-bitch."

Kurt quirked a brow, "Jealousy will get you nowhere. Trust me love blinded me in deep shit. And now I don't know where to begin."

Rich sauntered to his desk, picked up a small pile and handed it to Kurt, "Here– start by paying me back. I have part of her last company credit card bill to share with you."

"What's this?" Kurt reviewed it, paying close attention to the last charges– *A gas station in Philadelphia*–.

"No, I'm not responsible for her spending habits, yet. Looks like she got her monies' worth," he handed it back. "Problem is–did you get yours?" he flashed a wry smile.

Just then Sarah barged in.

They both turned. She excused the lawyer with a wave of her hand. The power her stride exuded, her guise, and her self-assured disposition demanded their undivided attention. Kurt dug his hands deep into his front pockets, toying with Amanda's watch, reminding him his time was slipping away. He stared impassive into Sarah's enraged cool eyes.

After delivering a peck on Rich's cheek, she turned to Kurt, her motherly expectation bordered on evil stepmother.

"So Kurt, what the hell is going on here? NYCB will be ruined. Why would you throw all this away?" She spread her arms wide. "You're giving up everything for a woman who a week ago wouldn't give you the time of day? Kurt, think about your career, we can hire another anchorwoman for you to banter with. You are the face of NYCB. Why throw it all away? Have you lost all control of your senses?" her eyes were wild with petition.

Kurt glanced down at the gray carpet and then up to the white grid ceiling as if the answers to her impeding questions would jump up to him or fall from the sky."I can't stay here without her. I can't partner with someone else. A new anchorwoman is not like buying a puppy. Besides you'll both know soon enough–. I crossed the bridge by exposing my sources – I had too. There is no more Kurt Kilawee–Anchorman for *'The New Edge on Truth'*."

His hands steepled over his nose and mouth, he expelled a whoosh of air. "I've been acting crazy the last five months. It's her. I'm crazy about her. I can't stand it when she's not near me. You two caused it. I was fine by myself. I didn't need or want competition or an Anchorwoman, and now I'm screwed. You forced me to watch her every move day and night. This is your fault even more than mine. I would have never met Amanda Lindas if you didn't hire her from Chicago. Now I have to find her or live my pathetic existence in the victim-witness program without her!" His emotions exposed his deep burning anguish. Nothing mattered except saving her.

Sarah and Rich stood together watching Kurt crumble under the extreme pressure he placed upon himself. A man they had known for his stature and urbane temperament fell apart before their eyes.

Sarah reacted first pulling him back to the leather chair before he collapsed to the floor.

"Are you okay? Can we get you a drink? Rich get him a drink." She knelt low to get Kurt's attention. Distraught his hands covered his face. "Kurt listen, we knew you had it bad for each other. We saw you from the sound booth. I told you to make your move. We didn't know Antonio Casali had a hit out on him. Things happened out of our control. We can fix this together. NYCB needs you. You're the face of NYCB."

Not ashamed that his emotions about Mandy had sprung loose, but frustrated that he couldn't free himself from her spell. He was torn about leaving his New York City lifestyle behind and everything that meant success to him–his career, his apartment, his adult friends and fans–everything was here except her. She was gone.

Rich handed him scotch. Kurt should have rejected it, but he took it like a baby accepting a pacifier. It would hold him until he heard her voice again, smelled her fresh scent, touched her smooth skin, tasted her sweet urgent kisses, and gazed into her icy-blue eyes.

It was urgent for him to leave. Philadelphia was about two hours away. The drink went down smooth, Kurt stood as soon as his long legs could support him. Ignoring Sarah's pleas he asked, "Rich did Mandy leave any forwarding addresses for her paperwork?"

Rich fiddled with the paper stacks on his desk. Pulling from the top of a stack he handed Kurt her letter of resignation. "This is all I have. Her employee file has the only other information–which by the way is mysteriously missing."

"It's in a safe place." Kurt skimmed the resignation not finding anything that he hadn't already known. Just looking at the swoop of her scripted A and L sent small shivers through him. He hoped he'd see that signature on a marriage license soon. He wanted to study the whole stack– to check over her contract, hoping she had hired good lawyers to review it for her severance. As long as her indictment papers on Rich hadn't passed into the court system, she was safe to get a financial compensation package especially since Kurt's leaving jeopardized the likelihood of the networks' success.

He hated for Sarah to suffer, but Rich deserved jail time. He only wished that he could cuff Rich and run him in himself. Rich wasn't all bad just another misguided soul who accepted dirty money for his personal gain and inherent greed.

Sarah touched Kurt's arm, "I hope you find her. Finding love like you feel is hard to come by. She just needs time to realize running from love is crazier than facing it. We wish you luck," her smile sincere while Rich remained indifferent; pricking Kurt's anger.

The lawyer came back with several documents printed up in triplicates. Kurt signed willingly and hastily.

With one last threat, Kurt pointed a finger at Rich, "If I find out you had anything to do with Mandy being chased or harmed, I will come back and shoot you myself." With no apparent regrets, Kurt left NYCB.

At his apartment, Kurt handed Jeremy copies of Amanda's file and his travel itinerary. First stop was Philadelphia, to meet and interrogate his future sister-in-law, then possibly Florida to speak to the man who caused most of his future wife's issues. Maybe Kurt could extract advice on how to handle her tantrums. Someone had to help him.

Then to Chicago to take cover under his father's protection, if he kept moving there was less chance of meeting his untimely demise. Hard to run from an enemy without a face, maybe they would assume he was running scared from New York, so it appeared he wouldn't testify at the trial. The attorney general's office said they would notify him if they needed his statement at the trial, until then he was advised to leave New York and stay alive. The latter he hoped to achieve while he sought true love.

The cold November air whipped outside his Kips Bay apartment, Kurt dressed in his long black wool jacket with his gray plaid scarf tucked in ascot style, he waved farewell using his fedora to Jeremy and Belinda. He spun away in his icy-blue Mercedes to find his woman. With her black stilettos placed strategically on the passenger seat reminding him that his Cinderella looked hot in *fuck-me* shoes.

His desire to have Mandy never dwindled even when he was challenged by adversity and aversion in the face of her older sister. Dory led him to believe their father was protecting Mandy.

As he squealed away from Dory's chicken infested condo, he left about a hundred dollars worth of rubber in her driveway; he raced to a pay phone to vent, "Hey Jeremy, this is Kurt. Did we hear from my wayward wife yet? Has she contacted Belinda?"

"No, how did it go with her sister?"

"What a royal bitch!"

"Oh very well huh? Tell me what happened?"

"She wouldn't tell me anything just yelled at me for ruining her sister's career and breaking her heart. Telling me I should be ashamed of the way I run around with gangly women, and that I think I'm some sort of stud gift to women. And on and on and on..."

"So you made friends huh? Any clues spark your interest?" Jeremy switched the subject to get him to focus on the task at hand.

"Well maybe a long shot, she had a diploma hanging on her wall from Parker Sr. High, and yearbooks on a shelf with the same Viking emblem. I'm guessing it's in Wisconsin or Illinois. See if Belinda can find any information on it. I'm heading straight for Miami to punch their father for being such a bastard raising women to be suspicious of men. Damn it! Now, I'm looking forward to the victim-witness protection just so we don't have to associate with her family." Frustration rolled freely from his lips.

Jeremy snickered at his predicament. "Man you better *settle your jets*. Go hold her shoes for awhile, get your bloodhound senses back and no drinking. I will talk with you the halfway mark. What do you think two days?"

"Yeah, I was going to stop in at my parent's house, but I don't trust them anymore than I trust her family." Kurt openly admitted.

"Well, don't do anything rash. I don't want to hear in the national news– Unemployed Anchorman rubs out Golden Anchorwoman's Father."

"Well maybe if I do, it will flush her out and she'd be grateful he finally got what he deserves."

"No Kurt, no, Mandy loves her dad. Just because he wasn't a great husband doesn't mean he was an awful dad. You hear me?"

"Yes, mother. Talk to you in a couple days; get Belinda searching that school. Thanks for letting me vent."

His goals were set– get to Miami, get Archibald Lindas to expose Mandy's hideout, and maybe get his blessing for marriage. Hopefully Mandy would be in his arms and his bed by Thanksgiving. He was looking forward to something to be thankful for.

The Miami sunshine would be a welcomed blessing. He could work on relaxing and get a tan. Or was it relax and working on his tan. Anyway, the Florida sunshine was calling his name. Maybe she was there hiding out. It certainly was a possibility. He hoped her dad would be more conducive to his visit than that sister of hers. The one thing the sister had that appealed to him was similar icy-blue eyes. His chest cinched when she opened her apartment door. At least she let him in; he hadn't totally lost his touch with the opposite sex.

In Miami in record time, he asked around to find the white condo complex owned and operated by none other than Archibald Cury Lindas. A plethora of white stucco buildings intermittently divided by pale peach and gray buildings lined up along *South Beach* facing the ocean on Collins.

The buildings were more muted than he imagined, he turned off Washington around 16th street bringing him closer to Espanola Way a Spanish influenced area with burnt-orange tiled roofs and charming striped awnings. Laden in Art Deco style mixed with a Bohemian festive flair, rich flora and fauna depicted luxury along with swaying palms on the first-class trendy shopping of Ocean Drive. He could easily fit into this lifestyle with the ocean lapping the sand and the erotic smell of suntanned oiled bodies.

Finally after getting turned around his unintentional extended tour ended. He drove up to a guard gated complex that exuded posh luxury that even impressed him. If it were up to him he would drag Mandy down to see her father at least twice a year. Especially to avoid winter in the windy city where he dreaded telling her she was going to have to live with him and his parents. Until it was decided whether his testimony was needed to help put twelve mob guys in prison.

A tall dark Latino guard instructed him to drive around to building D and walk up a flight of stairs to the center penthouse suite. It matched the address Kurt had in his Mandy file, easy enough.

He wished he had more time to look a little more presentable. First impressions are always key, and the hardest to repeat. Wearing white jeans, a turquoise T-shirt, and a white blazer with his sleeves scrunched up to his forearms, he was as together as he could get. Even wearing boat shoes, without socks, Jeremy would be proud.

He had stayed in a motel the night before and had a day's worth of beard growth, sort of the new Miami Vice look.

Maybe he'd check into getting a detective job, maybe Mandy could work the local news or radio station. Miami was not New York, but maybe she'd do it. Who was he trying to kid? He was addicted to her, so he'd have to follow her lead.

Taking the steps two at a time Kurt was anxious to meet the man that left a bad impression of men on his daughters. Brushing his hair back, he kept his mirrored sunglasses on to shade his apprehension. He rang the bell, pacing with his hands on his hips for what seemed like hours. Finally a beautiful tanned blonde dressed in a fluorescent pink bikini opened the door, triggering his male libido almost instantly. All those curves could cause a major slip up. He cleared his throat. "Hi, I'm Kurt Kilawee, is Mr. Lindas home?"

He wanted to flash his badge and barge in just to avoid her flesh. Flesh made him weak. Before Mandy, he would have tried to get the bikini clad woman in several compromising positions, but his mission in life had changed. Unfortunately his eyesight was still 20/20.

Keeping his shades on, he prohibited his roving eyes from offending his host and hostess. The penthouse decor transported him into a large contemporary McKnight painting. Including the Art-deco styled rotunda entrance. The walls were soft peach bordered with tall white baseboards and topped with white crown molding wrapped around the dome ceiling. His eyes scanned to the dome center, landing on a masterpiece painting of a voluptuous nude woman surrounded by those creepy cupid cherubs. Kurt used his time wisely remembering Amanda's curves.

"I see you have an interest in the arts." A deep baritone voice interrupted his thoughts.

Immediately Kurt's attention shifted from the heavenly body down to the blush breccia-oniciata marbled foyer inlaid with a shell medallion.

Lifting his sunglasses to the top of his head, he hoped the thirty-something female had left, so he could focus on his silver haired host.

Mr. Lindas was fashionably dressed in white cotton slacks and a tropical blue shirt with white palm leaves. Nearly a native to Florida, his tan face reminded Kurt of George Hamilton. A good looking sturdy man they were close to eye to eye physically. Kurt hoped they'd see eye to eye on Amanda.

With steady eye contact, Kurt extended a firm handshake. "Hi, I'm Kurt Kilawee." His confidence exuded as if he was President of the United States and her father was a dignitary meeting him on his terms.

"Good firm handshake. I'm impressed. I've been expecting you. Archie Lindas, Amanda's father. Just call me Art. Come follow me to the pool, you must be tired from your long drive? Philadelphia is a ways to travel," he said hinting at who had given him the heads up. "Can I get you a drink?"

Kurt was parched, but Jeremy's words of warning 'no drinking' forced out the words, "A club soda with a lime, please."

He followed Art to the open patio with an Olympic sized pool with no less than a dozen bathing beauties lounging around it.

"Hmmm, playing it safe, good idea," Art said as if he had read Kurt's mind. "I must apologize for my eldest daughter she says your visit was more of an attack than a cordial visit. Let's hope our visit is more productive and conducive to a mature understanding." He slicked back his silver hair and placed a white mesh fedora on his head taking the seat at the head of large rectangular glass patio table. He picked up his cocktail and motioned to Kurt. "Please have a seat."

Kurt obliged his jovial host. He sat three chairs away, feeling the need to stretch his long legs. Strategically the wide white Doric pillars blocked his view of the scantily clad bathing beauties. They lined the pool scattered on lounge chairs like confetti. The smell of suntan lotion infused with the tropical Miami breeze.

This heavenly setting was a true test of his attention span. Kurt sucked the club soda down unsure if he was quenching his thirst or trying to put out his fiery male instinct. *Keep focused, Kurt. Doesn't matter what those girls are not wearing they are his girls not for your window shopping bad habits.*

Mr. Lindas was astute to Kurt's apparent insatiable thirst. "Is there something else I can get you? Maybe a real drink and a cool dip in the pool? My house is yours for as long as you think you can handle the pleasure. In fact, I'm having a couple parties this week. And since you're a celebrity I'd like you to be my guest of honor. We can get better acquainted."

Kurt leaned forward resting his forearms on his thighs thereby eliminating his view of the pool entirely and getting the sun out of his eyes simultaneously. "Thank you, Mr. Lindas, I appreciate your hospitality, but I am no longer a celebrity, and I didn't come to visit you per se, I'm here looking for Amanda. I don't have a lot of time to find her. I was hoping you could tell me where she is, since your... other daughter." He wanted to say *the super bitch*, but he refrained repeating his pet name for her. "Dory wasn't very helpful; in fact she was downright rude and spiteful. My suspicion is that she was not just lashing out at me, but somehow lashing out at all men. Which brings me to my next point, I am in love with Mandy, and she loves me. She is in danger and I need to protect her. Do you understand me Mr. Lindas?" He kept his voice low and controlled with direct eye contact.

A young suntan oiled beauty approached with a box of Cuban cigars and offered one to Kurt breaking the cozy poolside chat. He declined although he was quite impressed with the extraordinary offer. The longer he stayed the more impressed he became with his future father-in-law. He was a man free to have as many vices as he desired at his beckon call. A man's man would believe this place was as close to Heaven that any man could get. Art was a virile, confident, and sophisticated man, he took two cigars and handed one to Kurt, apparently he didn't take 'no' for an answer.

He clipped his cigar and handed the cutter to Kurt. "Call me Art. Let's try to be friends first before we discuss my daughters. They are both old enough to make their own decisions. My ex-wife and I have raised them with strong decision making skills." Art lit his cigar with the convenient lighter held by another half-dressed entourage disciple.

She proceeded to leaning forward giving Kurt a full cleavage shot as she lit his cigar. Caught off guard by her healthy display Kurt's throat closed from the provocative sight. He choked. His eyes widen, red faced he gasped for some fresh smokeless air while accepting a glass of lemon water from the girl who caused the kinetic reaction in the first place. This meeting wasn't going the way he had envisioned.

With a mocking twinkle in his eyes directed at Kurt, Art Lindas continued his speech. "So you see Kurt, if my baby girl is in love with you, then she will tell you. She's not the type to lie or hide her emotions. You won't need my approval to marry her. According to my eldest daughter, Mandy is under the impression you are like her dear old-man. You spend time with me and we shall see. Be my guest. Collect your belongings and stay here–let's say a week." He took a long puff of his expensive cigar smugly satisfied with his generous offer.

Kurt leaned back into the overly cushioned chair stretching his strong legs crossing them at the ankles, realizing he was going to get to know

Mandy's father whether she wanted him to or not. Why fight it? His carnal mind entertained the thought of having his cake and eating it too.

But, his bruised and broken pride and heart refused. He had to have Mandy; other women were insufficient replacements, no matter how fleshy, smooth, and sexy they appeared on the surface they were poisonous to him—off limits.

Unsure if this was a setup to test his integrity to stay true to her, Kurt felt that any moment she would come around the corner to nail him. He lowered his sunglasses contemplating his open invitation.

"Okay Art, I accept your generous invitation, but under a couple of conditions." He pushed the envelope engaging his goal; he tipped his head and blew perfect smoke rings. The bathing beauties swarmed closer like bees to a colorful flower. One took it upon herself to massage his tight aching shoulders. Driving for several days took its toll on his neck muscles. Another brought him a larger club soda and lime. And yet another brought him a crystal ashtray. All the amenities of a peaceful loving home, he could get use to this external facade, but internally he wanted more.

Amanda had filled his empty void for six months—no longer could he accept mediocrity or the status quo. Politely he removed the tender fingers away from his neck.

"Okay, Mr. Kilawee, you have been around my daughter too much. There are always conditions with her, name your price."

"I'll stay, but none of these pool extras are allowed by my room, and you let me talk to Amanda today, so I know she's okay with my visit. If she says no—then I'll stay at my hotel."

"Well, I can guarantee these ladies will keep their distance if you keep yours. As far as you speaking to Mandy, I'm afraid that's entirely up to her."

Kurt shifted uncomfortably. "So you know where she is and that she's safe?"

"Yes, I have spoken to her every day since the murder of that Italian she was quite taken with. Except for one night when she was detained in a hotel room, I hear with you." He swished the girls away with a small wave of his hand. He leaned forward. In a harsh whisper, he said. "As a rule, I don't get involved with my daughters' love affairs, but I do have my concerns about you. You remind me of myself. If you are a player— then I suggest you save everyone a lot of heartache and by all means play through. I wished my father and father-in-law would have sat me down and told me to play through, as you see I've done some irreparable damage to my family. I love my girls and I still love their mother, but unfortunately they don't trust me. Be man enough to admit if she's just a passing fling then let her pass, she's been hurt enough by me. Do we understand each other, Mr. Kilawee?"

Visibly shaken, Kurt wiped the sweat from his drenched forehead; the infamous Florida humidity was killing him. A stiff drink and a dip in the pool, all of a sudden sounded like an insanely ingenious idea. Even Carmine Lucchesi didn't unnerve him as much as Art. "Do you mind if I take you up on that drink and the dip in pool?"

Kurt stood and puffed nervously on his cigar. He hoped he wasn't committing a trespass that would make Amanda angry. He asked again, "Is there any chance that I can talk with her today?"

Archie removed his hat and fanned himself, "You are incorrigible, let me see if she will agree."

Kurt placed his cigar in the crystal ashtray, rubbing his hands together, his excitement expanded to a higher level of exoneration.

"Between you and me, I don't think an early celebration is recommended, she is quite stubborn."

Kurt stopped and put his hands on his hips, "You don't have to tell me that, after the last six months of being around her–she wrote the book on stubbornness."

Art stood, "Yeah, her mother edited it. You've had fair warning. Go get your things, I will join you for a swim, without the ladies if you prefer, they seem to make you nervous like a famished mouse near a baited trap. That's a good sign."

"Oh nervous, you think?" Kurt said removing his jacket exposing his sweaty wet shirt, "I never used to be this way. I think it is safer without the girls."

A rich laughter rumbled from Art's chest. "I think Mandy will find your response gratifying. I will send my butler out to get your drink order." He patted Kurt on the shoulder. "You are an agreeable young man. I cannot say that my daughter will be as agreeable."

Chapter 22

"Hello Mandy, how are you?" Art said smoothly without warning signs that this was anything other than his daily call.

"Hi Dad, I'm fine. No signs of any corruption here, you know Janesville, not much commotion. Some runaway pheasants, a few deer and car collisions, no one was hurt. And, oh I read in the *Gazette* Dan Dean and Matt Sweeney each bowled a three hundred. I think this is Dan's third time. My friend Dee-Dee did it twice. Hell, tonight I'm going to celebrate with them and a few other friends."

"Sounds good, be careful, its Friday night fish fry and the crowds can be rambunctious. You and Gramps going to *Benedetti's*? Is it still his favorite place?"

"Yeah, it's my favorite fish place, and who can resist the huge grasshopper ice cream. Afterwards I'm meeting Cyndi, and *Rainbow Bridge Band* downtown at Rocky's. Shelly and Deb will meet me, I need to get out. I'm stir-crazy." Melancholy traced her words.

Art looked out his living room picture window showcasing the splendor of his peach tiled patio, turquoise pool, and into the distance the deep blue Atlantic Ocean. He puffed steadily on his fine Cuban cigar, hesitating on his next comment.

"Hey Dad, you there?"

"Oh yes, maybe you should come here. Someone, a little crazy, is visiting me. I thought maybe you'd want to speak with him. He's awfully anxious and direct. Quite impressive; he's a larger than life character in person than on TV."

Amanda felt a bitter chill race up her spine. Kurt was in sunny Florida while she was freezing her ass off in Wisconsin. Where was the poetic justice in this world? Damn him. Why didn't he just leave things the way they were or are? Damn him. What was she going to do? "What is he doing there?" she said flat.

"Right now he's out at my private pool applying lotion to that– how did your sister describe it– that rockin' bod." Art laughed, "Looks like a healthy prime example of the male species."

"Dad, is that necessary?" Her embarrassment met his chiding. But her mind flashed instant photos of ecstasy. From the night Kurt was shirtless in his bedroom to their night at the Excelsior. But then the ecstasy faded. He lied, forcing her to lie to save his life.

Lies, lies, lies.

"So is he enjoying your company of female specimens?" she cooed, with sugar-coated bitterness. She heard him puff his afternoon cigar, an expensive habit she hoped he didn't turn Kurt onto. Not that it mattered; she wouldn't be in Kurt's life anyway.

Laughter poured through the phone, "Funny you should ask, he requested their absence at the pool, and by his room. He was sweating like a pig on a hot summer's day. Not so cool and collected as he wants me to believe."

"His room? He's staying with you–just great! Not wanting half-naked women hanging on him? You have an imposter."

"He's adamant that he wants you. He wants to talk. Will you?"

Amanda began to pace to and fro on the worn linoleum kitchen floor. Her floppy bunny slippers took a beating from her nervous energy. Should she or shouldn't she? What would it help? And for that matter what would it hurt? She hurt. She didn't want to hurt. And she didn't want Kurt to hurt either. Why couldn't he just move on? Sighing heavily, she asked, "What do you think I should do Dad?"

Silently he puffed. He watched the lovesick exhausted man lying out on a comfortable lounge chair appearing to have fallen asleep as soon as he hit the chair. That man had just traveled three days or more in search of love for his daughter. Did he, as her father, want to encourage her to take a chance on getting hurt? Maybe she'd find love in the hands of this player, or possibly a reformed player who had finally met his match. Or maybe he wasn't a real player after all. "Baby girl, I don't want to sway you either way, but he seems sincere in his actions. He's resting now. Let me talk with him some more. Give me a week. Okay?"

"Okay, but don't trust him–he's an investigator. Don't leave him to his own devices. If he's looking for something he'll find it and he won't quit until he's satisfied."

"Thanks for the warning, I will try not to let down my guard, but maybe you should think about letting down yours. It seems to me he is quite satisfied in pursuing you."

That night, Amanda decided it was safe to let down her guard and have some fun. Janesville didn't' have the club scene like New York or Chicago, but rural blue-collar and farm people know how to dance and party hard. She felt safe around her high school and college buddies. Many stayed in the safe GMAD town; they got married and were happy raising their children in the quaint community. Nothing wrong with it–it just wasn't ideal for her life. She always dreamed of the big city and the rush of satisfaction that comes from striving for her dreams. Damn, she was so close, until she met Kurt.

Yet she had to admit, he challenged her to be a better reporter with the competition that flourished between them. Perhaps he deserved credit for coercing her into being the best she was capable of being.

After a whole weekend of drinking and dancing at the hallway sized bars, depression crept upon her. Plenty of men had asked her to dance and helped her on and off the dance bar at *Looking Glass*. Although she had suffered through dour hangovers, the alcohol diffused her broken spirit and heart.

She didn't want just any man, she wanted Kurt. And she didn't want him unless she didn't have to share him.

Throughout her self-inflicted incarceration she continued to call her mom and dad letting them know she was okay strapped to her farm girl roots. She even toyed with joining a bowling league. Well not really joining, but subbing once or twice to break up the monotony she called her life.

Gramps teased, "Do you really want bowling to interfere with your drinking?"

"Well, Gramps there isn't much for me to do except be your assistant extraordinaire putting up preserves, cleaning the barn, milking cows, and feeding those obnoxious chickens and Billy goats." She smiled and rubbed his bald head.

Gramps had all the updated equipment, so it was a no brainer. The stench of cows and chickens got real intense when she woke from her drunken stupors.

Maybe she was too hard on Kurt about his drinking bouts. At least drinking numbed her during the lonely nights when she craved the taste of his salty skin and his tender lips feeding hers. She missed his strong crushing arms, his chest brushing arousing cologne against her nose, while his lovemaking tantalized her to orgasmic seizures. Seeing the aftermath in his mesmerizing calm emerald eyes, his soft whispers and caresses lulled and comforted her. Wanting him was all wrong, but the sultry burning desire felt so right.

She shunned romantic interaction with other men. Cautiously she always watched over her shoulder. Not knowing when or where her New York stalkers would attack. She spoke with Belinda and Jeremy several times. They were her lifeline to the exciting world she had left behind.

As the days and nights passed, the beautiful autumn foliage reminded her that Thanksgiving was approaching; *damn it* she was going to miss the Macy's parade in person. Her booby prize was her mother and sister had plans to visit. For their visit to keep her mind off Kurt, her shot-to-hell career, and pathetic existence; she repainted the interior of Gramps' four bedroom farmhouse.

The rooms were quaint with dark-oak trim and doors, Gramps insisted on various shades of green. *Like Wisconsin needed more green*, she thought. Admittedly she loved Wisconsin's seasons, well with the exception of too much winter. This visit reminded her of when Nana had passed, Amanda was fifteen and devastated, she and Dory stayed with Gramps to help him while their parents pursued their careers.

Now she enjoyed Sunday Packers football with him in front of his 25" TV set. Gramps enjoyed watching the VHS tapes of her short-lived news career. Amanda wished she had covered the elections and she was equally sure Kurt did too.

Ronald Reagan and George Bush won by a landslide! She was happy with that. America was in dire need of strong leaders.

The news tapes rekindled her admiration for Kurt as she watched his professional mannerisms with his antics. Jeremy did awesome close-ups of Kurt's effulgent green eyes. She remembered their hours in makeup and caught herself singing his favorite Police songs. "Every Little Thing She Does is Magic" and "Every Breath You Take".

Was he singing them to her all that time? The part about asking her to marry him in an old fashion way amused her.

From her father's vague reports, Kurt was enjoying his celebrity time and the sunshine while she watched snow flurries whirl around the barren farmyard. In the biting cold, her grandfather butchered a turkey and some chickens; she grudgingly helped pluck feathers. This was a far cry from black tie affairs and cocktail charity functions with her debonair, albeit being paid to be there, escort Kurt.

"Gramps do you think I'm being overly cautious about hiding?"

Gramps stopped and looked at her, blood dripping like a horror film gone wrong on his leather gloves and leather apron, "Do you really want this old fool's opinion?" his warm words blew forth steam clouds into the chilly air.

The freezing wind tossed her wavy hair about, smiling she said, "I wouldn't ask, if I didn't want it."

"Sweetheart, I have never met the man you're pining after, but I do know how a man looks at a woman he loves. I loved Nana for fifty years and not a day goes by that I don't miss that look in her eyes. You and that young man have that look. It's televised to the public. Any woman, in her right mind, would crave the attention that man wants to give you. It would be a shame not to allow love to take its course. I know you're unhappy here. Killing chickens and milking cows was never your dream, or living with a sentimental old fool. If you want my advice– let your father tell him where you are–give love a chance. You know the saying– *it is better to have loved and lost, than never to have loved at all.* I say– *it is better to love and be loved for as long as your heart can stand it.* I miss your nana and some days it hurts like hell." He pounded a fist to his heart, "but I am glad I didn't miss loving her when I had the chance."

Tears trailed down Amanda's blush red cheeks. She knew he was right, but there was more at stake than just loving and being loved, there was fear. Fear of death, and fear of losing Kurt to another woman while they lived. Why did she fall for Kurt? Why was Tony murdered?

So confused, now, she had a drinking problem and possibly a bowling average. *God this is not the plan– not my dream!*

With added fierceness, she clipped the chicken wings, dipped it into the boiling water pot over the fire, and plucked feathers with her slippery blood soaked gloves. She answered her complaint, *Deal with it Amanda! It's not your plan that matters–it's God's plan.*

The meteorologist on WGN Chicago station predicted snow for the twenty-second of November, Thanksgiving. Amanda finished her painting projects and removed furniture from the overcrowded rooms. She stacked the furniture securely in the barn, so it wouldn't tumble onto the Queen Anne dining set Nana had left her. She covered the furniture with padded moving blankets in corner of the large barn that housed the cows and the two destructive goats. She named the naughty goats Kurt and Flirt. When she tried to work they'd nip at her for treats.

While she waited for the milking machines to do their work, she'd uncovered the table and a chair to do journaling. She daydreamed about Kurt having a great time with her dad. Her dad was a great guy, lots of fun, full of surprises; good and bad. She learned to accept him the way he was. But as for accepting a husband that way; well that was a whole new therapy session ballgame. A psycho game she was damn sure she didn't want to play.

Thanksgiving came with one hitch. Her mother and sister insisted that she was better off alone like them.

Irritated Gramps voiced his vehement opinion, "You two are doing more damage than molting hens in a henhouse attacking the rooster. You're attacking a rooster who isn't allowed to defend himself. Jaded women will be the death of the human race." He huffed away to his woodworking shed.

Around the first of December Wisconsinites were blindsided by horrific blizzards. After the accumulation of three to four feet, Amanda stopped hoping it would end, and instead she entertained thoughts of visiting her father in Miami and having hot passionate sex with Kurt. Her dad offered several times–along with petitioning her to speak to Kurt. She denied herself both privileges. *What was she going to say anyway? Hey Kurt, I miss you; let's have hot suntan oiled sex.*

To keep her mind off lovemaking scenes of them together, she worked the farm, cleaned house, and even did Cookie Day with Gramps and her friends with children. After cooking and cleaning weather permitting she spent nights dancing to her favorite band, *Rainbow Bridge*. Dancing was her only outlet; sexual flings were not her style. Several gorgeous guys in their close knit circle loved dancing too. Some wanted more than she was willing to give, and that included a few bartenders that persistently asked her to after bar-time breakfast at the *Oasis*. Sadly she declined remembering the last handsome bartender she was involved with.

By mid-December, on a routine below zero day; Amanda decided to drive into town for food and alcohol at Woodman's Grocery and get supplies at Farm-n-Fleet. Bundled up in her fury hooded parka, her scarf wrapped snug exposing only her eyes to the seventeen below wind-chill factor; she hoped her eyes wouldn't freeze.

Seated in her Ford pickup, she revved the engine to warm it; she glanced down at the passenger seat. A frozen severed cow's head stared glassy eyed at her. Her mouth agape sucked in her fuzzy scarf. She thought she screamed, but she couldn't hear herself. Frozen with fright, her heart rampaged in her chest. Involuntarily she revved the engine; her hands stayed glued to the steering wheel. Fear swept into every crevice of her body, mind, and soul.

The mob had found her.

This warning was deadly. Stuck in a shock coma she didn't hear Gramps screaming her name.

"Mandy! Amanda! What's going on? Please stop revving the engine!" He reached in and yanked out the key. That's when he saw the cow's head. Things like this never happened in Janesville.

With all his strength he pried her hands off the steering wheel. Dragging her into the house was easier than getting her to quit screaming and shaking.

"Mandy, sweetheart please stop you're hurting my good ear with your wailing, please sit, stop screaming. I'll call the police. Who do you think would pull such a prank? Anyone you met in town recently? Were you followed after bar-time? An after bar party? Please give me some clues, so I can tell the police." Gramps brought her a glass of water and a Valium he had leftover from dental surgery. "Here Sweetie take this, it should calm your nerves."

Trembling, she dropped the pill and spilled the water. He got another and helped her like a toddler using a cup for the first time, still spilling, but together they got the job done. "Go lie down on the sofa, and I'll call the police."

Amanda obeyed; she listened to him relaying the details.

Gramps explained afterwards, "They'll send an officer tomorrow morning, they're shorthanded with the semi-trucks jackknifing on Hwy 12 and 14, and Interstate 90 has a pile up. Yesterday's temps melted the snow leaving black ice conditions this morning. Apparently a frozen cow's head doesn't take precedence over live stranded people. You know frostbite and hypothermia can set in fast."

"Yeah, Gramps Wisconsin winters are not for wimps, being a Cheese Head and beer drinker takes courage and a bit of crazy. Gotta lov'em," she said drifting into a Valium slumber.

The next morning Amanda woke in the exact spot Gramps had left her. Starving she floated towards the rich smell of freshly brewed coffee. Overly warm from sleeping in her parka, she shed down to her Packer T-shirt and jeans. She poured herself a hot mug. She inhaled its sweet aroma, cradling it in her chilled hands. She gazed down at a note left on the nook table.

Mandy, Went into town to finish errands, please take care of chores. Remember police coming to do report. Love Gramps

Instant fear gripped her mind, she shook it off. The live cows still needed milking, the chickens needed feeding. Kurt and Flirt needed their breakfast too, even though she was sure they had snacked on the gate rope again. There was nothing they wouldn't eat. Oh well, such is the life of a farmer's granddaughter. She drank the last of the coffee, put on her bunny slippers; too hot for her parka, she'd endure the cold barn without it.

Looking out the window she studied the three inches of fresh snow covering her cow infested truck. The round thermometer connected to the outside window casing was in the red somewhere around thirty-five.

Oh wow, having a heat wave–a tropical heat wave, she murmured to herself as she shuffled to the big red barn, flanked by two silver silos, such an idyllic Wisconsin postcard moment. Wisconsinites would likely enjoy it for three or four more months– *ugh*!

Inside the barn, she leaned into the warmth of Daisy's body to attach the milking machine. Mindlessly, her thoughts drifted. Everyone who owned cows at one time or another had a cow named Daisy–how original Gramps. Her mind played tricks, she wasn't sure if she had heard the creaking of the barn door first or the goats butting their newly roped secured gate, but something startled her from her involuntary coma.

In a frozen fog a male voice addressed her by name and within seconds the click of cold metal cinched her left wrist. She jumped up almost knocking herself out on her assailant's chin. Twisting and squirming she tried to escape while the intruder covered her eyes and struggled to control her flailing arms.

She heard another click, but it wasn't on her other wrist, it was around her attacker's wrist. Struggling to face him, she yanked her left arm hard. The cold metal cut her wrist drawing blood.

When she faced him, there was no mistaking the fiery emerald eyes shadowed by a navy blue cop hat. It was Kurt. He was wearing a Janesville Police Department uniform.

Repeatedly her mouth opened and shut, she tried to speak intelligible audible words, but nothing came out.

First he spoke into a radio receiver, "Officer Kilawee reporting from Wallace Coleman residence out on Afton Road, I'm handling a domestic dispute, over." With his jaw clenched, he narrowed his eyes waiting for her response. His broad chest heaved visibly alerting her to his pent up anger.

The crackling police radio squawked back, "Do you need back up?"

He pulled her to his warm chest pressing her against his uniform belt. So tight she swore his holster was going to leave a permanent imprint in her hip. He pushed the radio lever keeping his eyes on hers; his warm breath thawed her cheeks from the outside as her anger swelled heating them from the inside. Her lower internal flame began burning just from his touch, his smell, and his elevated heart rate. She was toast.

Kurt squawked, "No, give me an hour; I can handle this dispute alone."

"Okay, sharp shooter; I got you covered, just an hour. Over"

Kurt tossed his radio to the straw covered floor. Still holding her close, she felt her ribs cracking.

His breathing labored, his eyes soften, his words came slow and calculated, "Now, that I have your attention, I have a couple of complaints about you Ms. Lindas. You're under arrest for grand larceny and future spousal abuse. How do you wish to plead or proceed?"

She palmed his chest pulling his hand with, wincing from her new handcuff cuts. "You're arresting me for spousal abuse?"

She caught a glimpse of his badge and then glanced at the name tag on the opposite side, an epiphany of horror crossed her mind, "You're a real cop!"

A wry grin spread on his suntanned face, "Hey respect the badge. I am a Police Officer. And you're still as brilliant and sexy as ever. This farming lifestyle suits you." He cupped her derrière with his free hand pressing her close. "Now, let's play catch-up. So, tell me why your grandfather called the police to file a report on a severed cow's head found in a 1984 Ford 4x4 red and white striped pickup?" She wiggled back from his grip. He continued his terse gripe and stepped towards her. "Well it could be worse; he could have called in a missing person's report or a homicide?"

Her heart rate soared.

"You're a cop? You're impersonating a cop that's a felony in any state!" She screamed riling the goats and cows creating a cacophony in the barn. She stomped her bunny slipper feet as the goats' loud baying interrupted her thoughts. She waved her right fist, "Knock it off Kurt and Flirt–stop!"

They settled just long enough for Kurt to voice his disdain, "What? You named a goat after me, my namesake is a goat? Really Amanda?" He placed his hands on his hips pulling her cuffed one with. His eyebrows raised and his lips tightened.

She yanked her left hand to her hip with his attached, smirked and squinted, "Yes, I named them both after you. They're both a big a pain in the ass. Why are you here? You must be crazy!"

He played tough tug-of-war pulling her hand back to his hip. Slowly he backed her up towards the stacked furniture away from the noisy pain-in-the-ass goats. Anger rose like a phoenix out of his inner cavern, he shot her a stern glare, "Crazy? Hell yes, what idiot do you know that follows a crazy woman through two metropolitan cities, crosses two continents, flies across the Atlantic Ocean not once, but twice," his fingers raised each time he articulated the word two. "What crazy bastard travels with the Italian and American mob henchmen breathing down his fucking neck while he's searching for you? If that's quintessential crazy then you've got the right guy. I wasn't always this crazy. I was a successful News Anchorman. I had all the wine, women, and excitement one man could stand. And then," he pointed an accusing finger, "you showed up– Miss Perfect Midwestern purity, with your cooing– *I-get-what-I-want-when-I-want-it*. With those icy-blue sultry eyes flashing hot and cold at your every whim poisoning me, wooing, and forcing me to want you more." He reached over and stroked her face and then her hair, "That perfect creamy complexion and those pouting lips, this wild untamable hair begging me to pay attention turning me into a crazy wanton fool. Yeah you've got the right guy."

He eyed her face, running his fingers through her soft spiral curls, making her insides ravenous and lustful for his hungry touch. His fingertips stroked her shoulder to her breast, grazing a pert nipple and followed down to her waist, settling on her hips with firm grip. "You left me naked and needy." Hot passion pulsated from his body. His sultry eyes narrowed, "You owe me. You said you are not a one night stand. I'm here to guarantee that."

With dominant passionate words, he slew her shredding her insides. A woman of many snide comebacks stood helpless and unable to conjure a satisfactory rebuke. He had her tongue-tied; strapped by his alpha-male strength. Hot tumultuous passion rose within; anticipation seized her, she wheezed for air. The cow stench and the fresh hay played havoc with her hitched breaths. She bit her lower lip so hard she thought she tasted blood.

His eyes lit up completely enthralled, he cupped her head and pulled her face close, "Don't bite your lip. You don't know what that does to me." He panted. "Don't tease me." Removing his free hand from her, he pulled his revolver out. With forced he placed the cold metal revolver in her hand, "Here, just shoot me." His demand yearning and unpretentious, "Do it! Just put me out of my fucking misery! I can't stand us apart. I might as well be dead."

"Okay, going all dramatic on me?" Her inside shaking transmitted to her timid hand clamped on his revolver, "You're crazy, I can't…"

Mechanically he unlatched his heavy police belt from his hips. It dropped to the barn floor with a thud, he kick it away along with his shoes. Using his strong left hand, he ripped open his shirt just enough to expose his tanned left pectoral, "Sure you can, you're killing me every day you run from us." His words sharp, he pounded his chest near his heart, "Shoot here, where it hurts the most. I'd rather be dead than keep feeling loneliness, unrequited desire, and jealousy every time you come within three feet of a bartender. Just put me out of my misery or make love to me for the rest of my life."

Okay not the proposal she was hoping for, but he was in shock–a complete whack job. Wisconsin winters could do that to anyone.

He unbuttoned his shirt pocket pulled out her love note, the single wrapped condom, her lost silver Gucci wristwatch, and the three carat princess cut emerald-diamond ring.

Her eyes lit up. He didn't give it to another woman? Confusion and sincere regret washed through her entire body, she released the pent-up air that suffocated her. "I can't…" was all she could squeeze out.

"WE won't be a one night stand, so you can choose this ring for a lifetime of one night stands with me, or the condom because I didn't come all the way from your father's Miami whorehouse for nothing. You make the call, Mandy," his eyebrows arched. "I happen to like morning sex. And you owe me that with the coffee you promised to bring back for *us*." He gritted his intense desire raging like a racehorse ready to be released from the start gate.

Still holding his gun, tears filled her blue pools, "No, you shoot me–I can't say – 'no' to you. And I don't know how to shoot a revolver." Her tears spilled down her cold cheeks. "And we're out of coffee."

Smiling he put the ring on her left ring finger. "I'm taking that as a– firm yes, Mrs. Kurt Kilawee." He took the gun from her trembling hand and tossed it into a pile of loose straw. The condom package sailed across the barn within the goats' reach. Unsure which goat ate it; he didn't show any remorse for doing so, "Now to get at what I came for," He planted an ardent kiss on her chilled lips.

She wasn't kissing back, not that she didn't want too, just the initial shock of his proposal left her numb. "Ah…what about the condom?"

"I'm all the protection you'll need. Amanda Kilawee, are you resisting arrest?" He unbuttoned his shirt all the way exposing his muscular physique. "Do I have to read you your Amanda rights?" He asked releasing his belt from his uniform slacks. "You better get started, this is a strip search and I want you naked before I read you your rights." Kurt stripped like a he knew the routine too well, like maybe he was moonlighting as a stripper cop still handcuffed with his right wrist to her left.

"You are crazy, it's freezing out here–you're on duty. This is a barn, and what happened to an old fashion proposal?"

"Baby we've already established that I'm crazy, about you. And it's freezing because it's winter in Wisconsin–your hideout choice. What planet are you from alien? Barns are good and old fashion. And besides– Jesus was born in a barn."

"Yeah, born in a barn, not conceived," she said starting her own striptease, using shimmying to get her jeans to her ankles.

"Circumstantial evidence–where's your proof?"

She helped him strip, running her cold hands on his body. "What does a city guy like you know about barns? Nice tan lines."

"Your cold hands aren't helping me get to where I want to be."

"Oh really and where is that?" She warmed her hands under his buff arms and removed his shirt as far possible. It hung off his right arm meeting her shirt dangling at their cuffed wrists.

"I see you're a Packer fan–that may cause a problem." He chatted

"Really Officer, how's that?" she quizzed him stroking his hard manhood.

He kissed her neck with his burning lips, gnawing. "I'm from a family of Bears," he growled playfully. His kisses crossed the swells of her creamy gooseflesh breasts. Taking his time, his tongue lightly brushed her hard cold nipples through her lacy bra. "Hmm, someone is catching a chill." Not one to waste a thrill, he took her nipples to peaks.

He created wetness in her molten sex; with his cool fingers he loosened her tightness brushing his thumb against her softness. An urgent need, within him pushed forward encouraging her to caress him more.

"Oh–I'm on the edge," he whispered releasing her breast from the manmade lace trap, "I want you– now and forever," he whispered his urgent demands.

Demands she wanted, she shuddered to his suave determined touch. He played her well. "Over there, go to the table," she rasped. His mouth devoured her neck and chest, hot ecstasy shot through her.

He hiked her up to his hips, her legs wrapped him; his length penetrated her with strong desire. Her sex pulsated around his.

God, he had all the right moves, she thought.

"You're good at this maneuvering thing–must be all the practice you've had?" she said.

His eyes darkened, "Babe, don't ruin this moment, I can't change the past." He placed her bottom on the edge of the blanket covered dining table, perfect height. Still intent on following through, he was relieved they didn't have to get down on the rough straw. "We're together now–no one else with us–this is our haven. With you this means so much more. Do you understand?"

She nodded, but still searched his face for the truth.

He knew she was searching, he had studied that look so many times watching her in action– she desired the truth. And he was willing to give her that and more.

"Listen; believe me the truth is here and willing to stay with you. I love you Amanda." His steady thrust coaxed to her to rescind her doubt. His hips tight against hers, he said. "This Super-hero wants to make love with just you." He focused on her rapt glow, "Look at me, Amanda Lindas-Kilawee you have the right to remain silent in anything you do, but moaning and screaming will be used against you by creating a force of justifiable pleasure. You will never need an attorney or any other man. I will fulfill your desires. You have the right to say–'I do'. Now that I've read your Amanda Rights do you understand that I love only you?"

She sighed, "Yes, I do. Now stop the happy-talk already. Do your job."

He joined her on the table. Her body arched into his putting her over the edge. He rasped, "Tell me you love me–and no conditions–just say it."

Losing her mind and her breath at the same time, she tried to slow his hip movements. The uncontrolled emotions she never wanted to feel for him kicked her common sense to the curb.

He begged her; he needed to hear the truth. Her eyes writhed with ecstasy. Hard and steady, he put her legs on his shoulders and taunted her, his words thick and low. "Come on Baby, it's time. Tell the truth."

Breaking their heated moment, she tried to pull back, "But what about safe sex?"

He smiled, "This is not an interview–no questions–making love with your husband is the safest sex. Tell me you love me." He continued his slow calculated lovemaking until she gasped.

Involuntary shudders quivered through her, she confessed, "Okay, I love you, I love you, now stop, oh my god. No don't stop!" He quickened his thrust pushing her over the ecstasy edge. She released with him.

He covered her with his hot muscular body, his face wrenched with heated fervor. "Oh, yeah."

Intertwined in a lovers' embrace, he sprinkled kisses on her neck and face until the mooing of the un-milked cows and the crackling police radio brought them back to the reality of the freezing barn in the dead of a Wisconsin winter.

"Officer Kilawee, do you need back up for that domestic disturbance? Repeat do you need back up? Over."

Amanda slapped his back with her free hand, and hollered, "Yeah, he sure does."

Kurt scrunched his face at her smiling face. "You liar–" he said finding her left hand in their tangled shirts. He kissed her ring finger. "I've got my back up, Baby. You're coming home with me. You're under arrest."

Chapter 23

Happily ever after didn't start immediately, nor is it an automatic given in any relationship. Kurt realized this as they suffered technical difficulties getting his future wife packed. She wouldn't separate company with her bunny slippers–almost resorting to tears.

Their main obstacle was the handcuffs. In the barn, he made a major mistake leaving his pants and contents unguarded while being detained by erotic desire. The famished goats broke through their ineffective gate. Flirt ate the handcuff keys for breakfast.

A couple of hours later, Kurt hoisted his future wife's bulging luggage into the truck bed with her dangling like a bangle charm.

"Let's go before we get caught in a snowstorm," he said opening the driver's door. At least he heeded the forethought of cuffing his right to her left giving him the mobility to drive.

Without notice as he helped her in, her bloodcurdling scream ripped his eardrum. Amanda froze midway, her eyes fixated on the frozen cow head.

Singlehanded he flipped her over his shoulder and yanked her out, "It is dead. Babe you're okay." He tried to calm her nerves along with his. "Now look at me," lovingly he stood her and stroked her face, "we have to work together to remove it." His speech was slow and direct as if she were a first grader. The calm woman he once knew blew a gasket.

"No! I'm not going near that thing. Let's take the police car!" she screamed and stomped her feet. Her arms flailed, he pulled rank by clamping their attached arms down to his side then he managed to capture her freehand.

"Amanda! Stop acting like a child! The cow head is dead. We have to remove it together, unless you want to end up like it." He linked his fingers with hers to stop the cold metal cuff from digging into his wrist.

How could an idea seem great at the inception in one's mind somehow turn into the worst idea ever? Kurt thought, while he pulled her to the other side of the truck and opened the passenger door.

In order to remove it, he needed leverage. Thankfully it was still frozen, yet gruesome it turned his stomach–just another idea that rapidly went rancid.

He didn't dare confess his participation on how the cow head came to its present placement. Desperate situations, call for desperate measures. Enough said.

Willfully taking on the Super-hero role, he had to save his damsel in distress and drive her to the *Church on the Side of the Road* in Rockton, Illinois. Another secret agenda she was not privy to.

Amanda pounded her frustrations out on his back as he squished her to the truck side while he assessed their peculiar predicament.

For leverage he stood on the seat edge with one foot and extended his other onto the door armrest. Strength and agility on his side, he hoped the armrest would support his weight. He shifted Amanda from the truck side to behind the door stretching his arm and hers to the limit. Holding the window rim, he reached in, gripped the frozen cow nose pretending it was a large roast. Using brute strength he pushed it through his straddled legs and out the door.

Mission accomplished cow's head out and future wife almost settled. Now – their hour journey to Rockton was possible. Gingerly he climbed off the makeshift jungle gym; shooting her a stern look, he said, "Is everybody happy now?" his eyebrows rose with sarcastic retribution.

Back into the truck through the driver's side, Amanda went willingly. She had no choice, or so it seemed, to back out of their "I do" deal.

She sat close to him on the bench seat, he believed she wanted to.

The first fifteen minutes of their journey was silent contentment, great sex had a way of keeping their other issues at bay.

His right hand rested on his thigh forcing her left to do the same. He wasn't sorry about the cuffs. As a backup plan they guaranteed that she'd have to go with him regardless of what transpired in the barn. He was more than happy about the barn incident. And the sponge baths afterwards ranked pretty high on his list too.

Earlier he had explained to his partner and the Janesville Chief of Police that a leave of absence was unavoidable based upon his participation in the upcoming trials in New York. Stuck wearing his uniform and under time constraints, he couldn't stop at his Victorian Stone Manor on ST. Lawrence Street near the Rock County Court House. Another incidental he failed to reveal. Well, he would eventually. She hated secrets. And he knew it.

"So how did you find me? Who screwed up?" Her hand rubbed his thigh.

His eyes flashed in her direction promoting more suspicion than not. "Wouldn't you like to know? A Super-hero doesn't expose his sources."

She slapped his leg, "Hey I deserve to know who the rat is in my circle of friends and family." Seriousness was confirmed in her eyes.

"No need for violence. You know I stayed at your dad's place."

"Yeah, I noticed your tan lines earlier." She smiled. "And I have an unrelated question for you?"

"No, I didn't *do*–any of his scantily clad women," he answered before she asked. "Remember we're not mixing the past in our future."

"Thanks for the graphics, but that wasn't even close to my question." She rolled her eyes. "I'm curious, how does an Irishman tan so well?"

His smile grew, "Maybe if someone did her research she'd know that I am also Italian and Indian."

"Oh, I missed the memo that required me to research your ancestral background. I should have guessed all the 'I's involve match your ego."

"My ego? Joanie, ah, Belinda says we both have ego issues. Sometimes she makes sense. She's staying in my apartment until..." he stopped to keep a lid on his secret can of worms.

"Until when? Are we ever going back to New York? I missed the Macy's parade, skating at Rockefeller Plaza, and all the Christmas decorations, damn Mafia!" She slumped into his shoulder.

He kept his eyes on the road contemplating what part of the truth he should share. Life was complicated. He loved New York and his pad was near perfection. Then there was the Apthorp property that Anna willed to Amanda. He hadn't mentioned it. Amanda had skipped town before he had the chance. But selfishly he refused Tony's memory to taint today. To appease her, he had to stretch the truth. "We will go back–eventually."

"Eventually is not a good word–look at me."

He glanced over, "Why are you going to flash me? I can't watch your girls; and the road." His eyes cut back to the snow drifting across County G knowing black ice was probable. He had witnessed too many accidents and fatalities the day before. Being a police officer had its drawbacks.

"Flash you? Yeah, hold onto that fantasy. Anyway what else did Belinda say about your ego? Wait, no...who ratted me out? Stop changing the subject."

"She said that as individuals we are damn good reporters, but together we're dynamite. She says you're spoiled rotten. I have the tendency to believe her on both counts."

"Me spoiled? I bet she said you're spoiled. Better get your facts straight Officer Kilawee. I can't believe you're a cop." She said dismayed, "A cop, I'm engaged to a cop. I fell for an Anchorman, and I'm marrying a cop. How does that happen?" she looked disgruntled and confused.

"Repeating is good; soak it in, but respect the badge Baby. A Police Officer is a very honorable profession. It is the closest profession to a Super-hero other than a Firefighter. And it is what I do–not who I am. I am an awesome private investigator, journalist, and still the same Super-hero you fell for, just a little more humble, so there."

"Boy, you're never going to forget that are you?"

"Nope," he patted his breast pocket, "I have it in writing – your handwriting. Thank you, it kept me sane searching for you. Joanie says I'm addicted. You're my crack heroin. I can't believe I slipped and called her Joanie to her face. I meant it in a good way, but she evil-eyed me and asked if I wanted another drink–in a glass." He chuckled to himself.

"Drinking again? Why?" Amanda pulled her hand away to hug her waist forgetting they were attached. His warm hand on her jean covered thigh moved close to her warm center. She squirmed to his forward touch.

"I think a certain farm-girl should worry about her own drinking before she questions mine. I've been watching the last three weeks and I think you…" he didn't finish his sentence before she removed his hand from its comfortable resting place.

"You what? You knew where I was for three weeks? And you watched me– what the hell! You're a poor excuse for a man. I felt spooked, I stopped going out." She knuckled his thigh giving him a Charlie-horse.

"Ouch! Was that necessary?" he hollered and inadvertently swerved the truck. "Stop that, I'm driving."

"Was it necessary for you to stalk me? You scare me."

"I wasn't the one who played this hide-n-seek bullshit."

She tried crossing her arms in rebellion; he flexed his arm tight not letting her move. Twisting her arm she turned her back to him the best she could. She pouted and tried to hide her disappointment.

Wordless, his blurt was unintentional. Spying was a habit, a cautionary tactic. To marry her; he wanted to be sure she wasn't considering their love as a passing fling. A fling, he couldn't deal with, he was addicted to her in too many ways.

"Babe listen, I'm sorry. I just wanted to be sure you were serious about us as I am. My admiration and respect for you grows every moment I'm near you." He stroked her backside and tried to link her hand with his. "I took the job with the department, so I could get close to you. I didn't know how you'd react to my being a police officer. I have to support us. You are a big time spender with awesomely hot moves. I saw your last company credit card bill. Wow you went wild in Rome, in more ways than one." He sequestered a small snicker. " '*Amanda Goes Wild in Rome*' can't wait for that flick to come out."

"Humph," she grunted leaning her back on him, knees bent she set her feet on the seat. "So using double entendres is how you justify spying and pointing out my faults?"

"Right or wrong, I saw you getting drunk and dancing almost every night except Mondays. You're a fulltime job Babe." He lifted their joined arms over her head and snuggled her close resting his hand on the swell of her breast. "Don't waste our happy reunion on anger."

"You're such a piece of work." she bantered. Staying mad at him wasn't easy.

"You're stuck with me now. See the headlines: Kurt Kilawee Anchorman marries Midwestern farm-girl." He veered off County G onto Highway 11 heading east towards I-90. Keeping his driving hand steady, he brushed her nipple with his thumb. He enjoyed her immediate reaction to his touch. "Do you forgive me?"

"Why? What's in it for me if I do?"

"Whatever you want?" He tightened his arm around her.

"Answer me this– What was your fascination dating the stick models with big lips without breast?" She looked over her shoulder to get a glimpse of his reaction with her lips protruding. "Don't lie. I know when you're lying." She kept her lips puckered and scooted down until her head rested in his lap.

"Oh, are we really going there?"

"Well, you know me I wouldn't ask if I didn't want to know." She turned her head towards groin area.

He squirmed, "Hey watch it–getting a little too close for me to keep driving. Watch those pretty fresh lips don't make me pull off the road. We'll have plenty of time for that on our honeymoon." He put her face in the V of his hand; pulling her up he kissed her puckered moist lips. "I think you know the fascination with the full lips–it's just a guy thing."

"Well, if we are going to be married…"

"There is no–*if*. It is–*when*. And we will be, very soon." He kissed her again to mark his point.

She sat up turning onto her knees wearing a quizzical look, "What do you mean very soon?" She wiggled the emerald ring on her finger nervously.

With gentle a knowing smile, he broke the news, "We are going to be married–in about…" he glanced at his watch. "In about thirty minutes in Rockton, Illinois."

A familiar uneasy glimmer of indignation rested in her eyes, "What? How did *we make* this decision? There should be six months to a year wait between engagement and wedding, not just a couple of hours."

Her reaction wasn't that surprising; she never did anything unplanned. Kurt was prepared for a full interview as she squinted decisively.

"So… you don't want to marry me? Besides, I waited six months."

Taking a deep breath, and exhaling a sigh, she said, "This is not about sex waiting. I would like to have a say in our wedding. At least my attire," she looked at her jeans, Packer shirt, and the plaid wool coat she couldn't put on entirely. "This is not exactly wedding attire." He stared at the road with due diligence as the snow blew across the highway. "Well, say something–are you wearing your uniform?"

"Well, it's the uniform or naked–you choose." He chuckled.

She tugged his hand from the bottom of the wheel. "Very funny, what about our lovely silver bracelets, a bit kinky for a wedding–ya think?"

He gripped her hand and pulled her back down. "Come on Mandy, sit still so we don't end up in a ditch. Besides kinky is subjective like the truth. It depends upon your perspective." Driving single-handed against the wind gusts crossing the barren fields was becoming more challenging as was his passenger.

"This, I have to hear," she scooted over to him giving his hand back to steady the steering wheel. Amanda knew Wisconsin's highways and back roads layered in drifting snow with black ice were dangerous. "So tell me– why is kinky like the truth?"

"Here it comes, let the interviewing begin." He chewed the inside of his mouth wondering if he should allow her interrogation or wait until they got to the church. Better get it out of the way, now. "There are different versions, levels, and perversions of the truth just as with kinky acts. You just have to decide which side you're on and how you like it."

"You're perverted, in your thought process. I should have known when you had the fetish for my *fuck-me* shoes."

He laughed. She didn't know he had them. "Now they fall under sexy– not kinky. And the handcuff idea wasn't mine." A mischievous glint danced in his eyes. "It was Shelly's. Listen, we will never do anything that you're not comfortable doing."

"Shelly really? I like that you bought my *fuck-me* shoes back from Belinda. You get high-heel fever often."

The devil danced in Kurt's eyes as he grinned. Silence loomed inside the truck, the harsh wind whistled around the truck. "Belinda's acute blabbing skills create proportional issues, her mouth verses her size just like her eating habits."

White Wedding, by Billy Idol played in Amanda's mind. "Well she didn't blab this. So, I have to marry you today huh?"

His smile dropped to a firm frown.

"No, the truth is– you don't have to marry me at all."

"Wow, a little miffed? Why are you upset with me–you obviously assumed I would jump at the chance to be your wife–like all women would? And you took advantage. Nice added fantasy touch, wearing the cop uniform, like women can't resist a man in uniform, right?"

Kurt smiled and shook his head, he had no clue where she was leading him, but he was along for the ride.

Either tolerate her twenty questions, or run along outside the truck in the freezing wind. He had witnessed her breakdown tougher men than him in newsroom interviews. She could get Gorbachev to break and stop the cold war if given the chance.

"Well Mr. Kilawee?"

He concentrated on the blinding storm, turning onto IL-75W after South Beloit, then onto Dearbourne Avenue. He had driven the route several times to finalize the wedding with Shelly and Pastor Doyle. What he didn't plan was being handcuffed, no time to get separated they were hooked facing a probable blizzard.

Cautious he entered the verbal wrestling ring with her, "Well, if the uniform worked for you, then I guess it worked for me too. And no, not all women would beg to be my wife, but some would be a bit more appreciative of my persistence. Instead of drilling me about the past we should be discussing the fact that you're a Packer fan and not a Bears fan. That will be a vein of discord in our marriage." Smug he waited for retaliation.

Dissension ruled her face, she scooted an arm's length away, and glared at him– "That is your assumption, not fact or truth. I'm not a Packer fan, my grandfather and ninety percent of my relatives are, but not me. So there."

He raised his eyebrows, "Really? Then what's with the Packer shirt, the green and gold rooms, the Packer memorabilia and the Vince Lombardi poster that watched us in the barn? I had fun in the barn."

"That's Gramps' stuff. I'm a 49er fan." She offered ignoring his barn comment.

"What? A 49er fan? How's that possible you were raised in Wisconsin and Chicago, and live New York? That's incomprehensible. I'm not sure I can marry someone that doesn't have an honest grip on football. The season is half the year. Why Forty-Whiners?"

Amanda paused and curled her legs under to get comfortable; her hand lost feeling dangling by his on the steering wheel. The seat-belt cut across her waist. A myriad of huge wet snowflakes dove into the windshield making the visibility worse slowing down traffic. The wipers swished them away as soon as they landed.

"I have two things to say then we are off football until the 49ers beat the Bears in January–Super-hero Joe Montana and fifteen wins. Now don't change the subject. Who sold me down the river?"

"So, Joe Montana–huh, he's like six-two and two hundred pounds, just an inch shorter than me, a little heavier, but not by much. So, I was right – you do like taller guys. Size does matter. Why did you date–" he stopped himself.

"Stop changing the subject– answer my question, damn it!"

"You're a real pain. No, it was not your father, indirectly maybe. I cased his office. I found a note pad with the top page torn off; I pencil shaded it to reveal phone numbers that were embossed in the page. One had 608, as an area code which matched with the information Belinda researched on Janesville. I called the number. The nicest person in your family answered. He referenced me as 'the rooster'," a snicker escaped. "Compared to the rest of your family, he's a saint. The other number was your mother's, she gave me an earache. But she confirmed that you were pining for me."

"I can't believe Gramps sold me down the river; the muddy Rock River." Defeated she leaned on his shoulder. "If you knew I was pining, why did you wait? I spent restless nights thinking I was being stalked. That damn cow's head finished me." She shuddered. "Do you think the mob is following us?"

Kurt rubbed his chin debating the truth again.

"Babe, if I found you, they can find you too. The cow's head was a warning that's all." He didn't lie, but it wasn't the whole truth either.

The wind rescinded, the snow turned to mist, heavy gray clouds lowered creating fog, not great for visibility, but an acceptable relief. Amanda's questions were minor compared to what he had expected.

A left onto Dearbourne Avenue, and then right on Prairie Hill Road, then another left onto Blackhawk Blvd. he careened the pickup into quaint Rockton about midday. The thick fog made it seem like dusk.

"Why are you going this way? You know I-90 is the way to Chicago?"

"It's a detour surprise." He said admiring her patience with his antics.

In front of a brown and white gothic-styled church, he stopped. The high pitched roof aligned to the right topped with a white steeple and a cross. The sign at the edge of the road gave away its identity before she could admire the wrought-iron arch entrance with a central large old-style lantern post.

The Church at the Side of the Road resembled a large gingerbread house from Santa's Village. The double red doors were dressed with twin holly wreaths. White lights on the green hedges twinkled through the new glistening snow that scattered around the courtyard. The misty fog and tall barren trees canopied the little chapel. A magical idyllic Christmas card scene waited to be disturbed. "It is times like this that make me fall in love with winter." She mused.

He watched her creamy face light up with an angelic glow, he was speechless, but he saw indifference stilled in her soft blue eyes.

His voice was barely a whisper. "Well, what about falling in love with me? Do you still want to marry me–today? We can cut the Packer shirt, so you can change into your wedding dress. I had Belinda and Shelly select you a designer gown." Emotion caught in his throat and moved his eyes to tears.

"Kurt this is beautiful, but if Belinda selected my dress it is probably black leather and lace. Although it would complement these kinky cuffs, it's not my style."

Some of her friends came out of the idyllic church– Vicki, Tami, Pam, Norma, Melissa, Rebecca and Nan. Then others drove up in their vehicles Sarah, Shelly, Deb, Darla, and Cyndi and Heather too. The girls were all dressed in red satin strapless gowns with pure white roses as their bouquets.

Kurt kissed her cheek, "No Baby, I wouldn't let Belinda do that. She tried, but I told her to select a white fitted strapless mermaid style gown. She knew your measurements from the designer clothing you left behind." He rubbed her tense shoulders. "Do you want to see it?"

"No." she said frozen emotionally, yet astounded by his generosity and his competence in wedding planning, she felt bitterness towards his secrecy. Too fast, too surreal, was she even ready for marriage?

She gazed at the emerald and diamonds gleaming on her left hand resting on his strong hand. She wanted him, more than any man, but fear inched its way into her heart. Could she trust this fairytale?

A wedding day is a magical day, but she wanted more than one day of magic. She wanted a marriage filled with love and commitment. Could Kurt deliver the promise of love and faithfulness and not just fulfill her fantasies? Tears pooled in her eyes, she tipped her head up to contain them.

Confused, Kurt saw a poignant change in her face, "Mandy don't. Don't cry Babe. This is a good surprise. I selected all of your friends as bridesmaids. Please don't say 'no'. No is so unacceptable." His labored breathing steamed the windows. "Maybe you need fresh air to clear your mind, everyone is waiting for us. If you see the dress you'll want to try it on. It has a cathedral length veil; Heather is prepared to do your hair and makeup. I promise I won't look. There's a place inside to dress behind a curtain. Being handcuffed is not all bad. Come with me."

"No."

"Mandy please, it's freezing and we have time constraints for the ceremony. Gramps is here to give you away. Your sister and Mom should be here too. Your dad couldn't make it, but we can get married again, so you can plan an official big bash–you can buy another dress whatever you want. But we have to get out of the truck today–like now. Okay?"

She lowered her eyes from the perfect scene. It faded like a dream as the windows fogged with every breath they shared. Her eyes studied his. Searching for the truth, the truth she desired to make her feel secure with the vow she believed was for life.

Could he keep his eyes and hands only on her and forsake all others? If she asked, he would just say yes, to momentarily appease her to obtain his goal. Why was he so adamant to marry her?

Her thoughts rushed like an express subway train: the day they met, their arguments in front of Jeremy, the AIDS telecast dubbing them as the high power 'Golden Couple', the yacht party, Antonio and Anna's deaths, and then the day she lied to Carmine in St. Peter's Basilica. A knot of anger and fear festered inside like a boil ready to burst, she had to lance it. She had to know the whole truth before she entered into a lifelong commitment.

"Kurt did you know when the hit was ordered on Antonio before it happened? Did you know who ordered it?" her dead stare was colder than the ice forming on the windows.

He swallowed hard and stared back, his poker-face intact, yet his breath hitched before he spoke reticently, "Why? What does it matter? Even if I did– I couldn't have stopped it. You have to believe me."

If the cold hard truth is what she wanted, then damn it – damn her – damn this whole life existence, he fought his emotions. Even from the grave Antonio was going to screw his plans. Tell the truth and live with her not trusting him or lie and not be able to live with his conscience. Those were his grim options.

He slammed his free hand on the steering wheel, "Damn it Amanda! This is our wedding day, a happy let's get our lives started day. But no, you never give up the interview. You constantly demand more, whether it matters or not. Will my answer change the fact that you love me?"

Shaking she balled her fists, gritted her teeth, her voice rattled, "Just tell the truth Kurt. I want to hear it from you. Did you or did you not know the hit was out on Antonio that night on the yacht? It does matter–it matters to me." Her tears ran down her face, her voice sharp and intense as an ice pick stabbing his heart.

His insides were raw with anger at himself for his overwhelming desire to have her. It was that way from the start, she was his love addiction, and he wasn't about to lose her, not to Tony, and not now. Time ticked away at his sanity, beads of sweat formed on his forehead, his throat was arid. He bit his lower lip; his hand raked his sandy-brown hair. *Courage is not doing something without fear; it is doing it in spite of fear.*

Wretched and spent by his emotions Kurt realized "do or die" and "now or never" were unpopular options. Words are powerful weapons mightier than a double-edged sword.

"Yes," he sighed. "I knew the hit was planned that night." His slow articulate words cut into her– .

More words trembled and tumbled forth, "I swear, my intention was to warn him. I tried, but all we fought about was you. He wouldn't believe me. He thought it was a ploy to get you away from him. Amanda – he was never in the mob, he was a causality of other men's hatred." Their tears dropped freely. Kurt cupped her face and rubbed the tears off her cheeks, "Baby I swear to you. I wanted you, but not at the expense of his life. It is in the police report. Gus confirmed what I said to Antonio. It had to be documented secretly, until the trial. I couldn't tell you or Anna. We were all targets. I had too much to lose. I followed you to Rome because I wanted to protect you. I was there when you lied to Carmine to save me. He thought I knew, but he believed you over his gut instinct."

Her eyes became large with shock. "You were there? At the Vatican? Where?"

"Behind a large column, near the front, with the two henchmen shoving their guns into my ribs, I thought they were going to kill us; but what you said set us free. After his thugs bruised my ribs, Carmine said I was lucky you told the truth, and that I didn't deserve you. They forced me to leave Rome, or he'd mess up my 'pretty boy' face. He said he hoped that I was half the man you thought I was. I hope I am." He searched her face. "I am not sorry, that I didn't tell you the whole truth. I had to protect you."

Her tears streamed down her cheeks splattering to his hands. He wiped her wet cheeks with gentle kisses. "Will you forgive me? I didn't want you to know just in case something happened, you don't tell lies well. I love that about you. Mandy, I love everything about you." He inhaled and released a shaky exhale.

Her head dropped. She didn't answer. Her silence was cruel.

The cold crept into their private space; the wedding guests disappeared into the church. Kurt turned the key to start the heater, just to hear something other than her disappointed silence.

He thought their guests assumed they were doing something nasty rather than having a heated discussion about truth. The darker side of the awful truth was the dreaded possibility of the victim-witness program.

"Amanda talk to me, say something. Scream– holler– just stop torturing me."

She looked up, "No one is torturing you, except yourself. You had the power to save a man's life! You could have taken me with you that night, but you put your gloating needs first. Tony would have listened to me. I risked my life to save yours. I lost my life, my dreams, my career and for what– lies, fairytales, and fantasies. And you think you're being tortured. You're not the one getting up every morning milking cows and collecting eggs in the bitter cold, wishing you were dead because the one you love is making a mockery of your love."

His free hand covered his face hiding his tears.

Stunned and shamed by her words, to say he was sorry again would only surface her bad memories of her father's trespasses against her mother. He knew that from his heated discussions with her sister and mother. The real truth wrestled deep inside to his lowest carnal animal instinct. He really wasn't sorry. And truthfully he was looking forward to their honeymoon sequestered in his bedroom at his parents' home.

He didn't want Tony dead, but he didn't want Tony to have her either. Why? Why had he allowed her to penetrate into the depths of his heart?

He slammed his fist on the dash. Flashes of her calming Tony at the club, their shared prized photos as the 'Golden Couple' on the road to stardom, her nailing him with the spiked heel of her *fuck-me* shoes, the coveted kiss after the yacht party, getting cuffed in front of her the morning of the murder, and their erotic night in Rome. All the memories choked him. He had never cried for the love of a woman.

Tough guys don't cry–they make others cry. He had accomplished that– he had screwed up again. He wanted to escape her tears, his legs eager to flee, so he could gather his bearings. Her saying 'no' was not in his plans. No was not the answer to their love.

Of course, his luck, nature decided to call. It was a viable excuse to get out of the truck. A strange ace in the hole, but it was the only move he had. He wiped his tears with the back of his hand, and spoke, "Okay this is inappropriate, but I have to answer to nature's call, and I need your cooperation." He tugged lightly on her hand.

She wiped the traces of tears from her face checking back into reality. "Really? Now?" she rolled her eyes and scooted to the edge of the driver seat while he stepped out. Using the door as his shield for one of the most humbling moments in his life, he had never released himself in front of a woman before. But his options were limited.

Amanda turned up the radio trying not to focus on their intimate situation. She dreaded the thought that she too would need to use the little girl's room soon. What was she going to do– with him?

He finished and slipped back into the truck. Nudging her over, sheepishly he commented, "I suppose you may have to do the same. I know they have restrooms inside, care to venture in?" His eyes sparkled like the emerald on her finger.

She swallowed delicately, "I suppose you will escort me considering our entanglement. This is the second most embarrassing event in my life, thank you Mr. Kilawee for orchestrating both. You sure you don't want to put this on national news?" She elbowed him to exit.

"Wait, I don't appreciate your tone or the reserved standoffish look on your face. We are not starting over as work associates." She had another thing coming–he wasn't about to accept her cold-shoulder treatment. It was bad enough he was freezing his balls off sitting in the cold truck.

Another wedding party was gathering at the Church, and he needed to explain their tardiness to their guests. He spotted Dory and another strikingly beautiful woman exit a red Cadillac in his outside mirror. He assumed she was the Mother Witch of his vixen bride.

Amanda shoved him, "Come on, get the lead out pretty boy, I have to go." She too had noticed her mother approaching the double red doors in an elegant red skirt suit. Her sister was wearing a bridesmaid dress matching the others.

He shook his head. "No, we are not moving until you say that you love me," his words snappish, his face stern.

"What do you want from me?"

"The truth!"

"Oh, oh so now the TRUTH is important." Amanda heaved the words she felt meant nothing to him.

"The truth is always important. I was a top news journalist for God's sake Amanda, I lost my life too. We're not leaving this vehicle until I hear the truth from you. Do you love me? And don't lie. I know when you're lying. I know you lied to Carmine– I don't know what you said, but it proves some lies are good. Now is not the time to lie–not to me. I watched you calm and coddle the savage beast in Tony. And I was forced by gunpoint to watch you calm a coldblooded killer." A fierce wanting in his eyes, unmasked his desire for her. "Use your technique on me, calm my inner beast and coddle my inner child. I deserve that from you. Give me satisfaction with the truth. You know the worst tragedy is an unsatisfied man. Unrequited love, remember?"

"I calmed them to protect you–."

"Then protect me now. Protect my breaking heart. Say you love me!"

"My love won't solve or cure you're capacity to tell lies."

"Oh, Miss Truth Seeker, be a good example. Teach the truth–show me how a pro does it."

"Kurt, I have to use the restroom."

"Well, that's nice, but not the words I want to hear."

"Kurt!" She raised her voice threatening him.

"Amanda!" he was louder and more forceful.

Some of the guests gathered close, having to leave the warmth of the church until the other wedding finished.

Amanda pushed hard on his solid chest.

"Don't expend your energy or you may have an accident." He warned holding her hands on his chest. "Now, we both know you can't out muscle me, you may be able to out write me or verbally abuse me, but I am physically stronger than you. Tell me the truth and I'll carry you to the restroom. Deal?"

"I'm not dealing with you."

"You are going to deal with us. We happen to be handcuffed together and I desire the truth now and for the rest of our lives." He edged closer ready to claim her lips, and her body if that's what it took to hear the words he heard her breathlessly confess early that day. "Deal with me, I love you. I want a chance to share happiness with you."

Biting back her lip, she had to appease him to get relief. The cold was not helping her full bladder, the more she thought the more urgent her body begged. Then the stirring heat from his chest wicked its way through her hands creating a desire that only he could quench. She could say the words–they came easier every time she did. She felt them. But he set some high standards and she questioned her ability to consistently meet them. He was high maintenance. A dominate man, a frightened boy, and spoiled rotten child inside one sexy hunk of a guy. What more could she want?

"Okay, one condition."

"No." he stared her down.

Sure the spoiled rotten child had to surface, irrational, bullying, and tough.

"Really? Just one thing."

"No. All or nothing."

"You're not playing fair."

"I'm not playing. Life is not fair get used to it! Tell me the truth and you are free to go– to the restroom–change your clothes–walk down the aisle–say 'I do', and go home with your handsome Super-hero husband. That would be me, in case you're confused." He knew he won. He loved winning.

"Fine, I love you."

"No– say it the way you said it this morning–you were so much more convincing." His lighthearted mischief beckoned her.

"Well, I was in the throes of passion, things have changed since then."

"Nothing has changed. The truth doesn't change what is – It is what is. Just because we have differences, doesn't mean we can't love and live peacefully." He crunched his nose at her, almost touching hers. "Okay, one more time from the top–say it and I will take you to freedom."

She put her cold hands on his warm cheeks and brushed her soft lips on his, "I love you." She kissed him deeply and unconditionally.

With that confession, Kurt popped open the door, scooped her up under her bottom, flipped her over his strong shoulder and carried her to the church.

They muddled through the embarrassment of the restroom shenanigans.

Quickly her girlfriends cut off her shirt and helped her dress in the finest gown she'd ever worn. Kurt kept his back turned and maneuvered his arm with hers. The mermaid-style crystal and pearl embellished gown fit perfectly, she only wished Belinda and Jeremy could be there. But under the dire circumstances, she was happy to know they were safe. Her veil in place, her hair up, ringlets framing her face, she was a blushing celebrated bride.

Kurt covered his eyes as her friends guided them into Pastor Doyle's office still linked by their silver bracelets.

Pastor Doyle addressed them, "Please everyone leave, except the bride and groom. With all the commotion I feel it is my duty to counsel you both into a peaceful resolve. In my twenty years as a minister I have never witnessed such a strange match. Meeting you, Kurt prior to this day I believed you were sane. Neither of you should coerce the other into matrimony." He glanced at the cuffs.

"See, I told you the cuffs were kinky." Amanda muttered.

"That being said," the pastor continued. "The vows you're about to take should not to be taken lightly. The vows you make are to God as well as to each other. And God will not be made a mockery. Saying 'I do' to each other means you will keep the covenant between God, man, and woman sacred. It means your marriage bed is undefiled; you are to cling to one another and walk away from anyone who tries to interfere. The vow you make today," he addressed Amanda, "is the same bond we make to Christ, allowing him to be the Lord of our lives. Kurt, the vow you make today is the same, but with added responsibility of protection, faithfulness, provision, and loyalty that you will be the spiritual guide of your household and love your wife as Christ does. Are you willing, without handcuffs, to accept your vows?"

Just then the church handyman entered with a large bolt cutter. He snipped the single chain between them. Immediately they rubbed their sore wrists and relished the physical freedom.

They looked at each other, knowing now they were free to leave.

Kurt lowered down on one knee, "Baby I love you, you're perfect for me. You're the brightest most beautiful woman I have ever known. Will you be my wife, marry me today?"

A warm Spirit filled the room and their hearts–comforting their fears. They folded into each other's arms; willingly and unconditionally.

"Yes, I will."

The pastor guided Amanda to her grandfather's arm while Kurt rushed to replace his uniform with his black Armani tuxedo, a white crisp shirt with a black bow-tie.

With a single red rose in his lapel, Kurt stood at the altar with Tom McCarthy as his best man in Jeremy's absence. Kurt promised Jeremy the best man slot for their larger celebration to come when Kurt's family and Amanda's father could attend.

His angelic bride approached the altar, Amanda Lindas fulfilled his dreams; she was his perfect match.

Saying their vows she only stumbled once over the 'obey'. He saw the subtle pertness in her eyes. Quirking his brow, he looked for reassurance. She smiled as she said "I do" giving him the security he desired.

When it was time to exchange the rings, Kurt had her grandmother's gold band from Gramps. But he had overlooked one detail; he didn't have a wedding band for him.

Gramps stood and removed his own wedding band. He had worn it for fifty years, he handed it to Amanda, "Here Sweetheart this one is guaranteed to last. It brought me good luck and perfect love. It will do the same for you both."

It was a perfect fit on Kurt's virgin ring finger.

Lifting her veil, Kurt gladly kissed his bride.

"Ladies and Gentlemen, may I introduce to you Mr. and Mrs. Kurt Kilawee."

Shelly whispered in her ear, "Ah, Amanda–you just married a cop."

"Yep, I married a *real* Super-hero," Amanda clutched Kurt's lapels and pulled his lips down to meet hers.

THE BEGINNING OF THE HAPPY ENDING

EPILOGUE – THE REST OF THE STORY

Later that same evening; Kurt and Amanda Kilawee arrived in Chicago, stopping only once to purchase champagne for their wedding night rendezvous in his bedroom suite in his parents' house on North Lake Shore Drive.

The "Windy City" was clothed in a layer of velvety snow adding to the ambiance of the circular drive sprinkled with blue spruces covered in white twinkling Christmas lights. The white Georgian-styled mansion was perfect symmetry. An oversized red double door entry flanked by four large lower windows and four second story windows. Each window had black shutters and adorned with lighted wreaths with large red bows. Centered on top in the gray slate roof were three dormer windows. The house-length porch had smooth Doric columns adding more grandeur and balance to the Chicago Commissioner's home. Amanda was enamored by the wealth and warmth the home exuded. "You live here?" was all she could muster.

"No, remember me, I live in Kips Bay near Murray Hill in New York City. My parents'–your in-laws live here. And we my dear will live here under house protection until some evil men are brought to justice." He patted her knee waking her from her enthralled trance. "Are you ready for this?"

They walked hand and hand up the snow dusted walkway to the front steps guarded by white lighted angels, like the angels in Rockefeller Plaza. Kurt scooped Mandy up into his arms. He was hoping his parents didn't wait up, but who was he trying to kid. His mother may not speak to him because she didn't get to attend the ceremony, but she'd be awake.

The red door opened, his parents stood in matching Christmas robes, hugging each other's waists.

"Merry Christmas, Mom, Dad." Kurt said first, kissing his mom on the cheek, he walked in with his bride. He put Amanda down delicately, held her steady until she regained her footing. He even fluffed her dress. His mom fussed with the dress while his father's sharp eyes noted a telltale oddity.

"Nice silver bracelets you have on son. Care to explain–need some help to remove them?"

Kurt rubbed his wrist. He dreaded repeating the fiasco to his father, who would engage him to repeat it to his brothers for years to come. It was funny and unpredictable; of course, he'd omit the intimate encounter in the barn, although that was the best part.

Sometimes a journalist or writer has to leave out the best parts to protect themselves; this was one of those times. "Sure Dad we could use a key."

Amanda embraced her in-laws, feeling the warmth of their love. Living here wasn't going to be bad as Kurt had promised.

They shared a toast to the Bride and Groom with the expensive champagne chilled by the enormous crackling fireplace in the immaculate formal living area.

Amanda had no idea the wealth that Kurt had been raised in. It enlightened her as to why he was so demanding of himself and others. His mother, Nancy never once stopped catering to him or his father making sure they had food and fresh drinks. She was eloquent, understated and charming.

After drinks and light snacks she insisted that Amanda get the tour of the amazing mansion. Nothing was out of place and everything decorated in the classic style of the house. No doubt, Kurt's flair for decorating came from his mother. The den without exception exuded the masculinity of his larger than life father. It appeared that the Chicago Bears had misplaced their locker room and play review theatre in the spacious mansion.

Kurt amply warned her, "You could be in for a rude awakening if the Forty-niners continue their winning streak." His father frowned as if Kurt had cursed the Bears.

It was late, Amanda noted Kurt getting restless. She feared overtired, and that wasn't what she wanted from her groom on their wedding night. "Mr. and Mrs. Kilawee, your home is beautiful, thank you for your hospitality. We appreciate your protection, until my wayward husband gets himself out of his quandary. We've had a long day. See you in the morning? Come on Sweetheart, I know how ornery you get when you don't get your sleep." Amanda said coaxing Kurt to follow her lead.

Wrapping his arms around her from the back he nuzzled his face into her hair and whispered, "I like it better when you call me Super-hero and my ornery disposition at work wasn't because I didn't have sleep it was because I didn't have someone keeping me awake in my bed."

His parents overhead just enough, Nancy said, "We will leave you off the tour at Kurt's room."

Kurt guided Amanda into his room with his hand gently on the small of her back, he kissed his mother on the cheek, and gave his dad a smirk, "We won't be seeing you guys tomorrow, maybe by Christmas. I have plans with my wife. Dad, don't call us, we'll call you. Pretend we're not here. We'll come out for food eventually. Understand?"

His father laughed, "Yes, Son we were young once too."

"Good." Kurt nodded. "Good night Mom and Dad."

DESIRE FOR TRUTH

<u>*Christmas Morning December 25th, 1984*</u>

Amanda awoke first; content in her husband's strong corded arms she remembered it was Christmas. Moments later she slipped out of bed while he snoozed quietly. Busily she wrapped his Christmas gifts. Her mom had delivered one the day before. Amanda managed to have his wedding band custom designed by a jeweler that sold blue diamonds– the same blue shade of her eyes. They customized the ring to replicate her emerald ring, as a loving reminder that her eyes were always on him.

The other gifts were the Bvlgari watch with the diamond bezel, and his Mont Blanc writing pen she purchased in Rome an accolade to Rich's credit card, she had used her severance pay in advance.

Everything wrapped and placed under the real Christmas tree, his mom had decorated with his childhood ornaments and their first Christmas ornament keepsakes. Nancy was a jewel and a saint, any woman who runs a household and raises men–deserves that title.

Amanda slipped back into bed to give her strapping husband a loving charged wakeup call. Using her full lips she kissed his warm neck and proceeded to pecking kisses on his broad chest trailing to his navel. With the tip of her cool tongue, she traced his happy-trail; to his firm length.

His breath hitched, "Oh Baby, sweet Jesus, Merry Christmas to me?" Her moist tongue slid along his tan line. He gripped the sheets to his sides, excited that his bride was giving him an early Christmas gift. He whispered, "I love this kind of gift, one that keeps on giving like the jam of the month club? Oh, yeah…" Her hand flattened on his hard flexing abs holding him still.

"Shush no talking. No sports commentating." She scolded. He stopped talking as the hot warmth of her wet mouth met his tender flesh. His hips shifted forward she let him know she was happy that their marriage bed was undefiled; he was hers for the taking. And take him she did to a level of ecstasy that a woman in love could give to her man. She felt powerful that he accepted her gift of ultimate pleasure. The further she went the tighter he clutched the sheets.

A hard knock came on the door, "Son...are you up?"

Kurt struggled to push her away, but she continued the blissful trip, giving a love gift. With a soft moan Kurt whispered to her, "Yeah, I'm up."

Then with much composure, he delivered a louder annoyed, "Yes, Dad, I'm up."

Caught in the throes of erotic joy, the newlyweds shared hushed whispers and stifled laughter for the awkward moment.

Keith's deep voice rattled on the other side of the locked door, "You are coming to breakfast?"

Kurt gritted his teeth as Amanda brought him to the edge, in a saucy whisper he said, "Oh yeah, I'm coming." Then louder, he managed, "We'll be down soon." Just in time he hoisted Amanda to his chest by her upper arms. His eyes illuminated by love. His voice hoarse he whispered, "You are an incorrigible sexual nympho, I would spank you, but you'd enjoy it."

Before she could respond, he covered her mouth with greedy kisses, flipped her over quickly to bring her to a rockin' release. Instinctively he cupped her mouth softly to muffle her squeals. As he had suspected– his father had not left.

"Kurt, your mother has Christmas breakfast ready, so don't make a day of staying in bed, let Amanda come up for air. Your brothers and their families are on the way. You hear me?"

Kurt panted slowly working through his orgasm. "Yep, I hear ya." He collapsed putting all his body weight on her.

Amanda gave him a new memory to replace his memories of others. She vowed he'd forget his other encounters. It was her secret vendetta against the unknown.

On his elbows he lifted up still deep within her warmth, his hair fell across his Irish eyes twinkling a shade of Christmas green reflecting his appreciation. "Where did you learn that?"

She touched her index finger to her lips and tapped his nose, "Oh no, you don't. I can't change the past, but I can guarantee your future."

He laughed. "Okay, fair enough. Remember pay backs are a bitch." He ravished her lips and traveled to her nipples, giving her more of his appreciation, he felt her peak and release again before he ended his playful taunting. "Next time, you better use your own words."

"Or what you'll sue me for plagiarism? Besides who says there will be a next time?"

"Well, like the jam of the month– you know." He smiled hopeful.

"Get your facts straight; you said that–not me." He frowned. "You're such a big baby–."

"So, like it's a bad trait? I love getting my own way."

"Oh, newsflash!"

Within an hour they heard the family's golden retriever, Molly, playfully barking greetings to the tune of children laughing and muffled adult voices wishing "Merry Christmas".

That was until his brothers' caught on that he was still in his room; luckily Kurt and Amanda were fully dressed before they heard large footsteps on the wooden staircase.

"Hey Pretty Boy come on out, bring your playmate let us meet her." They teased.

Nancy scolded, "Come back to the breakfast table, I swear you boys will be the death of him yet, stop teasing. Kurt come on down, baby."

Slightly embarrassed, Kurt held Amanda's hand and led her down the spiral stairs. Both freshly showered and groomed to perfection, wearing jeans and the matching red cashmere sweaters, Kurt's mom insisted they wear for the family Christmas photos. Kurt also wore his new blue diamond wedding band with Gramp's gold band.

Stepping around the corner the 'Golden Couple' entered the large formal dining room, shock expanded on Amanda's face. She saw nothing but his massive brothers, Kevin and Kyle. He had mentioned he was the runt, but nothing prepared her for the big Chicago cops in uniform, one six-five the other six-seven. Kurt was definitely *Mama's Pretty Boy.*

Ruthlessly they teased and jabbed him. Kurt took it all in fun, but he never let loose of her hand, especially when they took turns giving her big bear hugs. His confidence never wavered; he stood his ground and bantered back. Respectful he stopped to kiss each sister-in-law on their cheeks. He became a jungle gym for his nieces and nephews when he knelt to hug them.

Pulling Mandy forward he introduced her, "Family this is the wife of the luckiest man in the world, meet Amanda, or Mandy, Mrs. Kurt Kilawee." He raised her hand in triumph.

At the bountiful Christmas breakfast table, Keith had Kurt say the family blessing as they all held hands. Amanda's heart swelled with pride. He was a champion among champions, how could she have ever doubted his sincerity. He knew what love was he was covered in it. It took meeting the woman he felt could fit into the schematics of his challenging strong family. It wasn't his fault–it was his nature.

Passing the food, Nancy prodded Kurt, "Honey did you tell Mandy about the charity event last year. You remember what we discovered when you came back from Miami?"

Kurt shook his head signaling a definite–no. "No Mom, she doesn't need to know. No Mom, please don't," he begged for her silence with a whine. His face flushed, he wanted to flee, but he sat cringing to his mother's tale.

"Well you see Mandy, Kurt came home for Easter. We always attend the Catholic Charity luncheon and dinner which he always attended like a good sport. But this past year, he refused to go because an acquaintance of mine had mentioned that he should meet her daughter, since she was a journalist, but..."

Kurt sat shaking his head, "Mom, come on– don't."

Amanda held his arm feeling his increased need to flee. "No, by all means please do continue Nancy. Do I happen to know this acquaintance?"

"Oh, so he did tell you?" Surprise and confusion filled the room. Everyone listened intently on the outcome.

Amanda shot him a stern look of distrust and gave him a sharp knuckle to his thigh under the table.

Kurt winced. "No, I can't say this story has passed between us."

"Well, anyway Kurt decided to give his boss Rich Underwood his ticket knowing he had a mutual friend attending, a Professor Houston, I believe."

Amanda's face pinked, her mouth opened and then closed. Words wouldn't form.

"Mom you know it is against the law to kill your child." Kurt said pointed. "You're killing me."

Nancy continued. "Long story short, my son decided to go carousing and drinking instead. Said he didn't want to meet a Midwestern bookworm journalist. Well, his boss Rich ends up hiring the casual blind date that my writer friend tried to set up. Then in June, Kurt starts ranting about the girl. I didn't associate it because he insisted on calling you–what was that name son?" A gleam of mischief glittered in her hazel-green eyes as she paused and placed her hand on her cheek.

Kurt propped his elbows on the table, covered his face, and then gazed at the ceiling searching for reprieve or salvation. "Mom, you're killing me. Dad, tell her to stop. This is not funny."

Too late, Keith was already chuckling, the irony cracked him up. The laughter multiplied at the family table, so jovial the children joined in as children often do.

"Oh, I remember...Mandy-Candy. He whined and complained about her. It dawned on me when he stopped home from Miami pouting and pining over you. I told him–none of this mess would have happened if he would have just trusted his mother."

Kurt stood assuming that Mandy was about to attack. His instincts were dead on. He looked into her icy glare thinking it might be a long while before he'd feel that gift that keeps on giving again. "Thanks Mom, big time," he said and escaped through the kitchen to the six car garage with Amanda at his heels.

"Kurt Kilawee stop and face the music!" Amanda hollered catching him in the garage. Indignation flashed in her eyes, she gripped her hips. "Mandy-Candy? And we could have avoided this mess if you would have just trusted your mom. You could have met me before Rich and Antonio. Oh the crap you put me through, Kurt Allen Kilawee!"

"I'm sorry," he planted his hands firmly on his hips. His face was as red as his sweater. "No–I am not sorry. I don't like blind dates!"

"No, state the facts, you don't like blind dates with Midwestern bookworm types–but hot models and playmates are acceptable? Is there anything else you want to share with me? Let's just cut to the truth, so we can avoid any more trouble."

"I brought your Christmas gift from New York, the one you weren't supposed to see until now." Slowly he turned her and pointed to the icy-blue Mercedes with a huge red bow. She melted a little into his chest. He folded his arms around her, and rested his chin on her head. "The one you stole from my locked garage."

"You stole my clothes. And tried to steal my story."

"Well, we have a lifetime to argue that scenario. There is something else in the glove compartment. It was handed to me to give to you. I think you're ready to see it."

Wonder replaced her anger. His generosity overwhelmed her, she had to forgive him. Who wouldn't? He was humble and sincere.

They walked over to the car, his arm around her shoulders, "Go ahead open the door." He released her.

Amanda sat, reached into the glove compartment, and found Anna's will. Tears came quickly, she missed her dear friend. And she thought none of this would have happened had she met Kurt before.

Everything in life has a purpose and every person you meet or choose not to meet could be the truth that you seek.

All the chance meetings meant everything to her; she realized she wouldn't have chosen to miss their journey to love.

With a heavy hearted sigh, Kurt squatted to hold her. "It's alright Baby, we're together now."

She allowed her husband to comfort her. She thought, I must have done something right to deserve him. Things do happen for a reason, our choices do affect our lives and others.

January 6th 1985, The San Francisco 49ers defeated the Chicago Bears 23-0. On January 20th the 49ers won the Super bowl against Miami-Dolphins 38-16, guaranteeing Amanda bragging rights towards Kurt's father and her father until the next football season.

New York Times reports February 5, 1985:
251 Underworld suspects go on trial in Naples, Italy. The first of three trials sent 640 people to Poggioronle Prison.

New York Times February 27th, 1985 Headline:

"Well, Babe here it is– *U.S. Indictment Says 9 Governed New York Mafia–list of Crimes Included 5 Murders.*" Kurt read aloud lying in bed wearing just jeans. Mandy listened brushing her freshly showered hair. "It says here, Rudolph W. Giuliani, US Attorney in Manhattan conducted the news conference in the Federal office building at 26 Federal Plaza across from the US court house at Poley Square, *'This case charges more mafia bosses in one indictment than ever before,'* Mr. Giuliani said. *He described the commission as, 'The Mafia ruling council here in New York and other cities.'*"

She went to their bed, slipped in under his arm and read the rest of the article with him. Her eyes danced. They were finally free. "So does this mean we can move back to New York City?"

Kurt rolled over on top of her, trapping her under his muscular body, "It means we can go wherever we want, but we stay out of other people's business. It also means I have to get a job to support us, so what are your plans?"

She hugged his neck, "Hmm, I think I will write novels based on my travels and personal experiences. I'll write stories that take people to wonderful places and share life's troubles with uplifting themes. Themes that make people think and dream about taking risks and lots of journeys. I can write wherever you want to work. Tell me–are you going back to being a cop?"

"What did I tell you about that word? Respect the badge." He kissed her lips, "If we stay here, I will do undercover work. It's dangerous, but I've gotten used to working with my father again. If we want to live in a laid back rural area and raise kids, we have a Victorian house in Janesville, you and mom can restore it. Or we can live in Miami in a condo that your dad lost to me– he bet I couldn't get you to marry me by Christmas. I could just lie around the pool and work on my tan." he grinned. "Then we have two places in New York. The Apthorp would be my first choice. I seriously doubt that Belinda will give up my orgy bathroom any time soon."

"Hey, I love that bathroom and my fantasy vision of you standing half-naked reflected in the mirrors."

"Why fantasized about me half-naked when you can have me *au naturel* now?" he sprinkled kisses on her neck.

"Kurt, I just got cleaned up. I have to meet with our mothers, the florist, the cake decorators, and rent the hall. I have an official wedding to plan. Belinda and the girls from Wisconsin are coming in to help. I have a busy schedule today, but tonight I'm all yours for date night."

His eyes reflected mischief, "Are you resisting house arrest? I knew you'd like planning our second wedding. I'll release you if we can use that gift that keeps on giving?"

She smiled back, "We'll see how you behave."

"I'm always good, even when I'm bad–I'm good. Will you wear your sexy *fuck-me* shoes? You never told me who bought the shoes the first time."

"I told you, I don't know who bought the shoes. Honestly, I thought it was you, since you were so infatuated with them. You are so bad."

"I can't help myself when I'm around you– I get high-heel fevers. You bring nasty out of me. Sure I can't convince you to stay home?"

June 22, 1985 Amanda and Kurt Kilawee's official wedding

The wedding was a spectacular event. Amanda wore her original designer strapless gown. Kurt was sharp and debonair in his black Armani Tuxedo. The groomsmen dressed in black tuxes and bridesmaids wore the red strapless tea length gowns again, except Belinda wore black. But this time Amanda's father showed up and walked his baby girl down the aisle. And he picked up the tab on the wedding, surprising Kurt.

The wedding marked the first time Florence and Art Lindas were together at an event since their bitter divorce. Amanda was petrified at first, but thankfully they got along in spite of their differences, making her second wedding one of her best days. The wedding pictures were a challenge with all their attendants. Kurt's huge brothers looked and acted like bodyguards ensuring peace, although they were the worst of the Irish, Italian, and Indian bunch.

Jeremy was the best man as promised; happy he was accepted as family. He was pleased to announce that since Kurt and Amanda's exodus of NYCB, he was promoted to stand in front of the camera instead of behind it.

Sharply dressed in his tuxedo, Jeremy took the microphone and stood. Next to Kurt at the wedding table, he articulated with is news anchor voice. "Ladies and gentleman and all my munchkin fans, I have a newsworthy story to share– I worked with Kurt for many years before Mandy-Candy came into the picture." He laughed and pointed at Mandy's chagrin. "Kurt was a royal pain, a true HMP–High Maintenance Pain. But I loved his determination and quirkiness. Then along comes Mandy– a smart, vibrant, witty woman that blew him out of the dating pool." Everyone laughed at the verbal picture Jeremy painted.

"But this hunky Anchorman refused to believe–he had met his match. I told him daily, she was unlike any woman he'd ever crossed paths with, and I warned him to straighten up and fly straight. But he refused. Well honestly, Mandy's ego wasn't any better–the biggest two egos I have ever met. They bickered, bantered, and challenged each other until I was ready to kill them. A trial separation at work was essential." He put his hand on Kurt's shoulder. "Dude it was me who had you transferred to the 'pee-on' team not Mandy. This toast is my confession of truth; an elusive idealism you both desired in your careers and life,"

Belinda stood and handed a brown bag to Jeremy. He removed a black glittery stiletto. Kurt and Amanda sat with their mouths agape. "And just like Cinderella had her glass slipper, this love story started with a magical pair of shoes. Kurt and Amanda, just to set the record straight– I bought Mandy these F-me shoes."

Kurt shook his head and under his breath he said, "You son-of-a-bitch."

Jeremy clamped his hand on Kurt's shoulder preventing him from standing. "Now hear me out, I knew you couldn't stand back and let another man buy the woman you loved– F-me shoes." Still pressing Kurt's shoulder, "This man loves this beautiful, strong woman with impeccable taste, and integrity. Every woman needs a good pair of kickass shoes. And she kicked your butt–good." The applause and roar of the crowd approved his back-story. "I could tell you a slew of Kurt stories. But, I believe the best is yet to come. I wish you both a lifetime of giving each other migraines. Remember Kurt, you promised, I get to name the second child. And Tom gets to name the first born. I wish you two the best that life can offer. Salute!"

The truth was out, mystery solved. Everyone stood to cheer the couple. Kurt put Jeremy in a headlock and knuckle rubbed his short afro.

Belinda helped Amanda put on the stilettos, Amanda stood on her chair exposing her legs catching Kurt's attention. He released Jeremy and hugged him, "Thanks man, I love those shoes."

The DJ played their wedding song, "One on One" by Hall and Oats. Kurt carried his bride to the dance floor. They kissed and danced across the large dance floor. Kurt whispered, "I told you this was our song."

THE END OF THE BEGINNING.

www.ingramcontent.com/pod-product-compliance
Lightning Source LLC
Chambersburg PA
CBHW070754280626
47162CB00016B/479